Henry David Thoreau (1817–62) haunted the woods and fields as a boy. At the age of sixteen, he went to Harvard, where he was a receptive student proficient in Greek, Latin, and the English classics. After graduation, he taught school for a time, but he soon turned to lecturing and writing. In 1845, he began his famous experiment in woodland living, which he recorded in *Walden*. During the first year of his hermitage, Thoreau was arrested for refusing to pay his poll tax, an episode that led to "On the Duty of Civil Disobedience." From 1849 to 1853, he made several brief trips that supplied the material for his posthumously published books, *Excursions*, *The Maine Woods*, and *A Yankee in Canada*.

W. S. Merwin is an acclaimed poet whose works include *A Mask for Janus* and *The Pupil*. He is also a playwright and renowned translator of poetry. The recipient of numerous literary awards, including the Pulitzer Prize in 1971, he lives in Hawaii.

Perry Miller (1905–63) received his Ph.D. from the University of Chicago. A towering figure in the field of American intellectual history, Miller was the author of numerous works, especially about colonial New England. Among his books are *The New England Mind* (1939), *Errand into the Wilderness* (1956), and the posthumously published *The Life of the Mind in America: From the Revolution to the Civil War* (1965), which won the Pulitzer Prize in History. Miller taught at Harvard from 1931 until his death.

WALDEN
or Life in the Woods
and
"On the Duty of Civil Disobedience"

HENRY DAVID THOREAU

With an Introduction by
W.S. MERWIN
and an Afterword by
Perry Miller

SIGNET CLASSICS

SIGNET CLASSICS
Published by New American Library, a division of
Penguin Group (USA) Inc., 375 Hudson Street,
New York, New York 10014, USA
Penguin Group (Canada), 90 Eglinton Avenue East, Suite 700, Toronto,
Ontario M4P 2Y3, Canada (a division of Pearson Penguin Canada Inc.)
Penguin Books Ltd., 80 Strand, London WC2R 0RL, England
Penguin Ireland, 25 St. Stephen's Green, Dublin 2,
Ireland (a division of Penguin Books Ltd.)
Penguin Group (Australia), 250 Camberwell Road, Camberwell, Victoria 3124,
Australia (a division of Pearson Australia Group Pty. Ltd.)
Penguin Books India Pvt. Ltd., 11 Community Centre, Panchsheel Park,
New Delhi - 110 017, India
Penguin Group (NZ), 67 Apollo Drive, Mairangi Bay,
Auckland 1311, New Zealand (a division of Pearson New Zealand Ltd.)
Penguin Books (South Africa) (Pty.) Ltd., 24 Sturdee Avenue,
Rosebank, Johannesburg 2196, South Africa

Penguin Books Ltd., Registered Offices:
80 Strand, London WC2R 0RL, England

Published by Signet Classics, an imprint of New American Library,
a division of Penguin Group (USA) Inc.

First Signet Classics Printing (Merwin Introduction), August 1999
10 9

Introduction copyright © W. S. Merwin, 1999
Afterword copyright © New American Library, a division of Penguin Group
(USA) Inc., 1960
All rights reserved

CONTENTS

Introduction

What is it, after all, this unsettling sequence of pages, memorable but elusive, that speaks to us—parts of it, to some of us—more pertinently in our own time than it did to all but a few of Thoreau's contemporaries, even among those who read it during his brief lifetime? It is not, evidently, a novel, although that word now is used with remarkable permissiveness. It seems scarcely to be a narrative at all, and yet it is, in several senses, a story, with a central character, and a quest sustaining it, and both the character and the occasions are partly fictions. It is not really a journal, though it is composed from one, and presents itself, off and on, in the form of a journal, with an observant and intimate passage through the seasons. Is it a memoir? If so, it leads us to ask what a memoir really is. Thoreau informs us at the start that he is going to tell us about himself, "the narrowness of my experience," and he remarks, as he does so, that "I, on my side, require of every writer, first or last, a simple and sincere account of his own life, and not merely what he has heard of other men's lives; some such account as he would send to his kindred from a distant land; for if he has lived sincerely it must have been in a distant land to me." But in fact he proceeds to tell us at least as much about what he thought of the experience of "Life in the Woods," and what it prompted him to think of, as about the experience itself, detailed as his account of that is in some of its particulars. So, is it an essay, a rumination, a sermon? With the vivid and admirable example of his older neighbor, Ralph Waldo Emerson, and Emerson's "Essays" so close to him, it is not surprising to realize that it is something of all these. And in the end, after his repeated re-castings and re-phrasings and re-orderings, it comes to us as a kind of prophetic book, not wholly at ease in time, something that by nature could never really be finished. Named for a body of water which in turn became a metaphor, whether that had any place in his original intentions or not.

There is a quality to prophetic books, and occasionally, no doubt, to their authors, that some are certain to find irritating, and there were those who found Thoreau aggravating and still do. I had a friend, a man of fine urbane learning, who loved to point out that Thoreau once accidentally started a disastrous fire in a neighbor's woodland. He told me with relish how many acres had been reduced to ashes. And that, he said, was at the same time that Thoreau was speaking with lofty disdain of his practical, hard-working fellow-citizens. ". . . always promising to pay," he was writing, "promising to pay, to-morrow, and dying to-day, insolvent . . . making yourselves sick, that you may lay up something against a sick day . . ." There are readers eager to insist that they cannot stand Thoreau, and even his kind and forbearing friend Emerson could not pretend that the younger man was easy to get along with, and as for intimacy, Emerson quoted a friend who said that he would as soon have taken an elm by the arm.

One of the criticisms of Thoreau, and of *Walden,* that is made most frequently by those with a mind to dismiss him, is that his "Life in the Woods" was really never anything of the kind. The whole thing was, they suggest, not only pretentious but virtually a fraud, and in fact all he had done was to magnify a kind of camping out in the backyard—a wooded backyard, indeed, on somebody else's property, out of earshot but within easy walking distance of his mother's back door, and her kitchen, in Concord. All of which is true (Thoreau himself, at the beginning of *Walden,* docs not claim to have lived farther than "a mile from any neighbor"), and it can be dwelt upon to deny the value of Thoreau's achievement, and denigrate his view of existence, if that is what anyone is determined to do. The land belonged to Emerson, who had lent it to Thoreau as a place for working on "A Week on the Concord and Merrimack Rivers." And it is true that Thoreau presents a portrait of his "Life in the Woods" that suggests a kind of autonomy which was more a matter of imagination than of fact—something which characterizes retreats of all kinds.

Thoreau resorted to the woods. He did not live there in unbroken withdrawal. He wrote from the vantage of being there. *Walden* is not simply an account of an extended camping-out. It is what Thoreau finds to say of that time of his life, those deliberate circumstances that he had chosen and partly made. It was his reflections that finally became the book which has since been discovered, and repeatedly returned to, and treasured as a kind of necessity.

Now that we know something about him, and a succession of remarkable studies of his life and of the evolution of his sentences has reached a considerable length, it is not easy to remember that Thoreau, in a way, was considered a nobody by many of the citizens of Concord. Emerson and one or two others recognized his originality, his perspicacity, something of his insight, but Emerson already had a reputation and a devoted following; many of Thoreau's neighbors had property and positions; and what did he have, or do? Not much, it seemed. He came early to recognize that some of his awkwardness in his social life was bound up with his own dissatisfactions, with looking for something, while all around him his fellow citizens seemed to take their lives as they found them, for all practical purposes. He was one of those inconvenient and uncomfortable figures, a seeker. "I long ago," he announces, "lost a hound, a bay horse, and a turtle dove, and am still on their trail. Many are the travellers I have spoken to concerning them, describing their tracks and what calls they answered to. I have met one or two who had heard the hound, and the tramp of the horse, and even seen the dove disappear behind a cloud, and they seemed as anxious to recover them as if they had lost them themselves." It is a kind of writing that is almost certain to annoy somebody, whatever it is taken to mean, yet he was speaking not only for himself but for many who have read him since, at all ages of their lives, and for many who will never read him at all. It must have been hard for his neighbors to know what to make of him, what he could have in mind, what it all amounted to. He was, after all, a surveyor, but much of the time he seemed to be walking all over the countryside with apparently nothing to do.

Something that we are still far from understanding was coming into existence, taking form, between the conflicts that became the American Revolution, and the Civil War. Even within the structured catechisms of the Protestant sects that dominated the colonies and then the republic, the troublesome insistence of the individual conscience continued its prompting, its demands, and the isolation and improvisations of frontier and rural life encouraged the habit of paying attention to them. The Revolution itself brought to the surface a surge of feeling that had been growing in the colonies, which made the words "independence" and "liberty" seem to be the rightful legacy of the people there at that moment. For all the splendor of Jefferson's rhetoric, the Declaration of Independence and the phrasing of the Constitution could scarcely have echoed with such excitement if they had not appeared to represent to many in the colonies something they thought they recognized as their own. When the war had been won, and they stood, in a new sense, alone, the words began to raise questions about their strange place in history, in geography, and then in behavior, in law, in existence. The old codes and theologies imported with the language were still there, little changed, apparently, in many respects, like the language itself. Some would insist that they had not changed at all. But people's relations to them had changed and would never be the same. The Constitution was neither English law nor Roman law, though it drew upon precedents in both. And the creeds of the churches, despite the vehemence with which they were preached and professed, were held in the context of a new relativism, which was the condition and the ground of questions that were not new at all but had not been asked for a long time, if ever, so nakedly and so generally, and in full knowledge of the presence of the old assurances, the orthodox answers. What was happening has been described as the erosion of faith, which in the familiar sense it certainly was, and one of the recurring questions would concern the nature of faith itself. And the basic enigmas of life, what we live for, who we are, how we should live and why. For many, whether they recognized the direction or not, it was a time of moving away from

the fixed answers, out into the questions. It should
scarcely be surprising that so many of the major works
of American literature in the first half of the nineteenth
century addressed the great questions so directly, as
though they had only recently been discovered. For Melville, the nature of evil and innocence. For Emily Dickin-
son, the mystery of death in life. For Emerson, the
ground of the great questions themselves. It might be
said that all of them, and most obviously Whitman and
Thoreau, different as they were, left us prophetic books,
speaking from within about the soul's life in time, in a
moment of history.

Whitman's sympathy, actual and imagined, for his
time and his contemporary humans, directed the impulse
from which he wrote. The cast of Thoreau's tempera-
ment turned him another way. Thoreau's own loneliness
became one of his guides, and he developed a fine regard for distance. "I live in the angle of a leaden wall,"
he wrote, "into whose composition was poured a little
alloy of bell-metal. Often, in the repose of my mid-day,
there reaches my ears a confused *tintinnabulum* from
without. It is the noise of my contemporaries." He was,
as the tone might lead one to suspect, exaggerating. He
was aware of the events of his time despite the scorn he
professed for those who seemed to be helplessly absorbed in whatever it said in the day's papers. Slavery
in his time, and the controversy continuing around it,
kept him awake. During the agitation that followed John
Brown's raid on Harper's Ferry, while Brown was in jail
awaiting sentence, Thoreau convened his fellow citizens
of Concord and read them his "Plea for John Brown."
"I put a piece of paper and a pencil under my pillow,"
he told them, "and when I could not sleep I wrote in
the dark."

"I think that I love society as much as most," he says
at the beginning of the chapter called "Visitors," and
immediately we wonder about that. "I am no more
lonely than a single mullein or dandelion in a pasture,
or a bean leaf, or sorrel, or a horse-fly, or a humble-bee.
I am no more lonely than the Mill Brook, or a weathercock, or the north star, or the south wind, or an April
shower, or a January thaw, or the first spider in a new

house," he says, and what he is telling us is indeed essential, and rarely realized, but as he says it we may be aware of a distinction that he appears to overlook, which might be described as the restive loneliness that characterizes, it may be, much of sensate life, and certainly all humankind. His relations to and his separation from his neighbors and the society around him were never as simple as he would have us believe. But he followed his own marginal course to a place in his own imagination where what he said, even about human society, often has the ring of a startling recognition.

He tells us at length—and returns to the subject—why he "went to the woods," clearly feeling that in the world in which he had grown up, the act needed explanation. He may have been explaining it to himself as much as to everyone else, since in fact he could have no certainty that anyone else would read his explanations. It must have been important to him to point out that this was a philosophical retreat, and not what it might have seemed to many of the citizens of Concord: a social back-sliding into the shanty lives, the cultural and economic indigence, immigrant and indigenous, around the fringes of the town and of the civilization the town represented. It is not, as we know, that he went very far into the woods, into a territory of total strangers and foreign perils, or that he was ever cut off from social contact with friends, or from other reminders of how near his native village really was. He spoke with affection of those who came to visit him, and from the woods near his cabin he could hear not only the shriek and clatter of the train passing at some distance through the woods, but the rumble of wagons crossing over the bridges on their way to and from Concord. He could not, he noted, hear the sound of roosters in barnyards, and he considered getting a rooster of his own, for the sound.

What was he really doing there that he might not have done somewhere else? He said he had no wish to travel abroad, to leave Concord altogether, where he had already "traveled a good deal." He was convinced that every singular existence, if it could be clearly perceived, could reveal, within itself, the whole, all that there is. "I went to the woods," he says, "because I wished to live deliberately, to front only the essential facts of life, and see if I could not learn what it had to teach, and not, when I came to die, discover that I had not lived." The enterprise, one might argue, could have been pursued anywhere. Thoreau's choice of situation and circumstances was largely temperamental, the result of a regard for his own nature, and it took a form that was not, after all, without precedent in the course of human civilization at large; its oddity in Concord did say something about the society Thoreau inherited, and the limitations of its outlook. In age after age it has been considered comprehensible, even commendable, and in some places traditional, for some who are so impelled to withdraw from the rest of society and try "to live deliberately, to front only the essentials of life," and not, when they come to die, discover that they have not lived. And for many, a measure of solitude, a remove from the immediacy of human society, and the presence, and awareness of the presence, of the rest of existence, of which everyone is a part, have been the setting that seemed appropriate to such an aspiration. The "essentials" that Thoreau speaks of are not only the bare physical necessities of daily life, which he examines with a closeness and austerity that verge on the pedantic, but the plain awareness of the living moment itself. Such a regard for the essentials is an approach, a perspective, an acceptance, an attitude toward his own momentary nature, and toward the whole of that nature whose essentials are his own. In the course of his own century, and then in ours, the impulse for such retreats from the assumptions and traffic of society has become something of a commonplace. It has been blurred and cheapened sometimes in the process. The essentials have been accorded the status of clichés, and the retreat itself, in one form or another, has been commodified. Thoreau's own attitude toward the essentials, toward the nature which he shares with all that is mortal and, perhaps, immortal, remains as rare as it always was, the root of his language and the mark of his originality. In the great journals from which *Walden* was gathered there are passages about the things that he comes to see appearing to him first in his mind, and then before his eye, in the course of his day's walk.

It is the realization of an attitude not of aggressive intellectual extension and dominion, but of lucid, singular acceptance, and its articulation is at the heart of his authentic testament. The prose in which he embodies it seems to me sometimes to be akin to Traherne's "Centuries of Meditations," and Sir Thomas Browne, and sometimes to have an affinity with the best writing of Alfred Russell Wallace and Charles Darwin.

This attitude toward things was inseparable from the other aspect of his writing, in *Walden* and in the journals as a whole, which those who love his work return to with recurring gratitude: the manner in which he observes, and the language in which he portrays, the lives that touch upon his own. Of all the comments written about Thoreau that I have read, I love none more than E. B. White's playful, candid, exquisite essay "A Slight Sound at Evening," its title taken from one of those journal passages (there are so many) which never got into *Walden* but continue to startle and wake us. "A slight sound at evening lifts me up by the ears, and makes life seem inexpressibly serene and grand. It may be in Uranus, or it may be in the shutter." It is the recognition of something in those passages that again and again gives us the sense of waking—which was part of what he wanted. It was his ambition, he said, "to speak somewhere *without* bounds; like a man in a waking moment, to men in their waking moments," and though if one comes to Thoreau in one's youth and is stirred, first, by the splendor of his devotion to individual integrity, it may be that in the long run it will be the moments when he wakes to some life in front of him that one returns to with happy astonishment.

In June the partridge (*Tetrao umbellus*), which is so shy a bird, led her brood past my windows, from the woods in the rear to the front of my house . . . The young suddenly disperse on your approach, at a signal from the mother, as if a whirlwind had swept them away, and they so exactly resemble the dried leaves and twigs that many a traveller has placed his foot in the midst of a brood . . . without suspecting their neighborhood . . . I have held them in my open hand at such a time, and still their only care, obedient to their mother and their instinct, was to squat there without fear or trembling . . . The remarkably adult yet innocent expression of their open and serene eyes is very memorable . . . Such an eye was not born when the bird was, but is coeval with the sky it reflects.

Even when he spent his two years, off and on, by Walden Pond, the woods he went to live in were going. At the time that he had first known the pond, he says, "it was completely surrounded by thick and lofty pine and oak woods, and in some of its coves grape-vines had run over the trees next the water and formed bowers under which a boat could pass." But in the days of his own cabin not only had the railroad arrived, but the "dark, surrounding woods" were gone, and "the villagers, who scarcely know where it lies, instead of going to the pond to bathe or drink, are thinking to bring its water, which should be as sacred as the Ganges at least, to the village in a pipe, or wash their dishes with!" One of the essentials he confronted was human history, its innate dilemma. He saw it. And in the woods that were still there he saw the eye of the infant partridge and told us its true age.

—W. S. Merwin

W. S. Merwin was born in New York City in 1927 and is one of the most distinguished literary writers in America. He is the author of more than fifteen books of poetry, numerous plays, nearly twenty books of translation, and four books of prose. His many honors include the Pulitzer Prize, the Lenore Marshall Poetry Prize, the Aiken Taylor Award for Modern American Poetry, the Bollingen Prize, a Ford Foundation grant, the Governor's Award for Literature of the State of Hawaii, the Ruth Lilly Poetry Prize, the PEN Translation Prize, the Shelley Memorial Award, the first Tanning Prize, and a Lila Wallace–Reader's Digest Writers' Award, and fellowships from The Academy of American Poets, the Guggenheim Foundation, the National Endowment for the Arts, and the Rockefeller Foundation. He is a Chancellor of The Academy of American Poets and recently began a five-year term as judge of the Yale Series of Younger Poets Competition. He lives and works in Hawaii.

1. Economy

WHEN I wrote the following pages, or rather the bulk of them, I lived alone, in the woods, a mile from any neighbor, in a house which I had built myself, on the shore of Walden Pond, in Concord, Massachusetts, and earned my living by the labor of my hands only. I lived there two years and two months. At present I am a sojourner in civilized life again.

I should not obtrude my affairs so much on the notice of my readers if very particular inquiries had not been made by my townsmen concerning my mode of life, which some would call impertinent, though they do not appear to me at all impertinent, but, considering the circumstances, very natural and pertinent. Some have asked what I got to eat; if I did not feel lonesome; if I was not afraid; and the like. Others have been curious to learn what portion of my income I devoted to charitable purposes; and some, who have large families, how many poor children I maintained. I will therefore ask those of my readers who feel no particular interest in me to pardon me if I undertake to answer some of these questions in this book. In most books, the *I*, or first person, is omitted; in this it will be retained; that, in respect to egotism, is the main difference. We commonly do not remember that it is, after all, always the first person that is speaking. I should not talk so much about myself if there were anybody else whom I knew as well. Unfortunately, I am confined to this theme by the narrowness of my experience. Moreover, I, on my side, require of every writer, first or last, a simple and sincere account of his own life, and not merely what he has heard of other men's lives; some such account as he would send to his kindred from a distant land; for if he has lived sincerely it must have been in a distant land to me. Perhaps these pages are more particularly addressed to poor students. As for the rest of my readers, they will accept such portions as apply to them. I trust that none will stretch the seams in putting on the coat, for it may do good service to him whom it fits.

I would fain say something, not so much concerning the Chinese and Sandwich Islanders as you who read these pages, who are said to live in New England; something about your condition, especially your outward condition or circumstances in this world, in this town, what it is, whether it is necessary that it be as bad as it is, whether it cannot be improved as well as not. I have travelled a good deal in Concord; and everywhere, in shops, and offices, and fields, the inhabitants have appeared to me to be doing penance in a thousand remarkable ways. What I have heard of Bramins sitting exposed to four fires and looking in the face of the sun; or hanging suspended, with their heads downwards, over flames; or looking at the heavens over their shoulders "until it becomes impossible for them to resume their natural position, while from the twist of the neck nothing but liquids can pass into the stomach;" or dwelling, chained for life, at the foot of a tree; or measuring with their bodies, like caterpillars, the breadth of vast empires; or standing on one leg on the tops of pillars,—even these forms of conscious penance are hardly more incredible and astonishing than the scenes which I daily witness. The twelve labors of Hercules were trifling in comparison with those which my neighbors have undertaken; for they were only twelve, and had an end; but I could never see that these men slew or captured any monster or finished any labor. They have no friend Iolaus to burn with a hot iron the root of the hydra's head, but as soon as one head is crushed, two spring up.

I see young men, my townsmen, whose misfortune it is to have inherited farms, houses, barns, cattle, and farming tools; for these are more easily acquired than got rid of. Better if they had been born in the open pasture and suckled by a wolf, that they might have seen with clearer eyes what field they were called to labor in. Who made them serfs of the soil? Why should they eat their sixty acres, when man is condemned to eat only his peck of dirt? Why should they begin digging their graves as soon as they are born? They have got to live a man's life, pushing all these things before them, and get on as well as they can. How many a poor immortal soul have I met well-nigh crushed and smothered under its load, creeping down the road of life, pushing before it a barn seventy-five feet by forty, its Augean stables never cleansed, and one hundred acres of land, tillage, mowing, pasture, and wood-lot. The portionless, who struggle with no such unnecessary inherited encumbrances, find it labor enough to subdue and cultivate a few cubic feet of flesh.

But men labor under a mistake. The better part of the man is soon plowed into the soil for compost. By a seeming fate, commonly called necessity, they are employed, as it says in an old book, laying up treasures which moth and rust will corrupt and thieves break through and steal. It is a fool's life, as they will find when they get to the end of it, if not before. It is said that Deucalion and Pyrrha created men by throwing stones over their heads behind them:—

> Inde genus durum sumus, experiensque laborum,
> Et documenta damus quâ sumus origine nati.

Or, as Raleigh rhymes it in his sonorous way,—

> "From thence our kind hard-hearted is, enduring pain and care,
> Approving that our bodies of a stony nature are."

So much for a blind obedience to a blundering oracle, throwing the stones over their heads behind them, and not seeing where they fell.

Most men, even in this comparatively free country, through mere ignorance and mistake, are so occupied with the factitious cares and superfluously coarse labors of life that its finer fruits cannot be plucked by them. Their fingers, from excessive toil, are too clumsy and tremble too much for that. Actually, the laboring man has not leisure for a true integrity day by day; he cannot afford to sustain the manliest relations to men; his labor would be depreciated in the market. He has no time to be anything but a machine. How can he remember well his ignorance—which his growth requires—who has so often to use his knowledge? We should feed and clothe him gratuitously sometimes, and recruit him with our cordials, before we judge of him. The finest qualities of our nature, like the bloom on fruits, can be preserved only by the most delicate handling. Yet we do not treat ourselves nor one another thus tenderly.

Some of you, we all know, are poor, find it hard to live, are sometimes, as it were, gasping for breath. I have no doubt that some of you who read this book are unable to pay for all the dinners which you have actually eaten, or for the coats and shoes which are fast wearing or are already worn out, and have come to this page to spend borrowed or stolen time, robbing your creditors of an hour. It is very evident what mean and sneaking lives many of you live, for my sight has been whetted by experience; always on the limits, trying to get into business and trying to get out of debt, a very ancient slough, called by the Latins *aes alienum*, another's brass, for some of their coins were made of brass; still living, and dying, and buried by this other's brass; always promising to pay, promising to pay, to-morrow, and dying to-day, insolvent; seeking to curry favor, to get custom, by how many modes, only not state-prison offenses; lying, flattering, voting, contracting yourselves into a nutshell of civility, or dilating into an atmosphere of thin and vaporous generosity, that you may persuade your neighbor to let you make his shoes, or his hat, or his coat, or his carriage, or import his groceries for him; making yourselves sick, that you may lay up something against a sick day, something to be tucked away in an old chest, or in a stocking behind the plastering, or, more safely, in the brick bank; no matter where, no matter how much or how little.

I sometimes wonder that we can be so frivolous, I may almost say, as to attend to the gross but somewhat foreign form of servitude called Negro Slavery, there are so many keen and subtle masters that enslave both North and South. It is hard to have a Southern overseer; it is worse to have a Northern one; but worst of all when you are the slave-driver of yourself. Talk of a divinity in man! Look at the teamster on the highway, wending to market by day or night; does any divinity stir within him? His highest duty to fodder and water his horses! What is his destiny to him compared with the shipping interests? Does not he drive for Squire Make-a-stir? How godlike, how immortal, is he? See how he cowers and sneaks, how vaguely all the day he fears, not being immortal nor divine, but the slave and prisoner of his own opinion of himself, a fame won by his own deeds. Public opinion is a weak tyrant compared with our own private opinion. What a man thinks of himself, that it is which determines, or rather indicates, his fate. Self-emancipation even in the West Indian provinces of the fancy and imagination,—what Wilberforce is there to bring that about? Think, also, of the ladies of the land weaving toilet cushions against the last day, not to betray too green an interest in their fates! As if you could kill time without injuring eternity.

The mass of men lead lives of quiet desperation. What is called resignation is confirmed desperation. From the desperate city you go into the desperate country, and have to console yourself with the bravery of minks and muskrats. A stereotyped but unconscious despair is concealed even under what are called the games and amusements of mankind. There is no play in them, for this comes after work. But it is a characteristic of wisdom not to do desperate things.

When we consider what, to use the words of the catechism, is the chief end of man, and what are the true necessaries and means of life, it appears as if men had deliberately chosen the common mode of living because they preferred it to any other. Yet they honestly think there is no choice left. But alert and healthy natures remember that the sun rose clear. It is never too late to give up our prejudices. No way of thinking or doing, however ancient, can be trusted without proof. What everybody echoes or in silence passes by as true to-day may turn out to be falsehood to-morrow, mere smoke of opinion, which some had trusted for a cloud that would sprinkle fertilizing rain on their fields. What old people say you cannot do, you try and find that you can. Old deeds for old people, and new deeds for new. Old people did not know enough once, perchance, to fetch fresh fuel to keep the fire a-going; new people put a little dry wood under a pot, and are whirled round the globe with the speed of birds, in a way to kill old people, as the phrase is. Age is no better, hardly so well, qualified for an instructor as youth, for it has not profited so much as it has lost. One may almost doubt if the wisest man has learned anything of absolute value by living. Practically, the old have no very important advice to give the young, their own experience has been so partial, and their lives have been such miserable failures, for private reasons, as they must believe; and it may be that they have some faith left which belies that experience, and they are only less young than they were. I have lived some thirty years on this planet, and I have yet to hear the first syllable of valuable or even earnest advice from my seniors. They have told me nothing, and probably cannot tell me anything to the purpose. Here is life, an experiment to a great extent untried by me; but it does not avail me that they have tried it. If I have any experience which I think valuable, I am sure to reflect that this my Mentors said nothing about.

One farmer says to me, "You cannot live on vegetable food solely, for it furnishes nothing to make bones with;" and so he religiously devotes a part of his day to supplying his system with the raw material of bones; walking all the while he talks behind his oxen, which, with vegetable-made bones, jerk him and his lumbering plow along in spite of every obstacle. Some things are really necessaries of life in some circles, the most helpless and diseased, which in others are luxuries merely, and in others still are entirely unknown.

The whole ground of human life seems to some to have been gone over by their predecessors, both the heights and the valleys, and all things to have been cared for. According to Evelyn, "the wise Solomon prescribed ordinances for the very distance of trees; and the Roman prætors have decided how often you may go into your neighbor's land to gather the acorns which fall on it without trespass, and what share belongs to that neighbor." Hippocrates has even left directions how we should cut our nails; that is, even with the ends of the fingers neither shorter nor longer. Undoubtedly the very tedium and ennui which presume to have exhausted the variety and the joys of life are as old as Adam. But man's capacities have never been measured; nor are we to judge of what he can do by any precedents, so little has been tried. Whatever have been thy failures hitherto, "be not afflicted, my child, for who shall assign to thee what thou hast left undone?"

We might try our lives by a thousand simple tests; as, for instance, that the same sun that ripens my beans illumines at once a system of earths like ours. If I had remembered this it would have prevented some mistakes. This was not the light in which I hoed them. The stars are the apexes of what wonderful triangles! What distant and different beings in the various mansions of the universe are contemplating the same one at the same moment! Nature and human life are as various as our several constitutions. Who shall say what prospect life offers to another? Could a greater miracle take place than for us to look through each other's eyes for an instant? We should live in all the ages of the world in an hour; ay, in all the worlds of the ages. History, Poetry, Mythology!—I know of no reading of another's experience so startling and informing as this would be.

The greater part of what my neighbors call good I believe in my soul to be bad, and if I repent of anything, it is very likely to be my good behavior. What demon possessed me that I behaved so well? You may say the wisest thing you can, old man,—you who have lived seventy years, not without honor of a kind,—I hear an irresistible voice which invites me away from all that. One generation abandons the enterprises of another like stranded vessels.

I think that we may safely trust a good deal more than we do. We may waive just so much care of ourselves as we honestly bestow elsewhere. Nature is as well adapted to our weakness as to our strength. The incessant anxiety and strain of some is a well-nigh incurable form of disease. We are made to exaggerate the importance of what work we do; and yet how much is not done by us! or, what if we had been taken sick? How vigilant we are! determined not to live by faith if we can avoid it; all the day long on the alert, at night we unwillingly say our prayers and commit ourselves to uncertainties. So thoroughly and sincerely are we compelled to live, reverencing our life, and denying the possibility of change. This is the only way, we say; but there are as many ways as there can be drawn radii from one centre. All change is a miracle to contemplate; but it is a miracle which is taking place every instant. Confucious said, "To know that we know what we know, and that we do not know what we do not know, that is true knowledge." When one man has reduced a fact of the imagination to be a fact of his understanding, I foresee that all men will at length establish their lives on that basis.

Let us consider for a moment what most of the trouble and anxiety which I have referred to is about, and how much it is necessary that we be troubled, or at least careful. It would be some advantage to live a primitive and frontier life, though in the midst of an outward civilization, if only to learn what are the gross necessaries of life and what methods have been taken to obtain them; or even to look over the old day-books of the merchants, to see what it was that men most commonly bought at the stores, what they stored, that is, what are the grossest groceries. For the improvements of ages have had but little influence on the essential laws of man's existence; as our skeletons, probably, are not to be distinguished from those of our ancestors.

By the words, *necessary of life,* I mean whatever, of all that man obtains by his own exertions, has been from the first, or from long use has become, so important to human life that few, if any, whether from savageness, or poverty, or philosophy, ever attempt to do without it. To many creatures there is in this sense but one necessary of life, Food. To the bison of the prairie it is a few inches of palatable grass, with water to drink; unless he seeks the Shelter of the forest or the mountain's shadow. None of the brute creation requires more than Food and Shelter. The necessaries of life for man in this climate may, accurately enough, be distributed under the several heads of Food, Shelter, Clothing, and Fuel; for not till we have secured these are we prepared to entertain the true problems of life with freedom and a prospect of success. Man has invented, not only houses, but clothes

and cooked food; and possibly from the accidental discovery of the warmth of fire, and the consequent use of
it, at first a luxury, arose the present necessity to sit by
it. We observe cats and dogs acquiring the same second
nature. By proper Shelter and Clothing we legitimately
retain our own internal heat; but with an excess of these,
or of Fuel, that is, with an external heat greater than
our own internal, may not cookery properly be said to
begin? Darwin, the naturalist, says of the inhabitants of
Tierra del Fuego, that while his own party, who were
well clothed and sitting close to a fire, were far from too
warm, these naked savages, who were farther off, were
observed, to his great surprise, "to be streaming with
perspiration at undergoing such a roasting." So, we are
told, the New Hollander goes naked with impunity,
while the European shivers in his clothes. Is it impossible
to combine the hardiness of these savages with the intel-
lectualness of the civilized man? According to Liebig,
man's body is a stove, and food the fuel which keeps up
the internal combustion in the lungs. In cold weather we
eat more, in warm less. The animal heat is the result of
a slow combustion, and disease and death take place
when this is too rapid; or for want of fuel, or from some
defect in the draught, the fire goes out. Of course the
vital heat is not to be confounded with fire; but so much
for analogy. It appears, therefore, from the above list,
that the expression, *animal life,* is nearly synonymous
with the expression, *animal heat;* for while Food may be
regarded as the Fuel which keeps up the fire within us,—
and Fuel serves only to prepare that Food or to increase
the warmth of our bodies by addition from without,—
Shelter and Clothing also serve only to retain the *heat*
thus generated and absorbed.

The grand necessity, then, for our bodies, is to keep
warm, to keep the vital heat in us. What pains we accordingly take, not only with our Food, and Clothing,
and Shelter, but with our beds, which are our night-
clothes, robbing the nests and breasts of birds to prepare
this shelter within a shelter, as the mole has its bed of
grass and leaves at the end of its burrow! The poor man
is wont to complain that this is a cold world; and to cold,
no less physical than social, we refer directly a great part

of our ails. The summer, in some climates, makes possible to man a sort of Elysian life. Fuel, except to cook his Food, is then unnecessary; the sun is his fire, and many of the fruits are sufficiently cooked by its rays; while Food generally is more various, and more easily obtained, and Clothing and Shelter are wholly or half unnecessary. At the present day, and in this country, as I find by my own experience, a few implements, a knife, an axe, a spade, a wheelbarrow, etc., and for the studious, lamplight, stationery, and access to a few books, rank next to necessaries, and can all be obtained at a trifling cost. Yet some, not wise, go to the other side of the globe, to barbarous and unhealthy regions, and devote themselves to trade for ten or twenty years, in order that they may live,—that is, keep comfortably warm,— and die in New England at last. The luxuriously rich are not simply kept comfortably warm, but unnaturally hot; as I implied before, they are cooked, of course, *à la mode*.

Most of the luxuries, and many of the so-called comforts of life, are not only not indispensable, but positive hindrances to the elevation of mankind. With respect to luxuries and comforts, the wisest have ever lived a more simple and meagre life than the poor. The ancient philosophers, Chinese, Hindoo, Persian, and Greek, were a class than which none has been poorer in outward riches, none so rich in inward. We know not much about them. It is remarkable that *we* know so much of them as we do. The same is true of the more modern reformers and benefactors of their race. None can be an impartial or wise observer of human life but from the vantage ground of what *we* should call voluntary poverty. Of a life of luxury the fruit is luxury, whether in agriculture, or commerce, or literature, or art. There are nowadays professors of philosophy, but not philosophers. Yet it is admirable to profess because it was once admirable to live. To be a philosopher is not merely to have subtle thoughts, nor even to found a school, but so to love wisdom as to live according to its dictates, a life of simplicity, independence, magnanimity, and trust. It is to solve some of the problems of life, not only theoretically, but practically. The success of great scholars and thinkers is commonly a courtier-like success, not kingly, not manly. They make shift to live merely by conformity, practically as their fathers did, and are in no sense the progenitors of a nobler race of men. But why do men degenerate ever? What makes families run out? What is the nature of the luxury which enervates and destroys nations? Are we sure that there is none of it in our own lives? The philosopher is in advance of his age even in the outward form of his life. He is not fed, sheltered, clothed, warmed, like his contemporaries. How can a man be a philosopher and not maintain his vital heat by better methods than other men?

When a man is warmed by the several modes which I have described, what does he want next? Surely not more warmth of the same kind, as more and richer food, larger and more splendid houses, finer and more abundant clothing, more numerous, incessant, and hotter fires, and the like. When he has obtained those things which are necessary to life, there is another alternative than to obtain the superfluities; and that is, to adventure on life now, his vacation from humbler toil having commenced. The soil, it appears, is suited to the seed, for it has sent its radicle downward, and it may now send its shoot upward also with confidence. Why has man rooted himself thus firmly in the earth, but that he may rise in the same proportion into the heavens above?—for the nobler plants are valued for the fruit they bear at last in the air and light, far from the ground, and are not treated like the humbler esculents, which, though they may be biennials, are cultivated only till they have perfected their root, and often cut down at top for this purpose, so that most would not know them in their flowering season.

I do not mean to prescribe rules to strong and valiant natures, who will mind their own affairs whether in heaven or hell, and perchance build more magnificently and spend more lavishly than the richest, without ever impoverishing themselves, not knowing how they live,— if, indeed, there are any such, as has been dreamed; nor to those who find their encouragement and inspiration in precisely the present condition of things, and cherish it with the fondness and enthusiasm of lovers,—and, to

some extent, I reckon myself in this number; I do not
speak to those who are well employed, in whatever circumstances, and they know whether they are well employed or not;—but mainly to the mass of men who are
discontented, and idly complaining of the hardness of
their lot or of the times, when they might improve them.
There are some who complain most energetically and
inconsolably of any, because they are, as they say, doing
their duty. I also have in my mind that seemingly
wealthy, but most terribly impoverished class of all, who
have accumulated dross, but know not how to use it, or
get rid of it, and thus have forged their own golden or
silver fetters.

If I should attempt to tell how I have desired to spend
my life in years past, it would probably surprise those
of my readers who are somewhat acquainted with its
actual history; it would certainly astonish those who
know nothing about it. I will only hint at some of the
enterprises which I have cherished.

In any weather, at any hour of the day or night, I have
been anxious to improve the nick of time, and notch it
on my stick too; to stand on the meeting of two eterni-
ties, the past and future, which is precisely the present
moment; to toe that line. You will pardon some obscuri-
ties, for there are more secrets in my trade than in most
men's, and yet not voluntarily kept, but inseparable from
its very nature. I would gladly tell all that I know about
it, and never paint "No Admittance" on my gate.

I long ago lost a hound, a bay horse, and a turtle dove,
and am still on their trail. Many are the travellers I have
spoken concerning them, describing their tracks and
what calls they answered to. I have met one or two who
had heard the hound, and the tramp of the horse, and
even seen the dove disappear behind a cloud, and they
seemed as anxious to recover them as if they had lost
them themselves.

To anticipate, not the sunrise and the dawn merely,
but, if possible, Nature herself! How many mornings,
summer and winter, before yet any neighbor was stirring
about his business, have I been about mine! No doubt,
many of my townsmen have met me returning from this

enterprise, farmers starting for Boston in the twilight, or woodchoppers going to their work. It is true, I never assisted the sun materially in his rising, but, doubt not, it was of the last importance only to be present at it.

So many autumn, ay, and winter days, spent outside the town, trying to hear what was in the wind, to hear and carry it express! I well-nigh sunk all my capital in it, and lost my own breath into the bargain, running in the face of it. If it had concerned either of the political parties, depend upon it, it would have appeared in the Gazette with the earliest intelligence. At other times watching from the observatory of some cliff or tree, to telegraph any new arrival; or waiting at evening on the hill-tops for the sky to fall, that I might catch something, though I never caught much, and that, manna-wise, would dissolve again in the sun.

For a long time I was reporter to a journal, of no very wide circulation, whose editor has never yet seen fit to print the bulk of my contributions, and, as is too common with writers, I got only my labor for my pains. However, in this case my pains were their own reward.

For many years I was self-appointed inspector of snow-storms and rain-storms, and did my duty faithfully; surveyor, if not of highways, then of forest paths and all across-lot routes, keeping them open, and ravines bridged and passable at all seasons, where the public heel had testified to their utility.

I have looked after the wild stock of the town, which give a faithful herdsman a good deal of trouble by leaping fences; and I have had an eye to the unfrequented nooks and corners of the farm; though I did not always know whether Jonas or Solomon worked in a particular field to-day; that was none of my business. I have watered the red huckleberry, the sand cherry and the nettle-tree, the red pine and the black ash, the white grape and the yellow violet, which might have withered else in dry seasons.

In short, I went on thus for a long time (I may say it without boasting), faithfully minding my business, till it became more and more evident that my townsmen would not after all admit me into the list of town officers, nor make my place a sinecure with a moderate allowance. My accounts, which I can swear to have kept faithfully, I have, indeed, never got audited, still less accepted, still less paid and settled. However, I have not set my heart on that.

Not long since, a strolling Indian went to sell baskets at the house of a well-known lawyer in my neighborhood. "Do you wish to buy any baskets?" he asked. "No, we do not want any," was the reply. "What!" exclaimed the Indian as he went out the gate, "do you mean to starve us?" Having seen his industrious white neighbors so well off,—that the lawyer had only to weave arguments, and, by some magic, wealth and standing followed,—he had said to himself: I will go into business; I will weave baskets; it is a thing which I can do. Thinking that when he had made the baskets he would have done his part, and then it would be the white man's to buy them. He had not discovered that it was necessary for him to make it worth the other's while to buy them, or at least make him think that it was so, or to make something else which it would be worth his while to buy. I too had woven a kind of basket of a delicate texture, but I had not made it worth any one's while to buy them. Yet not the less, in my case, did I think it worth my while to weave them, and instead of studying how to make it worth men's while to buy my baskets, I studied rather how to avoid the necessity of selling them. The life which men praise and regard as successful is but one kind. Why should we exaggerate any one kind at the expense of the others?

Finding that my fellow-citizens were not likely to offer me any room in the court house, or any curacy or living anywhere else, but I must shift for myself, I turned my face more exclusively than ever to the woods, where I was better known. I determined to go into business at once, and not wait to acquire the usual capital, using such slender means as I had already got. My purpose in going to Walden Pond was not to live cheaply nor to live dearly there, but to transact some private business with the fewest obstacles; to be hindered from accomplishing which for want of a little common sense, a little enterprise and business talent, appeared not so sad as foolish.

I have always endeavored to acquire strict business habits; they are indispensable to every man. If your trade is with the Celestial Empire, then some small counting house on the coast, in some Salem harbor, will be fixture enough. You will export such articles as the country affords, purely native products, much ice and pine timber and a little granite, always in native bottoms. These will be good ventures. To oversee all the details yourself in person; to be at once pilot and captain, and owner and underwriter; to buy and sell and keep the accounts; to read every letter received, and write or read every letter sent; to superintend the discharge of imports night and day; to be upon many parts of the coast almost at the same time,—often the richest freight will be discharged upon a Jersey shore;—to be your own telegraph, unweariedly sweeping the horizon, speaking all passing vessels bound coastwise; to keep up a steady despatch of commodities, for the supply of such a distant and exorbitant market; to keep yourself informed of the state of the markets, prospects of war and peace everywhere, and anticipate the tendencies of trade and civilization,—taking advantage of the results of all exploring expeditions, using new passages and all improvements in navigation;—charts to be studied, the position of reefs and new lights and buoys to be ascertained, and ever, and ever, the logarithmic tables to be corrected, for by the error of some calculator the vessel often splits upon a rock that should have reached a friendly pier,—there is the untold fate of La Pérouse;—universal science to be kept pace with, studying the lives of all great discoverers and navigators, great adventurers and merchants, from Hanno and the Phœnicians down to our day; in fine, account of stock to be taken from time to time, to know how you stand. It is a labor to task the faculties of a man,—such problems of profit and loss, of interest, of tare and tret, and gauging of all kinds in it, as demand a universal knowledge.

I have thought that Walden Pond would be a good place for business, not solely on account of the railroad and the ice trade; it offers advantages which it may not be good policy to divulge; it is a good port and a good foundation. No Neva marshes to be filled; though you must everywhere build on piles of your own driving. It is said that a flood-tide, with a westerly wind, and ice in the Neva, would sweep St. Petersburg from the face of the earth.

As this business was to be entered into without the usual capital, it may not be easy to conjecture where those means, that will still be indispensable to every such undertaking, were to be obtained. As for Clothing, to come at once to the practical part of the question, perhaps we are led oftener by the love of novelty and a regard for the opinions of men, in procuring it, than by a true utility. Let him who has work to do recollect that the object of clothing is, first, to retain the vital heat, and secondly, in this state of society, to cover nakedness, and he may judge how much of any necessary or important work may be accomplished without adding to his wardrobe. Kings and queens who wear a suit but once, though made by some tailor or dressmaker to their majesties, cannot know the comfort of wearing a suit that fits. They are no better than wooden horses to hang the clean clothes on. Every day our garments become more assimilated to ourselves, receiving the impress of the wearer's character, until we hesitate to lay them aside without such delay and medical appliances and some such solemnity even as our bodies. No man ever stood the lower in my estimation for having a patch in his clothes; yet I am sure that there is greater anxiety, commonly, to have fashionable, or at least clean and unpatched clothes, than to have a sound conscience. But even if the rent is not mended, perhaps the worst vice betrayed is improvidence. I sometimes try my acquaintances by such tests as this,—Who could wear a patch, or two extra seams only, over the knee? Most behave as if they believed that their prospects for life would be ruined if they should do it. It would be easier for them to hobble to town with a broken leg than with a broken pantaloon. Often if an accident happens to a gentleman's legs, they can be mended; but if a similar accident happens to the legs of his pantaloons, there is no help for it; for he considers, not what is truly respectable, but what is respected. We know but few men, a great many coats and breeches. Dress a scarecrow in your last shift, you standing shiftless by, who would not soonest salute the scare-crow? Passing a cornfield the other day, close by a hat and coat on a stake, I recognized the owner of the farm. He was only a little more weatherbeaten than when I saw him last. I have heard of a dog that barked at every stranger who approached his master's premises with clothes on, but was easily quieted by a naked thief. It is an interesting question how far men would retain their relative rank if they were divested of their clothes. Could you, in such a case, tell surely of any company of civi-lized men which belonged to the most respected class? When Madam Pfeiffer, in her adventurous travels round the world, from east to west, had got so near home as Asiatic Russia, she says that she felt the necessity of wearing other than a traveling dress, when she went to meet the authorities, for she "was now in a civilized country, where . . . people are judged of by their clothes." Even in our democratic New England towns the accidental possession of wealth, and its manifestation in dress and equipage alone, obtain for the possessor almost universal respect. But they who yield such re-spect, numerous as they are, are so far heathen, and need to have a missionary sent to them. Beside, clothes introduced sewing, a kind of work which you may call endless; a woman's dress, at least, is never done.

A man who has at length found something to do will not need to get a new suit to do it in; for him the old will do, that has lain dusty in the garret for an indetermi-nate period. Old shoes will serve a hero longer than they have served his valet,—if a hero ever has a valet,—bare feet are older than shoes, and he can make them do. Only they who go to soirées and legislative halls must have new coats, coats to change as often as the man changes in them. But if my jacket and trousers, my hat and shoes, are fit to worship God in, they will do; will they not? Who ever saw his old clothes,—his old coat, actually worn out, resolved into its primitive elements, so that it was not a deed of charity to bestow it on some poor boy, by him perchance to be bestowed on some poorer still, or shall we say richer, who could do with less? I say, beware of all enterprises that require new clothes, and not rather a new wearer of clothes. If there is not a new man, how can the new clothes be made to fit? If you have any enterprise before you, try it in your old clothes. All men want, not something to *do with,* but something to *do,* or rather something to *be.* Perhaps we should never procure a new suit, however ragged or dirty the old, until we have so conducted, so enterprised or sailed in some way, that we feel like new men in the old, and that to retain it would be like keeping new wine in old bottles. Our moulting season, like that of the fowls, must be a crisis in our lives. The loon retires to solitary ponds to spend it. Thus also the snake casts its slough, and the caterpillar its wormy coat, by an internal industry and expansion; for clothes are but our outmost cuticle and mortal coil. Otherwise we shall be found sailing under false colors, and be inevitably cashiered at last by our own opinion, as well as that of mankind.

We don garment after garment, as if we grew like exogenous plants by addition without. Our outside and often thin and fanciful clothes are our epidermis, or false skin, which partakes not of our life, and may be stripped off here and there without fatal injury; our thicker garments, constantly worn, are our cellular integument, or cortex; but our shirts are our liber, or true bark, which cannot be removed without girdling and so destroying the man. I believe that all races at some seasons wear something equivalent to the shirt. It is desirable that a man be clad so simply that he can lay his hands on himself in the dark, and that he live in all respects so compactly and preparedly that, if an enemy take the town, he can, like the old philosopher, walk out the gate empty-handed without anxiety. While one thick garment is, for most purposes, as good as three thin ones, and cheap clothing can be obtained at prices really to suit customers; while a thick coat can be bought for five dollars, which will last as many years, thick pantaloons for two dollars, cowhide boots for a dollar and a half a pair, a summer hat for a quarter of a dollar, and a winter cap for sixty-two and a half cents, or a better be made at home at a nominal cost, where is he so poor that, clad in such a suit, *of his own earning,* there will not be found wise men to do him reverence?

When I ask for a garment of a particular form, my

tailoress tells me gravely, "They do not make them so now," not emphasizing the "They" at all, as if she quoted an authority as impersonal as the Fates, and I find it difficult to get made what I want, simply because she cannot believe that I mean what I say, that I am so rash. When I hear this oracular sentence, I am for a moment absorbed in thought, emphasizing to myself each word separately that I may come at the meaning of it, that I may find out by what degree of consanguinity *They* are related to *me,* and what authority they may have in an affair which affects me so nearly; and, finally, I am inclined to answer her with equal mystery, and without any more emphasis of the "they,"—"It is true, they did not make them so recently, but they do now." Of what use this measuring of me if she does not measure my character, but only the breadth of my shoulders, as it were a peg to hang the coat on? We worship not the Graces, nor the Parcæ, but Fashion. She spins and weaves and cuts with full authority. The head monkey at Paris puts on a traveller's cap, and all the monkeys in America do the same. I sometimes despair of getting anything quite simple and honest done in this world by the help of men. They would have to be passed through a powerful press first, to squeeze their old notions out of them, so that they would not soon get upon their legs again; and then there would be some one in the company with a maggot in his head, hatched from an egg deposited there nobody knows when, for not even fire kills these things, and you would have lost your labor. Nevertheless, we will not forget that some Egyptian wheat was handed down to us by a mummy.

On the whole, I think that it cannot be maintained that dressing has in this or any country risen to the dignity of an art. At present men make shift to·wear what they can get. Like shipwrecked sailors, they put on what they can find on the beach, and at a little distance, whether of space or time, laugh at each other's masquerade. Every generation laughs at the old fashions, but follows religiously the new. We are amused at beholding the costume of Henry VIII., or Queen Elizabeth, as much as if it was that of the King and Queen of the Cannibal Islands. All costume off a man is pitiful or grotesque. It is only the serious eye peering from and the sincere life passed within it which restrain laughter and consecrate the costume of any people. Let Harlequin be taken with a fit of the colic and his trappings will have to serve that mood too. When the soldier is hit by a cannon-ball, rags are as becoming as purple.

The childish and savage taste of men and women for new patterns keeps how many shaking and squinting through kaleidoscopes that they may discover the particular figure which this generation requires to-day. The manufacturers have learned that this taste is merely whimsical. Of two patterns which differ only by a few threads more or less of a particular color, the one will be sold readily, the other lie on the shelf, though it frequently happens that after the lapse of a season the latter becomes the most fashionable. Comparatively, tattooing is not the hideous custom which it is called. It is not barbarous merely because the printing is skin-deep and unalterable.

I cannot believe that our factory system is the best mode by which men may get clothing. The condition of the operatives is becoming every day more like that of the English; and it cannot be wondered at, since, as far as I have heard or observed, the principal object is, not that mankind may be well and honestly clad, but, unquestionably, that the corporations may be enriched. In the long run men hit only what they aim at. Therefore, though they should fail immediately, they had better aim at something high.

As for a Shelter, I will not deny that this is now a necessary of life, though there are instances of men having done without it for long periods in colder countries than this. Samuel Laing says that "the Laplander in his skin dress, and in a skin bag which he puts over his head and shoulders, will sleep night after night on the snow . . . in a degree of cold which would extinguish the life of one exposed to it in any woollen clothing." He had seen them asleep thus. Yet he adds, "They are not hardier than other people." But, probably, man did not live long on the earth without discovering the convenience which there is in a house, the domestic comforts, which phrase may have originally signified the satisfactions of the house more than of the family; though these must be extremely partial and occasional in those climates where the house is associated in our thoughts with winter or the rainy season chiefly, and two thirds of the year, except for a parasol, is unnecessary. In our climate, in the summer, it was formerly almost solely a covering at night. In the Indian gazettes a wigwam was the symbol of a day's march, and a row of them cut or painted on the bark of a tree signified that so many times they had camped. Man was not made so large limbed and robust but that he must seek to narrow his world, and wall in a space such as fitted him. He was at first bare and out of doors; but though this was pleasant enough in serene and warm weather, by daylight, the rainy season and the winter, to say nothing of the torrid sun, would perhaps have nipped his race in the bud if he had not made haste to clothe himself with the shelter of a house. Adam and Eve, according to the fable, wore the bower before other clothes. Man wanted a home, a place of warmth, of comfort, first of physical warmth, then the warmth of the affections.

We may imagine a time when, in the infancy of the human race, some enterprising mortal crept into a hollow in a rock for shelter. Every child begins the world again, to some extent, and loves to stay outdoors, even in wet and cold. It plays house, as well as horse, having an instinct for it. Who does not remember the interest with which when young he looked at shelving rocks, or any approach to a cave? It was the natural yearning of that portion of our most primitive ancestor which still survived in us. From the cave we have advanced to roofs of palm leaves, of bark and boughs, of linen woven and stretched, of grass and straw, of boards and shingles, of stone and tiles. At last, we know not what it is to live in the open air, and our lives are domestic in more senses than we think. From the hearth the field is a great distance. It would be well, perhaps, if we were to spend more of our days and nights without any obstruction between us and the celestial bodies, if the poet did not speak so much from under a roof, or the saint dwell there so long. Birds do not sing in caves, nor do doves cherish their innocence in dovecots.

However, if one designs to construct a dwelling-house,
it behooves him to exercise a little Yankee shrewdness,
lest after all he find himself in a workhouse, a labyrinth
without a clue, a museum, an almshouse, a prison, or a
splendid mausoleum instead. Consider first how slight a
shelter is absolutely necessary. I have seen Penobscot
Indians, in this town, living in tents of thin cotton cloth,
while the snow was nearly a foot deep around them, and
I thought that they would be glad to have it deeper to
keep out the wind. Formerly, when how to get my living
honestly, with freedom left for my proper pursuits, was
a question which vexed me even more than it does now,
for unfortunately I am become somewhat callous, I used
to see a large box by the railroad, six feet long by three
wide, in which the laborers locked up their tools at night;
and it suggested to me that every man who was hard
pushed might get such a one for a dollar, and, having
bored a few auger holes in it, to admit the air at least,
get into it when it rained and at night, and hook down
the lid, and so have freedom in his love, and in his soul
be free. This did not appear the worst, nor by any means
a despicable alternative. You could sit up as late as you
pleased, and, whenever you got up, go abroad without
any landlord or house-lord dogging you for rent. Many
a man is harassed to death to pay the rent of a larger
and more luxurious box who would not have frozen to
death in such a box as this. I am far from jesting. Economy is a subject which admits of being treated with lev-
ity, but it cannot so be disposed of. A comfortable house
for a rude and hardy race, that lived mostly out of doors,
was once made here almost entirely of such materials as
Nature furnished ready to their hands. Gookin, who was
superintendent of the Indians subject to the Massachusetts Colony, writing in 1674, says, "The best of their
houses are covered very neatly, tight and warm, with
barks of trees, slipped from their bodies at those seasons
when the sap is up, and made into great flakes, with
pressure of weighty timber, when they are green. . . .
The meaner sort are covered with mats which they make
of a kind of bulrush, and are also indifferently tight and
warm, but not so good as the former. . . . Some I have
seen, sixty or a hundred feet long and thirty feet

broad. . . . I have often lodged in their wigwams, and found them as warm as the best English houses." He adds that they were commonly carpeted and lined within with well-wrought embroidered mats, and were furnished with various utensils. The Indians had advanced so far as to regulate the effect of the wind by a mat suspended over the hole in the roof and moved by a string. Such a lodge was in the first instance constructed in a day or two at most, and taken down and put up in a few hours; and every family owned one, or its apartment in one.

In the savage state every family owns a shelter as good as the best, and sufficient for its coarser and simpler wants; but I think that I speak within bounds when I say that, though the birds of the air have their nests, and the foxes their holes, and the savages their wigwams, in modern civilized society not more than one half the families own a shelter. In the large towns and cities, where civilization especially prevails, the number of those who own a shelter is a very small fraction of the whole. The rest pay an annual tax for this outside garment of all, become indispensable summer and winter, which would buy a village of Indian wigwams, but now helps to keep them poor as long as they live. I do not mean to insist here on the disadvantage of hiring compared with owning, but it is evident that the savage owns his shelter because it costs so little, while the civilized man hires his commonly because he cannot afford to own it; nor can he, in the long run, any better afford to hire. But, answers one, by merely paying this tax the poor civilized man secures an abode which is a palace compared with the savage's. An annual rent of from twenty-five to a hundred dollars (these are the country rates) entitles him to the benefit of the improvements of centuries, spacious apartments, clean paint and paper, Rumford fireplace, back plastering, Venetian blinds, copper pump, spring lock, a commodious cellar, and many other things. But how happens it that he who is said to enjoy these things is so commonly a *poor* civilized man, while the savage, who has them not, is rich as a savage? If it is asserted that civilization is a real advance in the condition of man,—and I think that it is, though only the wise improve their advantages,—it must be shown that it has produced better dwellings without making them more costly; and the cost of a thing is the amount of what I will call life which is required to be exchanged for it, immediately or in the long run. An average house in this neighborhood costs perhaps eight hundred dollars, and to lay up this sum will take from ten to fifteen years of the laborer's life, even if he is not encumbered with a family,—estimating the pecuniary value of every man's labor at one dollar a day, for if some receive more, others receive less;—so that he must have spent more than half his life commonly before *his* wigwam will be earned. If we suppose him to pay a rent instead, this is but a doubtful choice of evils. Would the savage have been wise to exchange his wigwam for a palace on these terms?

It may be guessed that I reduce almost the whole advantage of holding this superfluous property as a fund in store against the future, so far as the individual is concerned, mainly to the defraying of funeral expenses. But perhaps a man is not required to bury himself. Nevertheless this points to an important distinction between the civilized man and the savage; and, no doubt, they have designs on us for our benefit, in making the life of a civilized people an *institution,* in which the life of the individual is to a great extent absorbed, in order to preserve and perfect that of the race. But I wish to show at what a sacrifice this advantage is at present obtained, and to suggest that we may possibly so live as to secure all the advantage without suffering any of the disadvantage. What mean ye by saying that the poor ye have always with you, or that the fathers have eaten sour grapes, and the children's teeth are set on edge?

"As I live, saith the Lord God, ye shall not have occasion any more to use this proverb in Israel.

"Behold all souls are mine; as the soul of the father, so also the soul of the son is mine: the soul that sinneth, it shall die."

When I consider my neighbors, the farmers of Concord, who are at least as well off as the other classes, I find that for the most part they have been toiling twenty, thirty, or forty years, that they may become the real owners of their farms, which commonly they have inherited with encumbrances, or else bought with hired money,—and we may regard one third of that toil as the cost of their houses,—but commonly they have not paid for them yet. It is true, the encumbrances sometimes outweigh the value of the farm, so that the farm itself becomes one great encumbrance, and still a man is found to inherit it, being well acquainted with it, as he says. On applying to the assessors, I am surprised to learn that they cannot at once name a dozen in the town who own their farms free and clear. If you would know the history of these homesteads, inquire at the bank where they are mortgaged. The man who has actually paid for his farm with labor on it is so rare that every neighbor can point to him. I doubt if there are three such men in Concord. What has been said of the merchants, that a very large majority, even ninety-seven in a hundred, are sure to fail, is equally true of the farmers. With regard to the merchants, however, one of them says pertinently that a great part of their failures are not genuine pecuniary failures, but merely failures to fulfil their engagements, because it is inconvenient; that is, it is the moral character that breaks down. But this puts an infinitely worse face on the matter, and suggests, beside, that probably not even the other three succeed in saving their souls, but are perchance bankrupt in a worse sense than they who fail honestly. Bankruptcy and repudiation are the springboards from which much of our civilization vaults and turns its somersets, but the savage stands on the unelastic plank of famine. Yet the Middlesex Cattle Show goes off here with *éclat* annually, as if all the joints of the agricultural machine were suent.

The farmer is endeavoring to solve the problem of a livelihood by a formula more complicated than the problem itself. To get his shoestrings he speculates in herds of cattle. With consummate skill he has set his trap with a hair spring to catch comfort and independence, and then, as he turned away, got his own leg into it. This is the reason he is poor; and for a similar reason we are all poor in respect to a thousand savage comforts, though surrounded by luxuries. As Chapman sings,—

"The false society of men—
—for earthly greatness
All heavenly comforts rarefies to air."

And when the farmer has got his house, he may not be
the richer but the poorer for it, and it be the house that
has got him. As I understand it, that was a valid objection urged by Momus against the house which Minerva
made, that she "had not made it movable, by which
means a bad neighborhood might be avoided," and it
may still be urged, for our houses are such unwieldy
property that we are often imprisoned rather than
housed in them; and the bad neighborhood to be
avoided is our own scurvy selves. I know one or two
families, at least, in this town, who, for nearly a generation, have been wishing to sell their houses in the outskirts and move into the village, but have not been able
to accomplish it, and only death will set them free.

Granted that the *majority* are able at last either to
own or hire the modern house with all its improvements.
While civilization has been improving our houses, it has
not equally improved the men who are to inhabit them.
It has created palaces, but it was not so easy to create
noblemen and kings. And *if the civilized man's pursuits
are no worthier than the savage's, if he is employed the
greater part of his life in obtaining gross necessaries and
comforts merely, why should he have a better dwelling
than the former?*

But how do the poor *minority* fare? Perhaps it will be
found that just in proportion as some have been placed
in outward circumstances above the savage, others have
been degraded below him. The luxury of one class is
counterbalanced by the indigence of another. On the
one side is the palace, on the other are the almshouse
and "silent poor." The myriads who built the pyramids
to be the tombs of the Pharaohs were fed on garlic, and
it may be were not decently buried themselves. The
mason who finishes the cornice of the palace returns at
night perchance to a hut not so good as a wigwam. It is
a mistake to suppose that, in a country where the usual
evidences of civilization exist, the condition of a very
large body of the inhabitants may not be as degraded as

that of savages. I refer to the degraded poor, not now to the degraded rich. To know this I should not need to look farther than to the shanties which everywhere border our railroads, that last improvement in civilization; where I see in my daily walks human beings living in sties, and all winter with an open door, for the sake of light, without any visible, often imaginable, wood-pile, and the forms of both old and young are permanently contracted by the long habit of shrinking from cold and misery, and the development of all their limbs and faculties is checked. It certainly is fair to look at that class by whose labor the works which distinguish this generation are accomplished. Such too, to a greater or less extent, is the condition of the operatives of every denomination in England, which is the great workhouse of the world. Or I could refer you to Ireland, which is marked as one of the white or enlightened spots on the map. Contrast the physical condition of the Irish with that of the North American Indian, or the South Sea Islander, or any other savage race before it was degraded by contact with the civilized man. Yet I have no doubt that that people's rulers are as wise as the average of civilized rulers. Their condition only proves what squalidness may consist with civilization. I hardly need refer now to the laborers in our Southern States who produce the staple exports of this country, and are themselves a staple production of the South. But to confine myself to those who are said to be in *moderate* circumstances.

Most men appear never to have considered what a house is, and are actually though needlessly poor all their lives because they think that they must have such a one as their neighbors have. As if one were to wear any sort of coat which the tailor might cut out for him, or, gradually leaving off palm-leaf hat or cap of woodchuck skin, complain of hard times because he could not afford to buy him a crown! It is possible to invent a house still more convenient and luxurious than we have, which yet all would admit that man could not afford to pay for. Shall we always study to obtain more of these things, and not sometimes to be content with less? Shall the respectable citizen thus gravely teach, by precept and example, the necessity of the young man's providing a certain number of superflous glow-shoes, and umbrellas, and empty guest chambers for empty guests, before he dies? Why should not our furniture be as simple as the Arab's or the Indian's? When I think of the benefactors of the race, whom we have apotheosized as messengers from heaven, bearers of divine gifts to man, I do not see in my mind any retinue at their heels, any car-load of fashionable furniture. Or what if I were to allow—would it not be a singular allowance?—that our furniture should be more complex than the Arab's, in proportion as we are morally and intellectually his superiors! At present our houses are cluttered and defiled with it, and a good housewife would sweep out the greater part into the dust hole, and not leave her morning's work undone. Morning work! By the blushes of Aurora and the music of Memnon, what should be man's *morning work* in this world? I had three pieces of limestone on my desk, but I was terrified to find that they required to be dusted daily, when the furniture of my mind was all undusted still, and I threw them out the window in disgust. How, then, could I have a furnished house? I would rather sit in the open air, for no dust gathers on the grass, unless where man has broken ground.

It is the luxurious and dissipated who set the fashions which the herd so diligently follow. The traveller who stops at the best houses, so called, soon discovers this, for the publicans presume him to be a Sardanapalus, and if he resigned himself to their tender mercies he would soon be completely emasculated. I think that in the rail-road car we are inclined to spend more on luxury than on safety and convenience, and it threatens without attaining these to become no better than a modern drawing room, with its divans, and ottomans, and sun-shades, and a hundred other oriental things, which we are taking west with us, invented for the ladies of the harem and the effeminate natives of the Celestial Empire, which Jonathan should be ashamed to know the names of. I would rather sit on a pumpkin and have it all to myself than be crowded on a velvet cushion. I would rather ride on earth in an ox cart, with a free circulation, than go to heaven in the fancy car of an excursion train and breathe a *malaria* all the way.

The very simplicity and nakedness of man's life in the primitive ages imply this advantage, at least, that they left him still but a sojourner in nature. When he was refreshed with food and sleep, he contemplated his journey again. He dwelt, as it were, in a tent in this world, and was either threading the valleys, or crossing the plains, or climbing the mountaintops. But lo! men have become the tools of their tools. The man who independently plucked the fruits when he was hungry is become a farmer; and he who stood under a tree for shelter, a housekeeper. We now no longer camp as for a night, but have settled down on earth and forgotten heaven. We have adopted Christianity merely as an improved method of *agri*-culture. We have built for this world a family mansion, and for the next a family tomb. The best works of art are the expression of man's struggle to free himself from this condition, but the effect of our art is merely to make this low state comfortable and that higher state to be forgotten. There is actually no place in this village for a work of *fine* art, if any had come down to us, to stand, for our lives, our houses and streets, furnish no proper pedestal for it. There is not a nail to hang a picture on, nor a shelf to receive the bust of a hero or a saint. When I consider how our houses are built and paid for, or not paid for, and their internal economy managed and sustained, I wonder that the floor does not give way under the visitor while he is admiring the gewgaws upon the mantelpiece, and let him through into the cellar to some solid and honest though earthy foundation. I cannot but perceive that this so-called rich and refined life is a thing jumped at, and I do not get on in the enjoyment of the *fine* arts which adorn it, my attention being wholly occupied with the jump; for I remember that the greatest genuine leap, due to human muscles alone, on record, is that of certain wandering Arabs, who are said to have cleared twenty-five feet on level ground. Without factitious support, man is sure to come to earth again beyond that distance. The first question which I am tempted to put to the proprietor of such great impropriety is, Who bolsters you? Are you one of the ninety-seven who fail, or the three who succeed? Answer me these questions, and then perhaps I may look at your baubles and find them ornamental. The cart before the horse is neither beautiful nor useful. Before we can adorn our houses with beautiful objects the walls must be stripped, and our lives must be stripped, and beautiful housekeeping and beautiful living be laid for a foundation: now, a taste for the beautiful is most cultivated out of doors, where there is no house and no housekeeper.

Old Johnson, in his "Wonder-Working Providence," speaking of the first settlers of this town, with whom he was contemporary, tells us that "they burrow themselves in the earth for their first shelter under some hillside, and, casting the soil aloft upon timber, they make a smoky fire against the earth, at the highest side." They did not "provide them houses," says he, "till the earth, by the Lord's blessing, brought forth bread to feed them," and the first year's crop was so light that "they were forced to cut their bread very thin for a long season." The secretary of the Province of New Netherland, writing in Dutch, in 1650, for the information of those who wished to take up land there, states more particularly that "those in New Netherland, and especially in New England, who have no means to build farm-houses at first according to their wishes, dig a square pit in the ground, cellar fashion, six or seven feet deep, as long and as broad as they think proper, case the earth inside with wood all round the wall, and line the wood with the bark of trees or something else to prevent the caving in of the earth; floor this cellar with plank, and wainscot it overhead for a ceiling, raise a roof of spars clear up, and cover the spars with bark or green sods, so that they can live dry and warm in these houses with their entire families for two, three, and four years, it being understood that partitions are run through those cellars which are adapted to the size of the family. The wealthy and principal men in New England, in the beginning of the colonies, commenced their first dwelling-houses in this fashion for two reasons: firstly, in order not to waste time in building, and not to want food the next season; secondly, in order not to discourage poor laboring peo-

ple whom they brought over in numbers from Fatherland. In the course of three or four years, when the
country became adapted to agriculture, they built themselves handsome houses, spending on them several
thousands."

In this course which our ancestors took there was a
show of prudence at least, as if their principle were to
satisfy the more pressing wants first. But are the more
pressing wants satisfied now? When I think of acquiring
for myself one of our luxurious dwellings, I am deterred,
for, so to speak, the country is not yet adapted to *human*
culture, and we are still forced to cut our *spiritual* bread
far thinner than our forefathers did their wheaten. Not
that all architectural ornament is to be neglected even
in the rudest periods; but let our houses first be lined
with beauty, where they come in contact with our lives,
like the tenement of the shell-fish, and not overlaid with
it. But, alas! I have been inside one or two of them, and
know what they are lined with.

Though we are not so degenerate but that we might
possibly live in a cave or a wigwam or wear skins to-day,
it certainly is better to accept the advantages, though so
dearly bought, which the invention and industry of mankind offer. In such a neighborhood as this, boards and
shingles, lime and bricks, are cheaper and more easily
obtained than suitable caves, or whole logs, or bark in
sufficient quantities, or even well-tempered clay or flat
stones. I speak understandingly on this subject, for I
have made myself acquainted with it both theoretically
and practically. With a little more wit we might use these
materials so as to become richer than the richest now
are, and make our civilization a blessing. The civilized
man is a more experienced and wiser savage. But to
make haste to my own experiment.

Near the end of March, 1845, I borrowed an axe and
went down to the woods by Walden Pond, nearest to
where I intended to build my house, and began to cut
down some tall, arrowy white pines, still in their youth,
for timber. It is difficult to begin without borrowing, but
perhaps it is the most generous course thus to permit
your fellow-men to have an interest in your enterprise.
The owner of the axe, as he released his hold on it, said

that it was the apple of his eye; but I returned it sharper than I received it. It was a pleasant hillside where I worked, covered with pine woods, through which I looked out on the pond, and a small open field in the woods where pines and hickories were springing up. The ice in the pond was not yet dissolved, though there were some open spaces, and it was all dark-colored and saturated with water. There were some slight flurries of snow during the days that I worked there; but for the most part when I came out on to the railroad, on my way home, its yellow sand-heap stretched away gleaming in the hazy atmosphere, and the rails shone in the spring sun, and I heard the lark and pewee and other birds already come to commence another year with us. They were pleasant spring days, in which the winter of man's discontent was thawing as well as the earth, and the life that had lain torpid began to stretch itself. One day, when my axe had come off and I had cut a green hickory for a wedge, driving it with a stone, and had placed the whole to soak in a pond-hole in order to swell the wood, I saw a striped snake run into the water, and he lay on the bottom, apparently without inconvenience, as long as I stayed there, or more than a quarter of an hour; perhaps because he had not yet fairly come out of the torpid state. It appeared to me that for a like reason men remain in their present low and primitive condition; but if they should feel the influence of the spring of springs arousing them, they would of necessity rise to a higher and more ethereal life. I had previously seen the snakes in frosty mornings in my path with portions of their bodies still numb and inflexible, waiting for the sun to thaw them. On the 1st of April it rained and melted the ice, and in the early part of the day, which was very foggy, I heard a stray goose groping about over the pond and cackling as if lost, or like the spirit of the fog.

So I went on for some days cutting and hewing timber, and also studs and rafters, all with my narrow axe, not having many communicable or scholar-like thoughts singing to myself,—

> Men say they know many things;
> But lo! they have taken wings,—

The arts and sciences,
And a thousand appliances;
The wind that blows
Is all that any body knows.

I hewed the main timbers six inches square, most of
the studs on two sides only, and the rafters and floor
timbers on one side, leaving the rest of the bark on, so
that they were just as straight and much stronger than
sawed ones. Each stick was carefully mortised or ten-
oned by its stump, for I had borrowed other tools by
this time. My days in the woods were not very long ones;
yet I usually carried my dinner of bread and butter, and
read the newspaper in which it was wrapped, at noon,
sitting amid the green pine boughs which I had cut off,
and to my bread was imparted some of their fragrance,
for my hands were covered with a thick coat of pitch.
Before I had done I was more the friend than the foe
of the pine tree, though I had cut down some of them,
having become better acquainted with it. Sometimes a
rambler in the wood was attracted by the sound of my
axe, and we chatted pleasantly over the chips which I
had made.

By the middle of April, for I made no haste in my
work, but rather made the most of it, my house was
framed and ready for the raising. I had already bought
the shanty of James Collins, an Irishman who worked
on the Fitchburg Railroad, for boards. James Collins'
shanty was considered an uncommonly fine one. When
I called to see it he was not at home. I walked about
the outside, at first unobserved from within, the window
was so deep and high. It was of small dimensions, with
a peaked cottage roof, and not much else to be seen,
the dirt being raised five feet all around as if it were a
compost heap. The roof was the soundest part, though
a good deal warped and made brittle by the sun. Doorsill
there was none, but a perennial passage for the hens
under the door-board. Mrs. C. came to the door and
asked me to view it from the inside. The hens were
driven in by my approach. It was dark, and had a dirt
floor for the most part, dank, clammy, and aguish, only
here a board and there a board which would not bear

removal. She lighted a lamp to show me the inside of the roof and the walls, and also that the board floor extended under the bed, warning me not to step into the cellar, a sort of dust hole two feet deep. In her own words, they were "good boards overhead, good boards all around, and a good window,"—of two whole squares originally, only the cat had passed out that way lately. There was a stove, a bed, and a place to sit, an infant in the house where it was born, a silk parasol, gilt-framed looking-glass, and a patent new coffee-mill nailed to an oak sapling, all told. The bargain was soon concluded, for James had in the meanwhile returned. I to pay four dollars and twenty-five cents to-night, he to vacate at five to-morrow morning, selling to nobody else meanwhile: I to take possession at six. It were well, he said, to be there early, and anticipate certain indistinct but wholly unjust claims on the score of ground rent and fuel. This he assured me was the only encumbrance. At six I passed him and his family on the road. One large bundle held their all,—bed, coffee-mill, looking-glass, hens,—all but the cat; she took to the woods and became a wild cat, and, as I learned afterward, trod in a trap set for woodchucks, and so became a dead cat at last.

I took down this dwelling the same morning, drawing the nails, and removed it to the pond-side by small cart-loads, spreading the boards on the grass there to bleach and warp back again in the sun. One early thrush gave me a note or two as I drove along the woodland path. I was informed treacherously by a young Patrick that neighbor Seeley, an Irishman, in the intervals of the carting, transferred the still tolerable, straight, and drivable nails, staples, and spikes to his pocket, and then stood when I came back to pass the time of day, and look freshly up, unconcerned, with spring thoughts, at the devastation; there being a dearth of work, as he said. He was there to represent spectatordom, and help make this seemingly insignificant event one with the removal of the gods of Troy.

I dug my cellar in the side of a hill sloping to the south, where a woodchuck had formerly dug his burrow, down through sumach and blackberry roots, and the lowest stain of vegetation, six feet square by seven deep, to a fine sand where potatoes would not freeze in any winter. The sides were left shelving, and not stoned; but the sun having never shone on them, the sand still keeps its place. It was but two hours' work. I took particular pleasure in this breaking of ground, for in almost all latitudes men dig into the earth for an equable temperature. Under the most splendid house in the city is still to be found the cellar where they store their roots as of old, and long after the superstructure has disappeared posterity remark its dent in the earth. The house is still but a sort of porch at the entrance of a burrow.

At length, in the beginning of May, with the help of some of my acquaintances, rather to improve so good an occasion for neighborliness than from any necessity, I set up the frame of my house. No man was ever more honored in the character of his raisers than I. They are destined, I trust, to assist at the raising of loftier structures one day. I began to occupy my house on the 4th of July, as soon as it was boarded and roofed, for the boards were carefully feather-edged and lapped, so that it was perfectly impervious to rain, but before boarding I laid the foundation of a chimney at one end, bringing two cartloads of stones up the hill from the pond in my arms. I built the chimney after my hoeing in the fall, before a fire became necessary for warmth, doing my cooking in the meanwhile out of doors on the ground, early in the morning: which mode I still think is in some respects more convenient and agreeable than the usual one. When it stormed before my bread was baked, I fixed a few boards over the fire, and sat under them to watch my loaf, and passed some pleasant hours in that way. In those days, when my hands were much employed, I read but little, but the least scraps of paper which lay on the ground, my holder, or tablecloth, afforded me as much entertainment, in fact answered the same purpose as the Iliad.

It would be worth the while to build still more deliberately than I did, considering, for instance, what foundation a door, a window, a cellar, a garret, have in the nature of man, and perchance never raising any superstructure until we found a better reason for it than our temporal necessities even. There is some of the same fitness in a man's building his own house that there is in a bird's building its own nest. Who knows but if men constructed their dwellings with their own hands, and provided food for themselves and families simply and honestly enough, the poetic faculty would be universally developed, as birds universally sing when they are so engaged? But alas! we do like cowbirds and cuckoos, which lay their eggs in nests which other birds have built, and cheer no traveller with their chattering and unmusical notes. Shall we forever resign the pleasure of construction to the carpenter? What does architecture amount to in the experience of the mass of men? I never in all my walks came across a man engaged in so simple and natural an occupation as building his house. We belong to the community. It is not the tailor alone who is the ninth part of a man; it is as much the preacher, and the merchant, and the farmer. Where is this division of labor to end? and what object does it finally serve? No doubt another *may* also think for me; but it is not therefore desirable that he should do so to the exclusion of my thinking for myself.

True, there are architects so called in this country, and I have heard of one at least possessed with the idea of making architectural ornaments have a core of truth, a necessity, and hence a beauty, as if it were a revelation to him. All very well perhaps from his point of view, but only a little better than the common dilettantism. A sentimental reformer in architecture, he began at the cornice, not at the foundation. It was only how to put a core of truth within the ornaments, that every sugarplum, in fact, might have an almond or caraway seed in it,—though I hold that almonds are most wholesome without the sugar,—and not how the inhabitant, the indweller, might build truly within and without, and let the ornaments take care of themselves. What reasonable man ever supposed that ornaments were something outward and in the skin merely,—that the tortoise got his spotted shell, or the shell-fish its mother-o'-pearl tints, by such a contract as the inhabitants of Broadway their Trinity Church? But a man has no more to do with the style of architecture of his house than a tortoise with that of its shell: nor need the soldier be so idle as to try to paint the precise *color* of his virtue on his standard. The enemy will find it out. He may turn pale when the trial comes. This man seemed to me to lean over the cornice, and timidly whisper his half truth to the rude occupants who really knew it better than he. What of architectural beauty I now see, I know has gradually grown from within outward, out of the necessities and character of the indweller, who is the only builder,—out of some unconscious truthfulness, and nobleness, without ever a thought for the appearance and whatever additional beauty of this kind is destined to be produced will be preceded by a like unconscious beauty of life. The most interesting dwellings in this country, as the painter knows, are the most unpretending, humble log huts and cottages of the poor commonly; it is the life of the inhabitants whose shells they are, and not any peculiarity in their surfaces merely, which makes them *picturesque;* and equally interesting will be the citizen's suburban box, when his life shall be as simple and as agreeable to the imagination, and there is as little straining after effect in the style of his dwelling. A great proportion of architectural ornaments are literally hollow, and a September gale would strip them off, like borrowed plumes, without injury to the substantials. They can do without *architecture* who have no olives nor wines in the cellar. What if an equal ado were made about the ornaments of style in literature, and the architects of our bibles spent as much time about their cornices as the architects of our churches do? So are made the *belles-lettres* and the *beaux-arts* and their professors. Much it concerns a man, forsooth, how a few sticks are slanted over him or under him, and what colors are daubed upon his box. It would signify somewhat, if, in any earnest sense, *he* slanted them and daubed it; but the spirit having departed out of the tenant, it is of a piece with constructing his own coffin,—the architecture of the grave,—and "carpenter" is but another name for "coffinmaker." One man says, in his despair or indifference to life, take up a handful of the earth at your feet, and paint your house that color. Is he thinking of his last and narrow house? Toss up a copper for it as well. What

an abundance of leisure he must have! Why do you take
up a handful of dirt? Better paint your house your own
complexion; let it turn pale or blush for you. An enterprise to improve the style of cottage architecture! When
you have got my ornaments ready, I will wear them.

Before winter I built a chimney, and shingled the sides
of my house, which were already impervious to rain,
with imperfect and sappy shingles made of the first slice
of the log, whose edges I was obliged to straighten with
a plane.

I have thus a tight shingled and plastered house, ten
feet wide by fifteen long, and eight-feet posts, with a
garret and a closet, a large window on each side, two
trap-doors, one door at the end, and a brick fireplace
opposite. The exact cost of my house, paying the usual
price for such materials as I used, but not counting the
work, all of which was done by myself, was as follows;
and I give the details because very few are able to tell
exactly what their houses cost, and fewer still, if any, the
separate cost of the various materials which compose
them:—

Boards	$8 03½,	mostly shanty boards.
Refuse shingles for roof and sides. . .	4 00	
Laths	1 25	
Two second-hand windows with glass	2 43	
One thousand old brick	4 00	
Two casks of lime. .	2 40	That was high.
Hair.	0 31	More than I needed.
Mantle-tree iron. . .	0 15	
Nails	3 90	
Hinges and screws .	0 14	
Latch	0 10	
Chalk	0 01	
Transportation . . .	1 40	{ I carried a good part on my back
In all	$28 12½	

These are all the materials, excepting the timber, stones, and sand, which I claimed by squatter's right. I have also a small woodshed adjoining, made chiefly of the stuff which was left after building the house.

I intend to build me a house which will surpass any on the main street in Concord in grandeur and luxury, as soon as it pleases me as much and will cost me no more than my present one.

I thus found that the student who wishes for a shelter can obtain one for a lifetime at an expense not greater than the rent which he now pays annually. If I seem to boast more than is becoming, my excuse is that I brag for humanity rather than for myself; and my shortcomings and inconsistencies do not affect the truth of my statement. Notwithstanding much cant and hypocrisy,— chaff which I find it difficult to separate from my wheat, but for which I am as sorry as any man,—I will breathe freely and stretch myself in this respect, it is such a relief to both the moral and physical system; and I am resolved that I will not through humility become the devil's attorney. I will endeavor to speak a good word for the truth. At Cambridge College the mere rent of a student's room, which is only a little larger than my own, is thirty dollars each year, though the corporation had the advantage of building thirty-two side by side and under one roof, and the occupant suffers the inconvenience of many and noisy neighbors, and perhaps a residence in the fourth story. I cannot but think that if we had more true wisdom in these respects, not only less education would be needed, because, forsooth, more would already have been acquired, but the pecuniary expense of getting an education would in a great measure vanish. Those conveniences which the student requires at Cambridge or elsewhere cost him or somebody else ten times as great a sacrifice of life as they would with proper management on both sides. Those things for which the most money is demanded are never the things which the student most wants. Tuition, for instance, is an important item in the term bill, while for the far more valuable education which he gets by associating with the most cultivated of his contemporaries no charge is made. The mode of founding a college is, commonly, to get up a

subscription of dollars and cents, and then, following
blindly the principles of a division of labor to its extreme,—a principle which should never be followed but
with circumspection,—to call in a contractor who makes
this a subject of speculation, and he employs Irishmen
or other operatives actually to lay the foundations, while
the students that are to be are said to be fitting themselves for it; and for these oversights successive generations have to pay. I think that it would be *better than
this,* for the students, or those who desire to be benefited
by it, even to lay the foundation themselves. The student
who secures his coveted leisure and retirement by systematically shirking any labor necessary to man obtains
but an ignoble and unprofitable leisure, defrauding himself of the experience which alone can make leisure fruit-
ful. "But," says one, "you do not mean that the students
should go to work with their hands instead of their
heads?" I do not mean that exactly, but I mean something which he might think a good deal like that; I mean
that they should not *play* life, or *study* it merely, while
the community supports them at this expensive game,
but earnestly *live* it from beginning to end. How could
youths better learn to live than by at once trying the
experiment of living? Methinks this would exercise their
minds as much as mathematics. If I wished a boy to
know something about the arts and sciences, for instance, I would not pursue the common course, which is
merely to send him into the neighborhood of some professor, where anything is professed and practised but the
art of life;—to survey the world through a telescope or
a microscope, and never with his natural eye; to study
chemistry, and not learn how his bread is made, or mechanics, and not learn how it is earned; to discover new
satellites to Neptune, and not detect the motes in his
eyes, or to what vagabond he is a satellite himself; or to
be devoured by the monsters that swarm all around him,
while contemplating the monsters in a drop of vinegar.
Which would have advanced the most at the end of a
month,—the boy who had made his own jackknife from
the ore which he had dug and smelted, reading as much
as would be necessary for this—or the boy who had attended the lectures on metallurgy at the Institute in the

meanwhile, and had received a Rodgers penknife from his father? Which would be most likely to cut his fingers? . . . To my astonishment I was informed on leaving college that I had studied navigation!—why, if I had taken one turn down the harbor I should have known more about it. Even the *poor* student studies and is taught only *political* economy, while that economy of living which is synonymous with philosophy is not even sincerely professed in our college. The consequence is, that while he is reading Adam Smith, Ricardo, and Say, he runs his father in debt irretrievably.

As with our colleges, so with a hundred "modern improvement;" there is an illusion about them; there is not always a positive advance. The devil goes on exacting compound interest to the last for his early share and numerous succeeding investments in them. Our inventions are wont to be pretty toys, which distract our attention from serious things. They are but improved means to an unimproved end, an end which it was already but too easy to arrive at; as railroads lead to Boston or New York. We are in great haste to construct a magnetic telegraph from Maine to Texas; but Maine and Texas, it may be, have nothing important to communicate. Either is in such a predicament as the man who was earnest to be introduced to a distinguished deaf woman, but when he was presented, and one end of her ear trumpet was put into his hand, had nothing to say. As if the main object were to talk fast and not to talk sensibly. We are eager to tunnel under the Atlantic and bring the Old World some weeks nearer to the New; but perchance the first news that will leak through into the broad, flapping American ear will be that the Princess Adelaide has the whooping cough. After all, the man whose horse trots a mile in a minute does not carry the most important messages; he is not an evangelist, nor does he come round eating locusts and wild honey. I doubt if Flying Childers ever carried a peck of corn to mill.

One says to me, "I wonder that you do not lay up money; you love to travel; you might take the cars and go to Fitchburg to-day and see the country." But I am wiser than that. I have learned that the swiftest traveller

is he that goes afoot. I say to my friend, Suppose we try
who will get there first. The distance is thirty miles; the
fare ninety cents. That is almost a day's wages. I remember when wages were sixty cents a day for laborers on
this very road. Well, I start now on foot, and get there
before night; I have travelled at that rate by the week
together. You will in the meanwhile have earned your
fare, and arrive there some time to-morrow, or possibly
this evening, if you are lucky enough to get a job in
season. Instead of going to Fitchburg, you will be working here the greater part of the day. And so, if the railroad reached round the world, I think that I should keep
ahead of you; and as for seeing the country and getting
experience of that kind, I should have to cut your acquaintance altogether.

Such is the universal law, which no man can ever out-
wit, and with regard to the railroad even we may say it
is as broad as it is long. To make a railroad round the
world available to all mankind is equivalent to grading
the whole surface of the planet. Men have an indistinct
notion that if they keep up this activity of joint stocks
and spades long enough all will at length ride somewhere, in next to no time, and for nothing; but though
a crowd rushes to the depot, and the conductor shouts
"All aboard!" when the smoke is blown away and the
vapor condensed, it will be perceived that a few are riding, but the rest are run over,—and it will be called, and
will be, "A melancholy accident." No doubt they can
ride at last who shall have earned their fare, that is, if
they survive so long, but they will probably have lost
their elasticity and desire to travel by that time. This
spending of the best part of one's life earning money in
order to enjoy a questionable liberty during the least
valuable part of it reminds me of the Englishman who
went to India to make a fortune first, in order that he
might return to England and live the life of a poet. He
should have gone up garret at once. "What!" exclaim a
million Irishmen starting up from all the shanties in the
land, "is not this railroad which we have built a good
thing?" Yes, I answer, *comparatively* good, that is, you
might have done worse; but I wish, as you are brothers

of mine, that you could have spent your time better than digging in this dirt.

Before I finished my house, wishing to earn ten or twelve dollars by some honest and agreeable method, in order to meet my unusual expenses, I planted about two acres and a half of light and sandy soil near it chiefly with beans, but also a small part with potatoes, corn, peas, and turnips. The whole lot contains eleven acres, mostly growing up to pines and hickories, and was sold the preceding season for eight dollars and eight cents an acre. One farmer said that it was "good for nothing but to raise cheeping squirrels on." I put no manure whatever on this land, not being the owner, but merely a squatter, and not expecting to cultivate so much again, and I did not quite hoe it all once. I got out several cords of stumps in plowing, which supplied me with fuel for a long time, and left small circles of virgin mould, easily distinguishable through the summer by the greater luxuriance of the beans there. The dead and for the most part unmerchantable wood behind my house, and the driftwood from the pond, have supplied the remainder of my fuel. I was obliged to hire a team and a man for the plowing, though I held the plow myself. My farm outgoes for the first season were, for implements, seed, work, etc., $14.72½. The seed corn was given me. This never costs anything to speak of, unless you plant more than enough. I got twelve bushels of beans, and eighteen bushels of potatoes, beside some peas and sweet corn. The yellow corn and turnips were too late to come to anything. My whole income from the farm was

	$23 44
Deducting the outgoes	14 72½
There are left.	$8 71½,

beside produce consumed and on hand at the time this estimate was made of the value of $4.50,—the amount on hand much more than balancing a little grass which I did not raise. All things considered, that is, considering the importance of a man's soul and of to-day, notwithstanding the short time occupied by my experiment, nay, partly even because of its transient character, I believe that that was doing better than any farmer in Concord did that year.

The next year I did better still, for I spaded up all the land which I required, about a third of an acre, and I learned from the experience of both years, not being in the least awed by many celebrated works on husbandry, Arthur Young among the rest, that if one would live simply and eat only the crop which he raised, and raise no more than he ate, and not exchange it for an insufficient quantity of more luxurious and expensive things, he would need to cultivate only a few rods of ground, and that it would be cheaper to spade up that than to use oxen to plow it, and to select a fresh spot from time to time than to manure the old, and he could do all his necessary farm work as it were with his left hand at odd hours in the summer; and thus he would not be tied to an ox, or horse, or cow, or pig, as at present. I desire to speak impartially on this point, and as one not interested in the success or failure of the present economical and social arrangements. I was more independent than any farmer in Concord, for I was not anchored to a house or farm, but could follow the bent of my genius, which is a very crooked one, every moment. Beside being better off than they already, if my house had been burned or my crops had failed, I should have been nearly as well off as before.

I am wont to think that men are not so much the keepers of herds as herds are the keepers of men, the former are so much the freer. Men and oxen exchange work; but if we consider necessary work only, the oxen will be seen to have greatly the advantage, their farm is so much the larger. Man does some of his part of the exchange work in his six weeks of haying, and it is no boy's play. Certainly no nation that lived simply in all respects, that is, no nation of philosophers, would commit so great a blunder as to use the labor of animals. True, there never was and is not likely, soon to be a nation of philosophers, nor am I certain it is desirable that there should be. However, *I* should never have broken a horse or bull and taken him to board for any work he might do for me, for fear I should become a horse-man or a herds-man merely; and if society seems to be the gainer by so doing, are we certain that what is one man's gain is not another's loss, and that the stable-boy has equal cause with his master to be satisfied? Granted that some public works would not have been constructed without this aid, and let man share the glory of such with the ox and horse; does it follow that he could not have accomplished works yet more worthy of himself in that case? When men begin to do, not merely unneces-sary or artistic, but luxurious and idle work, with their assistance, it is inevitable that a few do all the exchange work with the oxen, or, in other words, become the slaves of the strongest. Man thus not only works for the animal within him, but, for a symbol of this, he works for the animal without him. Though we have many sub-stantial houses of brick or stone, the prosperity of the farmer is still measured by the degree to which the barn overshadows the house. This town is said to have the largest houses for oxen, cows, and horses hereabouts, and it is not behindhand in its public buildings; but there are very few halls for free worship or free speech in this county. It should not be by their architecture, but why not even by their power of abstract thought, that nations should seek to commemorate themselves? How much more admirable the Bhagvat-Geeta than all the ruins of the East! Towers and temples are the luxury of princes. A simple and independent mind does not toil at the bidding of any prince. Genius is not a retainer to any emperor, nor is its material silver, or gold, or marble, except to a trifling extent. To what end, pray, is so much stone hammered? In Arcadia, when I was there, I did not see any hammering stone. Nations are possessed with an insane ambition to perpetuate the memory of themselves by the amount of hammered stone they leave. What if equal pains were taken to smooth and polish their manners? One piece of good sense would be more memorable than a monument as high as the moon. I love better to see stones in place. The grandeur of Thebes was a vulgar grandeur. More sensible is a rod of stone wall that bounds an honest man's field than a hundred-gated Thebes that has wandered farther from the true end of life. The religion and civilization which are barbaric and heathenish build splendid temples; but what you might call Christianity does not. Most of the stone a nation hammers goes toward its tomb only. It buries itself alive. As for the Pyramids, there is nothing to wonder at in them so much as the fact that so many men could be found degraded enough to spend their lives constructing a tomb for some ambitious booby, whom it would have been wiser and manlier to have drowned in the Nile, and then given his body to the dogs. I might possibly invent some excuse for them and him, but I have no time for it. As for the religion and love of art of the builders, it is much the same all the world over, whether the building be an Egyptian temple or the United States Bank. It costs more than it comes to. The mainspring is vanity, assisted by the love of garlic and bread and butter. Mr. Balcom, a promising young architect, designs it on the back of his Vitruvius, with hard pencil and ruler, and the job is let out to Dobson & Sons, stonecutters. When the thirty centuries begin to look down on it, mankind begin to look up at it. As for your high towers and monuments, there was a crazy fellow once in this town who undertook to dig through to China, and he got so far that, as he said, he heard the Chinese pots and kettles rattle; but I think that I shall not go out of my way to admire the hole which he made. Many are concerned about the monuments of the West and the East,—to know who built them. For my part, I should like to know who in those days did not build them,—who were above such trifling. But to proceed with my statistics.

By surveying, carpentry, and day-labor of various other kinds in the village in the meanwhile, for I have as many trades as fingers, I had earned $13.34. The expense of food for eight months, namely, from July 4th to March 1st, the time when these estimates were made, though I lived there more than two years,—not counting potatoes, a little green corn, and some peas, which I had raised, nor considering the value of what was on hand at the last date,—was

Rice.	$1 73½	
Molasses	1 73	Cheapest form of the saccharine.
Rye meal	1 04¾	
Indian meal . . .	0 99¾	Cheaper than rye.
Pork	0 22	
Flour	0 88	{ Costs more than Indian meal, both money and trouble.
Sugar	0 80	
Lard	0 65	
Apples	0 25	
Dried apple . . .	0 22	
Sweet potatoes	0 10	
One pumpkin . .	0 6	
One watermelon	0 2	
Salt	0 3	

All experiments which failed.

Yes, I did eat $8.74, all told; but I should not thus un-blushingly publish my guilt, if I did not know that most of my readers were equally guilty with myself, and that their deeds would look no better in print. The next year I sometimes caught a mess of fish for my dinner, and once I went so far as to slaughter a woodchuck which ravaged my bean-field,—effect his transmigration, as a Tartar would say,—and devour him, partly for experiment's sake; but though it afforded me a momentary enjoyment, notwithstanding a musky flavor, I saw that the longest use would not make that a good practice, however it might seem to have your woodchucks ready dressed by the village butcher.

Clothing and some incidental expenses within the same dates, though little can be inferred from this item, amounted to

$8 40¾

Oil and some household utensils . . 2 00

So that all the pecuniary outgoes, excepting for washing and mending, which for the most part were done out of the house, and their bills have not yet been received,—

and these are all and more than all the ways by which
money necessarily goes out in this part of the world,—were

House.	$28 12½
Farm one year	14 72½
Food eight months	8 74
Clothing, etc., eight months.	8 40¾
Oil, etc., eight months	2 00
In all	61 99¾

I address myself now to those of my readers who have
a living to get. And to meet this I have for farm produce sold

	$23 34
Earned by day-labor	13 34
In all	$36 78,

which subtracted from the sum of the outgoes leaves a
balance of $25.21¾ on the one side,—this being very nearly
the means with which I started, and the measure of expenses to be incurred,—and on the other, beside the leisure and independence and health thus secured, a
comfortable house for me as long as I choose to occupy it.

These statistics, however accidental and therefore un-
instructive they may appear, as they have a certain com-
pleteness, have a certain value also. Nothing was given
me of which I have not rendered some account. It appears from the above estimate, that my food alone cost
me in money about twenty-seven cents a week. It was,
for nearly two years after this, rye and Indian meal without yeast, potatoes, rice, a very little salt pork, molasses,
and salt; and my drink, water. It was fit that I should
live on rice, mainly, who loved so well the philosophy
of India. To meet the objections of some inveterate cav-
illers, I may as well state, that if I dined out occasionally,
as I always had done, and I trust shall have opportunities
to do again, it was frequently to the detriment of my
domestic arrangements. But the dining out, being, as I

have stated, a constant element, does not in the least affect a comparative statement like this.

I learned from my two years' experience that it would cost incredibly little trouble to obtain one's necessary food, even in this latitude; that a man may use as simple a diet as the animals, and yet retain health and strength. I have made a satisfactory dinner, satisfactory on several accounts, simply off a dish of purslane (*Portulaca oleracea*) which I gathered in my cornfield, boiled and salted. I give the Latin on account of the savoriness of the trivial name. And pray what more can a reasonable man desire, in peaceful times, in ordinary noons, than a sufficient number of ears of green sweet corn boiled, with the addition of salt? Even the little variety which I used was a yielding to the demands of appetite, and not of health. Yet men have come to such a pass that they frequently starve, not for want of necessaries, but for want of luxuries; and I know a good woman who thinks that her son lost his life because he took to drinking water only.

The reader will perceive that I am treating the subject rather from an economic than a dietetic point of view, and he will not venture to put my abstemiousness to the test unless he has a well-stocked larder.

Bread I at first made of pure Indian meal and salt, genuine hoe-cakes, which I baked before my fire out of doors on a shingle or the end of a stick of timber sawed off in building my house; but it was wont to get smoked and to have a piny flavor. I tried flour also; but have at last found a mixture of rye and Indian meal most convenient and agreeable. In cold weather it was no little amusement to bake several small loaves of this in succession, tending and turning them as carefully as an Egyptian his hatching eggs. They were a real cereal fruit which I ripened, and they had to my senses a fragrance like that of other noble fruits, which I kept in as long as possible by wrapping them in cloths. I made a study of the ancient and indispensable art of bread-making, consulting such authorities as offered, going back to the primitive days and first invention of the unleavened kind, when from the wildness of nuts and meats men first reached the mildness and refinement of this diet, and travelling gradually down in my studies through that accidental souring of the dough which, it is supposed, taught the leavening process, and through the various fermentations thereafter, till I came to "good, sweet, wholesome bread," the staff of life. Leaven, which some deem the soul of bread, the *spiritus* which fills its cellular tissue, which is religiously preserved like the vestal fire,—some precious bottleful, I suppose, first brought over in the Mayflower, did the business for America, and its influence is still rising, swelling, spreading, in cerealian billows over the land,—this seed I regularly and faithfully procured from the village, till at length one morning I forgot the rules, and scalded my yeast; by which accident I discovered that even this was not indispensable,—for my discoveries were not by the synthetic but analytic process,—and I have gladly omitted it since, though most housewives earnestly assured me that safe and wholesome bread without yeast might not be, and elderly people prophesied a speedy decay of the vital forces. Yet I find it not to be an essential ingredient, and after going without it for a year am still in the land of the living; and I am glad to escape the trivialness of carrying a bottleful in my pocket, which would sometimes pop and discharge its contents to my discomfiture. It is simpler and more respectable to omit it. Man is an animal who more than any other can adapt himself to all climates and circumstances. Neither did I put any salsoda, or other acid or alkali, into my bread. It would seem that I made it according to the recipe which Marcus Porcius Cato gave about two centuries before Christ. "Panem depsticium sic facito. Manus mortariumque bene lavato. Farinam in mortarium indito, aquae paulatim addito, subigitoque pulchre. Ubi bene subegeris, defingito, coquitoque sub testu." Which I take to mean, "Make kneaded bread thus. Wash your hands and trough well. Put the meal into the trough, add water gradually, and knead it thoroughly. When you have kneaded it well, mould it, and bake it under a cover," that is, in a baking-kettle. Not a word about leaven. But I did not always use this staff of life. At one time, owing to the emptiness of my purse, I saw none of it for more than a month.

Every New Englander might easily raise all his own bread-stuffs in this land of rye and Indian corn, and not depend on distant and fluctuating markets for them. Yet so far are we from simplicity and independence that, in Concord, fresh and sweet meal is rarely sold in the shops, and hominy and corn in a still coarser form are hardly used by any. For the most part the farmer gives to his cattle and hogs the grain of his own producing, and buys flour, which is at least no more wholesome, at a greater cost, at the store. I saw that I could easily raise my bushel or two of rye and Indian corn, for the former will grow on the poorest land, and the latter does not require the best, and grind them in a hand-mill, and so do without rice and pork; and if I must have some concentrated sweet, I found by experiment that I could make a very good molasses either of pumpkins or beets, and I knew that I needed only to set out a few maples to obtain it more easily still, and while these were growing I could use various substitutes beside those which I have named. "For," as the Forefathers sang,—

> "we can make liquor to sweeten our lips
> Of pumpkins and parsnips and walnut-tree chips."

Finally, as for salt, that grossest of groceries, to obtain this might be a fit occasion for a visit to the seashore, or, if I did without it altogether, I should probably drink the less water. I do not learn that the Indians ever troubled themselves to go after it.

Thus I could avoid all trade and barter, so far as my food was concerned, and having a shelter already, it would only remain to get clothing and fuel. The pantaloons which I now wear were woven in a farmer's family,—thank Heaven there is so much virtue still in man; for I think the fall from the farmer to the operative as great and memorable as that from the man to the farmer;—and in a new country, fuel is an encumbrance. As for a habitat, if I were not permitted still to squat, I might purchase one acre at the same price for which the land I cultivated was sold—namely, eight dollars and eight cents. But as it was, I considered that I enhanced the value of the land by squatting on it.

There is a certain class of unbelievers who sometimes ask me such questions as, if I think that I can live on vegetable food alone; and to strike at the root of the matter at once,—for the root is faith,—I am accustomed to answer such, that I can live on board nails. If they cannot understand that, they cannot understand much that I have to say. For my part, I am glad to hear of experiments of this kind being tried; as that a young man tried for a fortnight to live on hard, raw corn on the ear, using his teeth for all mortar. The squirrel tribe tried the same and succeeded. The human race is interested in these experiments, though a few old women who are incapacitated for them, or who own their thirds in mills, may be alarmed.

My furniture, part of which I made myself,—and the rest cost me nothing of which I have not rendered an account,—consisted of a bed, a table, a desk, three chairs, a looking-glass three inches in diameter, a pair of tongs and andirons, a kettle, a skillet, and a frying-pan, a dipper, a wash-bowl, two knives and forks, three plates, one cup, one spoon, a jug for oil, a jug for molasses, and a japanned lamp. None is so poor that he need sit on a pumpkin. That is shiftlessness. There is a plenty of such chairs as I like best in the village garrets to be had for taking them away. Furniture! Thank God, I can sit and I can stand without the aid of a furniture warehouse. What man but a philosopher would not be ashamed to see his furniture packed in a cart and going up country exposed to the light of heaven and the eyes of men, a beggarly account of empty boxes? That is Spaulding's furniture. I could never tell from inspecting such a load whether it belonged to a so-called rich man or a poor one; the owner always seemed poverty-stricken. Indeed, the more you have of such things the poorer you are. Each load looks as if it contained the contents of a dozen shanties; and if one shanty is poor, this is a dozen times as poor. Pray, for what do we *move* ever but to get rid of our furniture, our *exuviæ;* at last to go from this world to another newly furnished, and leave this to be burned? It is the same as if all these traps were buckled to a man's belt, and he could not

move over the rough country where our lines are cast
without dragging them,—dragging his trap. He was a
lucky fox that left his tail in the trap. The muskrat will
gnaw his third leg off to be free. No wonder man has
lost his elasticity. How often he is at a dead set! "Sir, if
I may be so bold, what do you mean by a dead set?" If
you are a seer, whenever you meet a man you will see
all that he owns, ay, and much that he pretends to dis-
own, behind him, even to his kitchen furniture and all
the trumpery which he saves and will not burn, and he
will appear to be harnessed to it and making what head-
way he can. I think that the man is at a dead set who
has got through a knot-hole or gateway where his sledge
load of furniture cannot follow him. I cannot but feel
compassion when I hear some trig, compact-looking
man, seemingly free, all girded and ready, speak of his
"furniture," as whether it is insured or not. "But what
shall I do with my furniture?" My gay butterfly is entan-
gled in a spider's web then. Even those who seem for a
long while not to have any, if you inquire more narrowly
you will find have some stored in somebody's barn. I
look upon England to-day as an old gentleman who is
travelling with a great deal of baggage, trumpery which
has accumulated from long housekeeping, which he has
not the courage to burn; great trunk, little trunk, band-
box, and bundle. Throw away the first three at least. It
would surpass the powers of a well man nowadays to
take up his bed and walk, and I should certainly advise
a sick one to lay down his bed and run. When I have
met an immigrant tottering under a bundle which contained his all,—looking like an enormous when which
had grown out of the nape of his neck.—I have pitied
him, not because that was his all, but because he had all
that to carry. If I have got to drag my trap, I will take
care that it be a light one and do not nip me in a vital
part. But perchance it would be wisest never to put one's
paw into it.

I would observe, by the way, that it costs me nothing
for curtains, for I have no gazers to shut out but the sun
and moon, and I am willing that they should look in.
The moon will not sour milk nor taint meat of mine,
nor will the sun injure my furniture or fade my carpet;

and if he is sometimes too warm a friend, I find it still
better economy to retreat behind some curtain which
nature has provided, than to add a single item to the
details of housekeeping. A lady once offered me a mat,
but as I had no room to spare within the house, nor
time to spare within or without to shake it, I declined
it, preferring to wipe my feet on the sod before my door.
It is best to avoid the beginnings of evil.

Not long since I was present at the auction of a dea-
con's effects, for his life had not been ineffectual:—

"The evil that men do lives after them."

As usual, a great proportion was trumpery which had
begun to accumulate in his father's day. Among the rest
was a dried tapeworm. And now, after lying half a century
in his garret and other dust holes, these things were not
burned; instead of a *bonfire,* or purifying destruction of
them, there was an *auction,* or increasing of them. The
neighbors eagerly collected to view them, bought them all,
and carefully transported them to their garrets and dust
holes, to lie there till their estates are settled, when they
will start again. When a man dies he kicks the dust.

The customs of some savage nations might, perchance,
be profitably imitated by us, for they at least go through
the semblance of casting their slough annually; they have
the idea of the thing, whether they have the reality or
not. Would it not be well if we were to celebrate such
a "busk," or "feast of first fruits," as Bartram describes
to have been the custom of the Mucclasse Indians?
"When a town celebrates the busk," says he, "having
previously provided themselves with new clothes, new
pots, pans, and other household utensils and furniture,
they collect all their worn out clothes and other despicable things, sweep and cleanse their houses, squares, and
the whole town, of their filth, which with all the remaining grain and other old provisions they cast together
into one common heap, and consume it with fire. After
having taken medicine, and fasted for three days, all the
fire in the town is extinguished. During this fast they
abstain from the gratification of every appetite and pas-

sion whatever. A general amnesty is proclaimed; all malefactors may return to their town."

"On the fourth morning, the high priest, by rubbing dry wood together, produces new fire in the public square, from whence every habitation in the town is supplied with the new and pure flame."

They then feast on the new corn and fruits, and dance and sing for three days, "and the four following days they receive visits and rejoice with their friends from neighboring towns who have in like manner purified and prepared themselves."

The Mexicans also practised a similar purification at the end of every fifty-two years, in the belief that it was time for the world to come to an end.

I have scarcely heard of a truer sacrament, that is, as the dictionary defines it, "outward and visible sign of an inward and spiritual grace," than this, and I have no doubt that they were originally inspired directly from Heaven to do thus, though they have no Biblical record of the revelation.

For more than five years I maintained myself thus solely by the labor of my hands, and I found that, by working about six weeks in a year, I could meet all the expenses of living. The whole of my winters, as well as most of my summers, I had free and clear for study. I have thoroughly tried school-keeping, and found that my expenses were in proportion, or rather out of proportion, to my income, for I was obliged to dress and train, not to say think and believe, accordingly, and I lost my time into the bargain. As I did not teach for the good of my fellow-men, but simply for a livelihood, this was a failure. I have tried trade but I found that it would take ten years to get under way in that, and that then I should probably be on my way to the devil. I was actually afraid that I might by that time be doing what is called a good business. When formerly I was looking about to see what I could do for a living, some sad experience in conforming to the wishes of friends being fresh in my mind to tax my ingenuity, I thought often and seriously of picking huckleberries; that surely I could do, and its small profits might suffice,—for my greatest skill has been to want but little,—so little capital it required, so little distraction from my wonted moods, I foolishly thought. While my acquaintances went unhesitatingly into trade or the professions, I contemplated this occupation as most like theirs; ranging the hills all summer to pick the berries which came in my way, and thereafter carelessly dispose of them; so, to keep the flocks of Admetus. I also dreamed that I might gather the wild herbs, or carry evergreens to such villagers as loved to be reminded of the woods, even to the city, by hay-cart loads. But I have since learned that trade curses everything it handles; and though you trade in messages from heaven, the whole curse of trade attaches to the business.

As I preferred some things to others, and especially valued my freedom, as I could fare hard and yet succeed well, I did not wish to spend my time in earning rich carpets or other fine furniture, or delicate cookery, or a house in the Grecian or the Gothic style just yet. If there are any to whom it is no interruption to acquire these things, and who know how to use them when acquired, I relinquish to them the pursuit. Some are "industrious," and appear to love labor for its own sake, or perhaps because it keeps them out of worse mischief; to such I have at present nothing to say. Those who would not know what to do with more leisure than they now enjoy, I might advise to work twice as hard as they do,—work till they pay for themselves, and get their free papers. For myself I found that the occupation of a day-laborer was the most independent of any, especially as it required only thirty or forty days in a year to support one. The laborer's day ends with the going down of the sun, and he is then free to devote himself to his chosen pursuit, independent of his labor; but his employer, who speculates from month to month, has no respite from one end of the year to the other.

In short, I am convinced, both by faith and experience, that to maintain one's self on this earth is not a hardship but a pastime, if we will live simply and wisely; as the pursuits of the simpler nations are still the sports of the more artificial. It is not necessary that a man should earn his living by the sweat of his brow, unless he sweats easier than I do.

One young man of my acquaintance, who has inherited some acres, told me that he thought he should live as I did, *if he had the means*. I would not have any one adopt *my* mode of living on any account; for, beside that before he has fairly learned it I may have found out another for myself, I desire that there may be as many different persons in the world as possible; but I would have each one be very careful to find out and pursue *his own* way, and not his father's or his mother's or his neighbor's instead. The youth may build or plant or sail, only let him not be hindered from doing that which he tells me he would like to do. It is by a mathematical point only that we are wise, as the sailor or the fugitive slave keeps the polestar in his eye; but that is sufficient guidance for all our life. We may not arrive at our port within a calculable period, but we would preserve the true course.

Undoubtedly, in this case, what is true for one is truer still for a thousand, as a large house is not proportionally more expensive than a small one, since one roof may cover, one cellar underlie, and one wall separate several apartments. But for my part, I preferred the solitary dwelling. Moreover, it will commonly be cheaper to build the whole yourself than to convince another of the advantage of the common wall; and when you have done this, the common partition, to be much cheaper, must be a thin one, and that other may prove a bad neighbor, and also not keep his side in repair. The only cooperation which is commonly possible is exceedingly partial and superficial; and what little true coöperation there is, is as if it were not, being a harmony inaudible to men. If a man has faith, he will coöperate with equal faith everywhere; if he has not faith, he will continue to live like the rest of the world, whatever company he is joined to. To coöperate in the highest as well as the lowest sense, means *to get our living together*. I heard it proposed lately that two young men should travel together over the world, the one without money, earning his means as he went, before the mast and behind the plow, the other carrying a bill of exchange in his pocket. It was easy to see that they could not long be companions or coöperate, since one would not *operate* at all. They would part at the first interesting crisis in their adventures. Above all, as I have implied, the man who goes alone can start to-day; but he who travels with another must wait till that other is ready, and it may be a long time before they get off.

But all this is very selfish, I have heard some of my townsmen say. I confess that I have hitherto indulged very little in philanthropic enterprises. I have made some sacrifices to a sense of duty, and among others have sacrificed this pleasure also. There are those who have used all their arts to persuade me to undertake the support of some poor family in the town; and if I had nothing to do—for the devil finds employment for the idle—I might try my hand at some such pastime as that. However, when I have thought to indulge myself in this respect, and lay their Heaven under an obligation by maintaining certain poor persons in all respects as comfortably as I maintain myself, and have even ventured so far as to make them the offer, they have one and all unhesitatingly preferred to remain poor. While my townsmen and women are devoted in so many ways to the good of their fellows, I trust that one at least may be spared to other and less humane pursuits. You must have a genius for charity as well as for anything else. As for Doing-good, that is one of the professions which are full. Moreover, I have tried it fairly, and, strange as it may seem, am satisfied that it does not agree with my constitution. Probably I should not consciously and deliberately forsake my particular calling to do the good which society demands of me, to save the universe from annihilation; and I believe that a like but infinitely greater steadfastness elsewhere is all that now preserves it. But I would not stand between any man and his genius; and to him who does this work, which I decline, with his whole heart and soul and life, I would say, Persevere, even if the world call it doing evil, as it is most likely they will.

I am far from supposing that my case is a peculiar one; no doubt many of my readers would make a similar defence. At doing something,—I will not engage that my neighbors shall pronounce it good,—I do not hesitate to say that I should be a capital fellow to hire; but what that is, it is for my employer to find out. What *good* I do, in the common sense of that word, must be aside from my main path, and for the most part wholly unintended. Men say, practically, Begin where you are and such as you are, without aiming mainly to become of more worth, and with kindness aforethought go about doing good. If I were to preach at all in this strain, I should say rather, Set about being good. As if the sun should stop when he had kindled his fires up to the splendor of a moon or a star of the sixth magnitude, and go about like a Robin Goodfellow, peeping in at every cottage window, inspiring lunatics, and tainting meats, and making darkness visible, instead of steadily increasing his genial heat and beneficence till he is of such brightness that no mortal can look him in the face, and then, and in the meanwhile too, going about the world in his own orbit, doing it good, or rather, as a truer philosophy has discovered, the world going about him getting good. When Phaëton, wishing to prove his heavenly birth by his beneficence, had the sun's chariot but one day, and drove out of the beaten track, he burned several blocks of houses in the lower streets of heaven, and scorched the surface of the earth, and dried up every spring, and made the great desert of Sahara, till at length Jupiter hurled him headlong to the earth with a thunderbolt, and the sun, through grief at his death, did not shine for a year.

There is no odor so bad as that which arises from goodness tainted. It is human, it is divine, carrion. If I knew for a certainty that a man was coming to my house with the conscious design of doing me good, I should run for my life, as from that dry and parching wind of the African deserts called the simoon, which fills the mouth and nose and ears and eyes with dust till you are suffocated, for fear that I should get some of his good done to me,—some of its virus mingled with my blood. No,—in this case I would rather suffer evil the natural way. A man is not a good *man* to me because he will feed me if I should be starving, or warm me if I should be freezing, or pull me out of a ditch if I should ever fall into one. I can find you a Newfoundland dog that will do as much. Philanthropy is not love for one's fel-

low-man in the broadest sense. Howard was no doubt
an exceedingly kind and worthy man in his way, and
has his reward; but, comparatively speaking, what are a
hundred Howards to *us,* if their philanthropy do not help
us in our best estate, when we are most worthy to be
helped? I never heard of a philanthropic meeting in
which it was sincerely proposed to do any good to me,
or the like of me.

The Jesuits were quite balked by those Indians who,
being burned at the stake, suggested new modes of tor-
ture to their tormentors. Being superior to physical suffering, it sometimes chanced that they were superior to
any consolation which the missionaries could offer; and
the law to do as you would be done by fell with less
persuasiveness on the ears of those who, for their part,
did not care how they were done by, who loved their
enemies after a new fashion, and came very near freely
forgiving them all they did.

Be sure that you give the poor the aid they most need,
though it be your example which leaves them far behind.
If you give money, spend yourself with it, and do not
merely abandon it to them. We make spurious mistakes
sometimes. Often the poor man is not so cold and hungry as he is dirty and ragged and gross. It is partly his
taste, and not merely his misfortune. If you give him
money, he will perhaps buy more rags with it. I was
wont to pity the clumsy Irish laborers who cut ice on
the pond, in such mean and ragged clothes, while I shiv-
ered in my more tidy and somewhat more fashionable
garments, till, one bitter cold day, one who had slipped
into the water came to my house to warm him, and I
saw him strip off three pairs of pants and two pairs of
stockings ere he got down to the skin, though they were
dirty and ragged enough, it is true, and that he could
afford to refuse the *extra* garments which I offered him,
he had so many *intra* ones. This ducking was the very
thing he needed. Then I began to pity myself, and I saw
that it would be a greater charity to bestow on me a
flannel shirt than a whole slop-shop on him. There are
a thousand hacking at the branches of evil to one who
is striking at the root, and it may be that he who bestows
the largest amount of time and money on the needy is

doing the most by his mode of life to produce that misery which he strives in vain to relieve. It is the pious slave-breeder devoting the proceeds of every tenth slave to buy a Sunday's liberty for the rest. Some show their kindness to the poor by employing them in their kitchens. Would they not be kinder if they employed themselves there? You boast of spending a tenth part of your income in charity; maybe you should spend the nine tenths so, and done with it. Society recovers only a tenth part of the property then. Is this owing to the generosity of him in whose possession it is found, or to the remissness of the officers of justice?

Philanthropy is almost the only virtue which is sufficiently appreciated by mankind. Nay, it is greatly overrated; and it is our selfishness which overrates it. A robust poor man, one sunny day here in Concord, praised a fellow-townsman to me, because, as he said, he was kind to the poor; meaning himself. The kind uncles and aunts of the races are more esteemed than its true spiritual fathers and mothers. I once heard a reverend lecturer on England, a man of learning and intelligence, after enumerating her scientific, literary, and political worthies, Shakespeare, Bacon, Cromwell, Milton, Newton, and others, speak next of her Christian heroes, whom, as if his profession required it of him, he elevated to a place far above all the rest, as the greatest of the great. They were Penn, Howard, and Mrs. Fry. Everyone must feel the falsehood and cant of this. The last were not England's best men and women; only, perhaps, her best philanthropists.

I would not subtract anything from the praise that is due to philanthropy, but merely demand justice for all who by their lives and works are a blessing to mankind. I do not value chiefly a man's uprightness and benevolence, which are, as it were, his stem and leaves. Those plants of whose greenness withered we make herb tea for the sick serve but a humble use, and are most employed by quacks. I want the flower and fruit of a man; that some fragrance be wafted over from him to me, and some ripeness flavor our intercourse. His goodness must not be a partial and transitory act, but a constant superfluity, which costs him nothing and of which he is unconscious. This is a charity that hides a multitude of sins. The philanthropist too often surrounds mankind with the remembrance of his own cast-off griefs as an atmosphere, and calls it sympathy. We should impart our courage, and not our despair, our health and ease, and not our disease, and take care that this does not spread by contagion. From what southern plains comes up the voice of wailing? Under what latitudes reside the heathen to whom we would send light? Who is that intemperate and brutal man whom we would redeem? If anything ail a man, so that he does not perform his functions, if he have a pain in his bowels even,—for that is the seat of sympathy,—he forthwith sets about reforming—the world. Being a microcosm himself, he discovers—and it is a true discovery, and he is the man to make it—that the world has been eating green apples; to his eyes, in fact, the globe itself is a great green apple, which there is danger awful to think of that the children of men will nibble before it is ripe; and straightway his drastic philanthropy seeks out the Esquimau and the Patagonian, and embraces the populous Indian and Chinese villages; and thus, by a few years of philanthropic activity, the powers in the meanwhile using him for their own ends, no doubt, he cures himself of his dyspepsia, the globe acquires a faint blush on one or both of its cheeks, as if it were beginning to be ripe, and life loses its cruelty and is once more sweet and wholesome to live. I never dreamed of any enormity greater than I have committed. I never knew, and never shall know, a worse man than myself.

I believe that what so saddens the reformer is not his sympathy with his fellows in distress, but, though he be the holiest son of God, is his private ail. Let this be righted, let the spring come to him, the morning rise over his couch, and he will forsake his generous companions without apology. My excuse for not lecturing against the use of tobacco is, that I never chewed it, that is a penalty which reformed tobacco-chewers have to pay; though there are things enough I have chewed which I could lecture against. If you should ever be betrayed into any of these philanthropies, do not let your left hand know what your right hand does, for it is not worth knowing. Rescue the drowning and tie your shoestrings. Take your time, and set about some free labor.

Our manners have been corrupted by communication with the saints. Our hymn-books resound with a melodious cursing of God and enduring Him forever. One would say that even the prophets and redeemers had rather consoled the fears than confirmed the hopes of man. There is nowhere recorded a simple and irrepressible satisfaction with the gift of life, any memorable praise of God. All health and success does me good, however far off and withdrawn it may appear; all disease and failure helps to make me sad and does me evil, however much sympathy it may have with me or I with it. If, then, we would indeed restore mankind by truly Indian, botanic, magnetic, or natural means, let us first be as simple and well as Nature ourselves, dispel the clouds which hang over our own brows, and take up a little life into our pores. Do not stay to be an overseer of the poor, but endeavor to become one of the worthies of the world.

I read in the Gulistan, or Flower Garden, of Sheik Sadi of Shiraz, that "they asked a wise man, saying: Of the many celebrated trees which the Most High God has created lofty and umbrageous, they call none azad, or free, excepting the cypress, which bears no fruit; what mystery is there in this? He replied: Each has its appropriate produce, and appointed season, during the continuance of which it is fresh and blooming, and during their absence dry and withered; to neither of which states is the cypress exposed, being always flourishing; and of this nature are the azads, or religious independents.—Fix not thy heart on that which is transitory; for the Dijlah, or Tigris, will continue to flow through Bagdad after the race of caliphs is extinct: if thy hand has plenty, be liberal as the date tree; but if it affords nothing to give away, be an azad, or free man, like the cypress."

COMPLEMENTAL VERSES

THE PRETENSIONS OF POVERTY

Thou dost presume too much, poor needy wretch,
To claim a station in the firmament
Because thy humble cottage, or thy tub,

Nurses some lazy or pedantic virtue
In the cheap sunshine or by shady springs,
With roots and pot-herbs; where thy right hand,
Tearing those humane passions from the mind,
Upon whose stocks fair blooming virtues flourish,
Degradeth nature, and benumbeth sense,
And, Gorgon-like, turns active men to stone.
We not require the dull society
Of your necessitated temperance,
Or that unnatural stupidity
That knows nor joy nor sorrow; nor your forc'd
Falsely exalted passive fortitude
Above the active. This low abject brood,
That fix their seats in mediocrity,
Become your servile minds; but we advance
Such virtues only as admit excess,
Brave, bounteous acts, regal magnificence,
All-seeing prudence, magnanimity
That knows no bound, and that heroic virtue
For which antiquity hath left no name,
But patterns only, such as Hercules,
Achilles, Theseus. Back to thy loath'd cell;
And when thou seest the new enlightened sphere,
Study to know but what those worthies were.

                                        T. CAREW

2. Where I Lived, and What I Lived For

AT a certain season of our life we are accustomed to
consider every spot as the possible site of a house. I
have thus surveyed the country on every side within a
dozen miles of where I live. In imagination I have
bought all the farms in succession, for all were to be
bought, and I knew their price. I walked over each farmer's premises, tasted his wild apples, discoursed on husbandry with him, took his farm at his price, at any price,

mortgaging it to him in my mind; even put a higher price on it,—took everything but a deed of it,—took his word for his deed, for I dearly love to talk,—cultivated it, and him too to some extent, I trust, and withdrew when I had enjoyed it long enough, leaving him to carry it on. This experience entitled me to be regarded as a sort of real-estate broker by my friends. Wherever I sat, there I might live, and the landscape radiated from me accordingly. What is a house but a *sedes,* a seat?—better if a country seat. I discovered many a site for a house not likely to be soon improved, which some might have thought too far from the village, but to my eyes the village was too far from it. Well, there I might live, I said; and there I did live, for an hour, a summer and a winter life; saw how I could let the years run off, buffet the winter through, and see the spring come in. The future inhabitants of this region, wherever they may place their houses, may be sure that they have been anticipated. An afternoon sufficed to lay out the land into orchard, wood-lot, and pasture, and to decide what fine oaks or pines should be left to stand before the door, and whence each blasted tree could be seen to the best advantage; and then I let it lie, fallow perchance, for a man is rich in proportion to the number of things which he can afford to let alone.

My imagination carried me so far that I even had the refusal of several farms,—the refusal was all I wanted,—but I never got my fingers burned by actual possession. The nearest that I came to actual possession was when I bought the Hollowell place, and had begun to sort my seeds, and collected materials with which to make a wheelbarrow to carry it on or off with; but before the owner gave me a deed of it, his wife—every man has such a wife—changed her mind and wished to keep it, and he offered me ten dollars to release him. Now, to speak the truth, I had but ten cents in the world, and it surpassed my arithmetic to tell, if I was that man who had ten cents, or who had a farm, or ten dollars, or all together. However, I let him keep the ten dollars and the farm too, for I had carried it far enough; or rather, to be generous, I sold him the farm for just what I gave for it, and, as he was not a rich man, made him a present

of ten dollars, and still had my ten cents, and seeds, and
materials for a wheelbarrow left. I found thus that I had
been a rich man without any damage to my poverty. But
I retained the landscape, and I have since annually carried off what it yielded without a wheelbarrow. With
respect to landscapes,—

> "I am monarch of all I *survey,*
>   My right there is none to dispute."

I have frequently seen a poet withdraw, having enjoyed the most valuable part of a farm, while the crusty
farmer supposed that he had got a few wild apples only.
Why, the owner does not know it for many years when
a poet has put his farm in rhyme, the most admirable
kind of invisible fence, has fairly impounded it, milked
it, skimmed it, and got all the cream, and left the farmer
only the skimmed milk.

The real attractions of the Hollowell farm, to me,
were: its complete retirement, being about two miles
from the village, half a mile from the nearest neighbor,
and separated from the highway by a broad field; its
bounding on the river, which the owner said protected
it by its fogs from frosts in the spring, though that was
nothing to me; the gray color and ruinous state of the
house and barn, and the dilapidated fences, which put
such an interval between me and the last occupant; the
hollow and lichen-covered apple trees, gnawed by rabbits, showing what kind of neighbors I should have; but
above all, the recollection I had of it from my earliest
voyages up the river, when the house was concealed behind a dense grove of red maples, through which I heard
the house-dog bark. I was in haste to buy it, before the
proprietor finished getting out some rocks, cutting down
the hollow apple trees, and grubbing up some young
birches which had sprung up in the pasture, or, in short,
had made any more of his improvements. To enjoy these
advantages I was ready to carry it on; like Atlas, to take
the world on my shoulders,—I never heard what compensation he received for that,—and do all those things
which had no other motive or excuse but that I might
pay for it and be unmolested in my possession of it; for

I knew all the while that it would yield the most abundant crop of the kind I wanted, if I could only afford to let it alone. But it turned out as I have said.

All that I could say, then, with respect to farming on a large scale—I have always cultivated a garden—was, that I had had my seeds ready. Many think that seeds improve with age. I have no doubt that time discriminates between the good and the bad; and when at last I shall plant, I shall be less likely to be disappointed. But I would say to my fellows, once for all, As long as possible live free and uncommitted. It makes but little difference whether you are committed to a farm or the county jail.

Old Cato, whose "De Re Rusticâ" is my "Cultivator," says,—and the only translation I have seen makes sheer nonsense of the passage,—"When you think of getting a farm turn it thus in your mind, not to buy greedily; nor spare your pains to look at it, and do not think it enough, to go round it once. The oftener you go there the more it will please you, if it is good." I think I shall not buy greedily, but go round and round it as long as I live, and be buried in it first, that it may please me the more at last.

The present was my next experiment of this kind, which I purpose to describe more at length, for convenience putting the experience of two years into one. As I have said, I do not propose to write an ode to dejection, but to brag as lustily as chanticleer in the morning, standing on his roost, if only to wake my neighbors up.

When first I took up my abode in the woods, that is, began to spend my nights as well as days there, which, by accident, was on Independence Day, or the Fourth of July, 1845, my house was not finished for winter, but was merely a defence against the rain, without plastering or chimney, the walls being of rough, weather-stained boards, with wide chinks, which made it cool at night. The upright white hewn studs and freshly planed door and window casings give it a clean and airy look, especially in the morning, when its timbers were saturated with dew, so that I fancied that by noon some sweet gum would exude from them. To my imagination it retained throughout the day more or less of this auroral character, reminding me of a certain house on a mountain which I had visited a year before. This was an airy and unplastered cabin, fit to entertain a travelling god, and where a goddess might trail her garments. The winds which passed over my dwelling were such as sweep over the ridges of mountains, bearing the broken strains, or celestial parts only, of terrestrial music. The morning wind forever blows, the poem of creation is uninterrupted; but few are the ears that hear it. Olympus is but the outside of the earth everywhere.

The only house I had been the owner of before, if I except a boat, was a tent, which I used occasionally when making excursions in the summer, and this is still rolled up in my garret; but the boat, after passing from hand to hand, has gone down the stream of time. With this more substantial shelter about me, I had made some progress toward settling in the world. This frame, so slightly clad, was a sort of crystallization around me, and reacted on the builder. It was suggestive somewhat as a picture in outlines. I did not need to go outdoors to take the air, for the atmosphere within had lost none of its freshness. It was not so much within-doors as behind a door where I sat, even in the rainiest weather. The Harivansa says, "An abode without birds is like a meat without seasoning." Such was not my abode, for I found myself suddenly neighbor to the birds; not by having imprisoned one, but having caged myself near them. I was not only nearer to some of those which commonly frequent the garden and the orchard, but to those wilder and more thrilling songsters of the forest which never, or rarely, serenade a villager,—the wood thrush, the veery, the scarlet tanager, the field sparrow, the whippoor-will, and many others.

I was seated by the shore of a small pond, about a mile and a half south of the village of Concord and somewhat higher than it, in the midst of an extensive wood between that town and Lincoln, and about two miles south of that our only field known to fame, Concord Battle Grounds; but I was so low in the woods that the opposite shore, half a mile off, like the rest, covered with wood, was my most distant horizon. For the first week, whenever I looked out on the pond it impressed me like a tarn high up on the side of a mountain, its bottom far above the surface of other lakes, and, as the sun arose, I saw it throwing off its nightly clothing of mist, and here and there, by degrees, its soft ripples or its smooth reflecting surface was revealed, while the mists, like ghosts, were stealthily withdrawing in every direction into the woods, as at the breaking up of some nocturnal conventicle. The very dew seemed to hang upon the trees later into the day than usual, as on the sides of mountains.

This small lake was of most value as a neighbor in the intervals of a gentle rain-storm in August, when, both air and water being perfectly still, but the sky overcast, mid-afternoon had all the serenity of evening, and the wood thrush sang around, and was heard from shore to shore. A lake like this is never smoother than at such a time; and the clear portion of the air above it being shallow and darkened by clouds, the water, full of light and reflections, becomes a lower heaven itself so much the more important. From a hill-top near by, where the wood had been recently cut off, there was a pleasing vista southward across the pond, through a wide indentation in the hills which form the shore there, where their opposite sides sloping toward each other suggested a stream flowing out in that direction through a wooded valley, but stream there was none. That way I looked between and over the near green hills to some distant and higher ones in the horizon, tinged with blue. Indeed, by standing on tiptoe I could catch a glimpse of some of the peaks of the still bluer and more distant mountain ranges in the northwest, those true-blue coins from heaven's own mint, and also of some portion of the village. But in other directions, even from this point, I could not see over or beyond the woods which surrounded me. It is well to have some water in your neighborhood, to give buoyancy to and float the earth. One value even of the smallest well is, that when you look into it you see that earth is not continent but insular. This is as important as that it keeps butter cool. When I looked across the pond from this peak toward the Sudbury meadows, which in time of flood I distinguished elevated perhaps by a mirage in their seething valley, like a coin in a basin, all the earth beyond the pond appeared like a thin crust insulated and floated even by this small sheet of intervening water, and I was reminded that this on which I dwelt was but *dry land*.

Though the view from my door was still more contracted, I did not feel crowded or confined in the least. There was pasture enough for my imagination. The low shrub oak plateau to which the opposite shore arose stretched away toward the prairies of the West and the steppes of Tartary, affording ample room for all the roving families of men. "There are none happy in the world but beings who enjoy freely a vast horizon,"—said Damodara, when his herds required new and larger pastures.

Both place and time were changed, and I dwelt nearer to those parts of the universe and to those eras in history which had most attracted me. Where I lived was as far off as many a region viewed nightly by astronomers. We are wont to imagine rare and delectable places in some remote and more celestial corner of the system, behind the constellation of Cassiopeia's Chair, far from noise and disturbance. I discovered that my house actually had its site in such a withdrawn, but forever new and unprofaned, part of the universe. If it were worth the while to settle in those parts near to the Pleiades or the Hyades, to Aldebaran or Altair, then I was really there, or at an equal remoteness from the life which I had left behind, dwindled and twinkling with as fine a ray to my nearest neighbor, and to be seen only in moonless nights by him. Such was that part of creation where I had squatted;—

> "There was a shepherd that did live,
>   And held his thoughts as high
> As were the mounts whereon his flocks
>   Did hourly feed him by."

What should we think of the shepherd's life if his flocks always wandered to higher pastures than his thoughts?

Every morning was a cheerful invitation to make my life of equal simplicity, and I may say innocence, with Nature herself. I have been as sincere a worshipper of

Aurora as the Greeks. I got up early and bathed in the pond; that was a religious exercise, and one of the best things which I did. They say that characters were engraven on the bathing tub of King Tching-thang to this effect: "Renew thyself completely each day; do it again, and again, and forever again." I can understand that. Morning brings back the heroic ages. I was as much affected by the faint hum of a mosquito making its invisible and unimaginable tour through my apartment at earliest dawn, when I was sitting with door and windows open, as I could be by any trumpet that ever sang of fame. It was Homer's requiem; itself an Iliad and Odyssey in the air, singing its own wrath and wanderings. There was something cosmical about it; a standing advertisement, till forbidden, of the everlasting vigor and fertility of the world. The morning, which is the most memorable season of the day, is the awakening hour. Then there is least somnolence in us; and for an hour, at least, some part of us awakes which slumbers all the rest of the day and night. Little is to be expected of that day, if it can be called a day, to which we are not awakened by our Genius, but by the mechanical nudgings of some servitor, are not awakened by our own newly acquired force and aspirations from within, accompanied by the undulations of celestial music, instead of factory bells, and a fragrance filling the air—to a higher life than we fell asleep from; and thus the darkness bear its fruit, and prove itself to be good, no less than the light. That man who does not believe that each day contains an earlier, more sacred, and auroral hour than he has yet profaned, has despaired of life, and is pursuing a descending and darkening way. After a partial cessation of his sensuous life, the soul of man, or its organs rather, are reinvigorated each day, and his Genius tries again what noble life it can make. All memorable events, I should say, transpire in morning time and in a morning atmosphere. The Vedas say, "All intelligences awake with the morning." Poetry and art, and the fairest and most memorable of the actions of men, date from such an hour. All poets and heroes, like Memnon, are the children of Aurora, and emit their music at sunrise. To him whose elastic and vigorous thought keeps pace with the sun, the day is a perpetual morning. It matters not what the clocks say or the attitudes and labors of men. Morning is when I am awake and there is a dawn in me. Moral reform is the effort to throw off sleep. Why is it that men give so poor an account of their day if they have not been slumbering? They are not such poor calculators. If they had not been overcome with drowsiness, they would have performed something. The millions are awake enough for physical labor; but only one in a million is awake enough for effective intellectual exertion, only one in a hundred millions to a poetic or divine life. To be awake is to be alive. I have never yet met a man who was quite awake. How could I have looked him in the face?

We must learn to reawaken and keep ourselves awake, not by mechanical aids, but by an infinite expectation of the dawn, which does not forsake us in our soundest sleep. I know of no more encouraging fact than the unquestionable ability of man to elevate his life by a conscious endeavor. It is something to be able to paint a particular picture, or to carve a statue, and so to make a few objects beautiful; but it is far more glorious to carve and paint the very atmosphere and medium through which we look, which morally we can do. To affect the quality of the day, that is the highest of arts. Every man is tasked to make his life, even in its details, worthy of the contemplation of his most elevated and critical hour. If we refused, or rather used up, such paltry information as we get, the oracles would distinctly inform us how this might be done.

I went to the woods because I wished to live deliberately, to front only the essential facts of life, and see if I could not learn what it had to teach, and not, when I came to die, discover that I had not lived. I did not wish to live what was not life, living is so dear; nor did I wish to practise resignation, unless it was quite necessary. I wanted to live deep and suck out all the marrow of life, to live so sturdily and Spartan-like as to put to rout all that was not life, to cut a broad swath and shave close, to drive life into a corner, and reduce it to its lowest terms, and, if it proved to be mean, why then to get the whole and genuine meanness of it, and publish its meanness to the world; or if it were sublime, to know it by experience, and be able to give a true account of it in my next excursion. For most men, it appears to me, are in a strange uncertainty about it, whether it is of the devil or of God, and have *somewhat hastily* concluded that it is the chief end of man here to "glorify God and enjoy him forever."

Still we live meanly, like ants; though the fable tells us that we were long ago changed into men; like pygmies we fight with cranes; it is error upon error, and clout upon clout, and our best virtue has for its occasion a superfluous and evitable wretchedness. Our life is frittered away by detail. An honest man has hardly need to count more than his ten fingers, or in extreme cases he may add his ten toes, and lump the rest. Simplicity, simplicity, simplicity! I say, let your affairs be as two or three, and not a hundred or a thousand; instead of a million count half a dozen, and keep your accounts on your thumb-nail. In the midst of this chopping sea of civilized life, such are the clouds and storms and quicksands and thousand-and-one items to be allowed for, that a man has to live, if he would not founder and go to the bottom and not make his port at all, by dead reckoning, and he must be a great calculator indeed who succeeds. Simplify, simplify. Instead of three meals a day, if it be necessary eat but one; instead of a hundred dishes, five; and reduce other things in proportion. Our life is like a German Confederacy, made up of petty states, with its boundary forever fluctuating, so that even a German cannot tell you how it is bounded at any moment. The nation itself, with all its so-called internal improvements, which, by the way are all external and superficial, is just such an unwieldly and overgrown establishment, cluttered with furniture and tripped up by its own traps, ruined by luxury and heedless expense, by want of calculation and a worthy aim, as the million households in the land; and the only cure for it, as for them, is in a rigid economy, a stern and more than Spartan simplicity of life and elevation of purpose. It lives too fast. Men think that it is essential that the *Nation* have commerce, and export ice, and talk through a telegraph, and ride thirty miles an hour, without a doubt, whether *they* do or not; but whether we should live like baboons or like men, is a little uncertain. If we do not get out sleepers, and forge rails, and devote days and nights to the work, but go to tinkering upon our *lives* to improve *them,* who will build railroads? And if railroads are not built, how shall we get to heaven in season? But if we stay at home and mind our business, who will want railroads? We do not ride on the railroad; it rides upon us. Did you ever think what those sleepers are that underlie the railroad? Each one is a man, an Irishman, or a Yankee man. The rails are laid on them, and they are covered with sand, and the cars run smoothly over them. They are sound sleepers, I assure you. And every few years a new lot is laid down and run over; so that, if some have the pleasure of riding on a rail, others have the misfortune to be ridden upon. And when they run over a man that is walking in his sleep, a supernumerary sleeper in the wrong position, and wake him up, they suddenly stop the cars, and make a hue and cry about it, as if this were an exception. I am glad to know that it takes a gang of men for every five miles to keep the sleepers down and level in their beds as it is, for this is a sign that they may sometime get up again.

Why should we live with such hurry and waste of life? We are determined to be starved before we are hungry. Men say that a stitch in time saves nine, and so they take a thousand stitches to-day to save nine to-morrow. As for *work,* we haven't any of any consequence. We have the Saint Vitus' dance, and cannot possibly keep our heads still. If I should only give a few pulls at the parish bell-rope, as for a fire, that is, without setting the bell, there is hardly a man on his farm in the outskirts of Concord, notwithstanding that press of engagements which was his excuse so many times this morning, nor a boy, nor a woman, I might almost say, but would forsake all and follow that sound, not mainly to save property from the flames, but, if we will confess the truth, much more to see it burn, since burn it must, and we, be it known, did not set it on fire,—or to see it put out, and have a hand in it, if that is done as handsomely; yes, even if it were the parish church itself. Hardly a man takes a half-hour's nap after dinner, but when he wakes he holds up his head and asks, "What's the news?" as if the rest of mankind had stood his sentinels. Some give directions to be waked every half-hour, doubtless for no other purpose; and then, to pay for it, they tell what they have dreamed. After a night's sleep the news is as indispensable as the breakfast. "Pray tell me anything new that has happened to a man anywhere on this globe,"—and he reads it over his coffee and rolls, that a man has had his eyes gouged out this morning on the Wachito River; never dreaming the while that he lives in the dark unfathomed mammoth cave of this world, and has but the rudiment of an eye himself.

For my part, I could easily do without the post office. I think that there are very few important communications made through it. To speak critically, I never received more than one or two letters in my life—I wrote this some years ago—that were worth the postage. The penny-post is, commonly, an institution through which you seriously offer a man that penny for his thoughts which is so often safely offered in jest. And I am sure that I never read any memorable news in a newspaper. If we read of one man robbed, or murdered, or killed by accident, or one house burned, or one vessel wrecked, or one steamboat blown up, or one cow run over on the Western Railroad, or one mad dog killed, or one lot of grasshoppers in the winter,—we never need read of another. One is enough. If you are acquainted with the principle, what do you care for a myriad instances and applications? To a philosopher all *news,* as it is called, is gossip, and they who edit and read it are old women over their tea. Yet not a few are greedy after this gossip. There was such a rush, as I hear, the other day at one of the offices to learn the foreign news by the last arrival, that several large squares of plate glass belonging to the establishment were broken by the pressure,—news which I seriously think a ready wit might write a twelvemonth, or twelve years, beforehand with sufficient accuracy. As for Spain, for instance, if you know how to throw in Don Carlos and the Infanta, and Don Pedro and Seville and Granada, from time to time in the right proportions,—they may have changed the names a little since I saw the papers,—and serve up a bullfight when other entertainments fail, it will be true to the letter, and give us as good an idea of the exact state or ruin of things in Spain as the most succinct and lucid reports under this head in the newspapers: and as for England, almost the last significant scrap of news from that quarter was the revolution of 1649; and if you have learned the history of her crops for an average year, you never need attend to that thing again, unless your specula- tions are of a merely pecuniary character. If one may judge who rarely looks into the newspapers, nothing new does ever happen in foreign parts, a French revolution not excepted.

What news! how much more important to know what that is which was never old! "Kieou-he-yu (great digni- tary of the state of Wei) sent a man to Khoung-tseu to know his news. Khoung-tseu caused the messenger to be seated near him, and questioned him in these terms: What is your master doing? The messenger answered with respect: My master desires to diminish the number of his faults, but he cannot come to the end of them. The messenger being gone, the philosopher remarked: What a worthy messenger! What a worthy messenger!" The preacher, instead of vexing the ears of drowsy farm- ers on their day of rest at the end of the week,—for Sunday is the fit conclusion of an ill-spent week, and not the fresh and brave beginning of a new one,—with this one other draggle-tail of a sermon, should shout with thundering voice, "Pause! Avast! Why so seeming fast, but deadly slow?"

Shams and delusions are esteemed for soundest truths, while reality is fabulous. If men would steadily observe realities only, and not allow theselves to be deluded, life, to compare it with such things as we know, would be like a fairy tale and the Arabian Nights' Entertainments. If we respected only what is inevitable and has a right to be, music and poetry would resound along the streets. When we are unhurried and wise, we perceive that only great and worthy things have any permanent and abso- lute existence, that petty fears and petty pleasures are but the shadow of the reality. This is always exhilarating and sublime. By closing the eyes and slumbering, and consenting to be deceived by shows, men establish and confirm their daily life of routine and habit everywhere, which still is built on purely illusory foundations. Children, who play life, discern its true law and relations more clearly than men, who fail to live it worthily, but who think that they are wiser by experience, that is, by failure. I have read in a Hindoo book, that "there was a king's son, who, being expelled in infancy from his native city, was brought up by a forester, and, growing up to maturity in that state, imagined himself to belong to the barbarous race with which he lived. One of his father's ministers having discovered him, revealed to him what he was, and the misconception of his character was removed, and he knew himself to be a prince. So soul," continues the Hindoo philosopher, "from the circumstances in which it is placed, mistakes its own character, until the truth is revealed to it by some holy teacher, and then it knows itself to be *Brahme*." I perceive that we inhabitants of New England live this mean life that we do because our vision does not penetrate the surface of things. We think that that *is* which *appears* to be. If a man should walk through this town and see only the reality, where, think you, would the "Mill-dam" go to? If he should give us an account of the realities he beheld there, we should not recognize the place in his description. Look at a meeting-house, or a court-house, or a jail, or a shop, or a dwelling-house, and say what that thing really is before a true gaze, and they would all go to pieces in your account of them. Men esteem truth remote, in the outskirts of the system, behind the farthest star, before Adam and after the last man. In eternity there is indeed something true and sublime. But all these times and places and occasions are now and here. God himself culminates in the present moment, and will never be more divine in the lapse of all the ages. And we are enabled to apprehend at all what is sublime and noble only by the perpetual instilling and drenching of the reality that surrounds us. The universe constantly and obediently answers to our conceptions; whether we travel fast or slow, the track is laid for us. Let us spend our lives in conceiving then. The poet or the artist never yet had so fair and noble a design but some of his posterity at least could accomplish it.

Let us spend one day as deliberately as Nature, and not be thrown off the track by every nutshell and mosquito's wing that falls on the rails. Let us rise early and fast, or break fast, gently and without perturbation; let company come and let company go, let the bells ring and the children cry,—determined to make a day of it. Why should we knock under and go with the stream? Let us not be upset and overwhelmed in that terrible rapid and whirlpool called a dinner, situated in the meridian shallows. Weather this danger and you are safe, for the rest of the way is down hill. With unrelaxed nerves, with morning vigor, sail by it, looking another way, tied to the mast like Ulysses. If the engine whistles, let it whistle till it is hoarse for its pains. If the bell rings, why should we run? We will consider what kind of music they are like. Let us settle ourselves, and work and wedge our feet downward through the mud and slush of opinion, and prejudice, and tradition, and delusion, and appearance, that alluvion which covers the globe, through Paris and London, through New York and Boston and Concord, through Church and State, through poetry and philosophy and religion, till we come to a hard bottom and rocks in place, which we can call *reality*, and say, This is, and no mistake; and then begin, having a point d'appui, below freshet and frost and fire, a place where you might found a wall or a state, or set a lamppost safely, or perhaps a gauge, not a Nilometer, but a Realometer, that future ages might know how deep a freshet of shams and appearances had gathered from time to time. If you stand right fronting and face to face to a fact, you will see the sun glimmer on both its surfaces, as if it were a cimeter, and feel its sweet edge dividing you through the heart and marrow, and so you will happily conclude your mortal career. Be it life or death, we crave only reality. If we are really dying, let us hear the rattle in our throats and feel cold in the extremities; if we are alive, let us go about our business.

Time is but the stream I go a-fishing in. I drink at it; but while I drink I see the sandy bottom and detect how shallow it is. Its thin current slides away, but eternity remains. I would drink deeper; fish in the sky, whose bottom is pebbly with stars. I cannot count one. I know not the first letter of the alphabet. I have always been regretting that I was not as wise as the day I was born. The intellect is a cleaver; it discerns and rifts its way into the secret of things. I do not wish to be any more busy with my hands than is necessary. My head is hands and feet. I feel all my best faculties concentrated in it. My instinct tells me that my head is an organ for burrowing, as some creatures use their snout and fore paws, and with it I would mine and burrow my way through these hills. I think that the richest vein is somewhere hereabouts; so by the divining-rod and thin rising vapors I judge; and here I will begin to mine.

3. Reading

WITH a little more deliberation in the choice of their pursuits, all men would perhaps become essentially students and observers, for certainly their nature and destiny are interesting to all alike. In accumulating property for ourselves or our posterity, in founding a family or a state, or acquiring fame even, we are mortal; but in dealing with truth we are immortal, and need fear no change nor accident. The oldest Egyptian or Hindoo philosopher raised a corner of the veil from the statue of the divinity; and still the trembling robe remains raised, and I gaze upon as fresh a glory as he did, since it was I in him that was then so bold, and it is he in me that now reviews the vision. No dust has settled on that robe; no time has elapsed since that divinity was revealed. That time which we really improve, or which is improvable, is neither past, present, nor future.

My residence was more favorable, not only to thought, but to serious reading, than a university; and though I was beyond the range of the ordinary circulating library, I had more than ever come within the influence of those books which circulate round the world, whose sentences were first written on bark, and are now merely copied from time to time on to linen paper. Says the poet Mîr

Camar Uddîn Mast, "Being seated, to run through the region of the spiritual world; I have had this advantage in books. To be intoxicated by a single glass of wine; I have experienced this pleasure when I have drunk the liquor of the esoteric doctrines." I kept Homer's Iliad on my table through the summer, though I looked at his page only now and then. Incessant labor with my hands, at first, for I had my house to finish and my beans to hoe at the same time, made more study impossible. Yet I sustained myself by the prospect of such reading in future. I read one or two shallow books of travel in the intervals of my work, till that employment made me ashamed of myself, and I asked where it was then that _I_ lived.

The student may read Homer or Æschylus in the Greek without danger of dissipation or luxuriousness, for it implies that he in some measure emulate their heroes, and consecrate morning hours to their pages. The heroic books, even if printed in the character of our mother tongue, will always be in a language dead to degenerate times; and we must laboriously seek the meaning of each word and line, conjecturing a larger sense than common use permits out of what wisdom and valor and generosity we have. The modern cheap and fertile press, with all its translations, has done little to bring us nearer to the heroic writers of antiquity. They seem as solitary, and the letter in which they are printed as rare and curious, as ever. It is worth the expense of youthful days and costly hours, if you learn only some words of an ancient language, which are raised out of the trivialness of the street, to be perpetual suggestions and provocations. It is not in vain that the farmer remembers and repeats the few Latin words which he has heard. Men sometimes speak as if the study of the classics would at length make way for more modern and practical studies; but the adventurous student will always study classics, in whatever language they may be written and however ancient they may be. For what are the classics but the noblest recorded thoughts of man? They are the only oracles which are not decayed, and there are such answers to the most modern inquiry in them as Delphi and Dodona never gave. We might as well omit

to study Nature because she is old. To read well, that
is, to read true books in a true spirit, is a noble exercise,
and one that will task the reader more than any exercise
which the customs of the day esteem. It requires a train-
ing such as the athletes underwent, the steady intention
almost of the whole life to this object. Books must be
read as deliberately and reservedly as they were written.
It is not enough even to be able to speak the language
of that nation by which they are written, for there is a
memorable interval between the spoken and the written
language, the language heard and the language read. The
one is commonly transitory, a sound, a tongue, a dialect
merely, almost brutish, and we learn it unconsciously,
like the brutes, of our mothers. The other is the maturity
and experience of that; if that is our mother tongue, this
is our father tongue, a reserved and select expression,
too significant to be heard by the ear, which we must be
born again in order to speak. The crowds of men who
merely *spoke* the Greek and Latin tongues in the Middle
Ages were not entitled by the accident of birth to *read*
the works of genius written in those languages; for these
were not written in that Greek or Latin which they
knew, but in the select language of literature. They had
not learned the nobler dialects of Greece and Rome, but
the very materials on which they were written were
waste paper to them, and they prized instead a cheap
contemporary literature. But when the several nations
of Europe had acquired distinct though rude written languages of their own, sufficient for the purposes of their
rising literatures, then first learning revived, and scholars
were enabled to discern from that remoteness the treasures of antiquity. What the Roman and Grecian multitude could not *hear*, after the lapse of ages a few
scholars *read*, and a few scholars only are still reading it.

However much we may admire the orator's occasional
bursts of eloquence, the noblest written words are commonly as far behind or above the fleeting spoken language as the firmament with its stars is behind the
clouds. *There* are the stars, and they who can may read
them. The astronomers forever comment on and observe
them. They are not exhalations like our daily colloquies
and vaporous breath. What is called eloquence in the

forum is commonly found to be rhetoric in the study. The orator yields to the inspiration of a transient occasion, and speaks to the mob before him, to those who can *hear* him; but the writer, whose more equable life is his occasion, and who would be distracted by the event and the crowd which inspire the orator, speaks to the intellect and heart of mankind, to all in any age who can *understand* him.

No wonder that Alexander carried the Iliad with him on his expeditions in a precious casket. A written word is the choicest of relics. It is something at once more intimate with us and more universal than any other work of art. It is the work of art nearest to life itself. It may be translated into every language, and not only be read but actually breathed from all human lips;—not be represented on canvas or in marble only, but be carved out of the breath of life itself. The symbol of an ancient man's thought becomes a modern man's speech. Two thousand summers have imparted to the monuments of Grecian literature, as to her marbles, only a maturer golden and autumnal tint, for they have carried their own serene and celestial atmosphere into all lands to protect them against the corrosion of time. Books are the treasured wealth of the world and the fit inheritance of generations and nations. Books, the oldest and the best, stand naturally and rightfully on the shelves of every cottage. They have no cause of their own to plead, but while they enlighten and sustain the reader his common sense will not refuse them. Their authors are a natural and irresistible aristocracy in every society, and, more than kings or emperors, exert an influence on mankind. When the illiterate and perhaps scornful trader has earned by enterprise and industry his coveted leisure and independence, and is admitted to the circles of wealth and fashion, he turns inevitably at last to those still higher but yet inaccessible circles of intellect and genius, and is sensible only of the imperfection of his culture and the vanity and insufficiency of all his riches, and further proves his good sense by the pains which he takes to secure for his children that intellectual culture whose want he so keenly feels; and thus it is that he becomes the founder of a family.

Those who have not learned to read the ancient classics in the language in which they were written must have a very imperfect knowledge of the history of the human race; for it is remarkable that no transcript of them has ever been made into any modern tongue, unless our civilization itself may be regarded as such a transcript. Homer has never yet been printed in English, nor Æschylus, nor Virgil even,—works as refined, as solidly done, and as beautiful almost as the morning itself; for later writers, say what we will of their genius, have rarely, if ever, equalled the elaborate beauty and finish and the lifelong and heroic literary labors of the ancients. They only talk of forgetting them who never knew them. It will be soon enough to forget them when we have the learning and the genius which will enable us to attend to and appreciate them. That age will be rich indeed when those relics which we call Classics, and the still older and more than classic but even less known Scriptures of the nations, shall have still further accumulated, when the Vaticans shall be filled with Vedas and Zendavestas and Bibles, with Homers and Dantes and Shakespeares, and all the centuries to come shall have successively deposited their trophies in the forum of the world. By such a pile we may hope to scale heaven at last.

The works of the great poets have never yet been read by mankind, for only great poets can read them. They have only been read as the multitude read the stars, at most astrologically, not astronomically. Most men have learned to read to serve a paltry convenience, as they have learned to cipher in order to keep accounts and not be cheated in trade; but of reading as a noble intellectual exercise they know little or nothing; yet this only is reading, in a high sense, not that which lulls us as a luxury and suffers the nobler faculties to sleep the while, but what we have to stand on tip-top to read and devote our most alert and wakeful hours to.

I think that having learned our letters we should read the best that is in literature, and not be forever repeating our a-b-abs, and words of one syllable, in the fourth or fifth classes, sitting on the lowest and foremost form all our lives. Most men are satisfied if they read or hear read, and perchance have been convicted by the wisdom of one good book, the Bible, and for the rest of their lives vegetate and dissipate their faculties in what is called easy reading. There is a work in several volumes in our Circulating Library entitled "Little Reading," which I thought referred to a town of that name which I had not been to. There are those who, like cormorants and ostriches, can digest all sorts of this, even after the fullest dinner of meats and vegetables, for they suffer nothing to be wasted. If others are the machines to provide this provender, they are the machines to read it. They read the nine thousandth tale about Zebulon and Sophronia, and how they loved as none had ever loved before, and neither did the course of their true love run smooth,—at any rate, how it did run and stumble, and get up again and go on! how some poor unfortunate got up on to a steeple, who had better never have gone up as far as the belfry; and then, having needlessly got him up there, the happy novelist rings the bell for all the world to come together and hear, O dear! how he did get down again! For my part, I think that they had better metamorphose all such aspiring heroes of universal noveldom into man weather-cocks, as they used to put heroes among the constellations, and let them swing round there till they are rusty, and not come down at all to bother honest men with their pranks. The next time the novelist rings the bell I will not stir though the meeting-house burn down. "The Skip of the Tip-Toe-Hop, a Romance of the Middle Ages, by the celebrated author of 'Tittle-Tol-Tan,' to appear in monthly parts; a great rush; don't all come together." All this they read with saucer eyes, and erect and primitive curiosity, and with unwearied gizzard, whose corrugations even yet need no sharpening, just as some little four-year-old bencher his two-cent gilt-covered edition of Cinderella,—without any improvement, that I can see, in the pronunciation, or accent, or emphasis, or any more skill in extracting or inserting the moral. The result is dullness of sight, a stagnation of the vital circulations, and a general deliquium and sloughing off of all the intellectual faculties. This sort of gingerbread is baked daily and more sedulously than pure wheat or rye-and-Indian in almost every oven and finds a surer market.

The best books are not read even by those who are called good readers. What does our Concord culture amount to? There is in this town, with a very few exceptions, no taste for the best or for very good books even in English literature, whose words all can read and spell. Even the college-bred and so-called liberally educated men here and elsewhere have really little or no acquaintance with the English classics; and as for the recorded wisdom of mankind, the ancient classics and Bibles, which are accessible to all who will know of them, there are the feeblest efforts anywhere made to become acquainted with them. I know a woodchopper, of middle age, who takes a French paper, not for news as he says, for he is above that, but to "keep himself in practice," he being a Canadian by birth; and when I ask him what he considers the best thing he can do in this world, he says, beside this, to keep up and add to his English. This is about as much as the college-bred generally do or aspire to do, and they take an English paper for the purpose. One who has just come from reading perhaps one of the best English books will find how many with whom he can converse about it? Or suppose he comes from reading a Greek or Latin classic in the original, whose praises are familiar even to the so-called illiterate; he will find nobody at all to speak to, but must keep silence about it. Indeed, there is hardly the professor in our colleges, who, if he has mastered the difficulties of the language, has proportionally mastered the difficulties of the wit and poetry of a Greek poet, and has any sympathy to impart to the alert and heroic reader; and as for the sacred Scriptures, or Bibles of mankind, who in this town can tell me even their titles? Most men do not know that any nation but the Hebrews have had a scripture. A man, any man, will go considerably out of his way to pick up a silver dollar; but here are golden words, which the wisest men of antiquity have uttered, and whose worth the wise of every succeeding age have assured us of;—and yet we learn to read only as far as Easy Reading, the primers and class-books, and when we leave school, the "Little Reading," and story-books, which are for boys and beginners; and our reading, our conversation and thinking, are all on a very low level, worthy only of pygmies and manikins.

I aspire to be acquainted with wiser men than this our Concord soil has produced, whose names are hardly known here. Or shall I hear the name of Plato and never read his book? As if Plato were my townsman and I never saw him,—my next neighbor and I never heard him speak or attended to the wisdom of his words. But how actually is it? His Dialogues, which contain what was immortal in him, lie on the next shelf, and yet I never read them. We are underbred and low-lived and illiterate; and in this respect I confess I do not make any very broad distinction between the illiterateness of my townsman who cannot read at all and the illiterateness of him who has learned to read only what is for children and feeble intellects. We should be as good as the worthies of antiquity, but partly by first knowing how good they were. We are a race of tit-men, and soar but little higher in our intellectual flights than the columns of the daily paper.

It is not all books that are as dull as their readers. There are probably words addressed to our condition exactly, which, if we could really hear and understand, would be more salutary than the morning or the spring to our lives, and possibly put a new aspect on the face of things for us. How many a man has dated a new era in his life from the reading of a book! The book exists for us, perchance, which will explain our miracles and reveal new ones. The at present unutterable things we may find somewhere uttered. These same questions that disturb and puzzle and confound us have in their turn occurred to all the wise men; not one has been omitted; and each has answered them, according to his ability, by his words and his life. Moreover, with wisdom we shall learn liberality. The solitary hired man on a farm in the outskirts of Concord, who has had his second birth and peculiar religious experience, and is driven as he believes into silent gravity and exclusiveness by his faith, may think it is not true; but Zoroaster, thousands of years ago, travelled the same road and had the same experience; but he, being wise, knew it to be universal, and treated his neighbors accordingly, and is even said to have invented and established worship among men. Let him humbly commune with Zoroaster then, and through the liberalizing influence of all the worthies, with Jesus Christ himself, and let "our church" go by the board.

We boast that we belong to the Nineteenth Century and are making the most rapid strides of any nation. But consider how little this village does for its own culture. I do not wish to flatter my townsmen, nor to be flattered by them, for that will not advance either of us. We need to be provoked,—goaded like oxen, as we are, into a trot. We have a comparatively decent system of common schools, schools for infants only; but excepting the half-starved Lyceum in the winter, and latterly the puny beginning of a library suggested by the State, no school for ourselves. We spend more on almost any article of bodily aliment or ailment than on our mental aliment. It is time that we had uncommon schools, that we did not leave off our education when we begin to be men and women. It is time that villages were universities, and their elder inhabitants the fellows of universities, with leisure—if they are, indeed, so well off—to pursue liberal studies the rest of their lives. Shall the world be confined to one Paris or one Oxford forever? Cannot students be boarded here and get a liberal education under the skies of Concord? Can we not hire some Abélard to lecture to us? Alas! what with foddering the cattle and tending the store, we are kept from school too long, and our education is sadly neglected. In this country, the village should in some respects take the place of the nobleman of Europe. It should be the patron of the fine arts. It is rich enough. It wants only the magnanimity and refinement. It can spend money enough on such things as farmers and traders value, but it is thought Utopian to propose spending money for things which more intelligent men know to be of far more worth. This town has spent seventeen thousand dollars on a townhouse, thank fortune or politics, but probably it will not spend so much on living wit, the true meat to put into that shell, in a hundred years. The one hundred and twenty-five dollars annually subscribed for a Lyceum in the winter is better spent than any other equal sum raised in the town. If we live in the Nineteenth Century, why should we not enjoy the advantages which the Nineteenth Century offers? Why should our life be in any respect provincial? If we will read newspapers, why not skip the gossip of Boston and take the best newspaper in the world at once?—not be sucking the pap of "neutral family" papers, or browsing "Olive-Branches" here in New England. Let the reports of all the learned societies come to us, and we will see if they know anything. Why should we leave it to Harper & Brothers and Redding & Co. to select our reading? As the nobleman of cultivated taste surrounds himself with whatever conduces to his culture,—genius—learning—wit—books—paintings—statuary—music—philosophical instruments, and the like; so let the village do,—not stop short at a pedagogue, a parson, a sexton, a parish library, and three select-men, because our Pilgrim forefathers got through a cold winter once on a bleak rock with these. To act collectively is according to the spirit of our institutions; and I am confident that, as our circumstances are more flourishing, our means are greater than the nobleman's. New England can hire all the wise men in the world to come and teach her, and board them round the while, and not be provincial at all. That is the *uncommon* school we want. Instead of noblemen, let us have noble villages of men. If it is necessary, omit one bridge over the river, go round a little there, and throw one arch at least over the darker gulf of ignorance which surrounds us.

4. Sounds

BUT while we are confined to books, though the most select and classic, and read only particular written languages, which are themselves but dialects and provincial, we are in danger of forgetting the language which all things and events speak without metaphor, which alone is copious and standard. Much is published, but little printed. The rays which stream through the shutter will be no longer remembered when the shutter is wholly removed. No method nor discipline can supersede the necessity of being forever on the alert. What is a course of history or philosophy, or poetry, no matter how well selected, or the best society, or the most admirable routine of life, compared with the discipline of looking always at what is to be seen? Will you be a reader, a student merely, or a seer? Read your fate, see what is before you, and walk on into futurity.

I did not read books the first summer; I hoed beans. Nay, I often did better than this. There were times when I could not afford to sacrifice the bloom of the present moment to any work, whether of the head or hands. I love a broad margin to my life. Sometimes, in a summer morning, having taken my accustomed bath, I sat in my sunny doorway from sunrise till noon, rapt in a revery, amidst the pines and hickories and sumachs, in undisturbed solitude and stillness, while the birds sang around or flitted noiseless through the house, until by the sun falling in at my west window, or the noise of some travellers' wagon on the distant highway, I was reminded of the lapse of time. I grew in those seasons like corn in the night, and they were far better than any work of the hands would have been. They were not time subtracted from my life, but so much over and above my usual allowance. I realized what the Orientals mean by contemplation and the forsaking of works. For the most part, I minded not how the hours went. The day advanced as if to light some work of mine; it was morning, and lo, now it is evening, and nothing memorable is accomplished. Instead of singing like the birds, I silently smiled at my incessant good fortune. As the sparrow had its trill, sitting on the hickory before my door, so had I my chuckle or suppressed warble which he might hear out of my nest. My days were not days of the week, bearing the stamp of any heathen deity, nor were they minced into hours and fretted by the ticking of a clock; for I lived like the Puri Indians, of whom it is said that "for yesterday, to-day, and to-morrow they have only one word, and they express the variety of meaning by pointing backward for yesterday, forward for to-morrow, and overhead for the passing day." This was sheer idleness to my fellow-townsmen, no doubt; but if the birds and flowers had tried me by their standard, I should not have been found wanting. A man must find his occasions in himself, it is true. The natural day is very calm, and will hardly reprove his indolence.

I had this advantage, at least, in my mode of life, over those who were obliged to look abroad for amusement, to society and the theatre, that my life itself was become my amusement and never ceased to be novel. It was a drama of many scenes and without an end. If we were always, indeed, getting our living, and regulating our lives according to the last and best mode we had learned, we should never be troubled with ennui. Follow your genius closely enough, and it will not fail to show you a fresh prospect every hour. Housework was a pleasant pastime. When my floor was dirty, I rose early, and, setting all my furniture out of doors on the grass, bed and bedstead making but one budget, dashed water on the floor, and sprinkled white sand from the pond on it, and then with a broom scrubbed it clean and white; and by the time the villagers had broken their fast the morning sun had dried my house sufficiently to allow me to move in again, and my meditations were almost uninterrupted. It was pleasant to see my whole household effects out on the grass, making a little pile like a gypsy's pack, and my three-legged table, from which I did not remove the books and pen and ink, standing amid the pines and hickories. They seemed glad to get out themselves, and as if unwilling to be brought in. I was sometimes tempted to stretch an awning over them and take my seat there. It was worth the while to see the sun shine on these things, and hear the free wind blow on them; so much more interesting most familiar objects look out of doors than in the house. A bird sits on the next bough, life-everlasting grows under the table, and blackberry vines run round its legs; pine cones, chestnut burs, and strawberry leaves are strewn about. It looked as if this was the way these forms came to be transferred to our furniture, to tables, chairs, and bedsteads,—because they once stood in their midst.

My house was on the side of a hill, immediately on

the edge of the larger wood, in the midst of a young forest of pitch pines and hickories, and half a dozen rods from the pond, to which a narrow footpath led down the hill. In my front yard grew the strawberry, blackberry, and life-everlasting, johnswort and goldenrod, shrub oaks and sand cherry, blueberry and groundnut. Near the end of May, the sand cherry (*Cerasus pumila*) adorned the sides of the path with its delicate flowers arranged in umbels cylindrically about its short stems, which last, in the fall, weighed down with good-sized and handsome cherries, fell over in wreaths like rays on every side. I tasted them out of compliment to Nature, though they were scarcely palatable. The sumach (*Rhus glabra*) grew luxuriantly about the house, pushing up through the embankment which I had made, and growing five or six feet the first season. Its broad pinnate tropical leaf was pleasant though strange to look on. The large buds, suddenly pushing out late in the spring from dry sticks which had seemed to be dead, developed themselves as by magic into graceful green and tender boughs, an inch in diameter; and sometimes, as I sat at my window, so heedlessly did they grow and tax their weak joints, I heard a fresh and tender bough suddenly fall like a fan to the ground, when there was not a breath of air stirring, broken off by its own weight. In August, the large masses of berries, which, when in flower, had attracted many wild bees, gradually assumed their bright velvety crimson hue, and by their weight again bent down and broke the tender limbs.

As I sit at my window this summer afternoon, hawks are circling about my clearing; the tantivy of wild pigeons, flying by twos and threes athwart my view, or perching restless on the white pine boughs behind my house, gives a voice to the air; a fish hawk dimples the glassy surface of the pond and brings up a fish; a mink steals out of the marsh before my door and seizes a frog by the shore; the sedge is bending under the weight of the reed-birds flitting hither and thither; and for the last half-hour I have heard the rattle of railroad cars, now dying away and then reviving like the beat of a partridge, conveying travellers from Boston to the country.

For I did not live so out of the world as that boy, who, as I hear, was put out to a farmer in the east part of the town, but ere long ran away and came home again, quite down at the heel and homesick. He had never seen such a dull and out-of-the-way place; the folks were all gone off; why, you couldn't even hear the whistle! I doubt if there is such a place in Massachusetts now:—

> "In truth, our village has become a butt
>   For one of those fleet railroad shafts, and o'er
>   Our peaceful plain its soothing sound is—Concord."

The Fitchburg Railroad touches the pond about a hundred rods south of where I dwell. I usually go to the village along its causeway, and am, as it were, related to society by this link. The men on the freight trains, who go over the whole length of the road, bow to me as to an old acquaintance, they pass me so often, and apparently they take me for an employee; and so I am. I too would fain be a track-repairer somewhere in the orbit of the earth.

The whistle of the locomotive penetrates my woods summer and winter, sounding like the scream of a hawk sailing over some farmer's yard, informing me that many restless city merchants are arriving within the circle of the town, or adventurous country traders from the other side. As they come under one horizon, they shout their warning to get off the track to the other, heard sometimes through the circles of two towns. Here come your groceries, country: your rations, countrymen! Nor is there any man so independent on his farm that he can say them nay. And here's your pay for them! screams the countryman's whistle; timber like long battering-rams going twenty miles an hour against the city's walls, and chairs enough to seat all the weary and heavy-laden that dwell within them. With such huge and lumbering civility the country hands a chair to the city. All the Indian huckleberry hills are stripped, all the cranberry meadows are raked into the city. Up comes the cotton, down goes the woven cloth; up comes the silk, down goes the woolen; up come the books, but down goes the wit that writes them.

When I meet the engine with its train of cars moving off with planetary motion,—or, rather, like a comet, for the beholder knows not if with that velocity and with that direction it will ever revisit this system, since its orbit does not look like a returning curve,—with its steam cloud like a banner streaming behind in golden and silver wreaths, like many a downy cloud which I have seen, high in the heavens, unfolding its masses to the light,—as if this travelling demigod, this cloud-compeller, would ere long take the sunset sky for the livery of his train: when I hear the iron horse make the hills echo with his snore like thunder, shaking the earth with his feet, and breathing fire and smoke from his nostrils (what kind of winged horse or fiery dragon they will put into the new Mythology I don't know), it seems as if the earth had got a race now worthy to inhabit it. If all were as it seems, and men made the elements their servants for noble ends! If the cloud that hangs over the engine were the perspiration of heroic deeds, or as beneficent as that which floats over the farmer's fields, then the elements and Nature herself would cheerfully accompany men on their errands and be their escort.

I watch the passage of the morning cars with the same feeling that I do the rising of the sun, which is hardly more regular. Their train of clouds stretching far behind and rising higher and higher, going to heaven while the cars are going to Boston, conceals the sun for a minute and casts my distant field into the shade, a celestial train beside which the pretty train of cars which hugs the earth is but the barb of the spear. The stabler of the iron horse was up early this winter morning by the light of the stars amid the mountains, to fodder and harness his steed. Fire, too, was awakened thus early to put the vital heat in him and get him off. If the enterprise were as innocent as it is early! If the snow lies deep, they strap on his snowshoes, and, with the giant plow, plow a furrow from the mountains to the seaboard, in which the cars, like a following drill-barrow, sprinkle all the restless men and floating merchandise in the country for seed. All day the fire-steed flies over the country, stopping only that his master may rest, and I am awakened by his tramp and defiant snort at midnight, when in some remote glen in the woods he fronts the elements incased in ice and snow; and he will reach his stall only with the morning star, to start once more on his travels without rest or slumber. Or perchance, at evening, I hear him in his stable blowing off the superfluous energy of the day, that he may calm his nerves and cool his liver and brain for a few hours of iron slumber. If the enterprise were as heroic and commanding as it is protracted and unwearied!

Far through unfrequented woods on the confines of towns, where once only the hunter penetrated by day, in the darkest night dart these bright saloons without the knowledge of their inhabitants; this moment stopping at some brilliant station-house in town or city, where a social crowd is gathered, the next in the Dismal Swamp, scaring the owl and fox. The startings and arrivals of the cars are now the epochs in the village day. They go and come with such regularity and precision, and their whistle can be heard so far, that the farmers set their clocks by them, and thus one well-conducted institution regulates a whole country. Have not men improved somewhat in punctuality since the railroad was invented? Do they not talk and think faster in the depot than they did in the stage-office? There is something electrifying in the atmosphere of the former place. I have been astonished at the miracles it has wrought; that some of my neighbors, who, I should have prophesied, once for all, would never get to Boston by so prompt a conveyance, are on hand when the bell rings. To do things "railroad fashion" is now the byword; and it is worth the while to be warned so often and so sincerely by any power to get off its track. There is no stopping to read the riot act, no firing over the heads of the mob, in this case. We have constructed a fate, an *Atropos,* that never turns aside. (Let that be the name of your engine.) Men are advertised that at a certain hour and minute these bolts will be shot toward particular points of the compass; yet it interferes with no man's business, and the children go to school on the other track. We live the steadier for it. We are all educated thus to be sons of Tell. The air is full of invisible bolts. Every path but your own is the path of fate. Keep on your own track, then.

What recommends commerce to me is its enterprise and bravery. It does not clasp its hands and pray to Jupiter. I see these men every day go about their business with more or less courage and content, doing more even than they suspect, and perchance better employed than they could have consciously devised. I am less affected by their heroism who stood up for half an hour in the front line at Buena Vista, than by the steady and cheerful valor of the men who inhabit the snow-plow for their winter quarters; who have not merely the three-o'clock-in-the-morning courage, which Bonaparte thought was the rarest, but whose courage does not go to rest so early, who go to sleep only when the storm sleeps or the sinews of their iron steed are frozen. On this morning of the Great Snow, perchance, which is still raging and chilling men's blood, I heard the muffled tone of their engine bell from out the fog bank of their chilled breath, which announces that the cars *are coming*, without long delay, notwithstanding the veto of a New England north-east snow storm, and I behold the plowmen covered with snow and rime, their heads peering above the mould-board which is turning down other than daisies and the nests of field mice, like bowlders of the Sierra Nevada, that occupy an outside place in the universe.

Commerce is unexpectedly confident and serene, alert, adventurous, and unwearied. It is very natural in its methods withal, far more so than many fantastic enterprises and sentimental experiments, and hence its singular success. I am refreshed and expanded when the freight train rattles past me, and I smell the stores which go dispensing their odors all the way from Long Wharf to Lake Champlain, reminding me of foreign parts, of coral reefs, and Indian oceans, and tropical climes, and the extent of the globe. I feel more like a citizen of the world at the sight of the palm-leaf which will cover so many flaxen New England heads the next summer, the Manilla hemp and cocoanut husks, the old junk, gunny bags, scrap iron, and rusty nails. This carload of torn sails is more legible and interesting now than if they should be wrought into paper and printed books. Who can write so graphically the history of the storms they have weathered as these rents have done? They are proof-sheets which need no correction. Here goes lumber from the Maine woods, which did not go out to sea in the last freshet, risen four dollars on the thousand because of what did go out or was split up; pine, spruce, cedar,—first, second, third, and fourth qualities, so lately all of one quality, to wave over the bear, and moose, and caribou. Next rolls Thomaston lime, a prime lot, which will get far among the hills before it gets slacked. These rags in bales, of all hues and qualities, the lowest condition to which cotton and linen descend, the final result of dress,—of patterns which are now no longer cried up, unless it be in Milwaukee, as those splendid articles, English, French, or American prints, ginghams, muslins, etc., gathered from all quarters both of fashion and poverty, going to become paper of one color or a few shades only, on which, forsooth, will be written tales of real life, high and low, and founded on fact! This closed car smells of salt fish, the strong New England and commercial scent, reminding me of the Grand Banks and the fisheries. Who has not seen a salt fish, thoroughly cured for this world, so that nothing can spoil it, and putting the perseverance of the saints to the blush? with which you may sweep or pave the streets, and split your kindlings, and the teamster shelter himself and his lading against sun, wind, and rain behind it,—and the trader, as a Concord trader once did, hang it up by his door for a sign when he commences business, until at last his oldest customer cannot tell surely whether it be animal, vegetable, or mineral, and yet it shall be as pure as a snowflake, and if it be put into a pot and boiled, will come out an excellent dunfish for a Saturday's dinner. Next Spanish hides, with the tails still preserving their twist and the angle of elevation they had when the oxen that wore them were careering over the pampas of the Spanish Main,—a type of all obstinacy, and evincing how almost hopeless and incurable are all constitutional vices. I confess, that practically speaking, when I have learned a man's real disposition, I have no hopes of changing it for the better or worse in this state of existence. As the Orientals say, "A cur's tail may be warmed, and pressed, and bound round with ligatures, and after a twelve years' labor bestowed upon it, still it

will retain its natural form." The only effectual cure for
such inveteracies as these tails exhibit is to make glue
of them, which I believe is what is usually done with
them, and then they will stay put and stick. Here is a
hogshead of molasses or of brandy directed to John
Smith, Cuttingsville, Vermont, some trader among the
Green Mountains, who imports for the farmers near his
clearing, and now perchance stands over his bulkhead
and thinks of the last arrivals on the coast, how they
may affect the price for him, telling his customers this
moment, as he has told them twenty times before this
morning, that he expects some by the next train of prime
quality. It is advertised in the Cuttingsville Times.

While these things go up other things come down.
Warned by the whizzing sound, I look up from my book
and see some tall pine, hewn on far northern hills, which
has winged its way over the Green Mountains and the
Connecticut, shot like an arrow through the township
within ten minutes, and scarce another eye beholds it;
going

> "to be the mast
> Of some great ammiral."

And hark! here comes the cattle-train bearing the cattle
of a thousand hills, sheepcots, stables, and cow-yards in
the air, drovers with their sticks, and shepherd boys in
the midst of their flocks, all but the mountain pastures,
whirled along like leaves blown from the mountains by
the September gales. The air is filled with the bleating
of calves and sheep, and the hustling of oxen, as if a
pastoral valley were going by. When the old bell-wether
at the head rattles his bell, the mountains do indeed skip
like rams and the little hills like lambs. A carload of
drovers, too, in the midst, on a level with their droves
now, their vocation gone, but still clinging to their useless sticks as their badge of office. But their dogs, where
are they? It is a stampede to them; they are quite thrown
out; they have lost the scent. Methinks I hear them barking behind the Peterboro' Hills, or panting up the western slope of the Green Mountains. They will not be in
at the death. Their vocation, too, is gone. Their fidelity

and sagacity are below par now. They will slink back to
their kennels in disgrace, or perchance run wild and
strike a league with the wolf and the fox. So is your
pastoral life whirled past and away. But the bell rings,
and I must get off the track and let the cars go by;—

> What's the railroad to me?
> I never go to see
> Where it ends.
> It fills a few hollows,
> And makes banks for the swallows,
> It sets the sand a-blowing,
> And the blackberries a-growing,

but I cross it like a cart-path in the woods. I will not
have my eyes put out and my ears spoiled by its smoke
and steam and hissing.

Now that the cars are gone by and all the restless
world with them, and the fishes in the pond no longer
feel their rumbling, I am more alone than ever. For the
rest of the long afternoon, perhaps, my meditations are
interrupted only by the faint rattle of a carriage or team
along the distant highway.

Sometimes, on Sundays, I heard the bells, the Lincoln,
Acton, Bedford, or Concord bell, when the wind was
favorable, a faint, sweet, and, as it were, natural melody,
worth importing into the wilderness. At a sufficient distance over the woods this sound acquires a certain vibra-
tory hum, as if the pine needles in the horizon were the
strings of a harp which it swept. All sound heard at the
greatest possible distance produces one and the same
effect, a vibration of the universal lyre, just as the intervening atmosphere makes a distant ridge of earth interesting to our eyes by the azure tint it imparts to it.
There came to me in this case a melody which the air
had strained, and which had conversed with every leaf
and needle of the wood, that portion of the sound which
the elements had taken up and modulated and echoed
from vale to vale. The echo is, to some extent, an original sound, and therein is the magic and charm of it. It
is not merely a repetition of what was worth repeating

in the bell, but partly the voice of the wood; the same
trivial words and notes sung by a wood-nymph.

At evening, the distant lowing of some cow in the
horizon beyond the woods sounded sweet and melodious
and at first I would mistake it for the voices of certain
minstrels by whom I was sometimes serenaded, who
might be straying over hill and dale; but soon I was not
unpleasantly disappointed when it was prolonged into
the cheap and natural music of the cow. I do not mean
to be satirical, but to express my appreciation of those
youths' singing, when I state that I perceived clearly that
it was akin to the music of the cow, and they were at
length one articulation of Nature.

Regularly at half-past seven, in one part of the summer, after the evening train had gone by, the whip-poor-
wills chanted their vespers for half an hour, sitting on a
stump by my door, or upon the ridge-pole of the house.
They would begin to sing almost with as much precision
as a clock, within five minutes of a particular time, referred to the setting of the sun, every evening. I had a
rare opportunity to become acquainted with their habits.
Sometimes I heard four or five at once in different parts
of the wood, by accident one a bar behind another, and
so near me that I distinguished not only the cluck after
each note, but often that singular buzzing sound like a
fly in a spider's web, only proportionally louder. Sometimes one would circle round and round me in the woods
a few feet distant as if tethered by a string, when probably I was near its eggs. They sang at intervals throughout
the night, and were again as musical as ever just before
and about dawn.

When other birds are still, the screech owls take up
the strain, like mourning women their ancient u-lu-lu.
Their dismal scream is truly Ben Jonsonian. Wise midnight hags! It is no honest and blunt tu-whit tu-who of
the poets, but, without jesting, a most solemn graveyard
ditty, the mutual consolations of suicide lovers remembering the pangs and the delights of supernal love in the
infernal groves. Yet I love to hear their wailing, their
doleful responses, trilled along the woodside; reminding
me sometimes of music and singing birds; as if it were
the dark and tearful side of music, the regrets and sighs

that would fain be sung. They are the spirits, the low spirits and melancholy forebodings, of fallen souls that once in human shape night-walked the earth and did the deeds of darkness, now expiating their sins with their wailing hymns or threnodies in the scenery of their transgressions. They give me a new sense of the variety and capacity of that nature which is our common dwelling. *Oh-o-o-o-o that I never had been bor-r-r-r-n!* sighs one on this side of the pond, and circles with the restlessness of despair to some new perch on the gray oaks. Then— *that I never had been bor-r-r-r-n!* echoes another on the farther side with tremulous sincerity, and—*bor-r-r-r-n!* comes faintly from far in the Lincoln woods.

I was also serenaded by a hooting owl. Near at hand you could fancy it the most melancholy sound in Nature, as if she meant by this to stereotype and make permanent in her choir the dying moans of a human being,— some poor weak relic of mortality who has left hope behind, and howls like an animal, yet with human sobs, on entering the dark valley, made more awful by a certain gurgling melodiousness,—I find myself beginning with the letters *gl* when I try to imitate it,—expressive of a mind which has reached the gelatinous, mildewy stage in the mortification of all healthy and courageous thought. It reminded me of ghouls and idiots and insane howlings. But now one answers from far woods in a strain made really melodious by distance,—*Hoo hoo hoo, hoorer hoo;* and indeed for the most part it suggested only pleasing associations, whether heard by day or night, summer or winter.

I rejoice that there are owls. Let them do the idiotic and maniacal hooting for men. It is a sound admirably suited to swamps and twilight woods which no day illustrates, suggesting a vast and undeveloped nature which men have not recognized. They represent the stark twilight and unsatisfied thoughts which all have. All day the sun has shone on the surface of some savage swamp, where the single spruce stands hung with usnea lichens, and small hawks circulate above, and the chickadee lisps amid the evergreens, and the partridge and rabbit skulk beneath; but now a more dismal and fitting day dawns,

and a different race of creatures awakes to express the
meaning of Nature there.

Late in the evening I heard the distant rumbling of
wagons over bridges,—a sound heard farther than almost
any other at night,—the baying of dogs, and sometimes
again the lowing of some disconsolate cow in a distant
barn-yard. In the meanwhile all the shore rang with the
trump of bullfrogs, the sturdy spirits of ancient wine-
bibbers and wassailers, still unrepentant, trying to sing a
catch in their Stygian lake,—if the Walden nymphs will
pardon the comparison, for though there are almost no
weeds, there are frogs there,—who would fain keep up
the hilarious rules of their old festal tables, though their
voices have waxed hoarse and solemnly grave, mocking
at mirth, and the wine has lost its flavor, and become
only liquor to distend their paunches, and sweet intoxi-
cation never comes to drown the memory of the past,
but mere saturation and waterloggedness and distention.
The most aldermanic, with his chin upon a heart-leaf,
which serves for a napkin to his drooling chaps, under this
northern shore quaffs a deep draught of the once scorned
water, and passes round the cup with the ejaculation *tr-r-
r-oonk, tr-r-r-oonk, tr-r-r-oonk!* and straightway comes
over the water from some distant cove the same pass-
word repeated, where the next in seniority and girth has
gulped down to his mark; and when this observance has
made the circuit of the shores, then ejaculates the master
of ceremonies, with satisfaction, *tr-r-r-oonk!* and each in
his turn repeats the same down to the least distended,
leakiest, and flabbiest paunched, that there be no mistake; and then the bowl goes round again and again,
until the sun disperses the morning mist, and only the
patriarch is not under the pond, but vainly bellowing
troonk from time to time, and pausing for a reply.

I am not sure that I ever heard the sound of cock-
crowing from my clearing, and I thought that it might
be worth the while to keep a cockerel for his music
merely, as a singing bird. The note of this once wild
Indian pheasant is certainly the most remarkable of any
bird's, and if they could be naturalized without being
domesticated, it would soon become the most famous
sound in our woods, surpassing the clangor of the goose

and the hooting of the owl; and then imagine the cackling of the hens to fill the pauses when their lords' clari-
ons rested! No wonder that man added this bird to his
tame stock,—to say nothing of the eggs and drumsticks.
To walk in a winter morning in a wood where these
birds abounded, their native woods, and hear the wild
cockerels crow on the trees, clear and shrill for miles
over the resounding earth, drowning the feebler notes
of other birds,—think of it! It would put nations on the
alert. Who would not be early to rise, and rise earlier
and earlier every successive day of his life, till he became
unspeakably healthy, wealthy, and wise? This foreign
bird's note is celebrated by the poets of all countries
along with the notes of their native songsters. All climates agree with brave Chanticleer. He is more indigenous even than the natives. His health is ever good, his
lungs are sound, his spirits never flag. Even the sailor
on the Atlantic and Pacific is awakened by his voice; but
its shrill sound never roused me from my slumbers. I
kept neither dog, cat, cow, pig, nor hens, so that you
would have said there was a deficiency of domestic
sounds; neither the churn, nor the spinning-wheel, nor
even the singing of the kettle, nor the hissing of the urn,
nor children crying, to comfort one. An old-fashioned
man would have lost his senses or died of ennui before
this. Not even rats in the wall, for they were starved out,
or rather were never baited in,—only squirrels on the
roof and under the floor, a whip-poor-will on the ridge-
pole, a blue jay screaming beneath the window, a hare
or woodchuck under the house, a screech owl or a cat
owl behind it, a flock of wild geese or a laughing loon
on the pond, and a fox to bark in the night. Not even a
lark or an oriole, those mild plantation birds, ever visited
my clearing. No cockerels to crow nor hens to cackle in
the yard. No yard! but unfenced nature reaching up to
your very sills. A young forest growing up under your
windows, and wild sumachs and blackberry vines breaking through into your cellar; sturdy pitch pines rubbing
and creaking against the shingles for want of room, their
roots reaching quite under the house. Instead of a scuttle
or a blind blown off in the gale,—a pine tree snapped

off or torn up by the roots behind your house for fuel. Instead of no path to the front-yard gate in the Great Snow,—no gate—no front-yard,—and no path to the civilized world.

5. Solitude

THIS is a delicious evening, when the whole body is one sense, and imbibes delight through every pore. I go and come with a strange liberty in Nature, a part of herself. As I walk along the stony shore of the pond in my shirt-sleeves, though it is cool as well as cloudy and windy, and I see nothing special to attract me, all the elements are unusually congenial to me. The bullfrogs trump to usher in the night, and the note of the whip-poor-will is borne on the rippling wind from over the water. Sympathy with the fluttering alder and poplar leaves almost takes away my breath; yet, like the lake, my serenity is rippled but not ruffled. These small waves raised by the evening wind are as remote from storm as the smooth reflecting surface. Though it is now dark, the wind still blows and roars in the wood, the waves still dash, and some creatures lull the rest with their notes. The repose is never complete. The wildest animals do not repose, but seek their prey now; the fox, and skunk, and rabbit, now roam the fields and woods without fear. They are Nature's watchmen,—links which connect the days of animated life.

When I return to my house I find that visitors have been there and left their cards, either a bunch of flowers, or a wreath of evergreen, or a name in pencil on a yellow walnut leaf or a chip. They who come rarely to the woods take some little piece of the forest into their hands to play with by the way, which they leave, either intentionally or accidentally. One has peeled a willow wand, woven it into a ring, and dropped it on my table. I could always tell if visitors had called in my absence, either by the bended twigs or grass, or the print of their shoes, and generally of what sex or age or quality they were by some slight trace left, as a flower dropped, or a bunch of grass plucked and thrown away, even as far off as the railroad, half a mile distant, or by the lingering odor of a cigar or pipe. Nay, I was frequently notified of the passage of a traveller along the highway sixty rods off by the scent of his pipe.

There is commonly sufficient space about us. Our horizon is never quite at our elbows. The thick wood is not just at our door, nor the pond, but somewhat is always clearing, familiar and worn by us, appropriated and fenced in some way, and reclaimed from Nature. For what reason have I this vast range and circuit, some square miles of unfrequented forest, for my privacy, abandoned to me by men? My nearest neighbor is a mile distant, and no house is visible from any place but the hill-tops within half a mile of my own. I have my horizon bounded by woods all to myself; a distant view of the railroad where it touches the pond on the one hand, and of the fence which skirts the woodland road on the other. But for the most part it is as solitary where I live as on the prairies. It is as much Asia or Africa as New England. I have, as it were, my own sun and moon and stars, and a little world all to myself. At night there was never a traveller passed my house, or knocked at my door, more than if I were the first or last man; unless it were in the spring, when at long intervals some came from the village to fish for pouts,—they plainly fished much more in the Walden Pond of their own natures, and baited their hooks with darkness,—but they soon retreated, usually with light baskets, and left "the world to darkness and to me," and the black kernel of the night was never profaned by any human neighborhood. I believe that men are generally still a little afraid of the dark, though the witches are all hung, and Christianity and candles have been introduced.

Yet I experienced sometimes that the most sweet and tender, the most innocent and encouraging society may be found in any natural object, even for the poor misanthrope and most melancholy man. There can be no very black melancholy to him who lives in the midst of nature and has his senses still. There was never yet such a storm but it was Æolian music to a healthy and innocent ear. Nothing can rightly compel a simple and brave man to a vulgar sadness. While I enjoy the friendship of the seasons I trust that nothing can make life a burden to me. The gentle rain which waters my beans and keeps me in the house to-day is not drear and melancholy, but good for me too. Though it prevents my hoeing them, it is of far more worth than my hoeing. If it should continue so long as to cause the seeds to rot in the ground and destroy the potatoes in the low lands, it would still be good for the grass on the uplands, and, being good for the grass, it would be good for me. Sometimes, when I compare myself with other men, it seems as if I were more favored by the gods than they, beyond any deserts that I am conscious of; as if I had a warrant and surety at their hands which my fellows have not, and were especially guided and guarded. I do not flatter myself, but if it be possible they flatter me. I have never felt lonesome, or in the least oppressed by a sense of solitude, but once, and that was a few weeks after I came to the woods, when, for an hour, I doubted if the near neighborhood of man was not essential to a serene and healthy life. To be alone was something unpleasant. But I was at the same time conscious of a slight insanity in my mood, and seemed to foresee my recovery. In the midst of a gentle rain while these thoughts prevailed, I was suddenly sensible of such sweet and beneficent society in Nature, in the very pattering of the drops, and in every sound and sight around my house, an infinite and unaccountable friendliness all at once like an atmosphere sustaining me, as made the fancied advantages of human neighborhood insignificant, and I have never thought of them since. Every little pine needle expanded and swelled with sympathy and befriended me. I was so distinctly made aware of the presence of something kindred to me, even in scenes which we are accustomed to call wild and dreary, and also that the nearest of blood to me and humanest was not a person nor a villager, that I thought no place could ever be strange to me again.—

"Mourning untimely consumes the sad;
    Few are their days in the land of the living,
    Beautiful daughter of Toscar."

Some of my pleasantest hours were during the long
rain-storms in the spring or fall, which confined me to
the house for the afternoon as well as the forenoon,
soothed by their ceaseless roar and pelting; when an
early twilight ushered in a long evening in which many
thoughts had time to take root and unfold themselves.
In those driving northeast rains which tried the village
houses so, when the maids stood ready with mop and
pail in front entries to keep the deluge out, I sat behind
my door in my little house, which was all entry, and
thoroughly enjoyed its protection. In one heavy thunder-
shower the lightning struck a large pitch pine across the
pond, making a very conspicuous and perfectly regular
spiral groove from top to bottom, an inch or more deep,
and four or five inches wide, as you would groove a
walking-stick. I passed it again the other day, and was
struck with awe on looking up and beholding that mark,
now more distinct than ever, where a terrific and re-
sistless bolt came down out of the harmless sky eight
years ago. Men frequently say to me, "I should think
you would feel lonesome down there, and want to be
nearer to folks, rainy and snowy days and nights especially." I am tempted to reply to such,—This whole earth
which we inhabit is but a point in space. How far apart,
think you, dwell the two most distant inhabitants of yonder star, the breadth of whose disk cannot be appreciated by our instruments? Why should I feel lonely? Is
not our planet in the Milky Way? This which you put
seems to me not to be the most important question.
What sort of space is that which separates a man from
his fellows and makes him solitary? I have found that
no exertion of the legs can bring two minds much nearer
to one another. What do we want most to dwell near
to? Not to many men surely, the depot, the post-office,
the bar-room, the meeting-house, the school-house, the
grocery, Beacon Hill, or the Five Points, where men
most congregate, but to the perennial source of our life,
whence in all our experience we have found that to issue,

as the willow stands near the water and sends out its roots in that direction. This will vary with different natures, but this is the place where a wise man will dig his cellar. . . . I one evening overtook one of my townsmen, who has accumulated what is called "a handsome property,"—though I never got a *fair* view of it,—on the Walden road, driving a pair of cattle to market, who inquired of me how I could bring my mind to give up so many of the comforts of life. I answered that I was very sure I liked it passably well; I was not joking. And so I went home to my bed, and left him to pick his way through the darkness and the mud to Brighton,— or Bright-town,—which place he would reach some time in the morning.

Any prospect of awakening or coming to life to a dead man makes indifferent all times and places. The place where that may occur is always the same, and indescribably pleasant to all our senses. For the most part we allow only outlying and transient circumstances to make our occasions. They are, in fact, the cause of our distraction. Nearest to all things is that power which fashions their being. *Next* to us the grandest laws are continually being executed. *Next* to us is not the workman whom we have hired, with whom we love so well to talk, but the workman whose work we are.

"How vast and profound is the influence of the subtile powers of Heaven and of Earth!"

"We seek to perceive them, and we do not see them; we seek to hear them, and we do not hear them; identified with the substance of things, they cannot be separated from them."

"They cause that in all the universe men purify and sanctify their hearts, and clothe themselves in their holiday garments to offer sacrifices and oblations to their ancestors. It is an ocean of subtile intelligences. They are everywhere, above us, on our left, on our right; they environ us on all sides."

We are the subjects of an experiment which is not a little interesting to me. Can we not do without the society of our gossips a little while under these circumstances,—have our own thoughts to cheer us? Confucius says truly, "Virtue does not remain as an abandoned orphan; it must of necessity have neighbors."

With thinking we may be beside ourselves in a sane sense. By a conscious effort of the mind we can stand aloof from actions and their consequences; and all things, good and bad, go by us like a torrent. We are not wholly involved in Nature. I may be either the driftwood in the stream, or Indra in the sky looking down on it. I *may* be affected by a theatrical exhibition; on the other hand, I *may not* be affected by an actual event which appears to concern me more more. I only know myself as a human entity; the scene, so to speak, of thoughts and affections; and am sensible of a certain doubleness by which I can stand as remote from myself as from another. However intense my experience, I am conscious of the presence and criticism of a part of me, which, as it were, is not a part of me, but spectator, sharing no experience, but taking note of it; and that is no more I than it is you. When the play, it may be the tragedy, of life is over, the spectator goes his way. It was a kind of fiction, a work of the imagination only, so far as he was concerned. This doubleness may easily make us poor neighbors and friends sometimes.

I find it wholesome to be alone the greater part of the time. To be in company, even with the best, is soon wearisome and dissipating. I love to be alone. I never found the companion that was so companionable as solitude. We are for the most part more lonely when we go abroad among men than when we stay in our chambers. A man thinking or working is always alone, let him be where he will. Solitude is not measured by the miles of space that intervene between a man and his fellows. The really diligent student in one of the crowded hives of Cambridge College is as solitary as a dervis in the desert. The farmer can work alone in the field or the woods all day, hoeing or chopping, and not feel lonesome, because he is employed; but when he comes home at night he cannot sit down in a room alone, at the mercy of his thoughts, but must be where he can "see the folks," and recreate, and, as he thinks, remunerate himself for his day's solitude; and hence he wonders how the student can sit alone in the house all night and most of the day without ennui and "the blues," but he does not realize that the student, though in the house, is still at work in *his* field, and chopping in *his* woods, as the farmer in his, and in turn seeks the same recreation and society that the latter does, though it may be a more condensed form of it.

Society is commonly too cheap. We meet at very short intervals, not having had time to acquire any new value for each other. We meet at meals three times a day, and give each other a new taste of that old musty cheese that we are. We have had to agree on a certain set of rules, called etiquette and politeness, to make this frequent meeting tolerable and that we need not come to open war. We meet at the post-office, and at the sociable, and about the fireside every night; we live thick and are in each other's way, and stumble over one another, and I think that we thus lose some respect for one another. Certainly less frequency would suffice for all important and hearty communications. Consider the girls in a factory,—never alone, hardly in their dreams. It would be better if there were but one inhabitant to a square mile, as where I live. The value of a man is not in his skin, that we should touch him.

I have heard of a man lost in the woods and dying of famine and exhaustion at the foot of a tree, whose loneliness was relieved by the grotesque visions with which, owing to bodily weakness, his diseased imagination surrounded him, and which he believed to be real. So also, owing to bodily and mental health and strength, we may be continually cheered by a like but more normal and natural society, and come to know that we are never alone.

I have a great deal of company in my house; especially in the morning, when nobody calls. Let me suggest a few comparisons, that some one may convey an idea of my situation. I am no more lonely than the loon in the pond that laughs so loud, or than Walden Pond itself. What company has that lonely lake, I pray? And yet it has not the blue devils, but the blue angels in it, in the azure tint of its waters. The sun is alone, except in thick weather, when there sometimes appear to be two, but one is a mock sun. God is alone,—but the devil, he is far from being alone; he sees a great deal of company;

he is legion. I am no more lonely than a single mullein
or dandelion in a pasture, or a bean leaf, or sorrel, or a
horse-fly, or a humble-bee. I am no more lonely than
the Mill Brook, or a weathercock, or the north star, or
the south wind, or an April shower, or a January thaw,
or the first spider in a new house.

I have occasional visits in the long winter evenings,
when the snow falls fast and the wind howls in the wood,
from an old settler and original proprietor, who is reported to have dug Walden Pond, and stoned it, and
fringed it with pine woods; who tells me stories of old
time and of new eternity; and between us we manage to
pass a cheerful evening with social mirth and pleasant
views of things, even without apples or cider,—a most
wise and humorous friend, whom I love much, who
keeps himself more secret than ever did Goffe or Whal-
ley; and though he is thought to be dead, none can show
where he is buried. An elderly dame, too, dwells in my
neighborhood, invisible to most persons, in whose odor-
ous herb garden I love to stroll sometimes, gathering
simples and listening to her fables; for she has a genius
of unequalled fertility, and her memory runs back farther than mythology, and she can tell me the original of
every fable, and on what fact every one is founded, for
the incidents occurred when she was young. A ruddy
and lusty old dame, who delights in all weathers and
seasons, and is likely to outlive all her children yet.

The indescribable innocence and beneficence of Nature,—of sun and wind and rain, of summer and winter,—such health, such cheer, they afford forever! and
such sympathy have they ever with our race, that all
Nature would be affected, and the sun's brightness fade,
and the winds would sigh humanely, and the clouds rain
tears, and the woods shed their leaves and put on
mourning in midsummer, if any man should ever for a
just cause grieve. Shall I not have intelligence with the
earth? Am I not partly leaves and vegetable mould
myself?

What is the pill which will keep us well, serene, contented? Not my or thy great-grandfather's, but our great-
grandmother Nature's universal, vegetable, botanic medi-
cines, by which she has kept herself young always, outlived

so many old Parrs in her day, and fed her health with their decaying fatness. For my panacea, instead of one of those quack vials of a mixture dipped from Acheron and the Dead Sea, which come out of those long shallow black-schooner looking wagons which we sometimes see made to carry bottles, let me have a draught of undiluted morning air. Morning air! If men will not drink of this at the fountain-head of the day, why, then, we must even bottle up some and sell it in the shops, for the benefit of those who have lost their subscription ticket to morning time in this world. But remember, it will not keep quite till noonday even in the coolest cellar, but drive out the stopples long ere that and follow westward the steps of Aurora. I am no worshipper of Hygeia, who was the daughter of that old herb-doctor Æsculapius, and who is represented on monuments holding a serpent in one hand, and in the other a cup out of which the serpent sometimes drinks; but rather of Hebe, cupbearer to Jupiter, who was the daughter of Juno and wild lettuce, and who had the power of restoring gods and men to the vigor of youth. She was probably the only thoroughly sound-conditioned, healthy, and robust young lady that ever walked the globe, and wherever she came it was spring.

6. Visitors

I THINK that I love society as much as most, and am ready enough to fasten myself like a bloodsucker for the time to any full-blooded man that comes in my way. I am naturally no hermit, but might possibly sit out the sturdiest frequenter of the bar-room, if my business called me thither.

I had three chairs in my house; one for solitude, two for friendship, three for society. When visitors came in larger and unexpected numbers there was but the third chair for them all, but they generally economized the room by standing up. It is surprising how many great men and women a small house will contain. I have had twenty-five or thirty souls, with their bodies, at once under my roof, and yet we often parted without being aware that we had come very near to one another. Many of our houses, both public and private, with their almost innumerable apartments, their huge halls and their cellars for the storage of wines and other munitions of peace, appear to me extravagantly large for their inhabitants. They are so vast and magnificent that the latter seem to be only vermin which infest them. I am surprised when the herald blows his summons before some Tremont or Astor or Middlesex House, to see come creeping out over the piazza for all inhabitants a ridiculous mouse, which soon again slinks into some hole in the pavement.

One inconvenience I sometimes experienced in so small a house, the difficulty of getting to a sufficient distance from my guest when we began to utter the big thoughts in big words. You want room for your thoughts to get into sailing trim and run a course or two before they make their port. The bullet of your thought must have overcome its lateral and ricochet motion and fallen into its last and steady course before it reaches the ear of the hearer, else it may plow out again through the side of his head. Also, our sentences wanted room to unfold and form their columns in the interval. Individuals, like nations, must have suitable broad and natural boundaries, even a considerable neutral ground, between them. I have found it a singular luxury to talk across the pond to a companion on the opposite side. In my house we were so near that we could not begin to hear,—we could not speak low enough to be heard; as when you throw two stones into calm water so near that they break each other's undulations. If we are merely loquacious and loud talkers, then we can afford to stand very near together, cheek by jowl, and feel each other's breath; but if we speak reservedly and thoughtfully, we want to be farther apart, that all animal heat and moisture may have a chance to evaporate. If we would enjoy the most intimate society with that in each of us which is without, or above, being spoken to, we must not only be silent, but commonly so far apart bodily that we cannot possibly hear each other's voice in any case. Referred to this standard, speech is for the convenience of those who are hard of hearing; but there are many fine things which we cannot say if we have to shout. As the conversation began to assume a loftier and grander tone, we gradually shoved our chairs farther apart till they touched the wall in opposite corners, and then commonly there was not room enough.

My "best" room, however, my withdrawing room, always ready for company, on whose carpet the sun rarely fell, was the pine wood behind my house. Thither in summer days, when distinguished guests came, I took them, and a priceless domestic swept the floor and dusted the furniture and kept the things in order.

If one guest came he sometimes partook of my frugal meal, and it was no interruption to conversation to be stirring a hasty-pudding, or watching the rising and maturing of a loaf of bread in the ashes, in the meanwhile. But if twenty came and sat in my house there was nothing said about dinner, though there might be bread enough for two, more than if eating were a forsaken habit; but we naturally practised abstinence; and this was never felt to be an offence against hospitality, but the most proper and considerate course. The waste and decay of physical life, which so often needs repair, seemed miraculously retarded in such a case, and the vital vigor stood its ground. I could entertain thus a thousand as well as twenty; and if any ever went away disappointed or hungry from my house when they found me at home, they may depend upon it that I sympathized with them at least. So easy is it, though many housekeepers doubt it, to establish new and better customs in the place of the old. You need not rest your reputation on the dinners you give. For my own part, I was never so effectually deterred from frequenting a man's house, by any kind of Cerberus whatever, as by the parade one made about dining me, which I took to be a very polite and roundabout hint never to trouble him so again. I think I shall never revisit those scenes. I should be proud to have for the motto of my cabin those lines of Spenser which one of my visitors inscribed on a yellow walnut leaf for a card:—

> "Arrivèd there, the little house they fill,
>   Ne looke for entertainment where none was;
>   Rest is their feast, and all things at their will:
>   The noblest mind the best contentment has."

When Winslow, afterward governor of the Plymouth Colony, went with a companion on a visit of ceremony to Massasoit on foot through the woods, and arrived tired and hungry at his lodge, they were well received by the king, but nothing was said about eating that day. When the night arrived, to quote their own words,—"He laid us on the bed with himself and his wife, they at the one end and we at the other, it being only planks laid a foot from the ground and a thin mat upon them. Two more of his chief men, for want of room, pressed by and upon us; so that we were worse weary of our lodging than of our journey." At one o'clock the next day Massasoit "brought two fishes that he had shot," about thrice as big as a bream. "These being boiled, there were at least forty looked for a share in them; the most eat of them. This meal only we had in two nights and a day; and had not one of us bought a partridge, we had taken our journey fasting." Fearing that they would be lightheaded for want of food and also sleep, owing to "the savages' barbarous singing, (for they use to sing themselves asleep,)" and that they might get home while they had strength to travel, they departed. As for lodging, it is true they were but poorly entertained, though what they found an inconvenience was no doubt intended for an honor; but as far as eating was concerned, I do not see how the Indians could have done better. They had nothing to eat themselves, and they were wiser than to think that apologies could supply the place of food to their guests; so they drew their belts tighter and said nothing about it. Another time when Winslow visited them, it being a season of plenty with them, there was no deficiency in this respect.

As for men, they will hardly fail one anywhere. I had more visitors while I lived in the woods than at any other period of my life; I mean that I had some. I met several there under more favorable circumstances than I could anywhere else. But fewer came to see me on

trivial business. In this respect, my company was win-
nowed by my mere distance from town. I had withdrawn
so far within the great ocean of solitude, into which the
rivers of society empty, that for the most part, so far as
my needs were concerned, only the finest sediment was
deposited around me. Beside, there were wafted to me
evidences of unexplored and uncultivated continents on
the other side.

Who should come to my lodge this morning but a true
Homeric or Paphlagonian man,—he had so suitable and
poetic a name that I am sorry I cannot print it here,—
a Canadian, a wood chopper and post-maker, who can
hole fifty posts in a day, who made his last supper on a
woodchuck which his dog caught. He, too, has heard of
Homer, and, "if it were not for books," would "not
know what to do rainy days," though perhaps he has
not read one wholly through for many rainy seasons.
Some priest who could pronounce the Greek itself
taught him to read his verse in the Testament in his
native parish far away; and now I must translate to him,
while he holds the book, Achilles' reproof to Patroclus
for his sad countenance.—"Why are you in tears, Patroclus, like a young girl?"—

"Or have you alone heard some news from Phthia?
They say that Menœtius lives yet, son of Actor,
And Peleus lives, son of Æacus, among the Myrmidons,
Either of whom having died, we should greatly grieve."

He says, "That's good." He has a great bundle of white
oak bark under his arm for a sick man, gathered this
Sunday morning. "I suppose there's no harm in going
after such a thing to-day," says he. To him Homer was
a great writer, though what his writing was about he did
not know. A more simple and natural man it would be
hard to find. Vice and disease, which cast such a sombre
moral hue over the world, seemed to have hardly any
existence for him. He was about twenty-eight years old,
and had left Canada and his father's house a dozen years
before to work in the States, and earn money to buy a
farm with at last, perhaps in his native country. He was
cast in the coarsest mould; a stout but sluggish body, yet

gracefully carried, with a thick sunburnt neck, dark bushy hair, and dull sleepy blue eyes, which were occasionally lit up with expression. He wore a flat gray cloth cap, a dingy wool-colored greatcoat, and cowhide boots. He was a great consumer of meat, usually carrying his dinner to his work a couple of miles past my house,— for he chopped all summer,—in a tin pail; cold meats, often cold woodchucks, and coffee in a stone bottle which dangled by a string from his belt; and sometimes he offered me a drink. He came along early, crossing my bean-field, though without anxiety or haste to get to his work, such as Yankees exhibit. He wasn't a-going to hurt himself. He didn't care if he only earned his board. Frequently he would leave his dinner in the bushes, when his dog had caught a woodchuck by the way, and go back a mile and a half to dress it and leave it in the cellar of the house where he boarded, after deliberating first for half an hour whether he could not sink it in the pond safely till nightfall,—loving to dwell long upon these themes. He would say, as he went by in the morning, "How thick the pigeons are! If working every day were not my trade, I could get all the meat I should want by hunting,—pigeons, woodchucks, rabbits, partridges,—by gosh! I could get all I should want for a week in one day."

He was a skilful chopper, and indulged in some flourishes and ornaments in his art. He cut his trees level and close to the ground, that the sprouts which came up afterward might be more vigorous and a sled might slide over the stumps; and instead of leaving a whole tree to support his corded wood, he would pare it away to a slender stake or splinter which you could break off with your hand at last.

He interested me because he was so quiet and solitary and so happy withal; a well of good humor and contentment which overflowed at his eyes. His mirth was without alloy. Sometimes I saw him at his work in the woods, felling trees, and he would greet me with a laugh of inexpressible satisfaction, and a salutation in Canadian French, though he spoke English as well. When I approached him he would suspend his work, and with half-suppressed mirth lie along the trunk of a pine which he had felled, and, peeling off the inner bark, roll it up into a ball and chew it while he laughed and talked. Such an exuberance of animal spirits had he that he sometimes tumbled down and rolled on the ground with laughter at anything which made him think and tickled him. Looking round upon the trees he would exclaim,—"By George! I can enjoy myself well enough here chopping; I want no better sport." Sometimes, when at leisure, he amused himself all day in the woods with a pocket pistol, firing salutes to himself at regular intervals as he walked. In the winter he had a fire by which at noon he warmed his coffee in a kettle; and as he sat on a log to eat his dinner the chickadees would sometimes come round and alight on his arm and peck at the potato in his fingers; and he said that he "liked to have the little *fellers* about him."

In him the animal man chiefly was developed. In physical endurance and contentment he was cousin to the pine and the rock. I asked him once if he was not sometimes tired at night, after working all day; and he answered, with a sincere and serious look, "Gorrappit, I never was tired in my life." But the intellectual and what is called spiritual man in him were slumbering as in an infant. He had been instructed only in that innocent and ineffectual way in which the Catholic priests teach the aborigines, by which the pupil is never educated to the degree of consciousness, but only to the degree of trust and reverence, and a child is not made a man, but kept a child. When Nature made him, she gave him a strong body and contentment for his portion, and propped him on every side with reverence and reliance, that he might live out his threescore years and ten a child. He was so genuine and unsophisticated that no introduction would serve to introduce him, more than if you introduced a woodchuck to your neighbor. He had got to find him out as you did. He would not play any part. Men paid him wages for work, and so helped to feed and clothe him; but he never exchanged opinions with them. He was so simply and naturally humble—if he can be called humble who never aspires—that humility was no distinct quality in him, nor could he conceive of it. Wiser men were demigods to him. If you told him that such a one was coming, he did as if he thought that anything so grand would expect nothing of himself, but take all the responsibility on itself, and let him be forgotten still. He never heard the sound of praise. He particularly reverenced the writer and the preacher. Their performances were miracles. When I told him that I wrote considerably, he thought for a long time that it was merely the handwriting which I meant, for he could write a remarkably good hand himself. I sometimes found the name of his native parish handsomely written in the snow by the highway, with the proper French accent, and knew that he had passed. I asked him if he ever wished to write his thoughts. He said that he had read and written letters for those who could not, but he never tried to write thoughts,—no, he could not, he could not tell what to put first, it would kill him, and then there was spelling to be attended to at the same time!

I heard that a distinguished wise man and reformer asked him if he did not want the world to be changed; but he answered with a chuckle of surprise in his Canadian accent, not knowing that the question had ever been entertained before, "No, I like it well enough." It would have suggested many things to a philosopher to have dealings with him. To a stranger he appeared to know nothing of things in general; yet I sometimes saw in him a man whom I had not seen before, and I did not know whether he was as wise as Shakespeare or as simply ignorant as a child, whether to suspect him of a fine poetic consciousness or of stupidity. A townsman told me that when he met him sauntering through the village in his small close-fitting cap, and whistling to himself, he reminded him of a prince in disguise.

His only books were an almanac and an arithmetic, in which last he was considerably expert. The former was a sort of cyclopædia to him, which he supposed to contain an abstract of human knowledge, as indeed it does to a considerable extent. I loved to sound him on the various reforms of the day, and he never failed to look at them in the most simple and practical light. He had never heard of such things before. Could he do without factories? I asked. He had worn the home-made Vermont gray, he said, and that was good. Could he dis-

pense with tea and coffee? Did this country afford any
beverage beside water? He had soaked hemlock leaves
in water and drunk it, and thought that was better than
water in warm weather. When I asked him if he could
do without money, he showed the convenience of money
in such a way as to suggest and coincide with the most
philosophical accounts of the origin of this institution,
and the very derivation of the word *pecunia*. If an ox
were his property, and he wished to get needles and
thread at the store, he thought it would be inconvenient
and impossible soon to go on mortgaging some portion
of the creature each time to that amount. He could defend many institutions better than any philosopher, because, in describing them as they concerned him, he gave
the true reason for their prevalence, and speculation had
not suggested to him any other. At another time, hearing
Plato's definition of a man,—a biped without feathers,—
and that one exhibited a cock plucked and called it
Plato's man, he thought it an important difference that
the *knees* bent the wrong way. He would sometimes exclaim, "How I love to talk! By George, I could talk all
day!" I asked him once, when I had not seen him for
many months, if he had got a new idea this summer.
"Good Lord," said he, "a man that has to work as I do,
if he does not forget the ideas he has had, he will do
well. May be the man you hoe with is inclined to race;
then, by gorry, your mind must be there; you think of
weeds." He would sometimes ask me first on such occasions, if I had made any improvement. One winter day
I asked him if he was always satisfied with himself, wishing to suggest a substitute within him for the priest without, and some higher motive for living. "Satisfied!" said
he; "some men are satisfied with one thing, and some
with another. One man, perhaps, if he has got enough,
will be satisfied to sit all day with his back to the fire
and his belly to the table, by George!" Yet I never, by
any manœuvring, could get him to take the spiritual view
of things; the highest that he appeared to conceive of
was a simple expediency, such as you might expect an
animal to appreciate; and this, practically, is true of most
men. If I suggested any improvement in his mode of life,
he merely answered, without expressing any regret, that

it was too late. Yet he thoroughly believed in honesty and the like virtues.

There was a certain positive originality, however slight, to be detected in him, and I occasionally observed that he was thinking for himself and expressing his own opinion, a phenomenon so rare that I would any day walk ten miles to observe it, and it amounted to the re-origination of many of the institutions of society. Though he hesitated, and perhaps failed to express himself distinctly, he always had a presentable thought behind. Yet his thinking was so primitive and immersed in his animal life, that, though more promising than a merely learned man's, it rarely ripened to anything which can be reported. He suggested that there might be men of genius in the lowest grades of life, however permanently humble and illiterate, who take their own view always, or do not pretend to see at all; who are as bottomless even as Walden Pond was thought to be, though they may be dark and muddy.

Many a traveller came out of his way to see me and the inside of my house, and, as an excuse for calling, asked for a glass of water. I told them that I drank at the pond, and pointed thither, offering to lend them a dipper. Far off as I lived, I was not exempted from that annual visitation which occurs, methinks, about the first of April, when everybody is on the move; and I had my share of good luck, though there were some curious specimens among my visitors. Half-witted men from the almshouse and elsewhere came to see me; but I endeavored to make them exercise all the wit they had, and make their confessions to me; in such cases making wit the theme of our conversation; and so was compensated. Indeed, I found some of them to be wiser than the so-called *overseers* of the poor and selectmen of the town, and thought it was time that the tables were turned. With respect to wit, I learned that there was not much difference between the half and the whole. One day, in particular, an inoffensive, simple-minded pauper, whom with others I had often seen used as fencing stuff, standing or sitting on a bushel in the fields to keep cattle and himself from straying, visited me, and expressed a wish to live as I did. He told me, with the utmost simplicity

and truth, quite superior, or rather *inferior,* to anything
that is called humility, that he was "deficient in intellect." These were his words. The Lord had made him
so, yet he supposed the Lord cared as much for him as
for another. "I have always been so," said he, "from my
childhood; I never had much mind; I was not like other
children; I am weak in the head. It was the Lord's will,
I suppose." And there he was to prove the truth of his
words. He was a metaphysical puzzle to me. I have
rarely met a fellow-man on such promising ground,—it
was so simple and sincere and so true all that he said.
And, true enough, in proportion as he appeared to humble himself was he exalted. I did not know at first but it
was the result of a wise policy. It seemed that from such
a basis of truth and frankness as the poor weak-headed
pauper had laid, our intercourse might go forward to
something better than the intercourse of sages.

I had some guests from those not reckoned commonly
among the town's poor, but who should be; who are
among the world's poor, at any rate; guests who appeal,
not to your hospitality, but to your *hospitalality;* who
earnestly wish to be helped, and preface their appeal
with the information that they are resolved, for one
thing, never to help themselves. I require of a visitor
that he be not actually starving, though he may have the
very best appetite in the world, however he got it. Objects of charity are not guests. Men who did not know
when their visit had terminated, though I went about my
business again, answering them from greater and greater
remoteness. Men of almost every degree of wit called
on me in the migrating season. Some who had more wits
than they knew what to do with; runaway slaves with
plantation manners, who listened from time to time, like
the fox in the fable, as if they heard the hounds a-baying
on their track, and looked at me beseechingly, as much
as to say,—

"O Christian, will you send me back?"

One real runaway slave, among the rest, whom I helped
to forward toward the north star. Men of one idea, like
a hen with one chicken, and that a duckling; men of a

thousand ideas, and unkempt heads, like those hens
which are made to take charge of a hundred chickens,
all in pursuit of one bug, a score of them lost in every
morning's dew,—and become frizzled and mangy in consequence; men of ideas instead of legs, a sort of intellectual centipede that made you crawl all over. One man
proposed a book in which visitors should write their
names, as at the White Mountains; but, alas! I have too
good a memory to make that necessary.

I could not but notice some of the peculiarities of
my visitors. Girls and boys and young women generally
seemed glad to be in the woods. They looked in the
pond and at the flowers, and improved their time. Men
of business, even farmers, thought only of solitude and
employment, and of the great distance at which I dwelt
from something or other; and though they said that they
loved a ramble in the woods occasionally, it was obvious
that they did not. Restless committed men, whose time
was all taken up in getting a living or keeping it; ministers who spoke of God as if they enjoyed a monopoly
of the subject, who could not bear all kinds of opinions;
doctors, lawyers, uneasy housekeepers who pried into
my cupboard and bed when I was out,—how came
Mrs. ——to know that my sheets were not as clean as
hers?—young men who had ceased to be young, and had
concluded that it was safest to follow the beaten track
of the professions,—all these generally said that it was
not possible to do so much good in my position. Ay!
there was the rub. The old and infirm and the timid, of
whatever age or sex, thought most of sickness, and sudden accident and death; to them life seemed full of danger,—what danger is there if you don't think of any—
and they thought that a prudent man would carefully
select the safest position, where Dr. B. might be on hand
at a moment's warning. To them the village was literally
a *com-munity,* a league for mutual defence, and you
would suppose that they would not go a-huckleberrying
without a medicine chest. The amount of it is, if a man
is alive, there is always *danger* that he may die, though
the danger must be allowed to be less in proportion as
he is dead-and-alive to begin with. A man sits as many
risks as he runs. Finally, there were the self-styled re-

formers, the greatest bores of all, who thought that I
was forever singing,—

> This is the house that I built;
> This is the man that lives in the house that I built;

but they did not know that the third line was,—

> These are the folks that worry the man
> That lives in the house that I built.

I did not fear the hen-harriers, for I kept no chickens;
but I feared the men-harriers rather.

I had more cheering visitors than the last. Children come
a-berrying, railroad men taking a Sunday morning walk in
clean shirts, fishermen and hunters, poets and philosophers;
in short, all honest pilgrims, who came out to the woods
for freedom's sake, and really left the village behind, I
was ready to greet with,—"Welcome, Englishmen! welcome, Englishmen!" for I had had communication with
that race.

7. The Bean-Field

MEANWHILE my beans, the length of whose rows, added
together, was seven miles already planted, were impatient to be hoed, for the earliest had grown considerably
before the latest were in the ground; indeed they were
not easily to be put off. What was the meaning of this
so steady and self-respecting, this small Herculean labor,
I knew not. I came to love my rows, my beans, though
so many more than I wanted. They attached me to the
earth, and so I got strength like Antæus. But why should
I raise them? Only Heaven knows. This was my curious
labor all summer,—to make this portion of the earth's
surface, which had yielded only cinquefoil, blackberries,
johnswort, and the like, before, sweet wild fruits and
pleasant flowers, produce instead this pulse. What shall

I learn of beans or beans of me? I cherish them, I hoe them, early and late I have an eye to them; and this is my day's work. It is a fine broad leaf to look on. My auxiliaries are the dews and rains which water this dry soil, and what fertility is in the soil itself, which for the most part is lean and effete. My enemies are worms, cool days, and most of all woodchucks. The last have nibbled for me a quarter of an acre clean. But what right had I to oust johnswort and the rest, and break up their ancient herb garden? Soon, however, the remaining beans will be too tough for them, and go forward to meet new foes.

When I was four years old, as I well remember, I was brought from Boston to this my native town, through these very woods and this field, to the pond. It is one of the oldest scenes stamped on my memory. And now to-night my flute has waked the echoes over that very water. The pines still stand here older than I; or, if some have fallen, I have cooked my supper with their stumps, and a new growth is rising all around, preparing another aspect for new infant eyes. Almost the same johnswort springs from the same perennial root in this pasture, and even I have at length helped to clothe that fabulous landscape of my infant dreams, and one of the results of my presence and influence is seen in these bean leaves, corn blades, and potato vines.

I planted about two acres and a half of upland; and as it was only about fifteen years since the land was cleared, and I myself had got out two or three cords of stumps, I did not give it any manure; but in the course of the summer it appeared by the arrowheads which I turned up in hoeing, that an extinct nation had anciently dwelt here and planted corn and beans ere white men came to clear the land, and so, to some extent, had exhausted the soil for this very crop.

Before yet any woodchuck or squirrel had run across the road, or the sun had got above the shrub oaks, while all the dew was on, though the farmers warned me against it,—I would advise you to do all your work if possible while the dew is on,—I began to level the ranks of haughty weeds in my bean-field and throw dust upon their heads. Early in the morning I worked barefooted, dabbling like a plastic artist in the dewy and crumbling sand, but later in the day the sun blistered my feet. There the sun lighted me to hoe beans, pacing slowly backward and forward over that yellow gravelly upland, between the long green rows, fifteen rods, the one end terminating in a shrub oak copse where I could rest in the shade, the other in a blackberry field where the green berries deepened their tints by the time I had made another bout. Removing the weeds, putting fresh soil about the bean stems, and encouraging this weed which I had sown, making the yellow soil express its summer thought in bean leaves and blossoms rather than in wormwood and piper and millet grass, making the earth say beans instead of grass,—this was my daily work. As I had little aid from horses or cattle, or hired men or boys, or improved implements of husbandry, I was much slower, and became much more intimate with my beans than usual. But labor of the hands, even when pursued to the verge of drudgery, is perhaps never the worst form of idleness. It has a constant and imperishable moral, and to the scholar it yields a classic result. A very *agricola laboriosus* was I to travellers bound westward through Lincoln and Wayland to nobody knows where; they sitting at their ease in gigs, with elbows on knees, and reins loosely hanging in festoons; I the home-staying, laborious native of the soil. But soon my homestead was out of their sight and thought. It was the only open and cultivated field for a great distance on either side of the road, so they made the most of it; and sometimes the man in the field heard more of travellers' gossip and comment than was meant for his ear: "Beans so late! peas so late!"—for I continued to plant when others had begun to hoe,—the ministerial husbandman had not suspected it. "Corn, my boy, for fodder; corn for fodder." "Does he *live* there?" asks the black bonnet of the gray coat; and the hard-featured farmer reins up his grateful dobbin to inquire what you are doing where he sees no manure in the furrow, and recommends a little chip dirt, or any little waste stuff, or it may be ashes or plaster. But here were two acres and a half of furrows, and only a hoe for cart and two hands to draw it,—there being an aversion to other carts

and horses,—and chip dirt far away. Fellow-travellers as
they rattled by compared it aloud with the fields which
they had passed, so that I came to know how I stood in
the agricultural world. This was one field not in Mr. Colman's report. And, by the way, who estimates the value
of the crop which nature yields in the still wilder fields
unimproved by man? The crop of *English* hay is carefully weighed, the moisture calculated, the silicates and
the potash; but in all dells and pond-holes in the woods
and pastures and swamps grows a rich and various crop
only unreaped by man. Mine was, as it were, the con-
necting link between wild and cultivated fields; as some
states are civilized, and others half-civilized, and others
savage or barbarous, so my field was, though not in a
bad sense, a half-cultivated field. They were beans cheerfully returning to their wild and primitive state that I
cultivated, and my hoe played the *Ranz des Vaches* for
them. Near at hand, upon the topmost spray of a birch,
sings the brown thrasher—or red mavis, as some love to
call him—all the morning, glad of your society, that
would find out another farmer's field if yours were not
here. While you are planting the seed, he cries,—"Drop
it, drop it,—cover it up, cover it up,—pull it up, pull it
up, pull it up." But this was not corn, and so it was safe
from such enemies as he. You may wonder what his
rigamarole, his amateur Paganini performances on one
string or on twenty, have to do with your planting, and
yet prefer it to leached ashes or plaster. It was a cheap
sort of top dressing in which I had entire faith.

As I drew a still fresher soil about the rows with my
hoe, I disturbed the ashes of unchronicled nations who
in primeval years lived under these heavens, and their
small implements of war and hunting were brought to
the light of this modern day. They lay mingled with other
natural stones, some of which bore the marks of having
been burned by Indian fires, and some by the sun, and
also bits of pottery and glass brought hither by the recent cultivators of the soil. When my hoe tinkled against
the stones, that music echoed to the woods and the sky,
and was an accompaniment to my labor which yielded
an instant and immeasurable crop. It was no longer
beans that I hoed, nor I that hoed beans; and I remem-

bered with as much pity as pride, if I remembered at all, my acquaintances who had gone to the city to attend the oratorios. The nighthawk circled overhead in the sunny afternoons—for I sometimes made a day of it—like a mote in the eye, or in heaven's eye, falling from time to time with a swoop and a sound as if the heavens were rent, torn at last to very rags and tatters, and yet a seamless cope remained; small imps that fill the air and lay their eggs on the ground on bare sand or rocks on the tops of hills, where few have found them; graceful and slender like ripples caught up from the pond, as leaves are raised by the wind to float in the heavens; such kindredship is in nature. The hawk is aerial brother of the wave which he sails over and surveys, those his perfect air-inflated wings answering to the elemental unfledged pinions of the sea. Or sometimes I watched a pair of hen-hawks circling high in the sky, alternately soaring and descending, approaching and leaving one another, as if they were the embodiment of my own thoughts. Or I was attracted by the passage of wild pigeons from this wood to that, with a slight quivering winnowing sound and carrier haste; or from under a rotten stump my hoe turned up a sluggish portentous and outlandish spotted salamander, a trace of Egypt and the Nile, yet our contemporary. When I paused to lean on my hoe, these sounds and sights I heard and saw anywhere in the row, a part of the inexhaustible entertainment which the country offers.

On gala days the town fires its great guns, which echo like popguns to these woods, and some waifs of martial music occasionally penetrate thus far. To me, away there in my bean-field at the other end of the town, the big guns sounded as if a puffball had burst; and when there was a military turnout of which I was ignorant, I have sometimes had a vague sense all the day of some sort of itching and disease in the horizon, as if some eruption would break out there soon, either scarlatina or canker-rash, until at length some more favorable puff of wind, making haste over the fields and up the Wayland road, brought me information of the "trainers." It seemed by the distant hum as if somebody's bees had swarmed, and that the neighbors, according to Virgil's advice, by a

faint *tintinnabulum* upon the most sonorous of their domestic utensils, were endeavoring to call them down into
the hive again. And when the sound died quite away,
and the hum had ceased, and the most favorable breezes
told no tale, I knew that they had got the last drone of
them all safely into the Middlesex hive, and that now
their minds were bent on the honey with which it was
smeared.

I felt proud to know that the liberties of Massachusetts
and of our fatherland were in such safe keeping; and as
I turned to my hoeing again I was filled with an inexpressible confidence, and pursued my labor cheerfully
with a calm trust in the future.

When there were several bands of musicians, it
sounded as if all the village was a vast bellows, and all
the buildings expanded and collapsed alternately with a
din. But sometimes it was a really noble and inspiring
strain that reached these woods, and the trumpet that
sings of fame, and I felt as if I could spit a Mexican
with a good relish,—for why should we always stand for
trifles?—and looked round for a woodchuck or a skunk
to exercise my chivalry upon. These martial strains
seemed as far away as Palestine, and reminded me of a
march of crusaders in the horizon, with a slight tantivy
and tremulous motion of the elm tree tops which over-
hang the village. This was one of the *great* days; though
the sky had from my clearing only the same everlastingly
great look that it wears daily, and I saw no difference
in it.

It was a singular experience that long acquaintance
which I cultivated with beans, what with planting, and
hoeing, and harvesting, and threshing, and picking over
and selling them,—the last was the hardest of all,—I
might add eating, for I did taste. I was determined to
know beans. When they were growing, I used to hoe
from five o'clock in the morning till noon, and commonly spent the rest of the day about other affairs. Consider the intimate and curious acquaintance one makes
with various kinds of weeds,—it will bear some iteration
in the account, for there was no little iteration in the
labor,—disturbing their delicate organizations so ruthlessly, and making such invidious distinctions with his

hoe, levelling whole ranks of one species, and sedulously cultivating another. That's Roman wormwood,—that's pigweed,—that's sorrel,—that's piper-grass,—have at him, chop him up, turn his roots upward to the sun, don't let him have a fibre in the shade, if you do he'll turn himself t' other side up and be as green as a leek in two days. A long war, not with cranes, but with weeds, those Trojans who had sun and rain and dews on their side. Daily the beans saw me come to their rescue armed with a hoe, and thin the ranks of their enemies, filling up the trenches with weedy dead. Many a lusty crest-waving Hector, that towered a whole foot above his crowding comrades, fell before my weapon and rolled in the dust.

Those summer days which some of my contemporaries devoted to the fine arts in Boston or Rome, and others to contemplation in India, and others to trade in London or New York, I thus, with the other farmers of New England, devoted to husbandry. Not that I wanted beans to eat, for I am by nature a Pythagorean, so far as beans are concerned, whether they mean porridge or voting, and exchanged them for rice; but, perchance, as some must work in fields if only for the sake of tropes and expression, to serve a parable-maker one day. It was on the whole a rare amusement, which, continued too long, might have become a dissipation. Though I gave them no manure, and did not hoe them all once, I hoed them unusually well as far as I went, and was paid for it in the end, "there being in truth," as Evelyn says, "no compost or lætation whatsoever comparable to this continual motion, repastination, and turning of the mould with the spade." "The earth," he adds elsewhere, "especially if fresh, has a certain magnetism in it, by which it attracts the salt, power, or virtue (call it either) which gives it life, and is the logic of all the labor and stir we keep about it, to sustain us; all dungings and other sordid temperings being but the vicars succedaneous to this improvement." Moreover, this being one of those "worn-out and exhausted lay fields which enjoy their sabbath," had perchance, as Sir Kenelm Digby thinks likely, attracted "vital spirits" from the air. I harvested twelve bushels of beans.

But to be more particular, for it is complained that Mr. Colman has reported chiefly the expensive experiments of gentlemen farmers, my outgoes were,—

For a hoe.	$0 54	
Plowing, harrowing, and furrowing	7 50	Too much.
Beans for seed	3 12½	
Potatoes "	1 33	
Peas "	0 40	
Turnip seed. . . . . :	0 06	
White line for crow fence.	0 02	
Horse cultivator and boy three hours	1 00	
Horse and cart to get crop	0 75	
In all	$14 72½	

My income was (patremfamilias vendacem, non emacem esse oportet), from

Nine bushels and twelve quarts of beans sold	$16 94
Five " large potatoes.	2 50
Nine " small	2 25
Grass	1 00
Stalks	0 75
In all	$23 44
Leaving a pecuniary profit, as I have elsewhere said, of	$8 71½

This is the result of my experience in raising beans: Plant the common small white bush bean about the first of June, in rows three feet by eighteen inches apart, being careful to select fresh round and unmixed seed. First look out for worms, and supply vacancies by planting anew. Then look out for woodchucks, if it is an exposed place, for they will nibble off the earliest tender leaves almost clean as they go; and again, when the young tendrils make their appearance, they have notice of it, and will shear them off with both buds and young pods, sitting erect like a squirrel. But above all harvest as early as possible, if you would escape frosts and have a fair and salable crop; you may save much loss by this means.

This further experience also I gained: I said to myself, I will not plant beans and corn with so much industry another summer, but such seeds, if the seed is not lost, as sincerity, truth, simplicity, faith, innocence, and the like, and see if they will not grow in this soil, even with less toil and manurance, and sustain me, for surely it has not been exhausted for these crops. Alas! I said this to myself; but now another summer is gone, and another, and another, and I am obliged to say to you, Reader, that the seeds which I planted, if indeed they *were* the seeds of those virtues, were worm-eaten or had lost their vitality, and so did not come up. Commonly men will only be brave as their fathers were brave, or timid. This generation is very sure to plant corn and beans each new year precisely as the Indians did centuries ago and taught the first settlers to do, as if there were a fate in it. I saw an old man the other day, to my astonishment, making the holes with a hoe for the seventieth time at least, and not for himself to lie down in! But why should not the New Englander try new adventures, and not lay so much stress on his grain, his potato and grass crop, and his orchards,—raise other crops than these? Why concern ourselves so much about our beans for seed, and not be concerned at all about a new generation of men? We should really be fed and cheered if when we met a man we were sure to see that some of the qualities which I have named, which we all prize more than those other productions, but which are for the most part broadcast and floating in the air, had taken root and grown in him. Here comes such a subtile and ineffable quality, for instance, as truth or justice, though the slightest amount or new variety of it, along the road. Our ambassadors should be instructed to send home such seeds as these, and Congress help to distribute them over all the land. We should never stand upon ceremony with sincerity. We should never cheat and insult and banish one another by our meanness, if there were present the kernel of worth and friendliness. We should not meet thus in haste. Most men I do not meet at all, for they seem not to have time; they are busy

about their beans. We would not deal with a man thus
plodding ever, leaning on a hoe or a spade as a staff
between his work, not as a mushroom, but partially risen
out of the earth, something more than erect, like swallows alighted and walking on the ground:—

> "And as he spake, his wings would now and then
> Spread, as he meant to fly, then close again,—"

so that we should suspect that we might be conversing
with an angel. Bread may not always nourish us; but it
always does us good, it even takes stiffness out of our
joints, and makes us supple and buoyant, when we knew
not what ailed us, to recognize any generosity in man or
Nature, to share any unmixed and heroic joy.

Ancient poetry and mythology suggest, at least, that
husbandry was once a sacred art; but it is pursued with
irreverent haste and heedlessness by us, our object being
to have large farms and large crops merely. We have no
festival, nor procession, nor ceremony, not excepting our
Cattle-shows and so-called Thanksgivings, by which the
farmer expresses a sense of the sacredness of his calling,
or is reminded of its sacred origin. It is the premium
and the feast which tempt him. He sacrifices not to Ceres
and the Terrestrial Jove, but to the infernal Plutus
rather. By avarice and selfishness, and a grovelling habit,
from which none of us is free, of regarding the soil as
property, or the means of acquiring property chiefly, the
landscape is deformed, husbandry is degraded with us,
and the farmer leads the meanest of lives. He knows
Nature but as a robber. Cato says that the profits of
agriculture are particularly pious or just (*maximeque
pius quaestus*), and according to Varro the old Romans
"called the same earth Mother and Ceres, and thought
that they who cultivated it led a pious and useful life,
and that they alone were left of the race of King
Saturn."

We are wont to forget that the sun looks on our cultivated fields and on the prairies and forests without distinction. They all reflect and absorb his rays alike, and
the former make but a small part of the glorious picture
which he beholds in his daily course. In his view the

earth is all equally cultivated like a garden. Therefore we should receive the benefit of his light and heat with a corresponding trust and magnanimity. What though I value the seed of these beans, and harvest that in the fall of the year? This broad field which I have looked at so long looks not to me as the principal cultivator, but away from me to influences more genial to it, which water and make it green. These beans have results which are not harvested by me. Do they not grow for wood-chucks partly? The ear of wheat (in Latin *spica*, obso-letely *speca*, from *spe*, hope) should not be the only hope of the husbandman; its kernel or grain (*granum*, from *gerendo*, bearing) is not all that it bears. How, then, can our harvest fail? Shall I not rejoice also at the abundance of the weeds whose seeds are the granary of the birds? It matters little comparatively whether the fields fill the farmer's barns. The true husbandman will cease from anxiety, as the squirrels manifest no concern whether the woods will bear chestnuts this year or not, and finish his labor with every day, relinquishing all claim to the pro-duce of his fields, and sacrificing in his mind not only his first but his last fruits also.

8. The Village

AFTER hoeing, or perhaps reading and writing, in the forenoon, I usually bathed again in the pond, swimming across one of its coves for a stint, and washed the dust of labor from my person, or smoothed out the last wrin-kle which study had made, and for the afternoon was absolutely free. Every day or two I strolled to the village to hear some of the gossip which is incessantly going on there, circulating either from mouth to mouth, or from newspaper to newspaper, and which, taken in homeo-pathic doses, was really as refreshing in its way as the rustle of leaves and the peeping of frogs. As I walked in the woods to see the birds and squirrels, so I walked in the village to see the men and boys; instead of the

wind among the pines I heard the carts rattle. In one
direction from my house there was a colony of muskrats
in the river meadows; under the grove of elms and but-
tonwoods in the other horizon was a village of busy men,
as curious to me as if they had been prairie-dogs, each
sitting at the mouth of its burrow, or running over to a
neighbor's to gossip. I went there frequently to observe
their habits. The village appeared to me a great news
room; and on one side, to support it, as once at Redding & Company's on State Street, they kept nuts and
raisins, or salt and meal and other groceries. Some have
such a vast appetite for the former commodity, that is,
the news, and such sound digestive organs, that they can
sit forever in public avenues without stirring, and let it
simmer and whisper through them like the Etesian
winds, or as if inhaling ether, it only producing numbness
and insensibility to pain,—otherwise it would often be
painful to hear,—without affecting the consciousness. I
hardly ever failed, when I rambled through the village,
to see a row of such worthies, either sitting on a ladder
sunning themselves, with their bodies inclined forward
and their eyes glancing along the line this way and that,
from time to time, with a voluptuous expression, or else
leaning against a barn with their hands in their pockets,
like caryatides, as if to prop it up. They, being commonly
out of doors, heard whatever was in the wind. These are
the coarsest mills, in which all gossip is first rudely di-
gested or cracked up before it is emptied into finer
and more delicate hoppers within doors. I observed
that the vitals of the village were the grocery, the bar-
room, the post-office, and the bank; and, as a necessary
part of the machinery, they kept a bell, a big gun, and
a fire engine, at convenient places; and the houses were
so arranged as to make the most of mankind, in lanes
and fronting one another, so that every traveller had to
run the gauntlet, and every man, woman, and child
might get a lick at him. Of course, those who were stationed nearest to the head of the line, where they could
most see and be seen, and have the first blow at him,
paid the highest prices for their places; and the few straggling inhabitants in the outskirts, where long gaps in the
line began to occur, and the traveller could get over

walls or turn aside into cow-paths, and so escape, paid a very slight ground or window tax. Signs were hung out on all sides to allure him; some to catch him by the appetite, as the tavern and victualling cellar; some by the fancy, as the dry goods store and the jeweller's; and others by the hair or the feet or the skirts, as the barber, the shoemaker, or the tailor. Besides, there was a still more terrible standing invitation to call at every one of these houses, and company expected about these times. For the most part I escaped wonderfully from these dangers, either by proceeding at once boldly and without deliberation to the goal, as is recommended to those who run the gauntlet, or by keeping my thoughts on high things, like Orpheus, who, "loudly singing the praises of the gods to his lyre, drowned the voices of the Sirens, and kept out of danger." Sometimes I bolted suddenly, and nobody could tell my whereabouts, for I did not stand much about gracefulness, and never hesitated at a gap in a fence. I was even accustomed to make an irruption into some houses, where I was well entertained, and after learning the kernels and very last sieveful of news,—what had subsided, the prospects of war and peace, and whether the world was likely to hold together much longer,—I was let out through the rear avenues, and so escaped to the woods again.

It was very pleasant, when I stayed late in town, to launch myself into the night, especially if it was dark and tempestuous, and set sail from some bright village parlor or lecture room, with a bag of rye or Indian meal upon my shoulder, for my snug harbor in the woods, having made all tight without and withdrawn under hatches with a merry crew of thoughts, leaving only my outer man at the helm, or even tying up the helm when it was plain sailing. I had many a genial thought by the cabin fire "as I sailed." I was never cast away nor distressed in any weather, though I encountered some severe storms. It is darker in the woods, even in common nights, than most suppose. I frequently had to look up at the opening between the trees above the path in order to learn my route, and, where there was no cart-path, to feel with my feet the faint track which I had worn, or steer by the known relation of particular trees which I felt with my hands, passing between two pines for instance, not more than eighteen inches apart, in the midst of the woods, invariably, in the darkest night. Sometimes, after coming home thus late in a dark and muggy night, when my feet felt the path which my eyes could not see, dreaming and absent-minded all the way, until I was aroused by having to raise my hand to lift the latch, I have not been able to recall a single step of my walk, and I have thought that perhaps my body would find its way home if its master should forsake it, as the hand finds its way to the mouth without assistance. Several times, when a visitor chanced to stay into evening, and it proved a dark night, I was obliged to conduct him to the cart-path in the rear of the house, and then point out to him the direction he was to pursue, and in keeping which he was to be guided rather by his feet than his eyes. One very dark night I directed thus on their way two young men who had been fishing in the pond. They lived about a mile off through the woods, and were quite used to the route. A day or two after one of them told me that they wandered about the greater part of the night, close by their own premises, and did not get home till toward morning, by which time, as there had been several heavy showers in the meanwhile, and the leaves were very wet, they were drenched to their skins. I have heard of many going astray even in the village streets, when the darkness was so thick that you could cut it with a knife, as the saying is. Some who live in the outskirts, having come to town a-shopping in their wagons, have been obliged to put up for the night; and gentlemen and ladies making a call have gone half a mile out of their way, feeling the sidewalk only with their feet, and not knowing when they turned. It is a surprising and memorable, as well as valuable experience, to be lost in the woods any time. Often in a snow-storm, even by day, one will come out upon a well-known road and yet find it impossible to tell which way leads to the village. Though he knows that he has travelled it a thousand times, he cannot recognize a feature in it, but it is as strange to him as if it were a road in Siberia. By night, of course, the perplexity is infinitely greater. In our most trivial walks, we are constantly, though unconsciously, steering like pilots by certain well-known beacons and headlands, and if we go beyond our usual course we still carry in our minds the bearing of some neighboring cape; and not till we are completely lost, or turned round,—for a man needs only to be turned round once with his eyes shut in this world to be lost,—do we appreciate the vastness and strangeness of nature. Every man has to learn the points of compass again as often as he awakes, whether from sleep or any abstraction. Not till we are lost, in other words not till we have lost the world, do we begin to find ourselves, and realize where we are and the infinite extent of our relations.

One afternoon, near the end of the first summer, when I went to the village to get a shoe from the cobbler's, I was seized and put into jail, because, as I have elsewhere related, I did not pay a tax to, or recognize the authority of the State which buys and sells men, women, and children, like cattle, at the door of its senate-house. I had gone down to the woods for other purposes. But, wherever a man goes, men will pursue and paw him with their dirty institutions, and, if they can, constrain him to belong to their desperate odd-fellow society. It is true, I might have resisted forcibly with more or less effect, might have run "amok" against society; but I preferred that society should run "amok" against me, it being the desperate party. However, I was released the next day, obtained my mended shoe, and returned to the woods in season to get my dinner of huckleberries on Fair Haven Hill. I was never molested by any person but those who represented the State. I had no lock nor bolt but for the desk which held my papers, not even a nail to put over my latch or windows. I never fastened my door night or day, though I was to be absent several days; not even when the next fall I spent a fortnight in the woods of Maine. And yet my house was more respected than if it had been surrounded by a file of soldiers. The tired rambler could rest and warm himself by my fire, the literary amuse himself with the few books on my table, or the curious, by opening my closet door, see what was left of my dinner, and what prospect I had of a supper. Yet, though many people of every class came this way to the pond, I suffered no serious inconvenience from these sources, and I never missed anything but one small book, a volume of Homer, which perhaps was improperly gilded, and this I trust a soldier of our camp has found by this time. I am convinced, that if all men were to live as simply as I then did, thieving and robbery would be unknown. These take place only in communities where some have got more than is sufficient while others have not enough. The Pope's Homers would soon get properly distributed.

> "Nec bella fuerunt,
> Faginus astabat dum scyphus ante dapes."

> "Nor wars did men molest,
> When only beechen bowls were in request."

"You who govern public affairs, what need have you to employ punishments? Love virtue, and the people will be virtuous. The virtues of a superior man are like the wind; the virtues of a common man are like the grass; the grass, when the wind passes over it, bends."

9. The Ponds

SOMETIMES, having had a surfeit of human society and gossip, and worn out all my village friends, I rambled still farther westward than I habitually dwell, into yet more unfrequented parts of the town, "to fresh woods and pastures new," or, while the sun was setting, made my supper of huckleberries and blueberries on Fair Haven Hill, and laid up a store for several days. The fruits do not yield their true flavor to the purchaser of them, nor to him who raises them for the market. There is but one way to obtain it, yet few take that way. If you would know the flavor of huckleberries, ask the cow-boy or the partridge. It is a vulgar error to suppose that you have tasted huckleberries who never plucked them. A huckleberry never reaches Boston; they have not been known there since they grew on her three hills. The ambrosial and essential part of the fruit is lost with the bloom which is rubbed off in the market cart, and they become mere provender. As long as Eternal Justice reigns, not one innocent huckleberry can be transported thither from the country's hills.

Occasionally, after my hoeing was done for the day, I joined some impatient companion who had been fishing on the pond since morning, as silent and motionless as a duck or a floating leaf, and, after practising various kinds of philosophy, had concluded commonly, by the time I arrived, that he belonged to the ancient sect of Cœnobites. There was one older man, an excellent fisher and skilled in all kinds of woodcraft, who was pleased to look upon my house as a building erected for the convenience of fishermen; and I was equally pleased when he sat in my doorway to arrange his lines. Once in a while we sat together on the pond, he at one end of the boat, and I at the other; but not many words passed between us, for he had grown deaf in his later years, but he occasionally hummed a psalm, which harmonized well enough with my philosophy. Our intercourse was thus altogether one of unbroken harmony, far more pleasing to remember than if it had been carried on by speech. When, as was commonly the case, I had none to commune with, I used to raise the echoes by striking with a paddle on the side of my boat, filling the surrounding woods with circling and dilating sound, stirring them up as the keeper of a menagerie his wild beasts, until I elicited a growl from every wooded vale and hillside.

In warm evenings I frequently sat in the boat playing the flute, and saw the perch, which I seem to have charmed, hovering around me, and the moon travelling over the ribbed bottom, which was strewed with the wrecks of the forest. Formerly I had come to this pond adventurously, from time to time, in dark summer nights, with a companion, and, making a fire close to the water's edge, which we thought attracted the fishes, we caught pouts with a bunch of worms strung on a thread, and when we had done, far in the night, threw the burning brands high into the air skyrockets, which, coming down

into the pond, were quenched with a loud hissing, and
we were suddenly groping in total darkness. Through
this, whistling a tune, we took our way to the haunts of
men again. But now I had made my home by the shore.

Sometimes, after staying in a village parlor till the
family had all retired, I have returned to the woods, and,
partly with a view to the next day's dinner, spent the
hours of midnight fishing from a boat by moonlight, serenaded by owls and foxes, and hearing, from time to time,
the creaking note of some unknown bird close at hand.
These experiences were very memorable and valuable to
me,—anchored in forty feet of water, and twenty or
thirty rods from the shore, surrounded sometimes by
thousands of small perch and shiners, dimpling the surface with their tails in the moonlight, and communicating
by a long flaxen line with mysterious nocturnal fishes
which had their dwelling forty feet below, or sometimes
dragging sixty feet of line about the pond as I drifted in
the gentle night breeze, now and then feeling a slight
vibration along it, indicative of some life prowling about
its extremity, of dull uncertain blundering purpose there,
and slow to make up its mind. At length you slowly
raise, pulling hand over hand, some horned pout squeak-
ing and squirming to the upper air. It was very queer,
especially in dark nights, when your thoughts had wandered to vast and cosmogonal themes in other spheres,
to feel this faint jerk, which came to interrupt your
dreams and link you to Nature again. It seemed as if I
might next cast my line upward into the air, as well as
downward into this element, which was scarcely more
dense. Thus I caught two fishes as it were with one hook.

The scenery of Walden is on a humble scale, and,
though very beautiful, does not approach to grandeur,
nor can it much concern one who has not long fre-
quented it or lived by its shore; yet this pond is so remarkable for its depth and purity as to merit a particular
description. It is a clear and deep green well, half a mile
long and a mile and three quarters in circumference, and
contains about sixty-one and a half acres; a perennial
spring in the midst of pine and oak woods, without any
visible inlet or outlet except by the clouds and evapora-

tion. The surrounding hills rise abruptly from the water to the height of forty to eighty feet, though on the southeast and east they attain to about one hundred and one hundred and fifty feet respectively, within a quarter and a third of a mile. They are exclusively woodland. All our Concord waters have two colors at least; one when viewed at a distance, and another, more proper, close at hand. The first depends more on the light, and follows the sky. In clear weather, in summer, they appear blue at a little distance, especially if agitated, and at a great distance all appear alike. In stormy weather they are sometimes of a dark slate-color. The sea, however, is said to be blue one day and green another without any perceptible change in the atmosphere. I have seen our river, when, the landscape being covered with snow, both water and ice were almost as green as grass. Some consider blue "to be the color of pure water, whether liquid or solid." But, looking directly down into our waters from a boat, they are seen to be of very different colors. Walden is blue at one time and green at another, even from the same point of view. Lying between the earth and the heavens, it partakes of the color of both. Viewed from a hilltop it reflects the color of the sky; but near at hand it is of a yellowish tint next the shore where you can see the sand, then a light green, which gradually deepens to a uniform dark green in the body of the pond. In some lights, viewed even from a hilltop, it is of a vivid green next the shore. Some have referred this to the reflection of the verdure; but it is equally green there against the railroad sandbank, and in the spring, before the leaves are expanded, and it may be simply the result of the prevailing blue mixed with the yellow of the sand. Such is the color of its iris. This is that portion, also, where in the spring, the ice being warmed by the heat of the sun reflected from the bottom, and also transmitted through the earth, melts first and forms a narrow canal about the still frozen middle. Like the rest of our waters, when much agitated, in clear weather, so that the surface of the waves may reflect the sky at the right angle, or because there is more light mixed with it, it appears at a little distance of a darker blue than the sky itself; and at such a time, being on its surface, and looking with divided vision, so as to see the reflection, I have discerned a matchless and indescribable light blue, such as watered or changeable silks and sword blades suggest, more cerulean than the sky itself, alternating with the original dark green on the opposite sides of the waves, which last appeared but muddy in comparison. It is a vitreous greenish blue, as I remember it, like those patches of the winter sky seen through cloud vistas in the west before sundown. Yet a single glass of its water held up to the light is as colorless as an equal quantity of air. It is well known that a large plate of glass will have a green tint, owing, as the makers say, to its "body," but a small piece of the same will be colorless. How large a body of Walden water would be required to reflect a green tint I have never proved. The water of our river is black or a very dark brown to one looking directly down on it, and, like that of most ponds, imparts to the body of one bathing in it a yellowish tinge; but this water is of such crystalline purity that the body of the bather appears of an alabaster whiteness, still more unnatural, which, as the limbs are magnified and distorted withal, produces a monstrous effect, making fit studies for a Michael Angelo.

The water is so transparent that the bottom can easily be discerned at the depth of twenty-five or thirty feet. Paddling over it, you may see, many feet beneath the surface, the schools of perch and shiners, perhaps only an inch long, yet the former easily distinguished by their transverse bars, and you think that they must be ascetic fish that find a subsistence there. Once, in the winter, many years ago, when I had been cutting holes through the ice in order to catch pickerel, as I stepped ashore I tossed my axe back on to the ice, but, as if some evil genius had directed it, it slid four or five rods directly into one of the holes, where the water was twenty-five feet deep. Out of curiosity, I lay down on the ice and looked through the hole, until I saw the axe a little on one side, standing on its head, with its helve erect and gently swaying to and fro with the pulse of the pond; and there it might have stood erect and swaying till in the course of time the handle rotted off, if I had not disturbed it. Making another hole directly over it with

an ice chisel which I had, and cutting down the longest
birch which I could find in the neighborhood with my
knife, I made a slip-noose, which I attached to its end,
and, letting it down carefully, passed it over the knob of
the handle, and drew it by a line along the birch, and
so pulled the axe out again.

The shore is composed of a belt of smooth rounded
white stones like paving-stones, excepting one or two
short sand beaches, and is so steep that in many places
a single leap will carry you into water over your head;
and were it not for its remarkable transparency, that
would be the last to be seen of its bottom till it rose on
the opposite side. Some think it is bottomless. It is nowhere muddy, and a casual observer would say that
there were no weeds at all in it; and of noticeable plants,
except in the little meadows recently overflowed, which
do not properly belong to it, a closer scrutiny does not
detect a flag nor a bulrush, nor even a lily, yellow or
white, but only a few small heart-leaves and potamoget-
ons, and perhaps a water-target or two; all which however a bather might not perceive; and these plants are
clean and bright like the element they grow in. The stones
extend a rod or two into the water, and then the bottom
is pure sand, except in the deepest parts, where there is
usually a little sediment, probably from the decay of the
leaves which have been wafted on to it so many successive falls, and a bright green weed is brought up on
anchors even in the midwinter.

We have one other pond just like this, White Pond,
in Nine Acre Corner, about two and a half miles westerly; but, though I am acquainted with most of the ponds
within a dozen miles of this centre, I do not know a third
of this pure and well-like character. Successive nations
perchance have drank at, admired, and fathomed it, and
passed away, and still its water is green and pellucid as
ever. Not an intermitting spring! Perhaps on that spring
morning when Adam and Eve were driven out of Eden
Walden Pond was already in existence, and even then
breaking up in a gentle spring rain accompanied with
mist and a southerly wind, and covered with myriads of
ducks and geese, which had not heard of the fall, when
still such pure lakes sufficed them. Even then it had com-

menced to rise and fall, and had clarified its waters and colored them of the hue they now wear, and obtained a patent of Heaven to be the only Walden Pond in the world and distiller of celestial dews. Who knows in how many unremembered nations' literatures this has been the Castalian Fountain? or what nymphs presided over it in the Golden Age? It is a gem of the first water which Concord wears in her coronet.

Yet perchance the first who came to this well have left some trace of their footsteps. I have been surprised to detect encircling the pond, even where a thick wood has just been cut down on the shore, a narrow shelf-like path in the steep hillside, alternately rising and falling, approaching and receding from the water's edge, as old probably as the race of man here, worn by the feet of aboriginal hunters, and still from time to time unwittingly trodden by the present occupants of the land. This is particularly distinct to one standing on the middle of the pond in winter, just after a light snow has fallen, appearing as a clear undulating white line, unobscured by weeds and twigs, and very obvious a quarter of a mile off in many places where in summer it is hardly distinguishable close at hand. The snow reprints it, as it were, in clear white type alto-relievo. The ornamented grounds of villas which will one day be built here may still preserve some trace of this.

The pond rises and falls, but whether regularly or not, and within what period, nobody knows, though, as usual, many pretend to know. It is commonly higher in the winter and lower in the summer, though not corresponding to the general wet and dryness. I can remember when it was a foot or two lower, and also when it was at least five feet higher, than when I lived by it. There is a narrow sand-bar running into it, with very deep water on one side, on which I helped boil a kettle of chowder, some six rods from the main shore, about the year 1824, which it has not been possible to do for twenty-five years; and, on the other hand, my friends used to listen with incredulity when I told them, that a few years later I was accustomed to fish from a boat in a secluded cove in the woods, fifteen rods from the only shore they knew, which place was long since converted into a meadow. But the pond has risen steadily for two years, and now, in the summer of '52, is just five feet higher than when I lived there, or as high as it was thirty years ago, and fishing goes on again in the meadow. This makes a difference of level, at the outside, of six or seven feet; and yet the water shed by the surrounding hills is insignificant in amount, and this overflow must be referred to causes which affect the deep springs. This same summer the pond has begun to fall again. It is remarkable that this fluctuation, whether periodical or not, appears thus to require many years for its accomplishment. I have observed one rise and a part of two falls, and I expect that a dozen or fifteen years hence the water will again be as low as I have ever known it. Flint's Pond, a mile eastward, allowing for the disturbance occasioned by its inlet and outlets, and the smaller intermediate ponds also, sympathize with Walden, and recently attained their greatest height at the same time with the latter. The same is true, as far as my observation goes, of White Pond.

This rise and fall of Walden at long intervals serves this use at least; the water standing at this great height for a year or more, though it makes it difficult to walk round it, kills the shrubs and trees which have sprung up about its edge since the last rise,—pitch pines, birches, alders, aspens, and others,—and, falling again, leaves an unobstructed shore; for, unlike many ponds and all waters which are subject to a daily tide, its shore is cleanest when the water is lowest. On the side of the pond next my house a row of pitch pines, fifteen feet high, has been killed and tipped over as if by a lever, and thus a stop put to their encroachments; and their size indicates how many years have elapsed since the last rise to this height. By this fluctuation the pond asserts its title to a shore, and thus the *shore* is shorn, and the trees cannot hold it by right of possession. These are the lips of the lake, on which no beard grows. It licks its chaps from time to time. When the water is at its height, the alders, willows, and maples send forth a mass of fibrous red roots several feet long from all sides of their stems in the water, and to the height of three or four feet from the ground, in the effort to maintain themselves; and I have known the high blueberry bushes about the shore, which commonly produce no fruit, bear an abundant crop under these circumstances.

Some have been puzzled to tell how the shore became so regularly paved. My townsmen have all heard the tradition—the oldest people tell me that they heard it in their youth—that anciently the Indians were holding a pow-wow upon a hill here, which rose as high into the heavens as the pond now sinks deep into the earth, and they used much profanity, as the story goes, though this vice is one of which the Indians were never guilty, and while they were thus engaged the hill shook and suddenly sank, and only one old squaw, named Walden, escaped, and from her the pond was named. It has been conjectured that when the hill shook these stones rolled down its side and became the present shore. It is very certain, at any rate, that once there was no pond here, and now there is one; and this Indian fable does not in any respect conflict with the account of that ancient settler whom I have mentioned, who remembers so well when he first came here with his divining-rod, saw a thin vapor rising from the sward, and the hazel pointed steadily downward, and he concluded to dig a well here. As for the stones, many still think that they are hardly to be accounted for by the action of the waves on these hills; but I observe that the surrounding hills are remarkably full of the same kind of stones, so that they have been obliged to pile them up in walls on both sides of the railroad cut nearest the pond; and, moreover, there are most stones where the shore is most abrupt; so that, unfortunately, it is no longer a mystery to me. I detect the paver. If the name was not derived from that of some English locality,—Saffron Walden, for instance,—one might suppose that it was called originally *Walled-in* Pond.

The pond was my well ready dug. For four months in the year its water is as cold as it is pure at all times; and I think that it is then as good as any, if not the best, in the town. In the winter, all water which is exposed to the air is colder than springs and wells which are protected from it. The temperature of the pond water which had stood in the room where I sat from five o'clock in the afternoon till noon the next day, the sixth of March, 1846, the thermometer having been up to 65° or 70°

some of the time, owing partly to the sun on the roof, was 42°, or one degree colder than the water of one of the coldest wells in the village just drawn. The temperature of the Boiling Spring the same day was 45°, or the warmest of any water tried, though it is the coldest that I know of in summer, when, beside, shallow and stagnant surface water is not mingled with it. Moreover, in summer, Walden never becomes so warm as most water which is exposed to the sun, on account of its depth. In the warmest weather I usually placed a pailful in my cellar, where it became cool in the night, and remained so during the day; though I also resorted to a spring in the neighborhood. It was as good when a week old as the day it was dipped, and had no taste of the pump. Whoever camps for a week in summer by the shore of a pond, needs only bury a pail of water a few feet deep in the shade of his camp to be independent of the luxury of ice.

There have been caught in Walden pickerel, one weighing seven pounds,—to say nothing of another which carried off a reel with great velocity, which the fisherman safely set down at eight pounds because he did not see him,—perch and pouts, some of each weighing over two pounds, shiners, chivins or roach (*Leuciscus pulchellus*), a very few breams, and a couple of eels, one weighing four pounds,—I am thus particular because the weight of a fish is commonly its only title to fame, and these are the only eels I have heard of here;—also, I have a faint recollection of a little fish some five inches long, with silvery sides and a greenish back, somewhat dace-like in its character, which I mention here chiefly to link my facts to fable. Nevertheless, this pond is not very fertile in fish. Its pickerel, though not abundant, are its chief boast. I have seen at one time lying on the ice pickerel of at least three different kinds: a long and shallow one, steel-colored, most like those caught in the river; a bright golden kind, with greenish reflections and remarkably deep, which is the most common here; and another, golden-colored, and shaped like the last, but peppered on the sides with small dark brown or black spots, intermixed with a few faint blood-red ones, very much like a trout. The specific name *reticulatus* would not apply to this; it should be *guttatus*

rather. These are all very firm fish, and weigh more than
their size promises. The shiners, pouts, and perch also,
and indeed all the fishes which inhabit this pond, are
much cleaner, handsomer, and firmer-fleshed than those
in the river and most other ponds, as the water is purer,
and they can easily be distinguished from them. Probably
many ichthyologists would make new varieties of some
of them. There are also a clean race of frogs and tortoises, and a few mussels in it; muskrats and minks leave
their traces about it, and occasionally a travelling mud-
turtle visits it. Sometimes, when I pushed off my boat in
the morning, I disturbed a great mud-turtle which had
secreted himself under the boat in the night. Ducks and
geese frequent it in the spring and fall, the white-bellied
swallows (*Hirundo bicolor*) skim over it, and the peet-
weets (*Totanus macularius*) "teeter" along its stony
shores all summer. I have sometimes disturbed a fish
hawk sitting on a white pine over the water; but I doubt
if it is ever profaned by the wing of a gull, like Fair
Haven. At most, it tolerates one annual loon. These are
all the animals of consequence which frequent it now.

You may see from a boat, in calm weather, near the
sandy eastern shore, where the water is eight or ten feet
deep, and also in some other parts of the pond, some
circular heaps half a dozen feet in diameter by a foot in
height, consisting of small stones less than a hen's egg
in size, where all around is bare sand. At first you wonder if the Indians could have formed them on the ice
for any purpose, and so, when the ice melted, they sank
to the bottom; but they are too regular and some of
them plainly too fresh for that. They are similar to those
found in rivers; but as there are no suckers nor lampreys
here, I know not by what fish they could be made. Perhaps they are the nests of the chivin. These lend a pleasing mystery to the bottom.

The shore is irregular enough not to be monotonous.
I have in my mind's eye the western, indented with deep
bays, the bolder northern, and the beautifully scalloped
southern shore, where successive capes overlap each
other and suggest unexplored coves between. The forest
has never so good a setting, nor is so distinctly beautiful,
as when seen from the middle of a small lake amid hills

which rise from the water's edge; for the water in which it is reflected not only makes the best foreground in such a case, but, with its winding shore, the most natural and agreeable boundary to it. There is no rawness nor imperfection in its edge there, as where the axe has cleared a part, or a cultivated field abuts on it. The trees have ample room to expand on the water side, and each sends forth its most vigorous branch in that direction. There Nature has woven a natural selvage, and the eye rises by just gradations from the low shrubs of the shore to the highest trees. There are few traces of man's hand to be seen. The water laves the shore as it did a thousand years ago.

A lake is the landscape's most beautiful and expressive feature. It is earth's eye; looking into which the beholder measures the depth of his own nature. The fluviatile trees next the shore are the slender eyelashes which fringe it, and the wooded hills and cliffs around are its overhanging brows.

Standing on the smooth sandy beach at the east end of the pond, in a calm September afternoon, when a slight haze makes the opposite shore-line indistinct, I have seen whence came the expression, "the glassy surface of a lake." When you invert your head, it looks like a thread of finest gossamer stretched across the valley, and gleaming against the distant pine woods, separating one stratum of the atmosphere from another. You would think that you could walk dry under it to the opposite hills, and that the swallows which skim over might perch on it. Indeed, they sometimes dive below the line, as it were by mistake, and are undeceived. As you look over the pond westward you are obliged to employ both your hands to defend your eyes against the reflected as well as the true sun, for they are equally bright; and if, between the two, you survey its surface critically, it is literally as smooth as glass, except where the skater insects, at equal intervals scattered over its whole extent, by their motions in the sun produce the finest imaginable sparkle on it, or, perchance, a duck plumes itself, or, as I have said, a swallow skims so low as to touch it. It may be that in the distance a fish describes an arc of three or four feet in the air, and there is one bright flash

where it emerges, and another where it strikes the water;
sometimes the whole silvery arc is revealed; or here and
there, perhaps, is a thistle-down floating on its surface,
which the fishes dart at and so dimple it again. It is like
molten glass cooled but not congealed, and the few
motes in it are pure and beautiful like the imperfections
in glass. You may often detect a yet smoother and
darker water, separated from the rest as if by an invisible
cobweb, boom of the water nymphs, resting on it. From
a hilltop you can see a fish leap in almost any part; for
not a pickerel or shiner picks an insect from this smooth
surface but it manifestly disturbs the equilibrium of the
whole lake. It is wonderful with what elaborateness this
simple fact is advertised,—this piscine murder will out,—
and from my distant perch I distinguish the circling undulations when they are a half a dozen rods in diameter.
You can even detect a water-bug (*Gyrinus*) ceaselessly
progressing over the smooth surface a quarter of a mile
off; for they furrow the water slightly, making a conspicuous ripple bounded by two diverging lines, but the skaters glide over it without rippling it perceptibly. When
the surface is considerably agitated there are no skaters
nor water-bugs on it, but apparently, in calm days, they
leave their havens and adventurously glide forth from
the shore by short impulses till they completely cover it.
It is a soothing employment, on one of those fine days
in the fall when all the warmth of the sun is fully appreciated, to sit on a stump on such a height as this,
overlooking the pond, and study the dimpling circles
which are incessantly inscribed on its otherwise invisible
surface amid the reflected skies and trees. Over this
great expanse there is no disturbance but it is thus at
once gently smoothed away and assuaged, as, when a
vase of water is jarred, the trembling circles seek the
shore and all is smooth again. Not a fish can leap or an
insect fall on the pond but it is thus reported in circling
dimples, in lines of beauty, as it were the constant welling up of its fountain, the gentle pulsing of its life, the
heaving of its breast. The thrills of joy and thrills of pain
are undistinguishable. How peaceful the phenomena of
the lake! Again the works of man shine as in the spring.
Ay, every leaf and twig and stone and cobweb sparkles

now at mid-afternoon as when covered with dew in a spring morning. Every motion of an oar or an insect produces a flash of light; and if an oar falls, how sweet the echo!

In such a day, in September or October, Walden is a perfect forest mirror, set around with stones as precious to my eye as if fewer or rarer. Nothing so fair, so pure, and at the same time so large, as a lake, perchance, lies on the surface of the earth. Sky water. It needs no fence. Nations come and go-without defiling it. It is a mirror which no stone can crack, whose quicksilver will never wear off, whose gilding Nature continually repairs; no storms, no dust, can dim its surface ever fresh;—a mirror in which all impurity presented to it sinks, swept and dusted by the sun's hazy brush,—this the light dust-cloth,—which retains no breath that is breathed on it, but sends its own to float as clouds high above its surface, and be reflected in its bosom still.

A field of water betrays the spirit that is in the air. It is continually receiving new life and motion from above. It is intermediate in its nature between land and sky. On land only the grass and trees wave, but the water itself is rippled by the wind. I see where the breeze dashes across it by the streaks or flakes of light. It is remarkable that we can look down on its surface. We shall, perhaps, look down thus on the surface of air at length, and mark where a still subtler spirit sweeps over it.

The skaters and water-bugs finally disappear in the latter part of October, when the severe frosts have come; and then and in November, usually, in a calm day, there is absolutely nothing to ripple the surface. One November afternoon, in the calm at the end of a rain-storm of several days' duration, when the sky was still completely overcast and the air was full of mist, I observed that the pond was remarkably smooth, so that it was difficult to distinguish its surface; though it no longer reflected the bright tints of October, but the sombre November colors of the surrounding hills. Though I passed over it as gently as possible, the slight undulations produced by my boat extended almost as far as I could see, and gave a ribbed appearance to the reflections. But, as I was looking over the surface, I saw here and there at a distance

a faint glimmer, as if some skater insects which had escaped the frosts might be collected there, or, perchance,
the surface, being so smooth, betrayed where a spring
welled up from the bottom. Paddling gently to one of
these places, I was surprised to find myself surrounded
by myriads of small perch, about five inches long, of a
rich bronze color in the green water, sporting there, and
constantly rising to the surface and dimpling it, sometimes leaving bubbles on it. In such transparent and
seemingly bottomless water, reflecting the clouds, I
seemed to be floating through the air as in a balloon,
and their swimming impressed me as a kind of flight or
hovering, as if they were a compact flock of birds passing
just beneath my level on the right or left, their fins, like
sails, set all around them. There were many such schools
in the pond, apparently improving the short season before winter would draw an icy shutter over their broad
skylight, sometimes giving to the surface an appearance
as if a slight breeze struck it, or a few rain-drops fell
there. When I approached carelessly and alarmed them,
they made a sudden plash and rippling with their tails,
as if one had struck the water with a brushy bough, and
instantly took refuge in the depths. At length the wind
rose, the mist increased, and the waves began to run,
and the perch leaped much higher than before, half out
of water, a hundred black points, three inches long, at
once above the surface. Even as late as the fifth of December, one year, I saw some dimples on the surface,
and thinking it was going to rain hard immediately, the
air being full of mist, I made haste to take my place at
the oars and row homeward; already the rain seemed
rapidly increasing, though I felt none on my cheek, and
I anticipated a thorough soaking. But suddenly the dimples ceased, for they were produced by the perch, which
the noise of my oars had scared into the depths, and I
saw their schools dimly disappearing; so I spent a dry
afternoon after all.

An old man who used to frequent this pond nearly
sixty years ago, when it was dark with surrounding forests, tells me that in those days he sometimes saw it all
alive with ducks and other water-fowl, and that there
were many eagles about it. He came here a-fishing, and

used an old log canoe which he found on the shore. It was made of two white pine logs dug out and pinned together, and was cut off square at the ends. It was very clumsy, but lasted a great many years before it became water-logged and perhaps sank to the bottom. He did not know whose it was; it belonged to the pond. He used to make a cable for his anchor of strips of hickory bark tied together. An old man, a potter, who lived by the pond before the Revolution, told him once that there was an iron chest at the bottom, and that he had seen it. Sometimes it would come floating up to the shore; but when you went toward it, it would go back into deep water and disappear. I was pleased to hear of the old log canoe, which took the place of an Indian one of the same material but more graceful construction, which perchance had first been a tree on the bank, and then, as it were, fell into the water, to float there for a generation, the most proper vessel for the lake. I remember that when I first looked into these depths there were many large trunks to be seen indistinctly lying on the bottom, which had either been blown over formerly, or left on the ice at the last cutting, when wood was cheaper; but now they have mostly disappeared.

When I first paddled a boat on Walden, it was completely surrounded by thick and lofty pine and oak woods, and in some of its coves grape-vines had run over the trees next the water and formed bowers under which a boat could pass. The hills which form its shores are so steep, and the woods on them were then so high that, as you looked down from the west end, it had the appearance of an amphitheatre for some kind of sylvan spectacle. I have spent many an hour, when I was younger, floating over its surface as the zephyr willed, having paddled my boat to the middle, and lying on my back across the seats, in a summer forenoon, dreaming awake, until I was aroused by the boat touching the sand, and I arose to see what shore my fates had impelled me to; days when idleness was the most attractive and productive industry. Many a forenoon have I stolen away, preferring to spend thus the most valued part of the day; for I was rich, if not in money, in sunny hours and summer days, and spent them lavishly; nor do I re-

gret that I did not waste more of them in the workshop
or the teacher's desk. But since I left those shores the
woodchoppers have still further laid them waste, and
now for many a year there will be no more rambling
through the aisles of the wood, with occasional vistas
through which you see the water. My Muse may be ex-
cused if she is silent henceforth. How can you expect
the birds to sing when their groves are cut down?

Now the trunks of trees on the bottom, and the old
log canoe, and the dark surrounding woods, are gone,
and the villagers, who scarcely know where it lies, instead of going to the pond to bathe or drink, are thinking to bring its water, which should be as sacred as the
Ganges at least, to the village in a pipe, to wash their
dishes with!—to earn their Walden by the turning of a
cock or drawing of a plug! That devilish Iron Horse,
whose ear-rending neigh is heard throughout the town,
has muddied the Boiling Spring with his foot, and he it
is that has browsed off all the woods on Walden shore,
that Trojan horse, with a thousand men in his belly, introduced by mercenary Greeks! Where is the country's
champion, the Moore of Moore Hall, to meet him at the
Deep Cut and thrust an avenging lance between the ribs
of the bloated pest?

Nevertheless, of all the characters I have known, perhaps Walden wears best, and best preserves its purity.
Many men have been likened to it, but few deserve that
honor. Though the woodchoppers have laid bare first
this shore and then that, and the Irish have built their
sties by it, and the railroad has infringed on its border,
and the ice-men have skimmed it once, it is itself un-
changed, the same water which my youthful eyes fell on;
all the change is in me. It has not acquired one permanent wrinkle after all its ripples. It is perennially young,
and I may stand and see a swallow dip apparently to
pick an insect from its surface as of yore. It struck me
again to-night, as if I had not seen it almost daily for
more than twenty years,—Why, here is Walden, the
same woodland lake that I discovered so many years
ago; where a forest was cut down last winter another is
springing up by its shore as lustily as ever; the same
thought is welling up to its surface that was then; it is

the same liquid joy and happiness to itself and its Maker, ay, and it *may* be to me. It is the work of a brave man surely, in whom there was no guile! He rounded this water with his hand, deepened and clarified it in his thought, and in his will bequeathed it to Concord. I see by its face that it is visited by the same reflection; and I can almost say, Walden, is it you?

> It is no dream of mine,
> To ornament a line;
> I cannot come nearer to God and Heaven
> Than I live to Walden even.
> I am its stony shore,
> And the breeze that passes o'er;
> In the hollow of my hand
> Are its water and its sand,
> And its deepest resort
> Lies high in my thought.

The cars never pause to look at it; yet I fancy that the engineers and firemen and brakemen, and those passengers who have a season ticket and see it often, are better men for the sight. The engineer does not forget at night, or his nature does not, that he has beheld this vision of serenity and purity once at least during the day. Though seen but once, it helps to wash out State Street and the engine's soot. One proposes that it be called "God's Drop."

I have said that Walden has no visible inlet nor outlet, but it is on the one hand distantly and indirectly related to Flint's Pond, which is more elevated, by a chain of small ponds coming from that quarter, and on the other directly and manifestly to Concord River, which is lower, by a similar chain of ponds through which in some other geological period it may have flowed, and by a little digging, which God forbid, it can be made to flow thither again. If by living thus reserved and austere, like a hermit in the woods, so long, it has acquired such wonderful purity, who would not regret that the comparatively impure waters of Flint's Pond should be mingled with it, or itself should ever go to waste its sweetness in the ocean wave?

*   *   *

Flint's, or Sandy Pond, in Lincoln, our greatest lake
and inland sea, lies about a mile east of Walden. It is
much larger, being said to contain one hundred and
ninety-seven acres, and is more fertile in fish; but it is
comparatively shallow, and not remarkably pure. A walk
through the woods thither was often my recreation. It
was worth the while, if only to feel the wind blow on
your cheek freely, and see the waves run, and remember
the life of mariners. I went a-chestnutting there in the
fall, on windy days, when the nuts were dropping into
the water and were washed to my feet; and one day, as
I crept along its sedgy shore, the fresh spray blowing in
my face, I came upon the mouldering wreck of a boat,
the sides gone, and hardly more than the impression of
its flat bottom left amid the rushes; yet its model was
sharply defined, as if it were a large decayed pad, with
its veins. It was as impressive a wreck as one could imagine on the seashore, and had as good a moral. It is by
this time mere vegetable mould and undistinguishable
pond shore, through which rushes and flags have pushed
up. I used to admire the ripple marks on the sandy bottom, at the north end of this pond, made firm and hard
to the feet of the wader by the pressure of the water,
and the rushes which grew in Indian file, in waving lines,
corresponding to these marks, rank behind rank, as if
the waves had planted them. There also I have found,
in considerable quantities, curious balls, composed apparently of fine grass or roots, of pipewort perhaps, from
half an inch to four inches in diameter, and perfectly
spherical. These wash back and forth in shallow water
on a sandy bottom, and are sometimes cast on the shore.
They are either solid grass, or have a little sand in the
middle. At first you would say that they were formed by
the action of the waves, like a pebble; yet the smallest
are made of equally coarse materials, half an inch long,
and they are produced only at one season of the year.
Moreover, the waves, I suspect, do not so much construct as wear down a material which has already acquired consistency. They preserve their form when dry
for an indefinite period.

Flint's Pond! Such is the poverty of our nomenclature.

What right had the unclean and stupid farmer, whose
farm abutted on this sky water, whose shores he has
ruthlessly laid bare, to give his name to it? Some skin-
flint, who loved better the reflecting surface of a dollar,
or a bright cent, in which he could see his own brazen
face; who regarded even the wild ducks which settled in
it as trespassers; his fingers grown into crooked and
horny talons from the long habit of grasping harpy-
like;—so it is not named for me. I go not there to see
him nor to hear of him; who never *saw* it, who never
bathed in it, who never loved it, who never protected it,
who never spoke a good word for it, nor thanked God
that He had made it. Rather let it be named from the
fishes that swim in it, the wild fowl or quadrupeds which
frequent it, the wild flowers which grow by its shores, or
some wild man or child the thread of whose history is
interwoven with its own; not from him who could show
no title to it but the deed which a like-minded neighbor
or legislature gave him,—him who thought only of its
money value; whose presence perchance cursed all the
shores; who exhausted the land around it, and would
fain have exhausted the waters within it; who regretted
only that it was not English hay or cranberry meadow,—
there was nothing to redeem it, forsooth, in his eyes,—
and would have drained and sold it for the mud at its
bottom. It did not turn his mill, and it was no *privilege*
to him to behold it. I respect not his labors, his farm
where everything has its price, who would carry the landscape, who would carry his God, to market, if he could
get anything for him; who goes to market *for* his god as
it is; on whose farm nothing grows free, whose fields
bear no crops, whose meadows no flowers, whose trees
no fruits, but dollars; who loves not the beauty of his
fruits, whose fruits are not ripe for him till they are
turned to dollars. Give me the poverty that enjoys true
wealth. Farmers are respectable and interesting to me in
proportion as they are poor,—poor farmers. A model
farm! where the house stands like a fungus in a muck-
hcap, chambers for men, horses, oxen, and swine,
cleansed and uncleansed, all contiguous to one another;
Stocked with men! A great greasespot, redolent of ma-
nures and buttermilk! Under a high state of cultivation,

being manured with the hearts and brains of men! As if
you were to raise your potatoes in the churchyard! Such
is a model farm.

No, no; if the fairest features of the landscape are to
be named after men, let them be the noblest and worthiest men alone. Let our lakes receive as true names at
least as the Icarian Sea, where "still the shore" a "brave
attempt resounds."

Goose Pond, of small extent, is on my way to Flint's;
Fair Haven, an expansion of Concord River, said to contain some seventy acres, is a mile southwest; and White
Pond, of about forty acres, is a mile and a half beyond
Fair Haven. This is my lake country. These, with Concord River, are my water privileges; and night and day,
year in year out, they grind such grist as I carry to them.

Since the wood-cutters, and the railroad, and I myself
have profaned Walden, perhaps the most attractive, if
not the most beautiful, of all our lakes, the gem of the
woods, is White Pond;—a poor name from its common-
ness, whether derived from the remarkable purity of its
waters or the color of its sands. In these as in other
respects, however, it is a lesser twin of Walden. They
are so much alike that you would say they must be connected under ground. It has the same stony shore, and
its waters are of the same hue. As at Walden, in sultry
dog-day weather, looking down through the woods on
some of its bays which are not so deep but that the
reflection from the bottom tinges them, its waters are of
a misty bluish-green or glaucous color. Many years since
I used to go there to collect the sand by cartloads, to
make sandpaper with, and I have continued to visit it
ever since. One who frequents it proposes to call it Virid
Lake. Perhaps it might be called Yellow Pine Lake, from
the following circumstance. About fifteen years ago you
could see the top of a pitch pine, of the kind called
yellow pine hereabouts, though it is not a distinct species, projecting above the surface in deep water, many
rods from the shore. It was even supposed by some that
the pond had sunk, and this was one of the primitive
forest that formerly stood there. I find that even so long
ago as 1792, in a "Topographical Description of the

Town of Concord," by one of its citizens, in the Collec-
tions of the Massachusetts Historical Society, the author,
after speaking of Walden and White Ponds, adds, "In
the middle of the latter may be seen, when the water is
very low, a tree which appears as if it grew in the place
where it now stands, although the roots are fifty feet
below the surface of the water; the top of this tree is
broken off, and at that place measures fourteen inches
in diameter." In the spring of '49 I talked with the man
who lives nearest the pond in Sudbury, who told me that
it was he who got out this tree ten or fifteen years before. As near as he could remember, it stood twelve or
fifteen rods from the shore, where the water was thirty
or forty feet deep. It was in the winter, and he had been
getting out ice in the forenoon, and had resolved that in
the afternoon, with the aid of his neighbors, he would
take out the old yellow pine. He sawed a channel in the
ice toward the shore, and hauled it over and along and
out on to the ice with oxen; but, before he had gone far
in his work, he was surprised to find that it was wrong
end upward, with the stumps of the branches pointing
down, and the small end firmly fastened in the sandy
bottom. It was about a foot in diameter at the big end,
and he had expected to get a good saw-log, but it was
so rotten as to be fit only for fuel, if for that. He had
some of it in his shed then. There were marks of an axe
and of woodpeckers on the butt. He thought that it
might have been a dead tree on the shore, but was finally
blown over into the pond, and after the top had become
water-logged, while the butt-end was still dry and light,
had drifted out and sunk wrong end up. His father,
eighty years old, could not remember when it was not
there. Several pretty large logs may still be seen lying
on the bottom, where, owing to the undulation of the
surface, they look like huge water snakes in motion.

This pond has rarely been profaned by a boat, for
there is little in it to tempt a fisherman. Instead of the
white lily, which requires mud, or the common sweet
flag, the blue flag (*Iris versicolor*) grows thinly in the
pure water, rising from the stony bottom all around the
shore, where it is visited by hummingbirds in June; and
the color both of its bluish blades and its flowers and

especially their reflections, is in singular harmony with the glaucous water.

White Pond and Walden are great crystals on the surface of the earth, Lakes of Light. If they were permanently congealed, and small enough to be clutched, they would, perchance, be carried off by slaves, like precious stones, to adorn the heads of emperors; but being liquid, and ample, and secured to us and our successors forever, we disregard them, and run after the diamond of Kohinoor. They are too pure to have a market value; they contain no muck. How much more beautiful than our lives, how much more transparent than our characters, are they! We never learned meanness of them. How much fairer than the pool before the farmer's door, in which his ducks swim! Hither the clean wild ducks come. Nature has no human inhabitant who appreciates her. The birds with their plumage and their notes are in harmony with the flowers, but what youth or maiden conspires with the wild luxuriant beauty of Nature? She flourishes most alone, far from the towns where they reside. Talk of heaven! ye disgrace earth.

10. Baker Farm

SOMETIMES I rambled to pine groves, standing like temples, or like fleets at sea, full-rigged, with wavy boughs, and rippling with light, so soft and green and shady that the Druids would have forsaken their oaks to worship in them; or to the cedar wood beyond Flint's Pond, where the trees, covered with hoary blue berries, spiring higher and higher, are fit to stand before Valhalla, and the creeping juniper covers the ground with wreaths full of fruit; or to swamps where the usnea lichen hangs in festoons from the white spruce trees, and toadstools, round tables of the swamp gods, cover the ground, and more beautiful fungi adorn the stumps, like butterflies or shells, vegetable winkles; where the swamp-pink and dogwood grow, the red alder berry glows like eyes of imps, the waxwork grooves and crushes the hardest woods in its folds, and the wild holly berries make the beholder forget his home with their beauty, and he is dazzled and tempted by nameless other wild forbidden fruits, too fair for mortal taste. Instead of calling on some scholar, I paid many a visit to particular trees, of kinds which are rare in this neighborhood, standing far away in the middle of some pasture, or in the depths of a wood or swamp, or on a hilltop; such as the black birch, of which we have some handsome specimens two feet in diameter; its cousin, the yellow birch, with its loose golden vest, perfumed like the first; the beech, which has so neat a bole and beautifully lichen-painted, perfect in all its details, of which, excepting scattered specimens, I know but one small grove of sizable trees left in the township, supposed by some to have been planted by the pigeons that were once baited with beech-nuts near by; it is worth the while to see the silver grain sparkle when you split this wood; the bass; the hornbeam; the *Celtis occidentalis,* or false elm, of which we have but one well-grown; some taller mast of a pine, a shingle tree, or a more perfect hemlock than usual, standing like a pagoda in the midst of the woods; and many others I could mention. These were the shrines I visited both summer and winter.

Once it chanced that I stood in the very abutment of a rainbow's arch, which filled the lower stratum of the atmosphere, tingeing the grass and leaves around, and dazzling me as if I looked through colored crystal. It was a lake of rainbow light, in which, for a short while, I lived like a dolphin. If it had lasted longer it might have tinged my employments and life. As I walked on the railroad causeway, I used to wonder at the halo of light around my shadow, and would fain fancy myself one of the elect. One who visited me declared that the shadows of some Irishmen before him had no halo about them, that it was only natives that were so distinguished. Benvenuto Cellini tells us in his memoirs, that, after a certain terrible dream or vision which he had during his confinement in the castle of St. Angelo a resplendent light appeared over the shadow of his head at morning and evening, whether he was in Italy or France, and it

was particularly conspicuous when the grass was moist
with dew. This was probably the same phenomenon to
which I have referred, which is especially observed in the
morning, but also at other times, and even by moonlight.
Though a constant one, it is not commonly noticed, and,
in the case of an excitable imagination like Cellini's it
would be basis enough for superstition. Beside, he tells
us that he showed it to very few. But are they not indeed
distinguished who are conscious that they are regarded
at all?

I set out one afternoon to go a-fishing to Fair Haven,
through the woods, to eke out my scanty fare of vegetables. My way led through Pleasant Meadow, an adjunct
of the Baker Farm, that retreat of which a poet has since
sung, beginning,—

> "Thy entry is a pleasant field,
>   Which some mossy fruit trees yield
>   Partly to a ruddy brook,
>   By gliding musquash undertook,
>   And mercurial trout,
>   Darting about."

I thought of living there before I went to Walden. I
"hooked" the apples, leaped the brook, and scared the
musquash and the trout. It was one of those afternoons
which seem indefinitely long before one, in which many
events may happen, a large portion of our natural life,
though it was already half spent when I started. By the
way there came up a shower, which compelled me to
stand half an hour under a pine, piling boughs over my
head, and wearing my handkerchief for a shed; and when
at length I had made one cast over the pickerel-weed,
standing up to my middle in water, I found myself suddenly in the shadow of a cloud, and the thunder began
to rumble with such emphasis that I could do no more
than listen to it. The gods must be proud, thought I,
with such forked flashes to rout a poor unarmed fisherman. So I made haste for shelter to the nearest hut,
which stood half a mile from any road, but so much the
nearer to the pond, and had long been uninhabited:—

"And here a poet builded,
    In the completed years,
For behold a trivial cabin
    That to destruction steers."

So the Muse fables. But therein, as I found, dwelt now
John Field, an Irishman, and his wife, and several children, from the broad-faced boy who assisted his father
at his work, and now came running by his side from the
bog to escape the rain, to the wrinkled, sibyl-like, cone-
headed infant that sat upon its father's knee as in the
palaces of nobles, and looked out from its home in the
midst of wet and hunger inquisitively upon the stranger,
with the privilege of infancy, not knowing but it was the
last of a noble line, and the hope and cynosure of the
world, instead of John Field's poor starveling brat. There
we sat together under that part of the roof which leaked
the least, while it showered and thundered without. I
had sat there many times of old before the ship was built
that floated this family to America. An honest, hard-
working, but shiftless man plainly was John Field; and
his wife, she too was brave to cook so many successive
dinners in the recesses of that lofty stove; with round
greasy face and bare breast, still thinking to improve her
condition one day; with the never absent mop in one
hand, and yet no effects of it visible anywhere. The
chickens, which had also taken shelter here from the
rain, stalked about the room like members of the family,
too humanized, methought, to roast well. They stood
and looked in my eye or pecked at my shoe significantly.
Meanwhile my host told me his story, how hard he
worked "bogging" for a neighboring farmer, turning up
a meadow with a spade or bog hoe at the rate of ten
dollars an acre and the use of the land with manure for
one year, and his little broad-faced son worked cheerfully at his father's side the while, not knowing how poor
a bargain the latter had made. I tried to help him with
my experience, telling him that he was one of my nearest
neighbors, and that I too, who came a-fishing here, and
looked like a loafer, was getting my living like himself;
that I lived in a tight, light, and clean house, which
hardly cost more than the annual rent of such a ruin as

his commonly amounts to; and how, if he chose, he
might in a month or two build himself a palace of his
own; that I did not use tea, nor coffee, nor butter, nor
milk, nor fresh meat, and so did not have to work to get
them; again, as I did not work hard, I did not have to
eat hard, and it cost me but a trifle for my food; but as
he began with tea, and coffee, and butter, and milk, and
beef, he had to work hard to pay for them, and when
he had worked hard he had to eat hard again to repair
the waste of his system,—and so it was as broad as it
was long, indeed it was broader than it was long, for he
was discontented and wasted his life into the bargain;
and yet he had rated it as a gain in coming to America,
that here you could get tea, and coffee, and meat every
day. But the only true America is that country where
you are at liberty to pursue such a mode of life as may
enable you to do without these, and where the state does
not endeavor to compel you to sustain the slavery and
war and other superfluous expenses which directly or
indirectly result from the use of such things. For I pur-
posely talked to him as if he were a philosopher, or
desired to be one. I should be glad if all the meadows
on the earth were left in a wild state, if that were the
consequence of men's beginning to redeem themselves.
A man will not need to study history to find out what
is best for his own culture. But alas! the culture of an
Irishman is an enterprise to be undertaken with a sort
of moral bog hoe. I told him, that as he worked so hard
at bogging, he required thick boots and stout clothing,
which yet were soon soiled and worn out, but I wore
light shoes and thin clothing, which cost not half so
much, though he might think that I was dressed like a
gentleman (which, however, was not the case), and in
an hour or two, without labor, but as a recreation, I
could, if I wished, catch as many fish as I should want
for two days, or earn enough money to support me a
week. If he and his family would live simply, they might
all go a-huckleberrying in the summer for their amusement. John heaved a sigh at this, and his wife stared
with arms a-kimbo, and both appeared to be wondering
if they had capital enough to begin such a course with,
or arithmetic enough to carry it through. It was sailing

by dead reckoning to them, and they saw not clearly how to make their port so; therefore I suppose they still take life bravely, after their fashion, face to face, giving it tooth and nail, not having skill to split its massive columns with any fine entering wedge, and rout it in detail;—thinking to deal with it roughly, as one should handle a thistle. But they fight at an overwhelming disadvantage,—living, John Field, alas! without arithmetic, and failing so.

"Do you ever fish?" I asked. "Oh yes, I catch a mess now and then when I am lying by; good perch I catch." "What's your bait?" "I catch shiners with fishworms, and bait the perch with them." "You'd better go now, John," said his wife, with glistening and hopeful face; but John demurred.

The shower was now over, and a rainbow above the eastern woods promised a fair evening; so I took my departure. When I had got without I asked for a drink, hoping to get a sight of the well bottom, to complete my survey of the premises; but there, alas! are shallows and quicksands, and rope broken withal, and bucket irrecoverable. Meanwhile the right culinary vessel was selected, water was seemingly distilled, and after consultation and long delay passed out to the thirsty one,— not yet suffered to cool, not yet to settle. Such gruel sustains life here, I thought; so, shutting my eyes, and excluding the motes by a skilfully directed undercurrent, I drank to genuine hospitality the heartiest draught I could. I am not squeamish in such cases when manners are concerned.

As I was leaving the Irishman's roof after the rain, bending my steps again to the pond, my haste to catch pickerel, wading in retired meadows, in sloughs and bogholes, in forlorn and savage places, appeared for an instant trivial to me who had been sent to school and college; but as I ran down the hill toward the reddening west, with the rainbow over my shoulder, and some faint tinkling sounds borne to my ear through the cleansed air, from I know not what quarter, my Good Genius seemed to say,—Go fish and hunt far and wide day by day,—farther and wider,—and rest thee by many brooks and hearth-sides without misgiving. Remember thy Cre-

ator in the days of thy youth. Rise free from care before
the dawn, and seek adventures. Let the noon find thee
by other lakes, and the night overtake thee everywhere
at home. There are no larger fields than these, no worthier games than may here be played. Grow wild according to thy nature, like these sedges and brakes,
which will never become English hay. Let the thunder
rumble; what if it threaten ruin to farmers' crops? That
is not its errand to thee. Take shelter under the cloud,
while they flee to carts and sheds. Let not to get a living
be thy trade, but thy sport. Enjoy the land, but own it
not. Through want of enterprise and faith men are where
they are, buying and selling, and spending their lives
like serfs.

O Baker Farm!

> "Landscape where the richest element
> Is a little sunshine innocent." . . .

> "No one runs to revel
> On thy rail-fenced lea." . . .

> "Debate with no man hast thou,
>   With questions art never perplexed,
> As tame at the first sight as now,
>   In thy plain russet gabardine dressed." . . .

> "Come ye who love,
>   And ye who hate,
> Children of the Holy Dove,
>   And Guy Faux of the state,
> And hang conspiracies
> From the tough rafters of the trees!"

Men come tamely home at night only from the next
field or street, where their household echoes haunt, and
their life pines because it breathes its own breath over
again; their shadows, morning and evening, reach farther
than their daily steps. We should come home from far,
from adventures, and perils, and discoveries every day,
with new experience and character.

Before I had reached the pond some fresh impulse

had brought out·John Field, with altered mind, letting
go "bogging" ere this sunset. But he, poor man, disturbed only a couple of fins while I was catching a fair
string, and he said it was his luck; but when we changed
seats in the boat luck changed seats too. Poor John
Field!—I trust he does not read this, unless he will improve by it,—thinking to live by some derivative old-
country mode in this primitive new country,—to catch
perch with shiners. It is good bait sometimes, I allow.
With his horizon all his own, yet he a poor man, born
to be poor, with his inherited Irish poverty or poor life,
his Adam's grandmother and boggy ways, not to rise in
this world, he nor his posterity, till their wading webbed
bogtrotting feet get *talaria* to their heels.

11. Higher Laws

As I came home through the woods with my string of
fish, trailing my pole, it being now quite dark, I caught
a glimpse of a woodchuck stealing across my path, and
felt a strange thrill of savage delight, and was strongly
tempted to seize·and devour him raw; not that I was
hungry then, except for that wildness which he represented. Once or twice, however, while I lived·at the
pond, I found myself ranging the woods, like a half-
starved hound, with a strange abandonment, seeking
some kind of venison which I might devour, and no mor-
sel could have been too savage for me. The wildest
scenes had become unaccountably familiar. I found in
myself, and still find, an instinct toward a higher, or, as
it is named, spiritual life, as do most men, and another
toward a primitive rank and savage one, and I reverence
them both. I love the wild not less than the good. The
wildness and adventure that are in fishing still recommended it to me. I·like sometimes to take rank hold on
life and spend my day more as the animals do. Perhaps
I have owed to this employment and to hunting, when
quite young, my closest·acquaintance with Nature. They

early introduce us to and detain us in scenery with which
otherwise, at that age, we should have little acquaintance. Fishermen, hunters, wood-choppers, and others,
spending their lives in the fields and woods, in a peculiar
sense a part of Nature themselves, are often in a more
favorable mood for observing her, in the intervals of
their pursuits, than philosophers or poets even, who approach her with expectation. She is not afraid to exhibit
herself to them. The traveller on the prairie is naturally
a hunter, on the head waters of the Missouri and Columbia a trapper, and at the Falls of St. Mary a fisherman.
He who is only a traveller learns things at second-hand
and by the halves, and is poor authority. We are most
interested when science reports what those men already
know practically or instinctively, for that alone is a true
humanity, or account of human experience.

They mistake who assert that the Yankee has few
amusements, because he has not so many public holi-
days, and men and boys do not play so many games as
they do in England, for here the more primitive but solitary amusements of hunting, fishing, and the like have
not yet given place to the former. Almost every New
England boy among my contemporaries shouldered a
fowling-piece between the ages of ten and fourteen; and
his hunting and fishing grounds were not limited, like
the preserves of an English nobleman, but were more
boundless even than those of a savage. No wonder, then,
that he did not oftener stay to play on the common. But
already a change is taking place, owing, not to an increased humanity, but to an increased scarcity of game,
for perhaps the hunter is the greatest friend of the animals hunted, not excepting the Humane Society.

Moreover, when at the pond, I wished sometimes to
add fish to my fare for variety. I have actually fished
from the same kind of necessity that the first fishers did.
Whatever humanity I might conjure up against it was all
factitious, and concerned my philosophy more than my
feelings. I speak of fishing only now, for I had long felt
differently about fowling, and sold my gun before I went
to the woods. Not that I am less humane than others, but
I did not perceive that my feelings were much affected. I
did not pity the fishes nor the worms. This was habit.

As for fowling, during the last years that I carried a gun my excuse was that I was studying ornithology, and sought only new or rare birds. But I confess that I am now inclined to think that there is a finer way of studying ornithology than this. It requires so much closer attention to the habits of the birds, that, if for that reason only, I have been willing to omit the gun. Yet notwithstanding the objection on the score of humanity, I am compelled to doubt if equally valuable sports are ever substituted for these; and when some of my friends have asked me anxiously about their boys, whether they should let them hunt, I have answered, yes,—remembering that it was one of the best parts of my education,— *make* them hunters, though sportsmen only at first, if possible, mighty hunters at last, so that they shall not find game large enough for them in this or any vegetable wilderness,—hunters as well as fishers of men. Thus far I am of the opinion of Chaucer's nun, who

> "yave not of the text a pulled hen
> That saith that hunters ben not holy men."

There is a period in the history of the individual, as of the race, when the hunters are the "best men," as the Algonquins called them. We cannot but pity the boy who has never fired a gun; he is no more humane, while his education has been sadly neglected. This was my answer with respect to those youths who were bent on this pursuit, trusting that they would soon outgrow it. No humane being, past the thoughtless age of boyhood, will wantonly murder any creature which holds its life by the same tenure that he does. The hare in its extremity cries like a child. I warn you, mothers, that my sympathies do not always make the usual *philanthropic* distinctions.

Such is oftenest the young man's introduction to the forest, and the most original part of himself. He goes thither at first as a hunter and fisher, until at last, if he has the seeds of a better life in him, he distinguishes his proper objects, as a poet or naturalist it may be, and leaves the gun and fish-pole behind. The mass of men are still and always young in this respect. In some countries a hunting parson is no uncommon sight. Such a one might make a good shepherd's dog, but is far from being the Good Shepherd. I have been surprised to consider that the only obvious employment, except wood-chopping, ice-cutting, or the like business, which ever to my knowledge detained at Walden Pond for a whole half-day any of my fellow-citizens, whether fathers or children of the town, with just one exception, was fishing. Commonly they did not think that they were lucky, or well paid for their time, unless they got a long string of fish, though they had the opportunity of seeing the pond all the while. They might go there a thousand times before the sediment of fishing would sink to the bottom and leave their purpose pure; but no doubt such a clarifying process would be going on all the while. The Governor and his Council faintly remember the pond, for they went a-fishing there when they were boys; but now they are too old and dignified to go a-fishing, and so they know it no more forever. Yet even they expect to go to heaven at last. If the legislature regards it, it is chiefly to regulate the number of hooks to be used there; but they know nothing about the hook of hooks with which to angle for the pond itself, impaling the legislature for a bait. Thus, even in civilized communities, the embryo man passes through the hunter stage of development.

I have found repeatedly, of late years, that I cannot fish without falling a little in self-respect. I have tried it again and again. I have skill at it, and, like many of my fellows, a certain instinct for it, which revives from time to time, but always when I have done I feel that it would have been better if I had not fished. I think that I do not mistake. It is a faint intimation, yet so are the first streaks of morning. There is unquestionably this instinct in me which belongs to the lower orders of creation; yet with every year I am less a fisherman, though without more humanity or even wisdom; at present I am no fisherman at all. But I see that if I were to live in a wilderness I should again be tempted to become a fisher and hunter in earnest. Beside, there is something essentially unclean about this diet and all flesh, and I began to see where housework commences, and whence the endeavor, which costs so much, to wear a tidy and respectable appearance each day, to keep the house sweet and

free from all ill odors and sights. Having been a
butcher and scullion and cook, as well as the gentleman
for whom the dishes were served up, I can speak from
an unusually complete experience. The practical objection to animal food in my case was its uncleanness; and
besides, when I had caught and cleaned and cooked and
eaten my fish, they seemed not to have fed me essentially. It was insignificant and unnecessary, and cost more
than it came to. A little bread or a few potatoes would
have done as well, with less trouble and filth. Like many
of my contemporaries, I had rarely for many years used
animal food, or tea, or coffee, etc.; not so much because
of any ill effects which I had traced to them, as because
they were not agreeable to my imagination. The repug-
nance to animal food is not the effect of experience, but
is an instinct. It appeared more beautiful to live low and
fare hard in many respects; and though I never did so,
I went far enough to please my imagination. I believe
that every man who has ever been earnest to preserve
his higher or poetic faculties in the best condition has
been particularly inclined to abstain from animal food,
and from much food of any kind. It is a significant fact,
stated by entomologists,—I find it in Kirby and
Spence,—that "some insects in their perfect state,
though furnished with organs of feeding, make no use
of them;" and they lay it down as "a general rule, that
almost all insects in this state eat much less than in that
of larvæ. The voracious caterpillar when transformed
into a butterfly . . . and the gluttonous maggot when
become a fly" content themselves with a drop or two of
honey or some other sweet liquid. The abdomen under
the wings of the butterfly still represents the larva. This
is the tidbit which tempts his insectivorous fate. The
gross feeder is a man in the larva state; and there are
whole nations in that condition, nations without fancy
or imagination, whose vast abdomens betray them.

It is hard to provide and cook so simple and clean a
diet as will not offend the imagination; but this, I think,
is to be fed when we feed the body; they should both
sit down at the same table. Yet perhaps this may be
done. The fruits eaten temperately need not make us
ashamed of our appetites, nor interrupt the worthiest

pursuits. But put an extra condiment into your dish, and it will poison you. It is not worth the while to live by rich cookery. Most men would feel shame if caught preparing with their own hands precisely such a dinner, whether of animal or vegetable food, as is every day prepared for them by others. Yet till this is otherwise we are not civilized, and, if gentlemen and ladies, are not true men and women. This certainly suggests what change is to be made. It may be vain to ask why the imagination will not be reconciled to flesh and fat. I am satisfied that it is not. Is it not a reproach that man is a carnivorous animal? True, he can and does live, in a great measure, by preying on other animals; but this is a miserable way,—as any one who will go to snaring rabbits, or slaughtering lambs, may learn,—and he will be regarded as a benefactor of his race who shall teach man to confine himself to a more innocent and wholesome diet. Whatever my own practice may be, I have no doubt that it is a part of the destiny of the human race, in its gradual improvement, to leave off eating animals, as surely as the savage tribes have left off eating each other when they came in contact with the more civilized.

If one listens to the faintest but constant suggestions of his genius, which are certainly true, he sees not to what extremes, or even insanity, it may lead him; and yet that way, as he grows more resolute and faithful, his road lies. The faintest assured objection which one healthy man feels will at length prevail over the arguments and customs of mankind. No man ever followed his genius till it misled him. Though the result were bodily weakness, yet perhaps no one can say that the consequences were to be regretted, for these were a life in conformity to higher principles. If the day and the night are such that you greet them with joy, and life emits a fragrance like flowers and sweet-scented herbs, is more elastic, more starry, more immortal,—that is your success. All nature is your congratulation, and you have cause momentarily to bless yourself. The greatest gains and values are farthest from being appreciated. We easily come to doubt if they exist. We soon forget them. They are the highest reality. Perhaps the facts most astounding and most real are never communicated by man to man. The true harvest of my daily life is somewhat as intangible and indescribable as the tints of morning or evening. It is a little star-dust caught, a segment of the rainbow which I have clutched.

Yet, for my part, I was never unusually squeamish; I could sometimes eat a fried rat with a good relish, if it were necessary. I am glad to have drunk water so long, for the same reason that I prefer the natural sky to an opium-eater's heaven. I would fain keep sober always; and there are infinite degrees of drunkenness. I believe that water is the only drink for a wise man; wine is not so noble a liquor; and think of dashing the hopes of a morning with a cup of warm coffee, or of an evening with a dish of tea! Ah, how low I fall when I am tempted by them! Even music may be intoxicating. Such apparently slight causes destroyed Greece and Rome, and will destroy England and America. Of all ebriosity, who does not prefer to be intoxicated by the air he breathes? I have found it to be the most serious objection to coarse labors long continued, that they compelled me to eat and drink coarsely also. But to tell the truth, I find myself at present somewhat less particular in these respects. I carry less religion to the table, ask no blessing; not because I am wiser than I was, but, I am obliged to confess, because, however much it is to be regretted, with years I have grown more coarse and indifferent. Perhaps these questions are entertained only in youth, as most believe of poetry. My practice is "nowhere," my opinion is here. Nevertheless I am far from regarding myself as one of those privileged ones to whom the Ved refers when it says, that "he who has true faith in the Omnipresent Supreme Being may eat all that exists," that is, is not bound to inquire what is his food, or who prepares it; and even in their case it is to be observed, as a Hindoo commentator has remarked, that the Vedant limits this privilege to "the time of distress."

Who has not sometimes derived an inexpressible satisfaction from his food in which appetite had no share? I have been thrilled to think that I owed a mental perception to the commonly gross sense of taste, that I have been inspired through the palate, that some berries

which I had eaten on a hillside had fed my genius. "The
soul not being mistress of herself," says Thseng-tseu,
"one looks, and one does not see; one listens, and one
does not hear; one eats, and one does not know the
savor of food." He who distinguishes the true savor of
his food can never be a glutton; he who does not cannot
be otherwise. A puritan may go to his brown-bread crust
with as gross an appetite as ever an alderman to his
turtle. Not that food which entereth into the mouth de-
fileth a man, but the appetite with which it is eaten. It
is neither the quality nor the quantity, but the devotion
to sensual savors; when that which is eaten is not a viand
to sustain our animal, or inspire our spiritual life, but
food for the worms that possess us. If the hunter has a
taste for mud-turtles, muskrats, and other such savage
tidbits, the fine lady indulges a taste for jelly made of a
calf's foot, or for sardines from over the sea, and they
are even. He goes to the mill-pond, she to her preserve-
pot. The wonder is how they, how you and I, can live
this slimy, beastly life, eating and drinking.

Our whole life is startlingly moral. There is never an
instant's truce between virtue and vice. Goodness is the
only investment that never fails. In the music of the harp
which trembles round the world it is the insisting on this
which thrills us. The harp is the travelling patterer for
the Universe's Insurance Company, recommending its
laws, and our little goodness is all the assessment that
we pay. Though the youth at last grows indifferent, the
laws of the universe are not indifferent, but are forever
on the side of the most sensitive. Listen to every zephyr
for some reproof, for it is surely there, and he is unfortunate who does not hear it. We cannot touch a string or
move a stop but the charming moral transfixes us. Many
an irksome noise, go a long way off, is heard as music,
a proud, sweet satire on the meanness of our lives.

We are conscious of an animal in us, which awakens
in proportion as our higher nature slumbers. It is reptile
and sensual, and perhaps cannot be wholly expelled; like
the worms which, even in life and health, occupy our
bodies. Possibly we may withdraw from it, but never
change its nature. I fear that it may enjoy a certain
health of its own; that we may be well, yet not pure.

The other day I picked up the lower jaw of a hog, with white and sound teeth and tusks, which suggested that there was an animal health and vigor distinct from the spiritual. This creature succeeded by other means than temperance and purity. "That in which men differ from brute beasts," says Mencius, "is a thing very inconsiderable; the common herd lose it very soon; superior men preserve it carefully." Who knows what sort of life would result if we had attained to purify? If I knew so wise a man as could teach me purity I would go to seek him forthwith. "A command over our passions, and over the external senses of the body, and good acts, are declared by the Ved to be indispensable in the mind's approximation to God." Yet the spirit can for the time pervade and control every member and function of the body, and transmute what in form is the grossest sensuality into purity and devotion. The generative energy, which, when we are loose, dissipates and makes us unclean, when we are continent invigorates and inspires us. Chastity is the flowering of man; and what are called Genius, Heroism, Holiness, and the like, are but various fruits which succeed it. Man flows at once to God when the channel of purity is open. By turns our purity inspires and our impurity casts us down. He is blessed who is assured that the animal is dying out in him day by day, and the divine being established. Perhaps there is none but has cause for shame on account of the inferior and brutish nature to which he is allied. I fear that we are such gods or demigods only as fauns and satyrs, the divine allied to beasts, the creatures of appetite, and that, to some extent, our very life is our disgrace.—

"How happy's he who hath due place assigned
To his beasts and disafforested his mind!

. . . .

Can use his horse, goat, wolf, and ev'ry beast,
And is not ass himself to all the rest!
Else man not only is the herd of swine,
But he's those devils too which did incline
Them to a headlong rage, and made them worse."

All sensuality is one, though it takes many forms; all

purity is one. It is the same whether a man eat, or drink, or cohabit, or sleep sensually. They are but one appetite, and we only need to see a person do any one of these things to know how great a sensualist he is. The impure can neither stand nor sit with purity. When the reptile is attacked at one mouth of his burrow, he shows himself at another. If you would be chaste, you must be temperate. What is chastity? How shall a man know if he is chaste? He shall not know it. We have heard of this virtue, but we know not what it is. We speak conformably to the rumor which we have heard. From exertion come wisdom and purity; from sloth ignorance and sensuality. In the student sensuality is a sluggish habit of mind. An unclean person is universally a slothful one, one who sits by a stove, whom the sun shines on prostrate, who reposes without being fatigued. If you would avoid uncleanness, and all the sins, work earnestly, though it be at cleaning a stable. Nature is hard to be overcome, but she must be overcome. What avails it that you are Christian, if you are not purer than the heathen, if you deny yourself no more, if you are not more religious? I know of many systems of religion esteemed heathenish whose precepts fill the reader with shame, and provoke him to new endeavors, though it be to the performance of rites merely.

I hesitate to say these things, but it is not because of the subject,—I care not how obscene my *words* are,— but because I cannot speak of them without betraying my impurity. We discourse freely without shame of one form of sensuality, and are silent about another. We are so degraded that we cannot speak simply of the necessary functions of human nature. In earlier ages, in some countries, every function was reverently spoken of and regulated by law. Nothing was too trivial for the Hindoo lawgiver, however offensive it may be to modern taste. He teaches how to eat, drink, cohabit, void excrement and urine and the like, elevating what is mean, and does not falsely excuse himself by calling these things trifles.

Every man is the builder of a temple, called his body, to the god he worships, after a style purely his own, nor can he get off by hammering marble instead. We are all sculptors and painters, and our material is our own flesh and blood and bones. Any nobleness begins at once to refine a man's features, any meanness or sensuality to imbrute them.

John Farmer sat at his door one September evening, after a hard day's work, his mind still running on his labor more or less. Having bathed, he sat down to re-create his intellectual man. It was a rather cool evening, and some of his neighbors were apprehending a frost. He had not attended to the train of his thoughts long when he heard some one playing on a flute, and that sound harmonized with his mood. Still he thought of his work; but the burden of his thought was, that though this kept running in his head, and he found himself planning and contriving it against his will, yet it concerned him very little. It was no more than the scurf of his skin, which was constantly shuffled off. But the notes of the flute came home to his ears out of a different sphere from that he worked in, and suggested work for certain faculties which slumbered in him. They gently did away with the street, and the village, and the state in which he lived. A voice said to him,—Why do you stay here and live this mean moiling life, when a glorious existence is possible for you? Those same stars twinkle over other fields than these.—But how to come out of this condition and actually migrate thither? All that he could think of was to practise some new austerity, to let his mind descend into his body and redeem it, and treat himself with ever increasing respect.

12. Brute Neighbors

SOMETIMES I had a companion in my fishing, who came through the village to my house from the other side of the town, and the catching of the dinner was as much a social exercise as the eating of it.

Hermit. I wonder what the world is doing now. I have not heard so much as a locust over the sweet-fern these three hours. The pigeons are all asleep upon their

roosts,—no flutter from them. Was that a farmer's noon
horn which sounded from beyond the woods just now?
The hands are coming in to boiled salt beef and cider
and Indian bread. Why will men worry themselves so?
He that does not eat need not work. I wonder how much
they have reaped. Who would live there where a body
can never think for the barking of Bose? And oh, the
housekeeping! to keep bright the devil's door-knobs, and
scour his tubs this bright day! Better not keep a house.
Say, some hollow tree; and then for morning calls and
dinner-parties! Only a woodpecker tapping. Oh, they
swarm; the sun is too warm there; they are born too far
into life for me. I have water from the spring, and a loaf
of brown bread on the shelf.—Hark! I hear a rustling of
the leaves. Is it some ill-fed village hound yielding to the
instinct of the chase? or the lost pig which is said to be
in these woods, whose tracks I saw after the rain? It
comes on apace; my sumachs and sweet-briers tremble.—Eh, Mr. Poet, is it you? How do you like the world
to-day?

Poet. See those clouds; how they hang! That's the
greatest thing I have seen to-day. There's nothing like it
in old paintings, nothing like it in foreign lands,—unless
when we were off the coast of Spain. That's a true Medi-
terranean sky. I thought, as I have my living to get, and
have not eaten to-day, that I might go a-fishing. That's
the true industry for poets. It is the only trade I have
learned. Come, let's along.

Hermit. I cannot resist. My brown bread will soon be
gone. I will go with you gladly soon, but I am just con-
cluding a serious meditation. I think that I am near the
end of it. Leave me alone, then, for a while. But that
we may not be delayed, you shall be digging the bait
meanwhile. Angleworms are rarely to be met with in
these parts, where the soil was never fattened with manure; the race is nearly extinct. The sport of digging the
bait is nearly equal to that of catching the fish, when
one's appetite is not too keen; and this you may have
all to yourself to-day. I would advise you to set in the
spade down yonder among the ground-nuts, where you
see the johnswort waving. I think that I may warrant
you one worm to every three sods you turn up, if you

look well in among the roots of the grass, as if you were weeding. Or, if you choose to go farther, it will not be unwise, for I have found the increase of fair bait to be very nearly as the squares of the distances.

Hermit alone. Let me see; where was I? Methinks I was nearly in this frame of mind; the world lay about at this angle. Shall I go to heaven or a-fishing? If I should soon bring this meditation to an end, would another so sweet occasion be likely to offer? I was as near being resolved into the essence of things as ever I was in my life. I fear my thoughts will not come back to me. If it would do any good, I would whistle for them. When they make us an offer, is it wise to say, We will think of it? My thoughts have left no track, and I cannot find the path again. What was it that I was thinking of? It was a very hazy day. I will just try these three sentences of Confutsee; they may fetch that state about again. I know not whether it was the dumps or a budding ecstasy. Mem. There never is but one opportunity of a kind.

Poet. How now, Hermit, is it too soon? I have got just thirteen whole ones, beside several which are imperfect or undersized; but they will do for the smaller fry; they do not cover up the hook so much. Those village worms are quite too large; a shiner may make a meal off one without finding the skewer.

Hermit. Well, then, let's be off. Shall we to the Concord? There's good sport there if the water be not too high.

Why do precisely these objects which we behold make a world? Why has man just these species of animals for his neighbors; as if nothing but a mouse could have filled this crevice? I suspect that Pilpay & Co. have put animals to their best use, for they are all beasts of burden, in a sense, made to carry some portion of our thoughts.

The mice which haunted my house were not the common ones, which are said to have been introduced into the country, but a wild native kind not found in the village. I sent one to a distinguished naturalist, and it interested him much. When I was building, one of these had its nest underneath the house, and before I had laid

the second floor, and swept out the shavings, would
come out regularly at lunch time and pick up the crumbs
at my feet. It probably had never seen a man before;
and it soon became quite familiar, and would run over
my shoes and up my clothes. It could readily ascend the
sides of the room by short impulses, like a squirrel,
which it resembled in its motions. At length, as I leaned
with my elbow on the bench one day, it ran up my clothes,
and along my sleeve, and round and round the paper
which held my dinner, while I kept the latter close,
and dodged and played at bopeep with it; and when
at last I held still a piece of cheese between my thumb
and finger, it came and nibbled it, sitting in my hand, and
afterward cleaned its face and paws, like a fly, and
walked away.

A phœbe soon built in my shed, and a robin for protection in a pine which grew against the house. In June
the partridge (*Tetrao umbellus*), which is so shy a bird,
led her brood past my windows, from the woods in the
rear to the front of my house, clucking and calling to
them like a hen, and in all her behavior proving herself
the hen of the woods. The young suddenly disperse on
your approach, at a signal from the mother, as if a whirlwind had swept them away, and they so exactly resemble
the dried leaves and twigs that many a traveller has
placed his foot in the midst of a brood, and heard the
whir of the old bird as she flew off, and her anxious calls
and mewing, or seen her trail her wings to attract his
attention, without suspecting their neighborhood. The
parent will sometimes roll and spin round before you in
such a dishabille, that you cannot, for a few moments,
detect what kind of creature it is. The young squat still
and flat, often running their heads under a leaf, and
mind only their mother's directions given from a distance, nor will your approach make them run again and
betray themselves. You may even tread on them, or have
your eyes on them for a minute, without discovering
them. I have held them in my open hand at such a time,
and still their only care, obedient to their mother and
their instinct, was to squat there without fear or
trembling. So perfect is this instinct, that once, when I
had laid them on the leaves again, and one accidentally

fell on its side, it was found with the rest in exactly the same position ten minutes afterward. They are not callow like the young of most birds, but more perfectly developed and precocious even than chickens. The remarkably adult yet innocent expression of their open and serene eyes is very memorable. All intelligence seems reflected in them. They suggest not merely the purity of infancy, but a wisdom clarified by experience. Such an eye was not born when the bird was, but is coeval with the sky it reflects. The woods do not yield another such a gem. The traveller does not often look into such a limpid well. The ignorant or reckless sportsman often shoots the parent at such a time, and leaves these innocents to fall a prey to some prowling beast or bird, or gradually mingle with the decaying leaves which they so much resemble. It·is said that when hatched by a hen they will directly disperse on some alarm, and so are lost, for they never hear the mother's call which gathers them again. These were my hens and chickens.

It is remarkable how many creatures live wild and free though secret in the woods, and still sustain themselves in the neighborhood of towns, suspected by hunters only. How retired the otter manages to live here! He grows to be four feet long, as big as a small boy, perhaps without any human being getting a glimpse of him. I formerly saw the raccoon in the woods behind where my house is built, and probably still heard their whinnering at night. Commonly I rested an hour or two in the shade at noon, after planting, and ate my lunch, and read a little by a spring which was the source of a swamp and of a brook, oozing from under Brister's Hill, half a mile from my field. The approach to this was through a succession of descending grassy hollows, full of young pitch pines, into a larger wood about the swamp. There, in a very secluded and shaded spot, under a spreading white pine, there was yet a clean, firm sward to sit on. I had dug out the spring and made a well of clear gray water, where I could dip up a pailful without roiling it, and thither I went for this purpose almost every day in midsummer, when the pond was warmest. Thither, too, the woodcock led her brood, to probe the mud for worms, flying but a foot above them down the bank, while they

ran in a troop beneath; but at last, spying me, she would
leave her young and circle round and round me, nearer
and nearer till within four or five feet, pretending broken
wings and legs, to attract my attention, and get off her
young, who would already have taken up their march,
with faint, wiry peep, single file through the swamp, as
she directed. Or I heard the peep of the young when I
could not see the parent bird. There too the turtle doves
sat over the spring, or fluttered from bough to bough of
the soft white pines over my head; or the red squirrel,
coursing down the nearest bough, was particularly familiar and inquisitive. You only need sit still long enough
in some attractive spot in the woods that all its inhabitants may exhibit themselves to you by turns.

I was witness to events of a less peaceful character.
One day when I went out to my wood-pile, or rather
my pile of stumps, I observed two large ants, the one
red, the other much larger, nearly half an inch long, and
black, fiercely contending with one another. Having once
got hold they never let go, but struggled and wrestled
and rolled on the chips incessantly. Looking farther, I
was surprised to find that the chips were covered with
such combatants, that it was not a *duellum,* but a *bellum,*
a war between two races of ants, the red always pitted
against the black, and frequently two red ones to one
black. The legions of these Myrmidons covered all the
hills and vales in my wood-yard, and the ground was
already strewn with the dead and dying, both red and
black. It was the only battle which I have ever witnessed,
the only battle-field I ever trod while the battle was raging; internecine war; the red republicans on the one
hand, and the black imperialists on the other. On every
side they were engaged in deadly combat, yet without
any noise that I could hear, and human soldiers never
fought so resolutely. I watched a couple that were fast
locked in each other's embraces, in a little sunny valley
amid the chips, now at noonday prepared to fight till the
sun went down, or life went out. The smaller red champion had fastened himself like a vise to his adversary's
front, and through all the tumblings on that field never
for an instant ceased to gnaw at one of his feelers near
the root, having already caused the other to go by the

board; while the stronger black one dashed him from side to side, and, as I saw on looking nearer, had already divested him of several of his members. They fought with more pertinacity than bulldogs. Neither manifested the least disposition to retreat. It was evident that their battle-cry was "Conquer or die." In the meanwhile there came along a single red ant on the hillside of this valley, evidently full of excitement, who either had despatched his foe, or had not yet taken part in the battle; probably the latter, for he had lost none of his limbs; whose mother had charged him to return with his shield or upon it. Or perchance he was some Achilles, who had nourished his wrath apart, and had now come to avenge or rescue his Patroclus. He saw this unequal combat from afar,—for the blacks were nearly twice the size of the red,—he drew near with rapid pace till he stood on his guard within half an inch of the combatants; then, watching his opportunity, he sprang upon the black warrior, and commenced his operations near the root of his right fore leg, leaving the foe to select among his own members; and so there were three united for life, as if a new kind of attraction had been invented which put all other locks and cements to shame. I should not have wondered by this time to find that they had their respective musical bands stationed on some eminent chip, and playing their national airs the while, to excite the slow and cheer the dying combatants. I was myself excited somewhat even as if they had been men. The more you think of it, the less the difference. And certainly there is not the fight recorded in Concord history, at least, if in the history of America, that will bear a moment's comparison with this, whether for the numbers engaged in it, or for the patriotism and heroism displayed. For numbers and for carnage it was an Austerlitz or Dresden. Concord fight! Two killed on the patriots' side, and Luther Blanchard wounded! Why here every ant was a Buttrick,—"Fire, for God's sake fire!"—and thousands shared the fate of Davis and Hosmer. There was not one hireling there. I have no doubt that it was a principle they fought for, as much as our ancestors, and not to avoid a three-penny tax on their tea; and the results of this battle will be as important and memorable to those

whom it concerns as those of the battle of Bunker Hill,
at least.

I took up the chip on which the three I have particularly described were struggling, carried it into my house,
and placed it under a tumbler on my window-sill, in
order to see the issue. Holding a microscope to the first-
mentioned red ant, I saw that, though he was assiduously
gnawing at the near fore leg of his enemy, having severed his remaining feeler, his own breast was all torn
away, exposing what vitals he had there to the jaws of
the black warrior, whose breastplate was apparently too
thick for him to pierce; and the dark carbuncles of the
sufferer's eyes shone with ferocity such as war only could
excite. They struggled half an hour longer under the
tumbler, and when I looked again the black soldier had
severed the heads of his foes from their bodies, and the
still living heads were hanging on either side of him like
ghastly trophies at his saddle-bow, still apparently as
firmly fastened as ever, and he was endeavoring with
feeble struggles, being without feelers and with only the
remnant of a leg, and I know not how many other
wounds, to divest himself of them; which at length, after
half an hour or more, he accomplished. I raised the glass,
and he went off over the window-sill in that crippled
state. Whether he finally survived that combat, and spent
the remainder of his days in some Hôtel des Invalides,
I do not know; but I thought that his industry would not
be worth much thereafter. I never learned which party
was victorious, nor the cause of the war; but I felt for
the rest of that day as if I had had my feelings excited
and harrowed by witnessing the struggle, the ferocity
and carnage, of a human battle before my door.

Kirby and Spence tell us that the battles of ants have
long been celebrated and the date of them recorded,
though they say that Huber is the only modern author
who appears to have witnessed them. "Æneas Sylvius,"
say they, "after giving a very circumstantial account of
one contested with great obstinacy by a great and small
species on the trunk of a pear tree," adds that " 'this
action was fought in the pontificate of Eugenius the
Fourth, in the presence of Nicholas Pistoriensis, an eminent lawyer, who related the whole history of the battle

with the greatest fidelity.' A similar engagement between great and small ants is recorded by Olaus Magnus, in which the small ones, being victorious, are said to have buried the bodies of their own soldiers, but left those of their giant enemies a prey to the birds. This event happened previous to the expulsion of the tyrant Christiern the Second from Sweden." The battle which I witnessed took place in the Presidency of Polk, five years before the passage of Webster's Fugitive-Slave Bill.

Many a village Bose, fit only to course a mud-turtle in a victualling cellar, sported his heavy quarters in the woods, without the knowledge of his master, and ineffectually smelled at old fox burrows and woodchucks' holes; led perchance by some slight cur which nimbly threaded the wood, and might still inspire a natural terror in its denizens;—now far behind his guide, barking like a canine bull toward some small squirrel which had treed itself for scrutiny, then, cantering off, bending the bushes with his weight, imagining that he is on the track of some stray member of the jerbilla family. Once I was surprised to see a cat walking along the stony shore of the pond, for they rarely wander so far from home. The surprise was mutual. Nevertheless the most domestic cat, which has lain on a rug all her days, appears quite at home in the woods, and, by her sly and stealthy behavior, proves herself more native there than the regular inhabitants. Once, when berrying, I met with a cat with young kittens in the woods, quite wild, and they all, like their mother had their backs up and were fiercely spitting at me. A few years before I lived in the woods there was what was called a "winged cat" in one of the farmhouses in Lincoln nearest the pond, Mr. Gilian Baker's. When I called to see her in June, 1842, she was gone a-hunting in the woods, as was her wont (I am not sure whether it was a male or female, and so use the more common pronoun), but her mistress told me that she came into the neighborhood a little more than a year before, in April, and was finally taken into their house; that she was of a dark brownish-gray color, with a white spot on her throat, and white feet, and had a large bushy tail like a fox; that in the winter the fur grew thick and flatted out along her sides, forming strips ten or twelve inches long by two and a half wide, and under her chin like a muff, the upper side loose, the under matted like felt, and in the spring these appendages dropped off. They gave me a pair of her "wings," which I keep still. There is no appearance of a membrane about them. Some thought it was part flying squirrel or some other wild animal, which is not impossible, for, according to naturalists, prolific hybrids have been produced by the union of the marten and domestic cat. This would have been the right kind of cat for me to keep, if I had kept any; for why should not a poet's cat be winged as well as his horse?

In the fall the loon (*Colymbus glacialis*) came, as usual, to moult and bathe in the pond, making the woods ring with his wild laughter before I had risen. At rumor of his arrival all the Mill-dam sportsmen are on the alert, in gigs and on foot, two by two and three by three, with patent rifles and conical balls and spy-glasses. They come rustling through the woods like autumn leaves, at least ten men to one loon. Some station themselves on this side of the pond, some on that, for the poor bird cannot be omnipresent; if he dive here he must come up there. But now the kind October wind rises, rustling the leaves and rippling the surface of the water, so that no loon can be heard or seen, though his foes sweep the pond with spy-glasses, and make the woods resound with their discharges. The waves generously rise and dash angrily, taking sides with all water-fowl, and our sportsmen must beat a retreat to town and shop and unfinished jobs. But they were too often successful. When I went to get a pail of water early in the morning I frequently saw this stately bird sailing out of my cove within a few rods. If I endeavored to overtake him in a boat, in order to see how he would manœuvre, he would dive and be completely lost, so that I did not discover him again, sometimes, till the latter part of the day. But I was more than a match for him on the surface. He commonly went off in a rain.

As I was paddling along the north shore one very calm October afternoon, for such days especially they settle on to the lakes, like the milkweed down, having looked in vain over the pond for a loon, suddenly one, sailing

out from the shore toward the middle a few rods in front
of me, set up his wild laugh and betrayed himself. I
pursued with a paddle and he dived, but when he came
up I was nearer than before. He dived again, but I mis-
calculated the direction he would take, and we were fifty
rods apart when he came to the surface this time, for I
had helped to widen the interval; and again he laughed
long and loud, and with more reason than before. He
manœuvred so cunningly that I could not get within half
a dozen rods of him. Each time, when he came to the
surface, turning his head this way and that, he coolly
surveyed the water and the land, and apparently chose
his course so that he might come up where there was
the widest expanse of water and at the greatest distance
from the boat. It was surprising how quickly he made
up his mind and put his resolve into execution. He led
me at once to the widest part of the pond, and could
not be driven from it. While he was thinking one thing
in his brain, I was endeavoring to divine his thought in
mine. It was a pretty game, played on the smooth surface
of the pond, a man against a loon. Suddenly your adversary's checker disappears beneath the board, and the
problem is to place yours nearest to where his will appear again. Sometimes he would come up unexpectedly
on the opposite side of me, having apparently passed
directly under the boat. So long-winded was he and so
unweariable, that when he had swum farthest he would
immediately plunge again, nevertheless; and then no wit
could divine where in the deep pond, beneath the
smooth surface, he might be speeding his way like a fish,
for he had time and ability to visit the bottom of the
pond in its deepest part. It is said that loons have been
caught in the New York lakes eighty feet beneath the
surface, with hooks set for trout,—though Walden is
deeper than that. How surprised must the fishes be to
see this ungainly visitor from another sphere speeding
his way amid their schools! Yet he appeared to know
his course as surely under water as on the surface, and
swam much faster there. Once or twice I saw a ripple
where he approached the surface, just put his head out
to reconnoitre, and instantly dived again. I found that it
was as well for me to rest on my oars and wait his reap-

pearing as to endeavor to calculate where he would rise;
for again and again, when I was straining my eyes over
the surface one way, I would suddenly be startled by his
unearthly laugh behind me. But why, after displaying so
much cunning, did he invariably betray himself the moment he came up by that loud laugh? Did not his white
breast enough betray him? He was indeed a silly loon,
I thought. I could commonly hear the splash of the water
when he came up, and so also detected him. But after
an hour he seemed as fresh as ever, dived as willingly,
and swam yet farther than at first. It was surprising to
see how serenely he sailed off with unruffled breast
when he came to the surface, doing all the work with his
webbed feet beneath. His usual note was this demoniac
laughter, yet somewhat like that of a water-fowl; but
occasionally, when he had balked me most successfully
and come up a long way off, he uttered a long-drawn
unearthly howl, probably more like that of a wolf than
any bird; as when a beast puts his muzzle to the ground
and deliberately howls. This was his looning,—perhaps
the wildest sound that is ever heard here, making the
woods ring far and wide. I concluded that he laughed in
derision of my efforts, confident of his own resources.
Though the sky was by this time overcast, the pond was
so smooth that I could see where he broke the surface
when I did not hear him. His white breast, the stillness
of the air, and the smoothness of the water were all
against him. At length having come up fifty rods off, he
uttered one of those prolonged howls, as if calling on
the god of loons to aid him, and immediately there came
a wind from the east and rippled the surface, and filled
the whole air with misty rain, and I was impressed as if
it were the prayer of the loon answered, and his god
was angry with me; and so I left him disappearing far
away on the tumultuous surface.

For hours, in fall days, I watched the ducks cunningly
tack and veer and hold the middle of the pond, far from
the sportsman; tricks which they will have less need to
practise in Louisiana bayous. When compelled to rise
they would sometimes circle round and round and over
the pond at a considerable height, from which they could
easily see to other ponds and the river, like black motes

in the sky; and, when I thought they had gone off thither long since, they would settle down by a slanting flight of a quarter of a mile on to a distant part which was left free; but what beside safety they got by sailing in the middle of Walden I do not know, unless they love its water for the same reason that I do.

13. House-Warming

IN OCTOBER I went a-graping to the river meadows, and loaded myself with clusters more precious for their beauty and fragrance than for food. There, too, I admired, though I did not gather, the cranberries, small waxen gems, pendants of the meadow grass, pearly and red, which the farmer plucks with an ugly rake, leaving the smooth meadow in a snarl, heedlessly measuring them by the bushel and the dollar only, and sells the spoils of the meads to Boston and New York: destined to be *jammed,* to satisfy the tastes of lovers of Nature there. So butchers rake the tongues of bison out of the prairie grass, regardless of the torn and drooping plant. The barberry's brilliant fruit was likewise food for my eyes merely; but I collected a small store of wild apples for coddling, which the proprietor and travellers had overlooked. When chestnuts were ripe I laid up half a bushel for winter. It was very exciting at that season to roam the then boundless chestnut woods of Lincoln,— they now sleep their long sleep under the railroad,— with a bag on my shoulder, and a stick to open burs with in my hand, for I did not always wait for the frost, amid the rustling of leaves and the loud reproofs of the red squirrels and the jays, whose half-consumed nuts I sometimes stole, for the burs which they had selected were sure to contain sound ones. Occasionally I climbed and shook the trees. They grew also behind my house, and one large tree, which almost overshadowed it, was, when in flower, a bouquet which scented the whole neighborhood, but the squirrels and the jays got most of its fruit; the last coming in flocks early in the morning and picking the nuts out of the burs before they fell. I relinquished these trees to them and visited the more distant woods composed wholly of chestnut. These nuts, as far as they went, were a good substitute for bread. Many other substitutes might, perhaps, be found. Digging one day for fishworms, I discovered the ground-nut (*Apios tuberosa*) on its string, the potato of the aborigines, a sort of fabulous fruit, which I had begun to doubt if I had ever dug and eaten in childhood, as I had told, and had not dreamed it. I had often since seen its crimpled red velvety blossom supported by the stems of other plants without knowing it to be the same. Cultivation has well-nigh exterminated it. It has a sweetish taste, much like that of a frost-bitten potato, and I found it better boiled than roasted. This tuber seemed like a faint promise of Nature to rear her own children and feed them simply here at some future period. In these days of fatted cattle and waving grain-fields this humble root, which was once the *totem* of an Indian tribe, is quite forgotten, or known only by its flowering vine; but let wild Nature reign here once more, and the tender and luxurious English grains will probably disappear before a myriad of foes, and without the care of man the crow may carry back even the last seed of corn to the great cornfield of the Indian's God in the southwest, whence he is said to have brought it; but the now almost exterminated ground-nut will perhaps revive and flourish in spite of frosts and wildness, prove itself indigenous, and resume its ancient importance and dignity as the diet of the hunter tribe. Some Indian Ceres or Minerva must have been the inventor and bestower of it; and when the reign of poetry commences here, its leaves and string of nuts may be represented on our works of art.

Already, by the first of September, I had seen two or three small maples turned scarlet across the pond, beneath where the white stems of three aspens diverged, at the point of a promontory, next the water. Ah, many a tale their color told! And gradually from week to week the character of each tree came out, and it admired itself reflected in the smooth mirror of the lake. Each morning the manager of this gallery substituted some new picture, distinguished by more brilliant or harmonious coloring, for the old upon the walls.

The wasps came by thousands to my lodge in October, as to winter quarters, and settled on my windows within and on the walls overhead, sometimes deterring visitors from entering. Each morning, when they were numbed with cold, I swept some of them out, but I did not trouble myself much to get rid of them; I even felt complimented by their regarding my house as a desirable shelter. They never molested me seriously, though they bedded with me; and they gradually disappeared, into what crevices I do not know, avoiding winter and unspeakable cold.

Like the wasps, before I finally went into winter quarters in November, I used to resort to the northeast side of Walden, which the sun, reflected from the pitch pine woods and the stony shore, made the fireside of the pond; it is so much pleasanter and wholesomer to be warmed by the sun while you can be, than by an artificial fire. I thus warmed myself by the still glowing embers which the summer, like a departed hunter, had left.

When I came to build my chimney I studied masonry. My bricks, being second-hand ones, required to be cleaned with a trowel, so that I learned more than usual of the qualities of bricks and trowels. The mortar on them was fifty years old, and was said to be still growing harder; but this is one of those sayings which men love to repeat whether they are true or not. Such sayings themselves grow harder and adhere more firmly with age, and it would take many blows with a trowel to clean an old wiseacre of them. Many of the villages of Mesopotamia are built of second-hand bricks of a very good quality, obtained from the ruins of Babylon, and the cement on them is older and probably harder still. However that may be, I was struck by the peculiar toughness of the steel which bore so many violent blows without being worn out. As my bricks had been in a chimney before, though I did not read the name of Nebuchadnezzar on them, I picked out as many fireplace bricks as I could find, to save work and waste, and I filled the spaces between the bricks about the fireplace with stones

from the pond shore, and also made my mortar with the
white sand from the same place. I lingered most about
the fireplace, as the most vital part of the house. Indeed,
I worked so deliberately, that though I commenced at
the ground in the morning, a course of bricks raised a
few inches above the floor served for my pillow at night;
yet I did not get a stiff neck for it that I remember; my
stiff neck is of older date. I took a poet to board for a
fortnight about those times, which caused me to be put
to it for room. He brought his own knife, though I had
two, and we used to scour them by thrusting them into
the earth. He shared with me the labors of cooking. I
was pleased to see my work rising so square and solid
by degrees, and reflected, that, if it proceeded slowly, it
was calculated to endure a long time. The chimney is to
some extent an independent structure, standing on the
ground, and rising through the house to the heavens;
even after the house is burned it still stands sometimes,
and its importance and independence are apparent. This
was toward the end of summer. It was now November.

The north wind had already begun to cool the pond,
though it took many weeks of steady blowing to accomplish it, it is so deep. When I began to have a fire at
evening, before I plastered my house, the chimney carried smoke particularly well, because of the numerous
chinks between the boards. Yet I passed some cheerful
evenings in that cool and airy apartment, surrounded by
the rough brown boards full of knots, and rafters with
the bark on high overhead. My house never pleased my
eye so much after it was plastered, though I was obliged
to confess that it was more comfortable. Should not
every apartment in which man dwells be lofty enough to
create some obscurity overhead, where flickering shadows may play at evening about the rafters? These forms
are more agreeable to the fancy and imagination than
fresco paintings or other the most expensive furniture. I
now first began to inhabit my house, I may say, when I
began to use it for warmth as well as shelter. I had got a
couple of old fire-dogs to keep the wood from the hearth,
and it did me good to see the soot form on the back of
the chimney which I had built, and I poked the fire with

more right and more satisfaction than usual. My dwelling was small, and I could hardly entertain an echo in it; but it seemed larger for being a single apartment and remote from neighbors. All the attractions of a house were concentrated in one room; it was kitchen, chamber, parlor, and keeping-room; and whatever satisfaction parent or child, master or servant, derive from living in a house, I enjoyed it all. Cato says, the master of a family (*patremfamilias*) must have in his rustic villa "cellam oleariam, vinariam, dolia multa, uti lubeat caritatem expectare, et rei, et virtuti, et gloriae erit," that is, "an oil and wine cellar, many casks, so that it may be pleasant to expect hard times; it will be for his advantage, and virtue, and glory." I had in my cellar a firkin of potatoes, about two quarts of peas with the weevil in them, and on my shelf a little rice, a jug of molasses, and of rye and Indian meal a peck each.

I sometimes dream of a larger and more populous house, standing in a golden age, of enduring materials, and without gingerbread work, which shall still consist of only one room, a vast, rude, substantial, primitive hall, without ceiling or plastering, with bare rafters and purlins supporting a sort of lower heaven over one's head,— useful to keep off rain and snow, where the king and queen posts stand out to receive your homage, when you have done reverence to the prostrate Saturn of an older dynasty on stepping over the sill; a cavernous house, wherein you must reach up a torch upon a pole to see the roof; where some may live in the fireplace, some in the recess of the window, and some on settles, some at one end of the hall, some at another, and some aloft on rafters with the spiders, if they choose; a house which you have got into when you have opened the outside door, and the ceremony is over; where the weary traveller may wash, and eat, and converse, and sleep, without further journey; such a shelter as you would be glad to reach in a tempestuous night, containing all the essentials of a house, and nothing for house-keeping; where you can see all the treasures of the house at one view, and everything hangs upon its peg that a man should use; at once kitchen, pantry, parlor, chamber, storehouse, and garret; where you can see so necessary a

thing as a barrel or a ladder, so convenient a thing as a
cupboard, and hear the pot boil, and pay your respects
to the fire that cooks your dinner, and the oven that
bakes your bread, and the necessary furniture and utensils are the chief ornaments; where the washing is not
put out, nor the fire, nor the mistress, and perhaps you
are sometimes requested to move from off the trap-door,
when the cook would descend into the cellar, and so
learn whether the ground is solid or hollow beneath you
without stamping. A house whose inside is as open and
manifest as a bird's nest, and you cannot go in at the
front door and out at the back without seeing some of
its inhabitants; where to be a guest is to be presented
with the freedom of the house, and not to be carefully
excluded from seven eighths of it, shut up in a particular
cell, and told to make yourself at home there,—in solitary confinement. Nowadays the host does not admit you
to *his* hearth, but has got the mason to build one for
yourself somewhere in his alley, and hospitality is the
art of *keeping* you at the greatest distance. There is as
much secrecy about the cooking as if he had a design to
poison you. I am aware that I have been on many a
man's premises, and might have been legally ordered off,
but I am not aware that I have been in many men's
houses. I might visit in my old clothes a king and queen
who lived simply in such a house as I have described, if
I were going their way; but backing out of a modern
palace will be all that I shall desire to learn, if ever I
am caught in one.

It would seem as if the very language of our parlors
would lose all its nerve and degenerate into *palaver*
wholly, our lives pass at such remoteness from its sym-
bols, and its metaphors and tropes are necessarily so far
fetched, through slides and dumb-waiters, as it were; in
other words, the parlor is so far from the kitchen and
workshop. The dinner even is only the parable of a dinner, commonly. As if only the savage dwelt near enough
to Nature and Truth to borrow a trope from them. How
can the scholar, who dwells away in the North West
Territory or the Isle of Man, tell what is parliamentary
in the kitchen?

However, only one or two of my guests were ever

bold enough to stay and eat a hasty-pudding with me; but when they saw that crisis approaching they beat a hasty retreat rather, as if it would shake the house to its foundations. Nevertheless, it stood through a great many hasty-puddings.

I did not plaster till it was freezing weather. I brought over some whiter and cleaner sand for this purpose from the opposite shore of the pond in a boat, a sort of conveyance which would have tempted me to go much farther if necessary. My house had in the meanwhile been shingled down to the ground on every side. In lathing I was pleased to be able to send home each nail with a single blow of the hammer, and it was my ambition to transfer the plaster from the board to the wall neatly and rapidly. I remembered the story of a conceited fellow, who, in fine clothes, was wont to lounge about the village once, giving advice to workmen. Venturing one day to substitute deeds for words, he turned up his cuffs, seized a plasterer's board, and having loaded his trowel without mishap, with a complacent look toward the lathing overhead, made a bold gesture thitherward; and straightway, to his complete discomfiture, received the whole contents in his ruffled bosom. I admired anew the economy and convenience of plastering, which so effectually shuts out the cold and takes a handsome finish, and I learned the various casualties to which the plasterer is liable. I was surprised to see how thirsty the bricks were which drank up all the moisture in my plaster before I had smoothed it, and how many pailfuls of water it takes to christen a new hearth. I had the previous winter made a small quantity of lime by burning the shells of the *Unio fluviatilis,* which our river affords, for the sake of the experiment; so that I knew where my materials came from. I might have got good limestone within a mile or two and burned it myself, if I had cared to do so.

The pond had in the meanwhile skimmed over in the shadiest and shallowest coves, some days or even weeks before the general freezing. The first ice is especially interesting and perfect, being hard, dark, and transparent, and affords the best opportunity that ever offers for examining the bottom where it is shallow; for you can

lie at your length on ice only an inch thick, like a skater
insect on the surface of the water, and study the bottom
at your leisure, only two or three inches distant, like a
picture behind a glass, and the water is necessarily always smooth then. There are many furrows in the sand
where some creature has travelled about and doubled
on its tracks; and, for wrecks, it is strewn with the cases
of caddis-worms made of minute grains of white quartz.
Perhaps these have creased it, for you find some of their
cases in the furrows, though they are deep and broad
for them to make. But the ice itself is the object of most
interest, though you must improve the earliest opportunity to study it. If you examine it closely the morning
after it freezes, you find that the greater part of the
bubbles, which at first appeared to be within it, are
against its under surface, and that more are continually
rising from the bottom; while the ice is as yet comparatively solid and dark, that is, you see the water through
it. These bubbles are from an eightieth to an eighth of
an inch in diameter, very clear and beautiful, and you
see your face reflected in them through the ice. There
may be thirty or forty of them to a square inch. There
are also already within the ice narrow oblong perpendicular bubbles about half an inch long, sharp cones with
the apex upward; or oftener, if the ice is quite fresh,
minute spherical bubbles one directly above another,
like a string of beads. But these within the ice are not
so numerous nor obvious as those beneath. I sometimes
used to cast on stones to try the strength of the ice, and
those which broke through carried in air with them,
which formed very large and conspicuous white bubbles
beneath. One day when I came to the same place forty-
eight hours afterward, I found that those large bubbles
were still perfect, though an inch more of ice had
formed, as I could see distinctly by the seam in the edge
of a cake. But as the last two days had been very warm,
like an Indian summer, the ice was not now transparent,
showing the dark green color of the water, and the bottom, but opaque and whitish or gray, and though twice
as thick was hardly stronger than before, for the air bubbles had greatly expanded under this heat and run together, and lost their regularity; they were no longer one

directly over another, but often like silvery coins poured from a bag, one overlapping another, or in thin flakes, as if occupying slight cleavages. The beauty of the ice was gone, and it was too late to study the bottom. Being curious to know what position my great bubbles occupied with regard to the new ice, I broke out a cake containing a middling sized one, and turned it bottom upward. The new ice had formed around and under the bubble, so that it was included between the two ices. It was wholly in the lower ice, but close against the upper, and was flattish, or perhaps slightly lenticular, with a rounded edge, a quarter of an inch deep by four inches in diameter; and I was surprised to find that directly under the bubble the ice was melted with great regularity in the form of a saucer reversed, to the height of five eighths of an inch in the middle, leaving a thin partition there between the water and the bubble, hardly an eighth of an inch thick; and in many places the small bubbles in this partition had burst out downward, and probably there was no ice at all under the largest bubbles, which were a foot in diameter. I inferred that the infinite number of minute bubbles which I had first seen against the under surface of the ice were now frozen in likewise, and that each, in its degree, had operated like a burning-glass on the ice beneath to melt and rot it. These are the little air-guns which contribute to make the ice crack and whoop.

At length the winter set in in good earnest, just as I had finished plastering, and the wind began to howl around the house as if it had not had permission to do so till then. Night after night the geese came lumbering in in the dark with a clangor and a whistling of wings, even after the ground was covered with snow, some to alight in Walden, and some flying low over the woods toward Fair Haven, bound for Mexico. Several times, when returning from the village at ten or eleven o'clock at night, I heard the tread of a flock of geese, or else ducks, on the dry leaves in the woods by a pond-hole behind my dwelling, where they had come up to feed, and the faint honk or quack of their leader as they hurried off. In 1845 Walden froze entirely over for the first

time on the night of the 22d of December, Flint's and
other shallower ponds and the river having been frozen
ten days or more; in '46, the 16th; in '49, about the 31st;
and in '50, about the 27th of December; in '52, the 5th
of January; in '53, the 31st of December. The snow had
already covered the ground since the 25th of November,
and surrounded me suddenly with the scenery of winter.
I withdrew yet farther into my shell, and endeavored to
keep a bright fire both within my house and within my
breast. My employment out of doors now was to collect
the dead wood in the forest, bringing it in my hands or
on my shoulders, or sometimes trailing a dead pine tree
under each arm to my shed. An old forest fence which
had seen its best days was a great haul for me. I sacrificed it to Vulcan, for it was past serving the god Termi-
nus. How much more interesting an event is that man's
supper who has just been forth in the snow to hunt, nay,
you might say, steal, the fuel to cook it with! His bread
and meat are sweet. There are enough fagots and waste
wood of all kinds in the forest of most of our towns to
support many fires, but which at present warm none,
and, some think, hinder the growth of the young wood.
There was also the driftwood of the pond. In the course
of the summer I had discovered a raft of pitch pine logs
with the bark on, pinned together by the Irish when the
railroad was built. This I hauled up partly on the shore.
After soaking two years and then lying high six months
it was perfectly sound, though water-logged past drying.
I amused myself one winter day with sliding this piece-
meal across the pond, nearly half a mile, skating behind
with one end of a log fifteen feet long on my shoulder,
and the other on the ice; or I tied several logs together
with a birch withe, and then, with a longer birch or alder
which had a hook at the end, dragged them across.
Though completely waterlogged and almost as heavy as
lead, they not only burned long, but made a very hot
fire; nay, I thought that they burned better for the soaking, as if the pitch, being confined by the water, burned
longer, as in a lamp.

Gilpin, in his account of the forest borderers of England, says that "the encroachments of trespassers, and
the houses and fences thus raised on the borders of the

forest," were "considered as great nuisances by the old
forest law, and were severely punished under the name
of *purprestures,* as tending *ad terrorem ferarum—ad no-
cumentum forestae,* etc.," to the frightening of the game
and the detriment of the forest. But I was interested in
the preservation of the venison and the vert more than
the hunters or woodchoppers, and as much as though I
had been the Lord Warden himself; and if any part was
burned, though I burned it myself by accident, I grieved
with a grief that lasted longer and was more inconsolable
than that of the proprietors; nay, I grieved when it was
cut down by the proprietors themselves. I would that
our farmers when they cut down a forest felt some of
that awe which the old Romans did when they came to
thin, or let in the light to, a consecrated grove (*lucum
conlucare*), that is, would believe that it is sacred to some
god. The Roman made an expiatory offering, and
prayed, Whatever god or goddess thou art to whom this
grove is sacred, be propitious to me, my family, and
children, etc.

It is remarkable what a value is still put upon wood
even in this age and in this new country, a value more
permanent and universal than that of gold. After all our
discoveries and inventions no man will go by a pile of
wood. It is as precious to us as it was to our Saxon and
Norman ancestors. If they made their bows of it, we
make our gun-stocks of it. Michaux, more than thirty
years ago, says that the price of wood for fuel in New
York and Philadelphia "nearly equals, and sometimes
exceeds, that of the best wood in Paris, though this im-
mense capital annually requires more than three hundred thousand cords, and is surrounded to the distance
of three hundred miles by cultivated plains." In this town
the price of wood rises almost steadily, and the only
question is, how much higher it is to be this year than
it was the last. Mechanics and tradesmen who come in
person to the forest on no other errand, are sure to
attend the wood auction, and even pay a high price for
the privilege of gleaning after the woodchopper. It is
now many years that men have resorted to the forest
for fuel and the materials of the arts: the New Englander
and the New Hollander, the Parisian and the Celt, the

farmer and Robin Hood, Goody Blake and Harry Gill; in most parts of the world the prince and the peasant, the scholar and the savage, equally require still a few sticks from the forest to warm them and cook their food. Neither could I do without them.

Every man looks at his wood-pile with a kind of affection. I loved to have mine before my window, and the more chips the better to remind me of my pleasing work. I had an old axe which nobody claimed, with which by spells in winter days, on the sunny side of the house, I played about the stumps which I had got out of my bean-field. As my driver prophesied when I was plowing, they warmed me twice,—once while I was splitting them, and again when they were on the fire, so that no fuel could give out more heat. As for the axe, I was advised to get the village blacksmith to "jump" it; but I jumped him, and, putting a hickory helve from the woods into it, made it do. If it was dull, it was at least hung true.

A few pieces of fat pine were a great treasure. It is interesting to remember how much of this food for fire is still concealed in the bowels of the earth. In previous years I had often gone "prospecting" over some bare hillside, where a pitch pine wood had formerly stood, and got out the fat pine roots. They are almost indestructible. Stumps thirty or forty years old, at least, will still be sound at the core, though the sapwood has all become vegetable mould, as appears by the scales of the thick bark forming a ring level with the earth four or five inches distant from the heart. With axe and shovel you explore this mine, and follow the marrowy store, yellow as beef tallow, or as if you had struck on a vein of gold, deep into the earth. But commonly I kindled my fire with the dry leaves of the forest, which I had stored up in my shed before the snow came. Green hickory finely split makes the woodchopper's kindlings, when he has a camp in the woods. Once in a while I got a little of this. When the villagers were lighting their fires beyond the horizon, I too gave notice to the various wild inhabitants of Walden vale, by a smoky streamer from my chimney, that I was awake.—

Light-winged Smoke, Icarian bird,
Melting thy pinions in thy upward flight,
Lark without song, and messenger of dawn,
Circling above the hamlets as thy nest;
Or else, departing dream, and shadowy form
Of midnight vision, gathering up thy skirts;
By night star-veiling, and by day
Darkening the light and blotting out the sun;
Go thou my incense upward from this hearth,
And ask the gods to pardon this clear flame.

Hard green wood just cut, though I used but little of that, answered my purpose better than any other. I sometimes left a good fire when I went to take a walk in a winter afternoon; and when I returned, three or four hours afterward, it would be still alive and glowing. My house was not empty though I was gone. It was as if I had left a cheerful housekeeper behind. It was I and Fire that lived there; and commonly my housekeeper proved trustworthy. One day, however, as I was splitting wood, I thought that I would just look in at the window and see if the house was not on fire; it was the only time I remember to have been particularly anxious on this score; so I looked and saw that a spark had caught my bed, and I went in and extinguished it when it had burned a place as big as my hand. But my house occupied so sunny and sheltered a position, and its roof was so low, that I could afford to let the fire go out in the middle of almost any winter day.

The moles nested in my cellar, nibbling every third potato, and making a snug bed even there of some hair left after plastering and of brown paper; for even the wildest animals love comfort and warmth as well as man, and they survive the winter only because they are so careful to secure them. Some of my friends spoke as if I was coming to the woods on purpose to freeze myself. The animal merely makes a bed, which he warms with his body, in a sheltered place; but man, having discovered fire, boxes up some air in a spacious apartment, and warms that, instead of robbing himself, makes that his bed, in which he can move about divested of more cumbrous clothing, maintain a kind of summer in the midst of winter, and by means of windows even admit the light, and with a lamp lengthen out the day. Thus he goes a step or two beyond instinct, and saves a little time for the fine arts. Though, when I had been exposed to the rudest blasts a long time, my whole body began to grow torpid, when I reached the genial atmosphere of my house I soon recovered my faculties and prolonged my life. But the most luxuriously housed has little to boast of in this respect, nor need we trouble ourselves to speculate how the human race may be at last destroyed. It would be easy to cut their threads any time with a little sharper blast from the north. We go on dating from Cold Fridays and Great Snows; but a little colder Friday, or greater snow would put a period to man's existence on the globe.

The next winter I used a small cooking-stove for economy, since I did not own the forest; but it did not keep fire so well as the open fireplace. Cooking was then, for the most part, no longer a poetic, but merely a chemic process. It will soon be forgotten, in these days of stoves, that we used to roast potatoes in the ashes, after the Indian fashion. The stove not only took up room and scented the house, but it concealed the fire, and I felt as if I had lost a companion. You can always see a face in the fire. The laborer, looking into it at evening, purifies his thoughts of the dross and earthiness which they have accumulated during the day. But I could no longer sit and look into the fire, and the pertinent words of a poet recurred to me with new force.—

"Never, bright flame, may be denied to me
  Thy dear, life imaging, close sympathy.
  What but my hopes shot upward e'er so bright?
  What but my fortunes sunk so low in night?
  Why art thou banished from our hearth and hall,
  Thou who art welcomed and beloved by all?
  Was thy existence then too fanciful
  For our life's common light, who are so dull?
  Did thy bright gleam mysterious converse hold
  With our congenial souls? secrets too bold?

Well, we are safe and strong, for now we sit
Beside a hearth where no dim shadows flit,
Where nothing cheers nor saddens, but a fire
Warms feet and hands—nor does to more aspire;
By whose compact utilitarian heap
The present may sit down and go to sleep,
Nor fear the ghosts who from the dim past walked,
And with us by the unequal light of the old wood fire
    talked."

14. Former Inhabitants; and
Winter Visitors

I WEATHERED some merry snow-storms, and spent some cheerful winter evenings by my fireside, while the snow whirled wildly without, and even the hooting of the owl was hushed. For many weeks I met no one in my walks but those who came occasionally to cut wood and sled it to the village. The elements, however, abetted me in making a path through the deepest snow in the woods, for when I had once gone through the wind blew the oak leaves into my tracks, where they lodged, and by absorbing the rays of the sun melted the snow, and so not only made a dry bed for my feet, but in the night their dark line was my guide. For human society I was obliged to conjure up the former occupants of these woods. Within the memory of many of my townsmen the road near which my house stands resounded with the laugh and gossip of inhabitants, and the woods which border it were notched and dotted here and there with their little gardens and dwellings, though it was then much more shut in by the forest than now. In some places, within my own remembrance, the pines would scrape both sides of a chaise at once, and women and children who were compelled to go this way to Lincoln alone and on foot did it with fear, and often ran a good part of the distance. Though mainly but a humble route to neighboring villages, or for the woodman's team, it once amused the traveller more than now by its variety, and lingered longer in his memory. Where now firm open fields stretch from the village to the woods, it then ran through a maple swamp on a foundation of logs, the remnants of which, doubtless, still underlie the present dusty highway, from the Stratton, now the Alms-House, Farm, to Brister's Hill.

East of my bean-field, across the road, lived Cato Ingraham, slave of Duncan Ingraham, Esquire, gentleman, of Concord village, who built his slave a house, and gave him permission to live in Walden Woods;—Cato, not Uticensis, but Concordiensis. Some say that he was a Guinea Negro. There are a few who remember his little patch among the walnuts, which he let grow up till he should be old and need them; but a younger and whiter speculator got them at last. He too, however, occupies an equally narrow house at present. Cato's half-obliterated cellar-hole still remains, though known to few, being concealed from the traveller by a fringe of pines. It is now filled with the smooth sumach (*Rhus glabra*), and one of the earliest species of goldenrod (*Solidago stricta*) grows there luxuriantly.

Here, by the very corner of my field, still nearer to town, Zilpha, a colored woman, had her little house, where she spun linen for the townsfolk, making the Walden Woods ring with her shrill singing, for she had a loud and notable voice. At length, in the war of 1812, her dwelling was set on fire by English soldiers, prisoners on parole, when she was away, and her cat and dog and hens were all burned up together. She led a hard life, and somewhat inhumane. One old frequenter of these woods remembers, that as he passed her house one noon he heard her muttering to herself over her gurgling pot,—"Ye are all bones, bones!" I have seen bricks amid the oak copse there.

Down the road, on the right hand, on Brister's Hill, lived Brister Freeman, "a handy Negro," slave of Squire Cummings once,—there where grow still the apple trees which Brister planted and tended; large old trees now, but their fruit still wild and ciderish to my taste. Not long since I read his epitaph in the old Lincoln burying-ground, a little on one side, near the unmarked graves of some British grenadiers who fell in the retreat from Concord,—where he is styled "Sippio Brister,"—Scipio Africanus he had some title to be called,—"a man of color," as if he were discolored. It also told me, with staring emphasis, when he died; which was but an indirect way of informing me that he ever lived. With him dwelt Fenda, his hospitable wife, who told fortunes, yet pleasantly,—large, round, and black, blacker than any of the children of night, such a dusky orb as never rose on Concord before or since.

Farther down the hill, on the left, on the old road in the woods, are marks of some homestead of the Stratton family; whose orchard once covered all the slope of Brister's Hill, but was long since killed out by pitch pines, excepting a few stumps, whose old roots furnish still the wild stocks of many a thrifty village tree.

Nearer yet to town, you come to Breed's location, on the other side of the way, just on the edge of the wood; ground famous for the pranks of a demon not distinctly named in old mythology, who has acted a prominent and astounding part in our New England life, and deserves, as much as any mythological character, to have his biography written one day; who first comes in the guise of a friend or hired man, and then robs and murders the whole family,—New-England Rum. But history must not yet tell the tragedies enacted here; let time intervene in some measure to assuage and lend an azure tint to them. Here the most indistinct and dubious tradition says that once a tavern stood; the well the same, which tempered the traveller's beverage and refreshed his steed. Here then men saluted one another, and heard and told the news, and went their ways again.

Breed's hut was standing only a dozen years ago, though it had long been unoccupied. It was about the size of mine. It was set on fire by mischievous boys, one Election night, if I do not mistake. I lived on the edge of the village then, and had just lost myself over Davenant's "Gondibert," that winter that I labored with a lethargy,—which, by the way, I never knew whether

to regard as a family complaint, having an uncle who
goes to sleep shaving himself, and is obliged to sprout
potatoes in a cellar Sundays, in order to keep awake and
keep the Sabbath, or as the consequence of my attempt
to read Chalmers' collection of English poetry without
skipping. It fairly overcame my Nervii. I had just sunk
my head on this when the bells rung fire, and in hot
haste the engines rolled that way, led by a straggling
troop of men and boys, and I among the foremost, for
I had leaped the brook. We thought it was far south
over the woods,—we who had run to fires before,—barn,
shop, or dwelling-house, or all together. "It's Baker's
barn," cried one. "It is the Codman place," affirmed
another. And then fresh sparks went up above the wood,
as if the roof fell in, and we all shouted "Concord to
the rescue!" Wagons shot past with furious speed and
crushing loads, bearing, perchance, among the rest, the
agent of the Insurance Company, who was bound to go
however far; and ever and anon the engine bell tinkled
behind, more slow and sure; and rearmost of all, as it
was afterward whispered, came they who set the fire and
gave the alarm. Thus we kept on like true idealists, re-
jecting the evidence of our senses, until at a turn in the
road we heard the crackling and actually felt the heat of
the fire from over the wall, and realized, alas! that we were
there. The very nearness of the fire but cooled our ardor.
At first we thought to throw a frog-pond on to it; but
concluded to let it burn, it was so far gone and so worth-
less. So we stood round our engine, jostled one another,
expressed our sentiments through speaking-trumpets, or
in lower tone referred to the great conflagations which
the world has witnessed, including Bascom's shop, and,
between ourselves, we thought that, were we there in
season with our "tub," and a full frog-pond by, we could
turn that threatened last and universal one into another
flood. We finally retreated without doing any mischief,—
returned to sleep and "Gondibert." But as for "Gondibert," I would except that passage in the preface about
wit being the soul's powder,—"but most of mankind are
strangers to wit, as Indians are to powder."

It chanced that I walked that way across the fields the
following night, about the same hour, and hearing a low

moaning at this spot, I drew near in the dark, and discovered the only survivor of the family that I know, the heir of both its virtues and its vices, who alone was interested in this burning, lying on his stomach and looking over the cellar wall at the still smouldering cinders beneath, muttering to himself, as is his wont. He had been working far off in the river meadows all day, and had improved the first moments that he could call his own to visit the home of his fathers and his youth. He gazed into the cellar from all sides and points of view by turns, always lying down to it, as if there was some treasure, which he remembered, concealed between the stones, where there was absolutely nothing but a heap of bricks and ashes. The house being gone, he looked at what there was left. He was soothed by the sympathy which my mere presence implied, and showed me, as well as the darkness permitted, where the well was covered up; which, thank Heaven, could never be burned; and he groped long about the wall to find the well-sweep which his father had cut and mounted, feeling for the iron hook or staple by which a burden had been fastened to the heavy end,—all that he could now cling to,—to convince me that it was no common "rider." I felt it, and still remark it almost daily in my walks, for by it hangs the history of a family.

Once more, on the left, where are seen the well and lilac bushes by the wall, in the now open field, lived Nutting and Le Grosse. But to return toward Lincoln.

Farther in the woods than any of these, where the road approaches nearest to the pond, Wyman the potter squatted, and furnished his townsmen with earthenware, and left descendants to succeed him. Neither were they rich in worldly goods, holding the land by sufferance while they lived; and there often the sheriff came in vain to collect the taxes, and "attached a chip," for form's sake, as I have read in his accounts, there being nothing else that he could lay his hands on. One day in midsummer, when I was hoeing, a man who was carrying a load of pottery to market stopped his horse against my field and inquired concerning Wyman the younger. He had long ago bought a potter's wheel of him, and wished to know what had become of him. I had read of the potter's clay and wheel in Scripture, but it had never occurred to me that the pots we use were not such as had come down unbroken from those days, or grown on trees like gourds somewhere, and I was pleased to hear that so fictile an art was ever practiced in my neighborhood.

The last inhabitant of these woods before me was an Irishman, Hugh Quoil (if I have spelt his name with coil enough), who occupied Wyman's tenement,—Col. Quoil, he was called. Rumor said that he had been a soldier at Waterloo. If he had lived I should have made him fight his battles over again. His trade here was that of a ditcher. Napoleon went to St. Helena; Quoil came to Walden Woods. All I know of him is tragic. He was a man of manners, like one who had seen the world, and was capable of more civil speech than you could well attend to. He wore a greatcoat in midsummer, being affected with the trembling delirium, and his face was the color of carmine. He died in the road at the foot of Brister's Hill shortly after I came to the woods, so that I have not remembered him as a neighbor. Before his house was pulled down, when his comrades avoided it as "an unlucky castle," I visited it. There lay his old clothes curled up by use, as if they were himself, upon his raised plank bed. His pipe lay broken on the hearth, instead of a bowl broken at the fountain. The last could never have been the symbol of his death, for he confessed to me that, though he had heard of Brister's Spring, he had never seen it; and soiled cards, kings of diamonds, spades, and hearts, were scattered over the floor. One black chicken which the administrator could not catch, black as night and as silent, not even croaking, awaiting Reynard, still went to roost in the next apartment. In the rear there was the dim outline of a garden, which had been planted but had never received its first hoeing, owing to those terrible shaking fits, though it was now harvest time. It was overrun with Roman wormwood and beggar-ticks, which last stuck to my clothes for all fruit. The skin of a woodchuck was freshly stretched upon the back of the house, a trophy of his last Waterloo; but no warm cap or mittens would he want more.

Now only a dent in the earth marks the site of these

dwellings, with buried cellar stones, and strawberries, raspberries, thimble-berries, hazel-bushes, and sumachs growing in the sunny sward there; some pitch pine or gnarled oak occupies what was the chimney nook, and a sweet-scented black birch, perhaps, waves where the door-stone was. Sometimes the well dent is visible, where once a spring oozed; now dry and tearless grass; or it was covered deep,—not to be discovered till some late day,—with a flat stone under the sod, when the last of the race departed. What a sorrowful act must that be,—the covering up of wells! coincident with the opening of wells of tears. These cellar dents, like deserted fox burrows, old holes, are all that is left where once were the stir and bustle of human life, and "fate, free will, foreknowledge absolute," in some form and dialect or other were by turns discussed. But all I can learn of their conclusions amounts to just this, that "Cato and Brister pulled wool;" which is about as edifying as the history of more famous schools of philosophy.

Still grows the vivacious lilac a generation after the door and lintel and the sill are gone, unfolding its sweet-scented flowers each spring, to be plucked by the musing traveller; planted and tended once by children's hands, in front-yard plots,—now standing by wall-sides in retired pastures, and giving place to new-rising forests;— the last of that stirp, sole survivor of that family. Little did the dusky children think that the puny slip with its two eyes only, which they stuck in the ground in the shadow of the house and daily watered, would root itself so, and outlive them, and house itself in the rear that shaded it, and grown man's garden and orchard, and tell their story faintly to the lone wanderer a half-century after they had grown up and died,—blossoming as fair, and smelling as sweet, as in that first spring. I mark its still tender, civil, cheerful, lilac colors.

But this small village, germ of something more, why did it fail while Concord keeps its ground? Were there no natural advantages,—no water privileges, forsooth? Ay, the deep Walden Pond and cool Brister's Spring,— privilege to drink long and healthy draughts at these, all unimproved by these men but to dilute their glass. They were universally a thirsty race. Might not the basket, stable-broom, mat-making, corn-parching, linen-spinning, and pottery business have thrived here, making the wilderness to blossom like the rose, and a numerous posterity have inherited the land of their fathers? The sterile soil would at least have been proof against a lowland degeneracy. Alas! how little does the memory of these human inhabitants enhance the beauty of the landscape! Again, perhaps, Nature will try, with me for a first settler, and my house raised last spring to be the oldest in the hamlet.

I am not aware that any man has ever built on the spot which I occupy. Deliver me from a city built on the site of a more ancient city, whose materials are ruins, whose gardens cemeteries. The soil is blanched and accursed there, and before that becomes necessary the earth itself will be destroyed. With such reminiscences I repeopled the woods and lulled myself asleep.

At this season I seldom had a visitor. When the snow lay deepest no wanderer ventured near my house for a week or fortnight at a time, but there I lived as snug as a meadow mouse, or as cattle and poultry which are said to have survived for a long time buried in drifts, even without food; or like that early settler's family in the town of Sutton, in this State, whose cottage was completely covered by the great snow of 1717 when he was absent, and an Indian found it only by the hole which the chimney's breadth made in the drift, and so relieved the family. But no friendly Indian concerned himself about me; nor needed he, for the master of the house was at home. The Great Snow! How cheerful it is to hear of! When the farmers could not get to the woods and swamps with their teams, and were obliged to cut down the shade trees before their houses, and, when the crust was harder, cut off the trees in the swamps, ten feet from the ground, as it appeared the next spring.

In the deepest snows, the path which I used from the highway to my house, about half a mile long, might have been represented by a meandering dotted line, with wide intervals between the dots. For a week of even weather I took exactly the same number of steps, and of the same length, coming and going, stepping deliberately and with the precision of a pair of dividers in my own deep tracks,—to such routine the winter reduces us,—yet often they were filled with heaven's own blue. But no weather interfered fatally with my walks, or rather my going abroad, for I frequently tramped eight or ten miles through the deepest snow to keep an appointment with a beech tree, or a yellow birch, or an old acquaintance among the pines: when the ice and snow causing their limbs to droop, and so sharpening their tops, had changed the pines into fir trees; wading to the tops of the highest hills when the snow was nearly two feet deep on a level, and shaking down another snow-storm on my head at every step; or sometimes creeping and floundering thither on my hands and knees, when the hunters had gone into winter quarters. One afternoon I amused myself by watching a barred owl (*Strix nebulosa*) sitting on one of the lower dead limbs of a white pine, close to the trunk, in broad daylight, I standing within a rod of him. He could hear me when I moved and cronched the snow with my feet, but could not plainly see me. When I made most noise he would stretch out his neck, and erect his neck feathers, and open his eyes wide; but their lids soon fell again, and he began to nod. I too felt a slumberous influence after watching him half an hour, as he sat thus with his eyes half open, like a cat, winged brother of the cat. There was only a narrow slit left between their lids, by which he preserved a peninsular relation to me; thus, with half-shut eyes, looking out from the land of dreams, and endeavoring to realize me, vague object or mote that interrupted his visions. At length, on some louder noise or my nearer approach, he would grow uneasy and sluggishly turn about on his perch, as if impatient at having his dreams disturbed; and when he launched himself off and flapped through the pines, spreading his wings to unexpected breadth, I could not hear the slightest sound from them. Thus, guided amid the pine boughs rather by a delicate sense of their neighborhood than by sight, feeling his twilight way, as it were, with his sensitive pinions, he found a new perch, where he might in peace await the dawning of his day.

As I walked over the long causeway made for the

railroad through the meadows, I encountered many a
blustering and nipping wind, for nowhere has it freer
play; and when the frost had smitten me on one cheek,
heathen as I was, I turned to it the other also. Nor was
it much better by the carriage road from Brister's Hill.
For I came to town still, like a friendly Indian, when the
contents of the broad open fields were all piled up between the walls of the Walden road, and half an hour
sufficed to obliterate the tracks of the last traveller. And
when I returned new drifts would have formed, through
which I floundered, where the busy northwest wind had
been depositing the powdery snow round a sharp angle
in the road, and not a rabbit's track, nor even the fine
print, the small type, of a meadow mouse was to be seen.
Yet I rarely failed to find, even in mid-winter, some
warm and springy swamp where the grass and the skunk-
cabbage still put forth with perennial verdure, and some
hardier bird occasionally awaited the return of spring.

Sometimes, notwithstanding the snow, when I returned from my walk at evening I crossed the deep
tracks of a woodchopper leading from my door, and
found his pile of whittlings on the hearth, and my house
filled with the odor of his pipe. Or on a Sunday afternoon, if I chanced to be at home, I heard the cronching
of the snow made by the step of a long-headed farmer,
who from far through the woods sought my house, to
have a social "crack;" one of the few of his vocation who
are "men on their farms;" who donned a frock instead of
a professor's gown, and is as ready to extract the moral
out of church or state as to haul a load of manure from
his barn-yard. We talked of rude and simple times, when
men sat about large fires in cold, bracing weather, with
clear heads; and when other dessert failed, we tried our
teeth on many a nut which wise squirrels have long since
abandoned, for those which have the thickest shells are
commonly empty.

The one who came from farthest to my lodge, through
deepest snows and most dismal tempests, was a poet. A
farmer, a hunter, a soldier, a reporter, even a philosopher, may be daunted; but nothing can deter a poet, for
he is actuated by pure love. Who can predict his comings
and goings? His business calls him out at all hours, even

when doctors sleep. We made that small house ring with boisterous mirth and resound with the murmur of much sober talk, making amends then to Walden vale for the long silences. Broadway was still and deserted in comparison. At suitable intervals there were regular salutes of laughter, which might have been referred indifferently to the last-uttered or the forth-coming jest. We made many a "bran new" theory of life over a thin dish of gruel, which combined the advantages of conviviality with the clear-headedness which philosophy requires.

I should not forget that during my last winter at the pond there was another welcome visitor, who at one time came through the village, through snow and rain and darkness, till he saw my lamp through the trees, and shared with me some long winter evenings. One of the last of the philosophers,—Connecticut gave him to the world,—he peddled first her wares, afterwards, as he declares, his brains. These he peddles still, prompting God and disgracing man, bearing for fruit his brain only, like the nut its kernel. I think that he must be the man of the most faith of any alive. His words and attitude always suppose a better state of things than other men are acquainted with, and he will be the last man to be disappointed as the ages revolve. He has no venture in the present. But though comparatively disregarded now, when his day comes, laws unsuspected by most will take effect, and masters of families and rulers will come to him for advice.—

"How blind that cannot see serenity!"

A true friend of man; almost the only friend of human progress. An Old Mortality, say rather an Immortality, with unwearied patience and faith making plain the image engraven in men's bodies, the God of whom they are but defaced and leaning monuments. With his hospitable intellect he embraces children, beggars, insane, and scholars, and entertains the thought of all, adding to it commonly some breadth and elegance. I think that he should keep a caravansary on the world's highway, where philosophers of all nations might put up, and on his sign should be printed, "Entertainment for man, but not for his beast. Enter ye that have leisure and a quiet mind, who earnestly seek the right road." He is perhaps the sanest man and has the fewest crotchets of any I chance to know; the same yesterday and to-morrow. Of yore we had sauntered and talked, and effectually put the world behind us; for he was pledged to no institution in it, freeborn, *ingenuus*. Whichever way we turned, it seemed that the heavens and the earth had met together, since he enhanced the beauty of the landscape. A blue-robed man, whose fittest roof is the overarching sky which reflects his serenity. I do not see how he can ever die; Nature cannot spare him.

Having each some shingles of thought well dried, we sat and whittled them, trying our knives, and admiring the clear yellowish grain of the pumpkin pine. We waded so gently and reverently, or we pulled together so smoothly, that the fishes of thought were not scared from the stream, nor feared any angler on the bank, but came and went grandly, like the clouds which float through the western sky, and the mother-o'-pearl flocks which sometimes form and dissolve there. There we worked, revising mythology, rounding a fable here and there, and building castles in the air for which earth offered no worthy foundation. Great Looker! Great Expecter! to converse with whom was a New England Night's Entertainment. Ah! such discourse we had, hermit and philosopher, and the old settler I have spoken of,—we three,—it expanded and racked my little house; I should not dare to say how many pounds' weight there was above the atmospheric pressure on every circular inch; it opened its seams so that they had to be calked with much dulness thereafter to stop the consequent leak;—but I had enough of that kind of oakum already picked.

There was one other with whom I had "solid seasons," long to be remembered, at his house in the village, and who looked in upon me from time to time; but I had no more for society there.

There too, as everywhere, I sometimes expected the Visitor who never comes. The Vishnu Purana says, "The householder is to remain at eventide in his courtyard as long as it takes to milk a cow, or longer if he pleases, to await the arrival of a guest." I often performed this duty of hospitality, waited long enough to milk a whole herd of cows, but did not see the man approaching from the town.

15. Winter Animals

WHEN the ponds were firmly frozen, they afforded not only new and shorter routes to many points, but new views from their surfaces of the familiar landscape around them. When I crossed Flint's Pond, after it was covered with snow, though I had often paddled about and skated over it, it was so unexpectedly wide and so strange that I could think of nothing but Baffin's Bay. The Lincoln hills rose up around me at the extremity of a snowy plain, in which I did not remember to have stood before; and the fishermen, at an indeterminable distance over the ice, moving slowly about with their wolfish dogs, passed for sealers or Esquimaux, or in misty weather loomed like fabulous creatures, and I did not know whether they were giants or pygmies. I took this course when I went to lecture in Lincoln in the evening, travelling in no road and passing no house between my own hut and the lecture room. In Goose Pond, which lay in my way, a colony of muskrats dwelt, and raised their cabins high above the ice, though none could be seen abroad when I crossed it. Walden, being like the rest usually bare of snow, or with only shallow and interrupted drifts on it, was my yard where I could walk freely when the snow was nearly two feet deep on a level elsewhere and the villagers were confined to their streets. There, far from the village street, and except at very long intervals, from the jingle of sleigh-bells, I slid and skated, as in a vast mooseyard well trodden, overhung by oak woods and solemn pines bent down with snow or bristling with icicles.

For sounds in winter nights, and often in winter days, I heard the forlorn but melodious note of a hooting owl indefinitely far; such a sound as the frozen earth would yield if struck with a suitable plectrum, the very *lingua vernacula* of Walden Wood, and quite familiar to me at last, though I never saw the bird while it was making it. I seldom opened my door in a winter evening without hearing it; *Hoo hoo hoo, hoorer hoo,* sounded sonorously, and the first three syllables accented somewhat like *how der do;* or sometimes *hoo hoo* only. One night in the beginning of winter, before the pond froze over, about nine o'clock, I was startled by the loud honking of a goose, and, stepping to the door, heard the sound of their wings like a tempest in the woods as they flew low over my house. They passed over the pond toward Fair Haven, seemingly deterred from settling by my light, their commodore honking all the while with a regular beat. Suddenly an unmistakable cat owl from very near me, with the most harsh and tremendous voice I ever heard from any inhabitant of the woods, responded at regular intervals to the goose, as if determined to expose and disgrace this intruder from Hudson's Bay by exhibiting a greater compass and volume of voice in a native, and *boo-hoo* him out of Concord horizon. What do you mean by alarming the citadel at this time of night consecrated to me? Do you think I am ever caught napping at such an hour, and that I have not got lungs and a larynx as well as yourself? *Boo-hoo, boo-hoo, boo-hoo!* It was one of the most thrilling discords I ever heard. And yet, if you had a discriminating ear, there were in it the elements of a concord such as these plains never saw nor heard.

I also heard the whooping of the ice in the pond, my great bed-fellow in that part of Concord, as if it were restless in its bed and would fain turn over, were troubled with flatulency and bad dreams; or I was waked by the cracking of the ground by the frost, as if some one had driven a team against my door, and in the morning would find a crack in the earth a quarter of a mile long and a third of an inch wide.

Sometimes I heard the foxes as they ranged over the snow-crust, in moonlight nights, in search of a partridge or other game, barking raggedly and demoniacally like forest dogs, as if laboring with some anxiety, or seeking expression, struggling for light and to be dogs outright and run freely in the streets; for if we take the ages into our account, may there not be a civilization going on among brutes as well as men? They seemed to me to be rudimental, burrowing men, still standing on their defence, awaiting their transformation. Sometimes one came near to my window, attracted by my light, barked a vulpine curse at me, and then retreated.

Usually the red squirrel (*Sciurus Hudsonius*) waked me in the dawn, coursing over the roof and up and down the sides of the house, as if sent out of the woods for this purpose. In the course of the winter I threw out half a bushel of ears of sweet corn, which had not got ripe, on to the snow-crust by my door, and was amused by watching the motions of the various animals which were baited by it. In the twilight and the night the rabbits came regularly and made a hearty meal. All day long the red squirrels came and went, and afforded me much entertainment by their manœuvres. One would approach at first warily through the shrub oaks, running over the snow-crust by fits and starts like a leaf blown by the wind, now a few paces this way, with wonderful speed and waste of energy, making inconceivable haste with his "trotters," as if it were for a wager, and now as many paces that way, but never getting on more than half a rod at a time; and then suddenly pausing with a ludicrous expression and a gratuitous somerset, as if all the eyes in the universe were fixed on him,—for all the motions of a squirrel, even in the most solitary recesses of the forest, imply spectators as much as those of a dancing girl,—wasting more time in delay and circumspection than would have sufficed to walk the whole distance,— I never saw one walk,—and then suddenly, before you could say Jack Robinson, he would be in the top of a young pitch pine, winding up his clock and chiding all imaginary spectators, soliloquizing and talking to all the universe at the same time,—for no reason that I could ever detect, or he himself was aware of, I suspect. At length he would reach the corn, and selecting a suitable ear, frisk about in the same uncertain trigonometrical way to the topmost stick of my woodpile, before my window, where he looked me in the face, and there sit

for hours, supplying himself with a new ear from time
to time, nibbling at first voraciously and throwing the
half-naked cobs about; till at length he grew more dainty
still and played with his food, tasting only the inside of
the kernel, and the ear, which was held balanced over
the stick by one paw, slipped from his careless grasp and
fell to the ground, when he would look over at it with
a ludicrous expression of uncertainty, as if suspecting
that it had life, with a mind not made up whether to get
it again, or a new one, or be off; now thinking of corn,
then listening to hear what was in the wind. So the little
impudent fellow would waste many an ear in a forenoon;
till at last, seizing some longer and plumper one, considerably bigger than himself, and skillfully balancing it, he
would set out with it to the woods, like a tiger with a
buffalo, by the same zigzag course and frequent pauses,
scratching along with it as if it were too heavy for him
and falling all the while, making its fall a diagonal between a perpendicular and horizontal, being determined
to put it through at any rate;—a singularly frivolous and
whimsical fellow;—and so he would get off with it to
where he lived, perhaps carry it to the top of a pine tree
forty or fifty rods distant, and I would afterwards find
the cobs strewn about the woods in various directions.

At length the jays arrive, whose discordant screams
were heard long before, as they were warily making their
approach an eighth of a mile off, and in a stealthy and
sneaking manner they flit from tree to tree, nearer and
nearer, and pick up the kernels which the squirrels have
dropped. Then, sitting on a pitch pine bough, they attempt to swallow in their haste a kernel which is too big
for their throats and chokes them; and after great labor
they disgorge it, and spend an hour in the endeavor to
crack it by repeated blows with their bills. They were
manifestly thieves, and I had not much respect for them;
but the squirrels, though at first shy, went to work as if
they were taking what was their own.

Meanwhile also came the chickadees in flocks, which,
picking up the crumbs the squirrels had dropped, flew
to the nearest twig, and, placing them under their claws,
hammered away at them with their little bills, as if it
were an insect in the bark, till they were sufficiently re-

duced for their slender throats. A little flock of these
titmice came daily to pick a dinner out of my wood-pile,
or the crumbs at my door, with faint flitting lisping notes,
like the tinkling of icicles in the grass, or else with
sprightly *day day day,* or more rarely, in springlike days,
a wiry summery *phe-be* from the woodside. They were
so familiar that at length one alighted on an armful of
wood which I was carrying in, and pecked at the sticks
without fear. I once had a sparrow alight upon my shoulder for a moment while I was hoeing in a village garden,
and I felt that I was more distinguished by that circumstance than I should have been by any epaulet I could
have worn. The squirrels also grew at last to be quite
familiar, and occasionally stepped upon my shoe, when
that was the nearest way.

When the ground was not yet quite covered, and again
near the end of winter, when the snow was melted on
my south hillside and about my wood-pile, the partridges
came out of the woods morning and evening to feed
there. Whichever side you walk in the woods the partridge bursts away on whirring wings, jarring the snow
from the dry leaves and twigs on high, which comes sift-
ing down in the sunbeams like golden dust, for this brave
bird is not to be scared by winter. It is frequently covered up by drifts, and, it is said, "sometimes plunges
from on wing into the soft snow, where it remains concealed for a day or two." I used to start them in the
open land also, where they had come out of the woods
at sunset to "bud" the wild apple trees. They will come
regularly every evening to particular trees, where the
cunning sportsman lies in wait for them, and the distant
orchards next the woods suffer thus not a little. I am
glad that the partridge gets fed, at any rate. It is Nature's
own bird which lives on buds and diet-drink.

In dark winter mornings, or in short winter afternoons,
I sometimes heard a pack of hounds threading all the
woods with hounding cry and yelp, unable to resist the
instinct of the chase, and the note of the hunting-horn
at intervals, proving that man was in the rear. The woods
ring again, and yet no fox bursts forth on to the open
level of the pond, nor following pack pursuing their
Actæon. And perhaps at evening I see the hunters re-

turning with a single brush trailing from their sleigh for a trophy, seeking their inn. They tell me that if the fox would remain in the bosom of the frozen earth he would be safe, or if he would run in a straight line away no foxhound could overtake him; but, having left his pursuers far behind, he stops to rest and listen till they come up, and when he runs he circles round to his old haunts, where the hunters await him. Sometimes, however, he will run upon a wall many rods, and then leap off far to one side, and he appears to know that water will not retain his scent. A hunter told me that he once saw a fox pursued by hounds burst out on to Walden when the ice was covered with shallow puddles, run part way across, and then return to the same shore. Ere long the hounds arrived, but here they lost the scent. Sometimes a pack hunting by themselves would pass my door, and circle round my house, and yelp and hound without regarding me, as if afflicted by a species of madness, so that nothing could divert them from the pursuit. Thus they circle until they fall upon the recent trail of a fox, for a wise hound will forsake everything else for this. One day a man came to my hut from Lexington to inquire after his hound that made a large track, and had been hunting for a week by himself. But I fear that he was not the wiser for all I told him, for every time I attempted to answer his questions he interrupted me by asking, "What do you do here?" He had lost a dog, but found a man.

One old hunter who has a dry tongue, who used to come to bathe in Walden once every year when the water was warmest, and at such times looked in upon me, told me that many years ago he took his gun one afternoon and went out for a cruise in Walden Wood; and as he walked the Wayland road he heard the cry of hounds approaching, and ere long a fox leaped the wall into the road, and as quick as thought leaped the other wall out of the road, and his swift bullet had not touched him. Some way behind came an old hound and her three pups in full pursuit, hunting on their own account, and disappeared again in the woods. Late in the afternoon, as he was resting in the thick woods south of Walden, he heard the voice of the hounds far over toward Fair

Haven still pursuing the fox; and on they came, their hounding cry which made all the woods ring sounding nearer and nearer, now from Well Meadow, now from the Baker Farm. For a long time he stood still and listened to their music, so sweet to a hunter's ear, when suddenly the fox appeared, threading the solemn aisles with an easy coursing pace, whose sound was concealed by a sympathetic rustle of the leaves, swift and still, keeping the ground, leaving his pursuers far behind; and, leaping upon a rock amid the woods, he sat erect and listening, with his back to the hunter. For a moment compassion restrained the latter's arm; but that was a short-lived mood, and as quick as thought can follow thought his piece was levelled, and *whang!*—the fox, rolling over the rock, lay dead on the ground. The hunter still kept his place and listened to the hounds. Still on they came, and now the near woods resounded through all their aisles with their demoniac cry. At length the old hound burst into view with muzzle to the ground, and snapping the air as if possessed, and ran directly to the rock; but, spying the dead fox, she suddenly ceased her hounding, as if struck dumb with amazement, and walked round and round him in silence; and one by one her pups arrived and, like their mother, were sobered into silence by the mystery. Then the hunter came forward and stood in their midst, and the mystery was solved. They waited in silence while he skinned the fox, then followed the brush a while, and at length turned off into the woods again. That evening a Weston squire came to the Concord hunter's cottage to inquire for his hounds, and told how for a week they had been hunting on their own account from Weston woods. The Concord hunter told him what he knew and offered him the skin; but the other declined it and departed. He did not find his hounds that night, but the next day learned that they had crossed the river and put up at a farmhouse for the night, whence, having been well fed, they took their departure early in the morning.

The hunter who told me this could remember one Sam Nutting, who used to hunt bears on Fair Haven Ledges, and exchange their skins for rum in Concord village; who told him, even, that he had seen a moose there.

Nutting had a famous foxhound named Burgoyne,—he pronounced it Bugine,—which my informant used to borrow. In the "Wast Book" of an old trader of this town, who was also a captain, town-clerk, and representative, I find the following entry. Jan. 18th, 1742-3, "John Melven Cr. by 1 Grey Fox 0—2—3;" they are not now found here; and in his ledger, Feb. 7th, 1743, Hezekiah Stratton has credit "by ½ a Catt skin 0—1—4½;" of course, a wild-cat, for Stratton was a sergeant in the old French war, and would not have got credit for hunting less noble game. Credit is given for deerskins also, and they were daily sold. One man still preserves the horns of the last deer that was killed in this vicinity, and another has told me the particulars of the hunt in which his uncle was engaged. The hunters were formerly a numerous and merry crew here. I remember well one gaunt Nimrod who would catch up a leaf by the roadside and play a strain on it wilder and more melodious, if my memory serves me, than any hunting-horn.

At midnight, when there was a moon, I sometimes met with hounds in my path prowling about the woods, which would skulk out of my way, as if afraid, and stand silent amid the bushes till I had passed.

Squirrels and wild mice disputed for my store of nuts. There were scores of pitch pines around my house, from one to four inches in diameter, which had been gnawed by mice the previous winter,—a Norwegian winter for them, for the snow lay long and deep, and they were obliged to mix a large proportion of pine bark with their other diet. These trees were alive and apparently flourishing at midsummer, and many of them had grown a foot, though completely girdled; but after another winter such were without exception dead. It is remarkable that a single mouse should thus be allowed a whole pine tree for its dinner, gnawing round instead of up and down it; but perhaps it is necessary in order to thin these trees, which are wont to grow up densely.

The hares (*Lepus Americanus*) were very familiar. One had her form under my house all winter, separated from me only by the flooring, and she startled me each morning by her hasty departure when I began to stir,— thump, thump, thump, striking her head against the floor

timbers in her hurry. They used to come round my door
at dusk to nibble the potato parings which I had thrown
out, and were so nearly the color of the ground that
they could hardly be distinguished when still. Sometimes
in the twilight I alternately lost and recovered sight of
one sitting motionless under my window. When I opened
my door in the evening, off they would go with a squeak
and a bounce. Near at hand they only excited my pity.
One evening one sat by my door two paces from me, at
first trembling with fear, yet unwilling to move; a poor
wee thing, lean and bony, with ragged ears and sharp
nose, scant tail and slender paws. It looked as if Nature
no longer contained the breed of nobler bloods, but
stood on her last toes. Its large eyes appeared young
and unhealthy, almost dropsical. I took a step, and lo,
away it scud with an elastic spring over the snow-crust,
straightening its body and its limbs into graceful length,
and soon put the forest between me and itself,—the wild
free venison, asserting its vigor and the dignity of Nature. Not without reason was its slenderness. Such then
was its nature. (*Lepus, levipes,* lightfoot, some think.)

What is a country without rabbits and partridges?
They are among the most simple and indigenous animal
products; ancient and venerable families known to antiquity as to modern times; of the very hue and substance
of Nature, nearest allied to leaves and to the ground,—
and to one another; it is either winged or it is legged. It
is hardly as if you had seen a wild creature when a rabbit
or a partridge bursts away, only a natural one, as much
to be expected as rustling leaves. The partridge and the
rabbit are still sure to thrive, like true natives of the soil,
whatever revolutions occur. If the forest is cut off, the
sprouts and bushes which spring up afford them conceal-
ment, and they become more numerous than ever. That
must be a poor country indeed that does not support a
hare. Our woods teem with them both, and around every
swamp may be seen the partridge or rabbit walk, beset
with twiggy fences and horse-hair snares, which some
cow-boy tends.

16. The Pond in Winter

AFTER a still winter night I awoke with the impression that some question had been put to me, which I had been endeavoring in vain to answer in my sleep, as what—how—when—where? But there was dawning Nature, in whom all creatures live, looking in at my broad windows with serene and satisfied face, and no question on *her* lips. I awoke to an answered question, to Nature and daylight. The snow lying deep on the earth dotted with young pines, and the very slope of the hill on which my house is placed, seemed to say, Forward! Nature puts no questions and answers none which we mortals ask. She has long ago taken her resolution. "O Prince, our eyes contemplate with admiration and transmit to the soul the wonderful and varied spectacle of this universe. The night veils without doubt a part of this glorious creation; but day comes to reveal to us this great work, which extends from earth even into the plains of the ether."

Then to my morning work. First I take an axe and pail and go in search of water, if that be not a dream. After a cold and snowy night it needed a divining-rod to find it. Every winter the liquid and trembling surface of the pond, which was so sensitive to every breath, and reflected every light and shadow, becomes solid to the depth of a foot or a foot and a half, so that it will support the heaviest teams, and perchance the snow covers it to an equal depth, and it is not to be distinguished from any level field. Like the marmots in the surrounding hills, it closes its eyelids and becomes dormant for three months or more. Standing on the snow-covered plain, as if in a pasture amid the hills, I cut my way first through a foot of snow, and then a foot of ice, and open a window under my feet, where, kneeling to drink, I look down into the quiet parlor of the fishes, pervaded by a softened light as through a window of ground glass,

with its bright sanded floor the same as in summer; there
a perennial waveless serenity reigns as in the amber twilight sky, corresponding to the cool and even tempera-
ment of the inhabitants. Heaven is under our feet as well
as over our heads.

Early in the morning, while all things are crisp with
frost, men come with fishing-reels and slender lunch, and
let down their fine lines through the snowy field to take
pickerel and perch; wild men, who instinctively follow
other fashions and trust other authorities than their
townsmen, and by their goings and comings stitch towns
together in parts where else they would be ripped. They
sit and eat their luncheon in stout fear-naughts on the
dry oak leaves on the shore, as wise in natural lore as
the citizen is in artificial. They never consult with books,
and know and can tell much less than they have done.
The things which they practice are said not yet to be
known. Here is one fishing for pickerel with grown perch
for bait. You look into his pail with wonder as into a
summer pond, as if he kept summer locked up at home,
or knew where she had retreated. How, pray, did he get
these in midwinter? Oh, he got worms out of rotten logs
since the ground froze, and so he caught them. His life
itself passes deeper in nature than the studies of the
naturalist penetrate; himself a subject for the naturalist.
The latter raises the moss and bark gently with his knife
in search of insects; the former lays open logs to their
core with his axe, and moss and bark fly far and wide.
He gets his living by barking trees. Such a man has some
right to fish, and I love to see nature carried out in
him. The perch swallows the grub-worm, the pickerel
swallows the perch, and the fisherman swallows the pickerel; and so all the chinks in the scale of being are filled.

When I strolled around the pond in misty weather I
was sometimes amused by the primitive mode which
some ruder fisherman had adopted. He would perhaps
have placed alder branches over the narrow holes in the
ice, which were four or five rods apart and an equal
distance from the shore, and having fastened the end of
the line to a stick to prevent its being pulled through,
have passed the slack line over a twig of the alder, a
foot or more above the ice, and tied a dry oak leaf to

it, which, being pulled down, would show when he had a bite. These alders loomed through the mist at regular intervals as you walked half way round the pond.

Ah, the pickerel of Walden! when I see them lying on the ice, or in the well which the fisherman cuts in the ice, making a little hole to admit the water, I am always surprised by their rare beauty, as if they were fabulous fishes, they are so foreign to the streets, even to the woods, foreign as Arabia to our Concord life. They possess a quite dazzling and transcendent beauty which separates them by a wide interval from the cadaverous cod and haddock whose fame is trumpeted in our streets. They are not green like the pines, nor gray like the stones, nor blue like the sky; but they have, to my eyes, if possible, yet rarer colors, like flowers and precious stones, as if they were the pearls, the animalized *nuclei* or crystals of the Walden water. They, of course, are Walden all over and all through; are themselves small Waldens in the animal kingdom, Waldenses. It is surprising that they are caught here,—that in this deep and capacious spring, far beneath the rattling teams and chaises and tinkling sleighs that travel the Walden road, this great gold and emerald fish swims. I never chanced to see its kind in any market; it would be the cynosure of all eyes there. Easily, with a few convulsive quirks, they give up their watery ghosts, like a mortal translated before his time to the thin air of heaven.

As I was desirous to recover the long lost bottom of Walden Pond, I surveyed it carefully, before the ice broke up, early in '46, with compass and chain and sounding line. There have been many stories told about the bottom, or rather no bottom, of this pond, which certainly had no foundation for themselves. It is remarkable how long men will believe in the bottomlessness of a pond without taking the trouble to sound it. I have visited two such Bottomless Ponds in one walk in this neighborhood. Many have believed that Walden reached quite through to the other side of the globe. Some who have lain flat on the ice for a long time, looking down through the illusive medium, perchance with watery eyes into the bargain, and driven to hasty conclusions by the fear of catching cold in their breasts, have seen vast holes "into which a load of hay might be driven," if there were anybody to drive it, the undoubted source of the Styx and entrance to the Infernal Regions from these parts. Others have gone down from the village with a "fifty-six" and a wagon load of inch rope, but yet have failed to find any bottom; for while the "fifty-six" was resting by the way, they were paying out the rope in the vain attempt to fathom their truly immeasurable capacity for marvellousness. But I can assure my readers that Walden has a reasonably tight bottom at a not unreasonable, though at an unusual, depth. I fathomed it easily with a cod-line and a stone weighing about a pound and a half, and could tell accurately when the stone left the bottom, by having to pull so much harder before the water got underneath to help me. The greatest depth was exactly one hundred and two feet; to which may be added the five feet which it has risen since, making one hundred and seven. This is a remarkable depth for so small an area; yet not an inch of it can be spared by the imagination. What if all ponds were shallow? Would it not react on the minds of men? I am thankful that this pond was made deep and pure for a symbol. While men believe in the infinite some ponds will be thought to be bottomless.

A factory-owner, hearing what depth I had found, thought that it could not be true, for, judging from his acquaintance with dams, sand would not lie at so steep an angle. But the deepest ponds are not so deep in proportion to their area as most suppose, and, if drained, would not leave very remarkable valleys. They are not like cups between the hills; for this one, which is so unusually deep for its area, appears in a vertical section through its centre not deeper than a shallow plate. Most ponds, emptied, would leave a meadow no more hollow than we frequently see. William Gilpin, who is so admirable in all that relates to landscapes, and usually so correct, standing at the head of Loch Fyne, in Scotland, which he describes as "a bay of salt water, sixty or seventy fathoms deep, four miles in breadth," and about fifty miles long, surrounded by mountains, observes, "if we could have seen it immediately after the diluvian crash, or whatever convulsion of nature occasioned it,

before the waters gushed in, what a horrid chasm must
it have appeared!

> "So high as heaved the tumid hills, so low
>   Down sunk a hollow bottom broad and deep,
>   Capacious bed of waters."

But if, using the shortest diameter of Loch Fyne, we
apply these proportions to Walden, which, as we have
seen, appears already in a vertical section only like a
shallow plate, it will appear four times as shallow. So
much for the *increased* horrors of the chasm of Loch
Fyne when emptied. No doubt many a smiling valley
with its stretching cornfields occupies exactly such a
"horrid chasm," from which the waters have receded,
though it requires the insight and the far sight of the
geologist to convince the unsuspecting inhabitants of this
fact. Often an inquisitive eye may detect the shores of a
primitive lake in the low horizon hills, and no subsequent
elevation of the plain have been necessary to conceal their
history. But it is easiest, as they who work on the highways
know, to find the hollows by the puddles after a shower.
The amount of it is, the imagination, give it the least license, dives deeper and soars higher than Nature goes. So,
probably, the depth of the ocean will be found to be very
inconsiderable compared with its breadth.

As I sounded through the ice I could determine the
shape of the bottom with greater accuracy than is possible in surveying harbors which do not freeze over, and
I was surprised at its general regularity. In the deepest
part there are several acres more level than almost any
field which is exposed to the sun, wind, and plow. In
one instance, on a line arbitrarily chosen, the depth did
not vary more than one foot in thirty rods; and generally,
near the middle, I could calculate the variation for each
one hundred feet in any direction beforehand within
three or four inches. Some are accustomed to speak of
deep and dangerous holes even in quiet sandy ponds like
this, but the effect of water under these circumstances
is to level all inequalities. The regularity of the bottom
and its conformity to the shores and the range of the
neighboring hills were so perfect that a distant promon-

tory betrayed itself in the soundings quite across the pond, and its direction could be determined by observing the opposite shore. Cape becomes bar, and plain shoal, and valley and gorge deep water and channel.

When I had mapped the pond by the scale of ten rods to an inch, and put down the soundings, more than a hundred in all, I observed this remarkable coincidence. Having noticed that the number indicating the greatest depth was apparently in the centre of the map, I laid a rule on the map lengthwise, and then breadthwise, and found, to my surprise, that the line of greatest length intersected the line of greatest breadth *exactly* at the point of greatest depth, notwithstanding that the middle is so nearly level, the outline of the pond far from regular, and the extreme length and breadth were got by measuring into the coves; and I said to myself, Who knows but this hint would conduct to the deepest part of the ocean as well as of a pond or puddle? Is not this the rule also for the height of mountains, regarded as the opposite of valleys? We know that a hill is not highest at its narrowest part.

Of five coves, three, or all which had been sounded, were observed to have a bar quite across their mouths and deeper water within, so that the bay tended to be an expansion of water within the land not only horizontally but vertically, and to form a basin or independent pond, the direction of the two capes showing the course of the bar. Every harbor on the seacoast, also, has its bar at its entrance. In proportion as the mouth of the cove was wider compared with its length, the water over the bar was deeper compared with that in the basin. Given, then, the length and breadth of the cove, and the character of the surrounding shore, and you have almost elements enough to make out a formula for all cases.

In order to see how nearly I could guess, with this experience, at the deepest point in a pond, by observing the outlines of its surface and the character of its shores alone, I made a plan of White Pond, which contains about forty-one acres, and, like this, has no island in it, nor any visible inlet or outlet; and as the line of greatest breadth fell very near the line of least breadth, where two opposite capes approached each other and two opposite bays receded, I ventured to mark a point a short distance from the latter line, but still on the line of greatest length, as the deepest. The deepest part was found to be within one hundred feet of this, still farther in the direction to which I had inclined, and was only one foot deeper, namely, sixty feet. Of course, a stream running through, or an island in the pond, would make the problem much more complicated.

If we knew all the laws of Nature, we should need only one fact, or the description of one actual phenomenon, to infer all the particular results at that point. Now we know only a few laws, and our result is vitiated, not, of course, by any confusion or irregularity in Nature, but by our ignorance of essential elements in the calculation. Our notions of law and harmony are commonly confined to those instances which we detect; but the harmony which results from a far greater number of seemingly conflicting, but really concurring, laws, which we have not detected, is still more wonderful. The particular laws are as our points of view, as, to the traveller, a mountain outline varies with every step, and it has an infinite number of profiles, though absolutely but one form. Even when cleft or bored through it is not comprehended in its entireness.

What I have observed of the pond is no less true in ethics. It is the law of average. Such a rule of the two diameters not only guides us toward the sun in the system and the heart in man, but draw lines through the length and breadth of the aggregate of a man's particular daily behaviors and waves of life into his coves and inlets, and where they intersect will be the height or depth of his character. Perhaps we need only to know how his shores trend and his adjacent country or circumstances, to infer his depth and concealed bottom. If he is surrounded by mountainous circumstances, an Achillean shore, whose peaks overshadow and are reflected in his bosom, they suggest a corresponding depth in him. But a low and smooth shore proves him shallow on that side. In our bodies, a bold projecting brow falls off to and indicates a corresponding depth of thought. Also there is a bar across the entrance of our every cove, or particular inclination; each is our harbor for a season, in which we are detained and partially land-locked. These inclinations are not whimsical usually, but their form, size, and direction are determined by the promontories of the shore, the ancient axes of elevation. When this bar is gradually increased by storms, tides, or currents, or there is a subsidence of the waters, so that it reaches to the surface, that which was at first but an inclination in the shore in which a thought was harbored becomes an individual lake, cut off from the ocean, wherein the thought secures its own conditions,—changes, perhaps, from salt to fresh, becomes a sweet sea, dead sea, or a marsh. At the advent of each individual into this life, may we not suppose that such a bar has risen to the surface somewhere? It is true, we are such poor navigators that our thoughts, for the most part, stand off and on upon a harborless coast, are conversant only with the bights of the bays of poesy, or steer for the public ports of entry, and go into the dry docks of science, where they merely refit for this world, and no natural currents concur to individualize them.

As for the inlet or outlet of Walden, I have not discovered any but rain and snow and evaporation, though perhaps, with a thermometer and a line, such places may be found, for where the water flows into the pond it will probably be coldest in summer and warmest in winter. When the ice-men were at work here in '46-7, the cakes sent to the shore were one day rejected by those who were stacking them up there, not being thick enough to lie side by side with the rest; and the cutters thus discovered that the ice over a small space was two or three inches thinner than elsewhere, which made them think that there was an inlet there. They also showed me in another place what they thought was a "leach-hole," through which the pond leaked out under a hill into a neighboring meadow, pushing me out on a cake of ice to see it. It was a small cavity under ten feet of water; but I think that I can warrant the pond not to need soldering till they find a worse leak than that. One has suggested, that if such a "leach-hole" should be found, its connection with the meadow, if any existed, might be proved by conveying some colored powder or sawdust to the mouth of the hole, and then putting a strainer over the spring in the meadow, which would catch some of the particles carried through by the current.

While I was surveying, the ice, which was sixteen inches thick, undulated under a slight wind like water. It is well known that a level cannot be used on ice. At one rod from the shore its greatest fluctuation, when observed by means of a level on land directed toward a graduated staff on the ice, was three quarters of an inch, though the ice appeared firmly attached to the shore. It was probably greater in the middle. Who knows but if our instruments were delicate enough we might detect an undulation in the crust of the earth? When two legs of my level were on the shore and the third on the ice, and the sights were directed over the latter, a rise or fall of the ice of an almost infinitesimal amount made a difference of several feet on a tree across the pond. When I began to cut holes for sounding there were three or four inches of water on the ice under a deep snow which had sunk it thus far; but the water began immediately to run into these holes, and continued to run for two days in deep streams, which wore away the ice on every side, and contributed essentially, if not mainly, to dry the surface of the pond; for, as the water ran in, it raised and floated the ice. This was somewhat like cutting a hole in the bottom of a ship to let the water out. When such holes freeze, and a rain succeeds, and finally a new freezing forms a fresh smooth ice over all, it is beautifully mottled internally by dark figures, shaped somewhat like a spider's web, what you may call ice rosettes, produced by the channels worn by the water flowing from all sides to a centre. Sometimes, also, when the ice was covered with shallow puddles, I saw a double shadow of myself, one standing on the head of the other, one on the ice, the other on the trees or hillside.

While yet it is cold January, and snow and ice are thick and solid, the prudent landlord comes from the village to get ice to cool his summer drink; impressively, even pathetically, wise, to foresee the heat and thirst of July now in January,—wearing a thick coat and mittens! when so many things are not provided for. It may be that he lays up no treasures in this world which will cool his summer drink in the next. He cuts and saws the solid pond, unroofs the house of fishes, and carts off their very element and air, held fast by chains and stakes like corded wood, through the favoring winter air, to wintry cellars, to underlie the summer there. It looks like solidified azure, as, far off, it is drawn through the streets. These ice-cutters are a merry race, full of jest and sport, and when I went among them they were wont to invite me to saw pit-fashion with them, I standing underneath.

In the winter of '46-7 there came a hundred men of Hyperborean extraction swoop down on to our pond one morning, with many carloads of ungainly-looking farming tools,—sleds, plows, drill-barrows, turf-knives, spades, saws, rakes, and each man was armed with a double-pointed pike-staff, such as is not described in the New-England Farmer or the Cultivator. I did not know whether they had come to sow a crop of winter rye, or some other kind of grain recently introduced from Iceland. As I saw no manure, I judged that they meant to skim the land, as I had done, thinking the soil was deep and had lain fallow long enough. They said that a gentleman farmer, who was behind the scenes, wanted to double his money, which, as I understood, amounted to half a million already; but in order to cover each one of his dollars with another, he took off the only coat, ay, the skin itself, of Walden Pond in the midst of a hard winter. They went to work at once, plowing, harrowing, rolling, furrowing, in admirable order, as if they were bent on making this a model farm; but when I was looking sharp to see what kind of seed they dropped into the furrow, a gang of fellows by my side suddenly began to hook up the virgin mould itself, with a peculiar jerk, clean down to the sand, or rather the water,—for it was a very springy soil,—indeed all the *terra firma* there was,—and haul it away on sleds, and then I guessed that they must be cutting peat in a bog. So they came and went every day, with a peculiar shriek from the locomotive, from and to some point of the polar regions, as it seemed to me, like a flock of arctic snowbirds. But sometimes Squaw Walden had her revenge, and a hired man, walking behind his team, slipped through a crack in the ground down toward Tartarus, and he who was so brave before suddenly became but the ninth part of a man, almost gave up his animal heat, and was glad to take refuge in my house, and acknowledged that there was some virtue in a stove; or sometimes the frozen soil took a piece of steel out of a plowshare, or a plow got set in the furrow and had to be cut out.

To speak literally, a hundred Irishmen, with Yankee overseers, came from Cambridge every day to get out the ice. They divided it into cakes by methods too well known to require description, and these, being sledded to the shore, were rapidly hauled off on to an ice platform, and raised by grappling irons and block and tackle, worked by horses, on to a stack, as surely as so many barrels of flour, and there placed evenly side by side, and row upon row, as if they formed the solid base of an obelisk designed to pierce the clouds. They told me that in a good day they could get out a thousand tons, which was the yield of about one acre. Deep ruts and "cradleholes" were worn in the ice, as on *terra firma,* by the passage of the sleds over the same track, and the horses invariably ate their oats out of cakes of ice hollowed out like buckets. They stacked up the cakes thus in the open air in a pile thirty-five feet high on one side and six or seven rods square, putting hay between the outside layers to exclude the air; for when the wind, though never so cold, finds a passage through, it will wear large cavities, leaving slight supports or studs only here and there, and finally topple it down. At first it looked like a vast blue fort or Valhalla; but when they began to tuck the coarse meadow hay into the crevices, and this became covered with rime and icicles, it looked like a venerable moss-grown and hoary ruin, built of azure-tinted marble, the abode of Winter, that old man we see in the almanac,—his shanty, as if he had a design to estivate with us. They calculated that not twenty-five per cent. of this would reach its destination, and that two or three per cent. would be wasted in the cars. However, a still greater part of this heap had a different destiny from what was intended; for, either because the ice was found not to keep so well as was expected, containing more air than usual, or for some other reason, it never got to market. This heap, made in the winter of

'46-7 and estimated to contain ten thousand tons, was finally covered with hay and boards; and though it was unroofed the following July, and a part of it carried off, the rest remaining exposed to the sun, it stood over that summer and the next winter, and was not quite melted till September, 1848. Thus the pond recovered the greater part.

Like the water, the Walden ice, seen near at hand, has a green tint, but at a distance is beautifully blue, and you can easily tell it from the white ice of the river, or the merely greenish ice of some ponds, a quarter of a mile off. Sometimes one of those great cakes slips from the ice-man's sled into the village street, and lies there for a week like a great emerald, an object of interest to all passers. I have noticed that a portion of Walden which in the state of water was green will often, when frozen, appear from the same point of view blue. So the hollows about this pond will, sometimes, in the winter, be filled with a greenish water somewhat like its own, but the next day will have frozen blue. Perhaps the blue color of water and ice is due to the light and air they contain, and the most transparent is the bluest. Ice is an interesting subject for contemplation. They told me that they had some in the ice-houses at Fresh Pond five years old which was as good as ever. Why is it that a bucket of water soon becomes putrid, but frozen remains sweet forever? It is commonly said that this is the difference between the affections and the intellect.

Thus for sixteen days I saw from my window a hundred men at work like busy husbandmen, with teams and horses and apparently all the implements of farming, such a picture as we see on the first page of the almanac; and as often as I looked out I was reminded of the fable of the lark and the reapers, or the parable of the sower, and the like; and now they are all gone, and in thirty days more, probably, I shall look from the same window on the pure sea-green Walden water there, reflecting the clouds and the trees, and sending up its evaporations in solitude, and no traces will appear that a man has ever stood there. Perhaps I shall hear a solitary loon laugh as he dives and plumes himself, or shall see a lonely fisher in his boat, like a floating leaf, beholding his form reflected in the waves, where lately a hundred men securely labored.

Thus it appears that the sweltering inhabitants of Charleston and New Orleans, of Madras and Bombay and Calcutta, drink at my well. In the morning I bathe my intellect in the stupendous and cosmogonal philosophy of the Bhagvat-Geeta, since whose composition years of the gods have elapsed, and in comparison with which our modern world and its literature seem puny and trivial; and I doubt if that philosophy is not to be referred to a previous state of existence, so remote is its sublimity from our conceptions. I lay down the book and go to my well for water, and lo! there I meet the servant of the Bramin, priest of Brahma and Vishnu and Indra, who still sits in his temple on the Ganges reading the Vedas, or dwells at the root of a tree with his crust and water jug. I meet his servant come to draw water for his master, and our buckets as it were grate together in the same well. The pure Walden water is mingled with the sacred water of the Ganges. With favoring winds it is wafted past the site of the fabulous islands of Atlantis and the Hesperides, makes the periplus of Hanno, and floating by Ternate and Tidore and the mouth of the Persian Gulf, melts in the tropic gales of the Indian seas, and is landed in ports of which Alexander only heard the names.

17. Spring

THE opening of large tracts by the ice-cutters commonly causes a pond to break up earlier; for the water, agitated by the wind, even in cold weather, wears away the surrounding ice. But such was not the effect on Walden that year, for she had soon got a thick new garment to take the place of the old. This pond never breaks up so soon as the others in this neighborhood, on account both of its greater depth and its having no stream passing through it to melt or wear away the ice. I never knew

it to open in the course of a winter, not excepting that
of '52-3, which gave the ponds so severe a trial. It commonly opens about the first of April, a week or ten days
later than Flint's Pond and Fair Haven, beginning to
melt on the north side and in the shallower parts where
it began to freeze. It indicates better than any water
hereabouts the absolute progress of the season, being
least affected by transient changes of temperature. A
severe cold of a few days' duration in March may very
much retard the opening of the former ponds, while the
temperature of Walden increases almost uninterruptedly.
A thermometer thrust into the middle of Walden on the
6th of March, 1847, stood at 32°, or freezing point; near
the shore at 33°; in the middle of Flint's Pond, the same
day, at 32½°; at a dozen rods from the shore, in shallow
water, under ice a foot thick, at 36°. This difference of
three and a half degrees between the temperature of the
deep water and the shallow in the latter pond, and the
fact that a great proportion of it is comparatively shallow, show why it should break up so much sooner than
Walden. The ice in the shallowest part was at this time
several inches thinner than in the middle. In midwinter
the middle had been the warmest and the ice thinnest
there. So, also, every one who has waded about the
shores of a pond in summer must have perceived how
much warmer the water is close to the shore, where only
three or four inches deep, than a little distance out, and
on the surface where it is deep, than near the bottom.
In spring the sun not only exerts an influence through
the increased temperature of the air and earth, but its
heat passes through ice a foot or more thick, and is
reflected from the bottom in shallow water, and so also
warms the water and melts the under side of the ice, at
the same time that it is melting it more directly above,
making it uneven, and causing the air bubbles which it
contains to extend themselves upward and downward
until it is completely honeycombed, and at last disappears suddenly in a single spring rain. Ice has its grain
as well as wood, and when a cake begins to rot or
"comb," that is, assume the appearance of honeycomb,
whatever may be its position, the air cells are at right
angles with what was the water surface. Where there is

a rock or a log rising near to the surface the ice over it is much thinner, and is frequently quite dissolved by this reflected heat; and I have been told that in the experiment at Cambridge to freeze water in a shallow wooden pond, though the cold air circulated underneath, and so had access to both sides, the reflection of the sun from the bottom more than counterbalanced this advantage. When a warm rain in the middle of the winter melts off the snow ice from Walden, and leaves a hard dark or transparent ice on the middle, there will be a strip of rotten though thicker white ice, a rod or more wide, about the shores, created by.this reflected heat. Also, as I have said, the bubbles themselves within the ice operate as burning-glasses to melt the ice beneath.

The phenomena of the year take place every day in a pond on a small scale. Every morning, generally speaking, the shallow water is being warmed more rapidly than the deep, though it may not be made so warm after all, and every evening it is being cooled more rapidly until the morning. The day is an epitome of the year. The night is the winter, the morning and evening are the spring and fall, and the noon is the summer. The cracking and booming of the ice indicate a change of temperature. One pleasant morning after a cold night, February 24th, 1850, having gone to Flint's Pond to spend the day, I noticed with surprise, that when I struck the ice with the head of my axe, it resounded like a gong for many rods around, or as if I had struck on a tight drum-head. The pond began to boom about an hour after sunrise, when it felt the influence of the sun's rays slanted upon it from over the hills; it stretched itself and yawned like a waking man with a gradually increasing tumult, which was kept up three or four hours. It took a short siesta at noon, and boomed once more toward night, as the sun was withdrawing his influence. In the right stage of the weather a pond fires its evening gun with great regularity. But in the middle of the day, being full of cracks, and the air also being less elastic, it had completely lost its resonance, and probably fishes and muskrats could not then have been stunned by a blow on it. The fishermen say that the "thundering of the pond" scares the fishes and prevents their biting. The pond does not thun-

der every evening, and I cannot tell surely when to expect its thundering; but though I may perceive no
difference in the weather, it does. Who would have suspected so large and cold and thick-skinned a thing to be
so sensitive? Yet it has its law to which it thunders obedience when it should as surely as the buds expand in
the spring. The earth is all alive and covered with pap-
illæ. The largest pond is as sensitive to atmospheric
changes as the globule of mercury in its tube.

One attraction in coming to the woods to live was that
I should have leisure and opportunity to see the Spring
come in. The ice in the pond at length begins to be
honeycombed, and I can set my heel in it as I walk. Fogs
and rains and warmer suns are gradually melting the
snow; the days have grown sensibly longer; and I see
how I shall get through the winter without adding to my
wood-pile, for large fires are no longer necessary. I am
on the alert for the first signs of spring, to hear the
chance note of some arriving bird, or the striped squirrel's chirp, for his stores must be now nearly exhausted,
or see the woodchuck venture out of his winter quarters.
On the 13th of March, after I had heard the bluebird,
song sparrow, and red-wing, the ice was still nearly a
foot thick. As the weather grew warmer it was not sensibly worn away by the water, nor broken up and floated
off as in rivers, but, though it was completely melted for
half a rod in width about the shore, the middle was
merely honeycombed and saturated with water, so that
you could put your foot through it when six inches thick;
but by the next day, evening, perhaps, after a warm rain
followed by fog, it would have wholly disappeared, all
gone off with the fog, spirited away. One year I went
across the middle only five days before it disappeared
entirely. In 1845 Walden was first completely open on
the 1st of April; in '46, the 25th of March; in '47, the
8th of April; in '51, the 28th of March; in '52, the 18th
of April; in '53, the 23d of March; in '54, about the 7th
of April.

Every incident connected with the breaking up of the
rivers and ponds and the settling of the weather is particularly interesting to us who live in a climate of so great
extremes. When the warmer days come, they who dwell

near the river hear the ice crack at night with a startling whoop as loud as artillery, as if its icy fetters were rent from end to end, and within a few days see it rapidly going out. So the alligator comes out of the mud with quakings of the earth. One old man, who has been a close observer of Nature, and seems as thoroughly wise in regard to all her operations as if she had been put upon the stocks when he was a boy, and he had helped to lay her keel,—who has come to his growth, and can hardly acquire more of natural lore if he should live to the age of Methuselah,—told me—and I was surprised to hear him express wonder at any of Nature's operations, for I thought that there were no secrets between them—that one spring day he took his gun and boat, and thought that he would have a little sport with the ducks. There was ice still on the meadows, but it was all gone out of the river, and he dropped down without obstruction from Sudbury, where he lived, to Fair Haven Pond, which he found, unexpectedly, covered for the most part with a firm field of ice. It was a warm day, and he was surprised to see so great a body of ice remaining. Not seeing any ducks, he hid his boat on the north or back side of an island in the pond, and then concealed himself in the bushes on the south side, to await them. The ice was melted for three or four rods from the shore, and there was a smooth and warm sheet of water, with a muddy bottom, such as the ducks love, within, and he thought it likely that some would be along pretty soon. After he had lain still there about an hour he heard a low and seemingly very distant sound, but singularly grand and impressive, unlike anything he had ever heard, gradually swelling and increasing as if it would have a universal and memorable ending, a sullen rush and roar, which seemed to him all at once like the sound of a vast body of fowl coming in to settle there, and, seizing his gun, he started up in haste and excited; but he found, to his surprise, that the whole body of the ice had started while he lay there, and drifted in to the shore, and the sound he had heard was made by its edge grating on the shore,—at first gently nibbled and crumbled off, but at length heaving up and scattering its wrecks along the island to a considerable height before it came to a standstill.

At length the sun's rays have attained the right angle, and warm winds blow up mist and rain and melt the snowbanks, and the sun, dispersing the mist, smiles on a checkered landscape of russet and white smoking with incense, through which the traveller picks his way from islet to islet, cheered by the music of a thousand tinkling rills and rivulets whose veins are filled with the blood of winter which they are bearing off.

Few phenomena gave me more delight than to observe the forms which thawing sand and clay assume in flowing down the sides of a deep cut on the railroad through which I passed on my way to the village, a phenomenon not very common on so large a scale, though the number of freshly exposed banks of the right material must have been greatly multiplied since railroads were invented. The material was sand of every degree of fineness and of various rich colors, commonly mixed with a little clay. When the frost comes out in the spring, and even in a thawing day in the winter, the sand begins to flow down the slopes like lava, sometimes bursting out through the snow and overflowing it where no sand was to be seen before. Innumerable little streams overlap and interlace one with another, exhibiting a sort of hybrid product, which obeys half way the law of currents, and half way that of vegetation. As it flows it takes the forms of sappy leaves or vines, making heaps of pulpy sprays a foot or more in depth, and resembling, as you look down on them, the laciniated, lobed, and imbricated thalluses of some lichens; or you are reminded of coral, of leopards' paws or birds' feet, of brains or lungs or bowels, and excrements of all kinds. It is a truly *grotesque* vegetation, whose forms and color we see imitated in bronze, a sort of architectural foliage more ancient and typical than acanthus, chicory, ivy, vine, or any vegetable leaves; destined perhaps, under some circumstances, to become a puzzle to future geologists. The whole cut impressed me as if it were a cave with its stalactites laid open to the light. The various shades of the sand are singularly rich and agreeable, embracing the different iron colors, brown, gray, yellowish, and reddish. When the flowing mass reaches the drain at the foot of the bank it spreads out flatter into *strands,* the separate streams losing their semi-cylindrical form and gradually becoming more flat and broad, running together as they are more moist, till they form an almost flat *sand,* still variously and beautifully shaded, but in which you can trace the original forms of vegetation; till at length, in the water itself, they are converted into *banks,* like those formed off the mouths of rivers, and the forms of vegetation are lost in the ripple-marks on the bottom.

The whole bank, which is from twenty to forty feet high, is sometimes overlaid with a mass of this kind of foliage, or sandy rupture, for a quarter of a mile on one or both sides, the produce of one spring day. What makes this sand foliage remarkable is its springing into existence thus suddenly. When I see on the one side the inert bank,—for the sun acts on one side first,—and on the other this luxuriant foliage, the creation of an hour, I am affected as if in a peculiar sense I stood in the laboratory of the Artist who made the world and me,— had come to where he was still at work, sporting on this bank, and with excess of energy strewing his fresh designs about. I feel as if I were nearer to the vitals of the globe, for this sandy overflow is something such a foliaceous mass as the vitals of the animal body. You find thus in the very sands an anticipation of the vegetable leaf. No wonder that the earth expresses itself outwardly in leaves, it so labors with the idea inwardly. The atoms have already learned this law, and are pregnant by it. The overhanging leaf sees here its prototype. *Internally,* whether in the globe or animal body, it is a moist thick *lobe,* a word especially applicable to the liver and lungs and the *leaves* of fat (λείβω, *labor, lapsus,* to flow or slip downward, a lapsing; λοβός, *globus,* lobe, globe; also lap, flap, and many other words); *externally,* a dry thin *leaf,* even as the *f* and *v* are a pressed and dried *b.* The radicals of *lobe* are *lb,* the soft mass of the *b* (single-lobed, or B, double-lobed), with the liquid *l* behind it pressing it forward. In globe, *glb,* the guttural *g* adds to the meaning the capacity of the throat. The feathers and wings of birds are still drier and thinner leaves. Thus, also, you pass from the lumpish grub in the earth to the airy and fluttering butterfly. The very globe continually transcends and translates itself, and becomes winged in its orbit. Even ice begins with delicate crystal leaves, as if it had flowed into moulds which the fronds of water-plants have impressed on the watery mirror. The whole tree itself is but one leaf, and rivers are still vaster leaves whose pulp is intervening earth, and towns and cities are the ova of insects in their axils.

When the sun withdraws the sand ceases to flow, but in the morning the streams will start once more and branch and branch again into a myriad of others. You here see perchance how blood-vessels are formed. If you look closely you observe that first there pushes forward from the thawing mass a stream of softened sand with a drop-like point, like the ball of the finger, feeling its way slowly and blindly downward, until at last with more heat and moisture, as the sun gets higher, the moist fluid portion, in its effort to obey the law to which the most inert also yields, separates from the latter and forms for itself a meandering channel or artery within that, in which is seen a little silvery stream glancing like light-ning from one stage of pulpy leaves or branches to an-other, and ever and anon swallowed up in the sand. It is wonderful how rapidly yet perfectly the sand organizes itself as it flows, using the best material its mass affords to form the sharp edges of its channel. Such are the sources of rivers. In the silicious matter which the water deposits is perhaps the bony system, and in the still finer soil and organic matter the fleshy fibre or cellular tissue. What is man but a mass of thawing clay? The ball of the human finger is but a drop congealed. The fingers and toes flow to their extent from the thawing mass of the body. Who knows what the human body would expand and flow out to under a more genial heaven? Is not the hand a spreading *palm* leaf with its lobes and veins? The ear may be regarded, fancifully, as a lichen, *Umbilicaria,* on the side of the head, with its lobe or drop. The lip—*labium,* from *labor* (?)—laps or lapses from the sides of the cavernous mouth. The nose is a manifest congealed drop or stalactite. The chin is a still larger drop, the confluent dripping of the face. The

cheeks are a slide from the brows into the valley of the
face, opposed and diffused by the cheek bones. Each
rounded lobe of the vegetable leaf, too, is a thick and
now loitering drop, larger or smaller; the lobes are the
fingers of the leaf; and as many lobes as it has, in so
many directions it tends to flow, and more heat or other
genial influences would have caused it to flow yet
farther.

Thus it seemed that this one hillside illustrated the
principle of all the operations of Nature. The Maker of
this earth but patented a leaf. What Champollion will
decipher this hieroglyphic for us, that we may turn over
a new leaf at last? This phenomenon is more exhilarating
to me than the luxuriance and fertility of vineyards.
True, it is somewhat excrementitious in its character, and
there is no end to the heaps of liver, lights, and bowels,
as if the globe were turned wrong side outward; but this
suggests at least that Nature has some bowels, and there
again is mother of humanity. This is the frost coming
out of the ground; this is Spring. It precedes the green
and flowery spring, as mythology precedes regular poetry. I know of nothing more purgative of winter fumes
and indigestions. It convinces me that Earth is still in
her swaddling-clothes, and stretches forth baby fingers
on every side. Fresh curls spring from the baldest brow.
There is nothing inorganic. These foliaceous heaps lie
along the bank like the slag of a furnace, showing that
Nature is "in full blast" within. The earth is not a mere
fragment of dead history, stratum upon stratum like the
leaves of a book, to be studied by geologists and anti-
quaries chiefly, but living poetry like the leaves of a tree,
which precede flowers and fruit,—not a fossil earth, but
a living earth; compared with whose great central life all
animal and vegetable life is merely parasitic. Its throes
will heave our exuviæ from their graves. You may melt
your metals and cast them into the most beautiful
moulds you can; they will never excite me like the forms
which this molten earth flows out into. And not only it,
but the institutions upon it are plastic like clay in the
hands of the potter.

Ere long, not only on these banks, but on every hill
and plain and in every hollow, the frost comes out of

the ground like a dormant quadruped from its burrow, and seeks the sea with music, or migrates to other climes in clouds. Thaw with his gentle persuasion is more powerful than Thor with his hammer. The one melts, the other but breaks in pieces.

When the ground was partially bare of snow, and a few warm days had dried its surface somewhat, it was pleasant to compare the first tender signs of the infant year just peeping forth with the stately beauty of the withered vegetation which had withstood the winter,— life-everlasting, goldenrods, pin-weeds, and graceful wild grasses, more obvious and interesting frequently than in summer even, as if their beauty was not ripe till then; even cotton-grass, cat-tails, mulleins, johnswort, hard-hack, meadow-sweet, and other strong-stemmed plants, those unexhausted granaries which entertain the earliest birds,—decent weeds, at least, which widowed Nature wears. I am particularly attracted by the arching and sheaf-like top of the wool-grass; it brings back the summer to our winter memories, and is among the forms which art loves to copy, and which, in the vegetable kingdom, have the same relation to types already in the mind of man that astronomy has. It is an antique style, older than Greek or Egyptian. Many of the phenomena of Winter are suggestive of an inexpressible tenderness and fragile delicacy. We are accustomed to hear this king described as a rude and boisterous tyrant; but with the gentleness of a lover he adorns the tresses of Summer.

At the approach of spring the red squirrels got under my house, two at a time, directly under my feet as I sat reading or writing, and kept up the queerest chuckling and chirruping and vocal pirouetting and gurgling sounds that ever were heard; and when I stamped they only chirruped the louder, as if past all fear and respect in their mad pranks, defying humanity to stop them. No, you don't—chickaree—chickaree. They were wholly deaf to my arguments, or failed to perceive their force, and fell into a strain of invective that was irresistible.

The first sparrow of spring! The year beginning with younger hope than ever! The faint silvery warblings heard over the partially bare and moist fields from the bluebird, the song sparrow, and the red-wing, as if the last flakes of winter tinkled as they fell! What at such a time are histories, chronologies, traditions, and all written revelations? The brooks sing carols and glees to the spring. The marsh hawk, sailing low over the meadow, is already seeking the first slimy life that awakes. The sinking sound of melting snow is heard in all dells, and the ice dissolves apace in the ponds. The grass flames up on the hillsides like a spring fire,—*"et primitus oritur herba imbribus primoribus evocata,"*—as if the earth sent forth an inward heat to greet the returning sun; not yellow but green is the color of its flame;—the symbol of perpetual youth, the grass-blade, like a long green ribbon, streams from the sod into the summer, checked indeed by the frost, but anon pushing on again, lifting its spear of last year's hay with the fresh life below. It grows as steadily as the rill oozes out of the ground. It is almost identical with that, for in the growing days of June, when the rills are dry, the grass-blades are their channels, and from year to year the herds drink at this perennial green stream, and the mower draws from it betimes their winter supply. So our human life but dies down to its root, and still puts forth its green blade to eternity.

Walden is melting apace. There is a canal two rods wide along the northerly and westerly sides, and wider still at the east end. A great field of ice has cracked off from the main body. I hear a song sparrow singing from the bushes on the shore,—*olit, olit, olit,—chip, chip, chip, che char,—che wiss, wiss, wiss.* He too is helping to crack it. How handsome the great sweeping curves in the edge of the ice, answering somewhat to those of the shore, but more regular! It is unusually hard, owing to the recent severe but transient cold, and all watered or waved like a palace floor. But the wind slides eastward over its opaque surface in vain, till it reaches the living surface beyond. It is glorious to behold this ribbon of water sparkling in the sun, the bare face of the pond full of glee and youth, as if it spoke the joy of the fishes within it, and of the sands on its shore,—a silvery sheen as from the scales of a leuciscus, as it were all one active fish. Such is the contrast between winter and spring. Walden was dead and is alive again. But this spring it broke up more steadily, as I have said.

The change from storm and winter to serene and mild weather, from dark and sluggish hours to bright and elastic ones, is a memorable crisis which all things proclaim. It is seemingly instantaneous at last. Suddenly an influx of light filled my house, though the evening was at hand, and the clouds of winter still overhung it, and the eaves were dripping with sleety rain. I looked out the window, and lo! where yesterday was cold gray ice there lay the transparent pond already calm and full of hope as in a summer evening, reflecting a summer evening sky in its bosom, though none was visible overhead, as if it had intelligence with some remote horizon. I heard a robin in the distance, the first I had heard for many a thousand years, methought, whose note I shall not forget for many a thousand more,—the same sweet and powerful song as of yore. O the evening robin, at the end of a New England summer day! If I could ever find the twig he sits upon! I mean *he;* I mean *the twig.* This at least is not the *Turdus migratorius.* The pitch pines and shrub oaks about my house, which had so long drooped, suddenly resumed their several characters, looked brighter, greener, and more erect and alive, as if effectually cleansed and restored by the rain. I knew that it would not rain any more. You may tell by looking at any twig of the forest, ay, at your very wood-pile, whether its winter is past or not. As it grew darker, I was startled by the honking of geese flying low over the woods, like weary travellers getting in late from Southern lakes, and indulging at last in unrestrained complaint and mutual consolation. Standing at my door, I could hear the rush of their wings; when, driving toward my house, they suddenly spied my light, and with hushed clamor wheeled and settled in the pond. So I came in, and shut the door, and passed my first spring night in the woods.

In the morning I watched the geese from the door through the mist, sailing in the middle of the pond, fifty rods off, so large and tumultuous that Walden appeared like an artificial pond for their amusement. But when I stood on the shore they at once rose up with a great flapping of wings at the signal of their commander, and when they had got into rank circled about over my head, twenty-nine of them, and then steered straight to Canada, with a regular *honk* from the leader at intervals, trusting to break their fast in muddier pools. A "plump" of ducks rose at the same time and took the route to the north in the wake of their noisier cousins.

For a week I heard the circling, groping clangor of some solitary goose in the foggy mornings, seeking its companion, and still peopling the woods with the sound of a larger life than they could sustain. In April the pigeons were seen again flying express in small flocks, and in due time I heard the martins twittering over my clearing, though it had not seemed that the township contained so many that it could afford me any, and I fancied that they were peculiarly of the ancient race that dwelt in hollow trees ere white men came. In almost all climes the tortoise and the frog are among the precursors and heralds of this season, and birds fly with song and glancing plumage, and plants spring and bloom, and winds blow, to correct this slight oscillation of the poles and preserve the equilibrium of nature.

As every season seems best to us in its turn, so the coming in of spring is like the creation of Cosmos out of Chaos and the realization of the Golden Age.—

"Eurus ad Auroram Nabathaeaque regna recessit,
 Persidaque, et radiis juga subdita matutinis."

"The East-Wind withdrew to Aurora and the Nabathæan kingdom,
 And the Persian, and the ridges placed under the morning rays.

 • • • • • • • • • • •

 Man was born. Whether that Artificer of things,
 The origin of a better world, made him from the divine seed;
 Or the earth, being recent and lately sundered from the high
 Ether, retained some seeds of cognate heaven."

A single gentle rain makes the grass many shades

greener. So our prospects brighten on the influx of better thoughts. We should be blessed if we lived in the present always, and took advantage of every accident that befell us, like the grass which confesses the influence of the slightest dew that falls on it; and did not spend our time in atoning for the neglect of past opportunities, which we call doing our duty. We loiter in winter while it is already spring. In a pleasant spring morning all men's sins are forgiven. Such a day is a truce to vice. While such a sun holds out to burn, the vilest sinner may return. Through our own recovered innocence we discern the innocence of our neighbors. You may have known your neighbor yesterday for a thief, a drunkard, or a sensualist, and merely pitied or despised him, and despaired of the world; but the sun shines bright and warm this first spring morning, re-creating the world, and you meet him at some serene work, and see how his exhausted and debauched veins expand with still joy and bless the new day, feel the spring influence with the innocence of infancy, and all his faults are forgotten. There is not only an atmosphere of good will about him, but even a savor of holiness groping for expression, blindly and ineffectually perhaps, like a new-born instinct, and for a short hour the south hillsides echoes to no vulgar jest. You see some innocent fair shoots preparing to burst from his gnarled rind and try another year's life, tender and fresh as the youngest plant. Even he has entered into the joy of his Lord. Why the jailer does not leave open his prison doors,—why the judge does not dismiss his case,—why the preacher does not dismiss his congregation! It is because they do not obey the hint which God gives them, nor accept the pardon which he freely offers to all.

"A return to goodness produced each day in the tranquil and beneficent breath of the morning, causes that in respect to the love of virtue and the hatred of vice, one approaches a little the primitive nature of man, as the sprouts of the forest which has been felled. In like manner the evil which one does in the interval of a day prevents the germs of virtues which began to spring up again from developing themselves and destroys them.

"After the germs of virtue have thus been prevented

many times from developing themselves, then the beneficent breath of evening does not suffice to preserve
them. As soon as the breath of evening does not suffice
longer to preserve them, then the nature of man does
not differ much from that of the brute. Men seeing the
nature of this man like that of the brute, think that he
has never possessed the innate faculty of reason. Are
those the true and natural sentiments of man?"

"The Golden Age was first created which without any
    avenger
Spontaneously without law cherished fidelity and rectitude.
Punishment and fear were not; nor were threatening words
    read
On suspended brass; nor did the suppliant crowd fear
The words of their judge; but were safe without an avenger.
Not yet the pine felled on its mountains had descended
To the liquid waves that it might see a foreign world,
And mortals knew no shores but their own.
    .   .   .   .
There was eternal spring, and placid zephyrs with warm
Blasts soothed the flowers born without seed."

On the 29th of April, as I was fishing from the bank
of the river near the Nine-Acre-Corner bridge, standing
on the quaking grass and willow roots, where the muskrats lurk, I heard a singular rattling sound, somewhat
like that of the sticks which boys play with their fingers,
when, looking up, I observed a very slight and graceful
hawk, like a nighthawk, alternately soaring like a ripple
and tumbling a rod or two over and over, showing the
under side of its wings, which gleamed like a satin ribbon
in the sun, or like the pearly inside of a shell. This sight
reminded me of falconry and what nobleness and poetry
are associated with that sport. The merlin it seemed to
me it might be called; but I care not for its name. It was
the most ethereal flight I had ever witnessed. It did not
simply flutter like a butterfly, nor soar like the larger
hawks, but it sported with proud reliance in the fields of
air; mounting again and again with its strange chuckle, it
repeated its free and beautiful fall, turning over and over
like a kite, and then recovering from its lofty tumbling, as

if it had never set its foot on *terra firma*. It appeared to have no companion in the universe,—sporting there alone,—and to need none but the morning and the ether with which it played. It was not lonely, but made all the earth lonely beneath it. Where was the parent which hatched it, its kindred, and its father in the heavens? The tenant of the air, it seemed related to the earth but by an egg hatched some time in the crevice of a crag;—or was its native nest made in the angle of a cloud, woven of the rainbow's trimmings and the sunset sky, and lined with some soft midsummer haze caught up from earth? Its eyry now some cliffy cloud.

Beside this I got a rare mess of golden and silver and bright cupreous fishes, which looked like a string of jewels. Ah! I have penetrated to those meadows on the morning of many a first spring day, jumping from hummock to hummock, from willow root to willow root, when the wild river valley and the woods were bathed in so pure and bright a light as would have waked the dead, if they had been slumbering in their graves, as some suppose. There needs no stronger proof of immortality. All things must live in such a light. O Death, where was thy sting? O Grave, where was thy victory, then?

Our village life would stagnate if it were not for the unexplored forests and meadows which surround it. We need the tonic of wildness,—to wade sometimes in marshes where the bittern and the meadow-hen lurk, and hear the booming of the snipe; to smell the whispering sedge where only some wilder and more solitary fowl builds her nest, and the mink crawls with its belly close to the ground. At the same time that we are earnest to explore and learn all things, we require that all things be mysterious and unexplorable, that land and sea be infinitely wild, unsurveyed and unfathomed by us because unfathomable. We can never have enough of nature. We must be refreshed by the sight of inexhaustible vigor, vast and titanic features, the sea-coast with its wrecks, the wilderness with its living and its decaying trees, the thunder-cloud, and the rain which lasts three weeks and produces freshets. We need to witness our own limits transgressed, and some life pasturing freely where we never wander. We are cheered when we observe the vulture feeding on the carrion which disgusts and disheartens us, and deriving health and strength from the repast. There was a dead horse in the hollow by the path to my house, which compelled me sometimes to go out of my way, especially in the night when the air was heavy, but the assurance it gave me of the strong appetite and inviolable health of Nature was my compensation for this. I love to see that Nature is so rife with life that myriads can be afforded to be sacrificed and suffered to prey on one another; that tender organizations can be so serenely squashed out of existence like pulp,—tadpoles which herons gobble up, and tortoises and toads run over in the road; and that sometimes it has rained flesh and blood! With the liability to accident, we must see how little account is to be made of it. The impression made on a wise man is that of universal innocence. Poison is not poisonous after all, nor are any wounds fatal. Compassion is a very untenable ground. It must be expeditious. Its pleadings will not bear to be stereotyped.

Early in May, the oaks, hickories, maples, and other trees, just putting out amidst the pine woods around the pond, imparted a brightness like sunshine to the landscape, especially in cloudy days, as if the sun were breaking through mists and shining faintly on the hillsides here and there. On the third or fourth of May I saw a loon in the pond, and during the first week of the month I heard the whip-poor-will, the brown thrasher, the veery, the wood pewee, the chewink, and other birds. I had heard the wood thrush long before. The phœbe had already come once more and looked in at my door and window, to see if my house was cavern-like enough for her, sustaining herself on humming wings with clinched talons, as if she held by the air, while she surveyed the premises. The sulphur-like pollen of the pitch pine soon covered the pond and the stones and rotten wood along the shore, so that you could have collected a barrelful. This is the "sulphur showers" we hear of. Even in Calidas' drama of Sacontala, we read of "rills dyed yellow with the golden dust of the lotus." And so the seasons went rolling on into summer, as one rambles into higher and higher grass.

Thus was my first year's life in the woods completed; and the second year was similar to it. I finally left Walden September 6th, 1847.

18. Conclusion

To the sick the doctors wisely recommend a change of air and scenery. Thank Heaven, here is not all the world. The buckeye does not grow in New England, and the mocking-bird is rarely heard here. The wild goose is more of a cosmopolite than we; he breaks his fast in Canada, takes a luncheon in the Ohio, and plumes himself for the night in a southern bayou. Even the bison, to some extent, keeps pace with the seasons, cropping the pastures of the Colorado only till a greener and sweeter grass awaits him by the Yellowstone. Yet we think that if rail fences are pulled down, and stone walls piled up on our farms, bounds are henceforth set to our lives and our fates decided. If you are chosen town clerk, forsooth, you cannot go to Tierra del Fuego this summer: but you may go to the land of infernal fire nevertheless. The universe is wider than our views of it.

Yet we should oftener look over the tafferel of our craft, like curious passengers, and not make the voyage like stupid sailors picking oakum. The other side of the globe is but the home of our correspondent. Our voyaging is only great-circle sailing, and the doctors prescribe for diseases of the skin merely. One hastens to southern Africa to chase the giraffe; but surely that is not the game he would be after. How long, pray, would a man hunt giraffes if he could? Snipes and woodcocks also may afford rare sport; but I trust it would be nobler game to shoot one's self.—

"Direct your eye right inward, and you'll find
A thousand regions in your mind

Yet undiscovered. Travel them, and be
Expert in home-cosmography."

What does Africa,—what does the West stand for? Is
not our own interior white on the chart? black though
it may prove, like the coast, when discovered. Is it the
source of the Nile, or the Niger, or the Mississippi, or a
Northwest Passage around this continent, that we would
find? Are these the problems which most concern mankind? Is Franklin the only man who is lost, that his wife
should be so earnest to find him? Does Mr. Grinnell
know where he himself is? Be rather the Mungo Park,
the Lewis and Clark and Frobisher, of your own streams
and oceans; explore your own higher latitudes,—with
shiploads of preserved meats to support you, if they be
necessary; and pile the empty cans sky-high for a sign.
Were preserved meats invented to preserve meat
merely? Nay, be a Columbus to whole new continents
and worlds within you, opening new channels, not of
trade, but of thought. Every man is the lord of a realm
beside which the earthly empire of the Czar is but a
petty state, a hummock left by the ice. Yet some can be
patriotic who have no *self-respect,* and sacrifice the
greater to the less. They love the soil which makes their
graves, but have no sympathy with the spirit which may
still animate their clay. Patriotism is a maggot in their
heads. What was the meaning of that South-Sea Exploring Expedition, with all its parade and expense, but an
indirect recognition of the fact that there are continents
and seas in the moral world to which every man is an
isthmus or an inlet, yet unexplored by him, but that it
is easier to sail many thousand miles through cold and
storm and cannibals, in a government ship, with five hundred men and boys to assist one, than it is to explore
the private sea, the Atlantic and Pacific Ocean of one's
being alone.—

"Erret, et extremos alter scrutetur Iberos.
Plus habet hic vitae, plus habet ille viae."

Let them wander and scrutinize the outlandish Australians.
I have more of God, they more of the road.

It is not worth the while to go round the world to count the cats in Zanzibar. Yet do this even till you can do better, and you may perhaps find some "Symmes' Hole" by which to get at the inside at last. England and France, Spain and Portugal, Gold Coast and Slave Coast, all front on this private sea; but no bark from them has ventured out of sight of land, though it is without doubt the direct way to India. If you would learn to speak all tongues and conform to the customs of all nations, if you would travel farther than all travellers, be naturalized in all climes, and cause the Sphinx to dash her head against a stone, even obey the precept of the old philosopher, and Explore thyself. Herein are demanded the eye and the nerve. Only the defeated and deserters go to the wars, cowards that run away and enlist. Start now on that farthest western way, which does not pause at the Mississippi or the Pacific, nor conduct toward a worn-out China or Japan, but leads on direct, a tangent to this sphere, summer and winter, day and night, sun down, moon down, and at last earth down too.

It is said that Mirabeau took to highway robbery "to ascertain what degree of resolution was necessary in order to place one's self in formal opposition to the most sacred laws of society." He declared that "a soldier who fights in the ranks does not require half so much courage as a foot-pad,"—"that honor and religion have never stood in the way of a well-considered and a firm resolve." This was manly, as the world goes; and yet it was idle, if not desperate. A saner man would have found himself often enough "in formal opposition" to what are deemed "the most sacred laws of society," through obedience to yet more sacred laws, and so have tested his resolution without going out of his way. It is not for a man to put himself in such an attitude to society, but to maintain himself in whatever attitude he find himself through obedience to the laws of his being, which will never be one of opposition to a just government, if he should chance to meet with such.

I left the woods for as good a reason as I went there. Perhaps it seemed to me that I had several more lives to live, and could not spare any more time for that one. It is remarkable how easily and insensibly we fall into a particular route, and make a beaten track for ourselves. I had not lived there a week before my feet wore a path from my door to the pondside; and though it is five or six years since I trod it, it is still quite distinct. It is true, I fear, that others may have fallen into it, and so helped to keep it open. The surface of the earth is soft and impressible by the feet of men; and so with the paths which the mind travels. How worn and dusty, then, must be the highways of the world, how deep the ruts of tradition and conformity! I did not wish to take a cabin passage, but rather to go before the mast and on the deck of the world, for there I could best see the moonlight amid the mountains. I do not wish to go below now.

I learned this, at least, by my experiment: that if one advances confidently in the direction of his dreams, and endeavors to live the life which he has imagined, he will meet with a success unexpected in common hours. He will put some things behind, will pass an invisible boundary; new, universal, and more liberal laws will begin to establish themselves around and within him; or the old laws be expanded, and interpreted in his favor in a more liberal sense, and he will live with the license of a higher order of beings. In proportion as he simplifies his life, the laws of the universe will appear less complex, and solitude will not be solitude, nor poverty poverty, nor weakness weakness. If you have built castles in the air, your work need not be lost; that is where they should be. Now put the foundations under them.

It is a ridiculous demand which England and America make, that you shall speak so that they can understand you. Neither men nor toadstools grow so. As if that were important, and there were not enough to understand you without them. As if Nature could support but one order of understandings, could not sustain birds as well as quadrupeds, flying as well as creeping things, and *hush* and *whoa*, which Bright can understand, were the best English. As if there were safety in stupidity alone. I fear chiefly lest my expression may not be *extra-vagant* enough, may not wander far enough beyond the narrow limits of my daily experience, so as to be adequate to the truth of which I have been convinced. *Extra vagance!* it depends on how you are yarded. The migrating buf-

falo, which seeks new pastures in another latitude, is not
extravagant like the cow which kicks over the pail, leaps
the cowyard fence, and runs after her calf, in milking
time. I desire to speak somewhere *without* bounds; like
a man in a waking moment, to men in their waking moments; for I am convinced that I cannot exaggerate
enough even to lay the foundation of a true expression.
Who that has heard a strain of music feared then lest he
should speak extravagantly any more forever? In view of
the future or possible, we should live quite laxly and
undefined in front, our outlines dim and misty on that
side; as our shadows reveal an insensible perspiration
toward the sun. The volatile truth of our words should
continually betray the inadequacy of the residual statement. Their truth is instantly *translated;* its literal monument alone remains. The words which express our faith
and piety are not definite; yet they are significant and
fragrant like frankincense to superior natures.

Why level downward to our dullest perception always,
and praise that as common sense? The commonest sense
is the sense of men asleep, which they express by snor-
ing. Sometimes we are inclined to class those who are
once-and-a-half-witted with the half-witted, because we
appreciate only a third part of their wit. Some would
find fault with the morning red, if they ever got up early
enough. "They pretend," as I hear, "that the verses of
Kabir have four different senses; illusion, spirit, intellect,
and the exotic doctrine of the Vedas;" but in this part
of the world it is considered a ground for complaint if a
man's writings admit of more than one interpretation.
While England endeavors to cure the potato-rot, will not
any endeavor to cure the brain-rot, which prevails so
much more widely and fatally?

I do not suppose that I have attained to obscurity, but
I should be proud if no more fatal fault were found with
my pages on this score than was found with the Walden
ice. Southern customers objected to its blue color, which
is the evidence of its purity, as if it were muddy, and
preferred the Cambridge ice, which is white, but tastes
of weeds. The purity men love is like the mists which
envelop the earth, and not like the azure ether beyond.

Some are dinning in our ears that we Americans, and

moderns generally, are intellectual dwarfs compared with the ancients, or even the Elizabethan men. But what is that to the purpose? A living dog is better than a dead lion. Shall a man go and hang himself because he belongs to the race of pygmies, and not be the biggest pygmy that he can? Let every one mind his own business, and endeavor to be what he was made.

Why should we be in such desperate haste to succeed and in such desperate enterprises? If a man does not keep pace with his companions, perhaps it is because he hears a different drummer. Let him step to the music which he hears, however measured or far away. It is not important that he should mature as soon as an apple tree or an oak. Shall he turn his spring into summer? If the condition of things which we were made for is not yet, what were any reality which we can substitute? We will not be shipwrecked on a vain reality. Shall we with pains erect a heaven of blue glass over ourselves, though when it is done we shall be sure to gaze still at the true ethereal heaven far above, as if the former were not?

There was an artist in the city of Kouroo who was disposed to strive after perfection. One day it came into his mind to make a staff. Having considered that in an imperfect work time is an ingredient, but into a perfect work time does not enter, he said to himself, It shall be perfect in all respects, though I should do nothing else in my life. He proceeded instantly to the forest for wood, being resolved that it should not be made of unsuitable material; and as he searched for and rejected stick after stick, his friends gradually deserted him, for they grew old in their works and died, but he grew not older by a moment. His singleness of purpose and resolution, and his elevated piety, endowed him, without his knowledge, with perennial youth. As he made no compromise with Time, Time kept out of his way, and only sighed at a distance because he could not overcome him. Before he had found a stick in all respects suitable the city of Kouroo was a hoary ruin, and he sat on one of its mounds to peel the stick. Before he had given it the proper shape the dynasty of the Candahars was at an end, and with the point of the stick he wrote the name of the last of that race in the sand, and then resumed his work. By the time he had smoothed and polished the staff Kalpa was no longer the pole-star; and ere he had put on the ferule and the head adorned with precious stones, Brahma had awoke and slumbered many times. But why do I stay to mention these things? When the finishing stroke was put to his work, it suddenly expanded before the eyes of the astonished artist into the fairest of all the creations of Brahma. He had made a new system in making a staff, a world with full and fair proportions; in which, though the old cities and dynasties had passed away, fairer and more glorious ones had taken their places. And now he saw by the heap of shavings still fresh at his feet, that, for him and his work, the former lapse of time had been an illusion, and that no more time had elapsed than is required for a single scintillation from the brain of Brahma to fall on and inflame the tinder of a mortal brain. The material was pure, and his art was pure; how could the result be other than wonderful?

No face which we can give to a matter will stead us so well at last as the truth. This alone wears well. For the most part, we are not where we are, but in a false position. Through an infirmity of our natures, we suppose a case, and put ourselves into it, and hence are in two cases at the same time, and it is doubly difficult to get out. In sane moments we regard only the facts, the case that is. Say what you have to say, not what you ought. Any truth is better than make-believe. Tom Hyde, the tinker, standing on the gallows, was asked if he had anything to say. "Tell the tailors," said he, "to remember to make a knot in their thread before they take the first stitch." His companion's prayer is forgotten.

However mean your life is, meet it and live it; do not shun it and call it hard names. It is not so bad as you are. It looks poorest when you are richest. The faultfinder will find faults even in paradise. Love your life, poor as it is. You may perhaps have some pleasant, thrilling, glorious hours, even in a poor-house. The setting sun is reflected from the windows of the alms-house as brightly as from the rich man's abode; the snow melts before its door as early in the spring. I do not see but a quiet mind may live as contentedly there, and have as cheering thoughts, as in a palace. The town's poor seem to me often to live the most independent lives of any. Maybe they are simply great enough to receive without misgiving. Most think that they are above being supported by the town; but it oftener happens that they are not above supporting themselves by dishonest means, which should be more disreputable. Cultivate poverty like a garden herb, like sage. Do not trouble yourself much to get new things, whether clothes or friends. Turn the old; return to them. Things do not change; we change. Sell your clothes and keep your thoughts. God will see that you do not want society. If I were confined to a corner of a garret all my days, like a spider, the world would be just as large to me while I had my thoughts about me. The philosopher said: "From an army of three divisions one can take away its general, and put it in disorder; from the man the most abject and vulgar one cannot take away his thought." Do not seek so anxiously to be developed, to subject yourself to many influences to be played on; it is all dissipation. Humility like darkness reveals the heavenly lights. The shadows of poverty and meanness gather around us, "and lo! creation widens to our view." We are often reminded that if there were bestowed on us the wealth of Crœsus, our aims must still be the same, and our means essentially the same. Moreover, if you are restricted in your range by poverty, if you cannot buy books and newspapers, for instance, you are but confined to the most significant and vital experiences; you are compelled to deal with the material which yields the most sugar and the most starch. It is life near the bone where it is sweetest. You are defended from being a trifler. No man loses ever on a lower level by magnanimity on a higher. Superfluous wealth can buy superfluities only. Money is not required to buy one necessary of the soul.

I live in the angle of a leaden wall, into whose composition was poured a little alloy of bell-metal. Often, in the repose of my mid-day, there reaches my ears a confused *tintinnabulum* from without. It is the noise of my contemporaries. My neighbors tell me of their adventures with famous gentlemen and ladies, what notabilities they met at the dinner-table; but I am no more interested in such things than in the contents of the Daily Times. The interest and the conversation are about costume and manners chiefly; but a goose is a goose still, dress it as you will. They tell me of California and Texas, of England and the Indies, of the Hon. Mr. —— of Georgia or Massachusetts, all transient and fleeting phenomena, till I am ready to leap from their court-yard like the Mameluke bey. I delight to come to my bearings,—not walk in procession with pomp and parade, in a conspicuous place, but to walk even with the Builder of the universe, if I may,—not to live in this restless, nervous, bustling, trivial Nineteenth Century, but stand or sit thoughtfully while it goes by. What are men celebrating? They are all on a committee of arrangements, and hourly expect a speech from somebody. God is only the president of the day, and Webster is his orator. I love to weigh, to settle, to gravitate toward that which most strongly and rightfully attracts me,—not hang by the beam of the scale and try to weigh less,— not suppose a case, but take the case that is; to travel the only path I can, and that on which no power can resist me. It affords me no satisfaction to commence to spring an arch before I have got a solid foundation. Let us not play at kittly-benders. There is a solid bottom everywhere. We read that the traveller asked the boy if the swamp before him had a hard bottom. The boy replied that it had. But presently the traveller's horse sank in up to the girths, and he observed to the boy, "I thought you said that this bog had a hard bottom." "So it has," answered the latter, "but you have not got half way to it yet." So it is with the bogs and quicksands of society; but he is an old boy that knows it. Only what is thought, said, or done at a certain rare coincidence is good. I would not be one of those who will foolishly drive a nail into mere lath and plastering; such a deed would keep me awake nights. Give me a hammer, and let me feel for the furring. Do not depend on the putty. Drive a nail home and clinch it so faithfully that you can wake up in the night and think of your work with satisfaction,—a work at which you would not be ashamed to invoke the Muse. So will help you God, and

so only. Every nail driven should be as another rivet in
the machine of the universe, you carrying on the work.

Rather than love, than money, than fame, give me
truth. I sat at a table where were rich food and wine in
abundance, an obsequious attendance, but sincerity and
truth were not; and I went away hungry from the inhos-
pitable board. The hospitality was as cold as the ices. I
thought that there was no need of ice to freeze them.
They talked to me of the age of the wine and the fame
of the vintage; but I thought of an older, a newer, and
purer wine, of a more glorious vintage, which they had
not got, and could not buy. The style, the house and
grounds and "entertainment" pass for nothing with me.
I called on the king, but he made me wait in his hall,
and conducted like a man incapacitated for hospitality.
There was a man in my neighborhood who lived in a
hollow tree. His manners were truly regal. I should have
done better had I called on him.

How long shall we sit in our porticoes practising idle
and musty virtues, which any work would make impertinent? As if one were to begin the day with long-suffer-
ing, and hire a man to hoe his potatoes; and in the
afternoon go forth to practise Christian meekness and
charity with goodness aforethought! Consider the China
pride and stagnant self-complacency of mankind. This
generation inclines a little to congratulate itself on being
the last of an illustrious line; and in Boston and London
and Paris and Rome, thinking of its long descent, it
speaks of its progress in art and science and literature
with satisfaction. There are the Records of the Philosophical Societies, and the public Eulogies of *Great Men!*
It is the good Adam contemplating his own virtue. "Yes,
we have done great deeds, and sung divine songs, which
shall never die,"—that is, as long as *we* can remember
them. The learned societies and great men of Assyria,—
where are they? What youthful philosophers and experi-
mentalists we are! There is not one of my readers who
has yet lived a whole human life. These may be but the
spring months in the life of the race. If we have had the
seven-years' itch, we have not seen the seventeen-year
locust yet in Concord. We are acquainted with a mere
pellicle of the globe on which we live. Most have not

delved six feet beneath the surface, nor leaped as many above it. We know not where we are. Beside, we are sound asleep nearly half our time. Yet we esteem ourselves wise, and have an established order on the surface. Truly, we are deep thinkers, we are ambitious spirits! As I stand over the insect crawling amid the pine needles on the forest floor, and endeavoring to conceal itself from my sight, and ask myself why it will cherish those humble thoughts, and hide its head from me who might, perhaps, be its benefactor, and impart to its race some cheering information, I am reminded of the greater Benefactor and Intelligence that stands over me the human insect.

There is an incessant influx of novelty into the world, and yet we tolerate incredible dulness. I need only suggest what kind of sermons are still listened to in the most enlightened countries. There are such words as joy and sorrow, but they are only the burden of a psalm, sung with a nasal twang, while we believe in the ordinary and mean. We think that we can change our clothes only. It is said that the British Empire is very large and respectable, and that the United States are a first-rate power. We do not believe that a tide rises and falls behind every man which can float the British Empire like a chip, if he should ever harbor it in his mind. Who knows what sort of seventeen-year locust will next come out of the ground? The government of the world I live in was not framed, like that of Britain, in after-dinner conversations over the wine.

The life in us is like the water in the river. It may rise this year higher than man has ever known it, and flood the parched uplands; even this may be the eventful year, which will drown out all our muskrats. It was not always dry land where we dwell. I see far inland the banks which the stream anciently washed, before science began to record its freshets. Everyone has heard the story which has gone the rounds of New England, of a strong and beautiful bug which came out of the dry leaf of an old table of apple-tree wood, which had stood in a farmer's kitchen for sixty years, first in Connecticut, and afterward in Massachusetts,—from an egg deposited in the living tree many years earlier still, as appeared by count-

ing the annual layers beyond it; which was heard gnawing out for several weeks, hatched perchance by the heat
of an urn. Who does not feel his faith in a resurrection
and immortality strengthened by hearing of this? Who
knows what beautiful and winged life, whose egg has
been buried for ages under many concentric layers of
woodenness in the dead dry life of society, deposited at
first in the alburnum of the green and living tree, which
has been gradually converted into the semblance of its
well-seasoned tomb,—heard perchance gnawing out now
for years by the astonished family of man, as they sat
round the festive board,—may unexpectedly come forth
from amidst society's most trivial and handselled furniture, to enjoy its perfect summer life at last!

I do not say that John or Jonathan will realize all this;
but such is the character of that morrow which mere
lapse of time can never make to dawn. The light which
puts out our eyes is darkness to us. Only that day dawns
to which we are awake. There is more day to dawn. The
sun is but a morning star.

On the Duty of
Civil Disobedience

I HEARTILY accept the motto,—"That government is best which governs least;" and I should like to see it acted up to more rapidly and systematically. Carried out, it finally amounts to this, which also I believe,—"That government is best which governs not at all;" and when men are prepared for it, that will be the kind of government which they will have. Government is at best but an expedient; but most governments are usually, and all governments are sometimes, inexpedient. The objections which have been brought against a standing army, and they are many and weighty, and deserve to prevail, may also at last be brought against a standing government. The standing army is only an arm of the standing government. The government itself, which is only the mode which the people have chosen to execute their will, is equally liable to be abused and perverted before the people can act through it. Witness the present Mexican war, the work of comparatively a few individuals using the standing government as their tool; for, in the outset, the people would not have consented to this measure.

This American government,—what is it but a tradition, though a recent one, endeavoring to transmit itself unimpaired to posterity, but each instant losing some of its integrity? It has not the vitality and force of a single living man; for a single man can bend it to his will. It is a sort of wooden gun to the people themselves; and, if ever they should use it in earnest as a real one against each other, it will surely split. But it is not the less necessary for this; for the people must have some complicated machinery or other, and hear its din, to satisfy that idea of government which they have. Governments show thus how successfully men can be imposed on, even impose on themselves, for their own advantage. It is excellent,

we must all allow; yet this government never of itself
furthered any enterprise, but by the alacrity with which
it got out of its way. *It* does not keep the country free.
It does not settle the West. *It* does not educate. The
character inherent in the American people has done all
that has been accomplished; and it would have done
somewhat more, if the government had not sometimes
got in its way. For government is an expedient by which
men would fain succeed in letting one another alone;
and, as has been said, when it is most expedient, the
governed are most let alone by it. Trade and commerce,
if they were not made of India rubber, would never manage to bounce over the obstacles which legislators are
continually putting in their way; and, if one were to
judge these men wholly by the effects of their actions,
and not partly by their intentions, they would deserve
to be classed and punished with those mischievous persons who put obstructions on the railroads.

But, to speak practically and as a citizen, unlike those
who call themselves no-government men, I ask for, not
at once no government, but *at once* a better government.
Let every man make known what kind of government
would command his respect, and that will be one step
toward obtaining it.

After all, the practical reason why, when the power is
once in the hands of the people, a majority are permitted, and for a long period continue, to rule, is not because they are most likely to be in the right, nor because
this seems fairest to the minority, but because they are
physically the strongest. But a government in which the
majority rule in all cases cannot be based on justice,
even as far as men understand it. Can there not be a
government in which majorities do not virtually decide
right and wrong, but conscience?—in which majorities
decide only those questions to which the rule of expediency is applicable? Must the citizen ever for a moment,
or in the least degree, resign his conscience to the legislator? Why has every man a conscience, then? I think
that we should be men first, and subjects afterward. It
is not desirable to cultivate a respect for the law, so
much as for the right. The only obligation which I have
a right to assume, is to do at any time what I think

right. It is truly enough said, that a corporation has no conscience; but a corporation of conscientious men is a corporation *with* a conscience. Law never made men a whit more just; and, by means of their respect for it, even the well-disposed are daily made the agents of injustice. A common and natural result of an undue respect for law is, that you may see a file of soldiers, colonel, captain, corporal, privates, powder-monkeys and all, marching in admirable order over hill and dale to the wars, against their wills, aye, against their common sense and consciences, which makes it very steep marching indeed, and produces a palpitation of the heart. They have no doubt that it is a damnable business in which they are concerned; they are all peaceably inclined. Now, what are they? Men at all? or small moveable forts and magazines, at the service of some unscrupulous man in power? Visit the Navy Yard, and behold a marine, such a man as an American government can make, or such as it can make a man with its black arts,—a mere shadow and reminiscence of humanity, a man laid out alive and standing, and already, as one may say, buried under arms with funeral accompaniments, though it may be

> "Not a drum was heard, nor a funeral note,
>   As his corse to the ramparts we hurried;
> Not a soldier discharged his farewell shot
>   O'er the grave where our hero we buried."

The mass of men serve the State thus, not as men mainly, but as machines, with their bodies. They are the standing army, and the militia, jailers, constables, *posse comitatus,* &c. In most cases there is no free exercise whatever of the judgment or of the moral sense; but they put themselves on a level with wood and earth and stones; and wooden men can perhaps be manufactured that will serve the purpose as well. Such command no more respect than men of straw, or a lump of dirt. They have the same sort of worth only as horses and dogs. Yet such as these even are commonly esteemed good citizens. Others, as most legislators, politicians, lawyers, ministers, and office-holders, serve the State chiefly with their heads;

and, as they rarely make any moral distinctions, they are
as likely to serve the devil, without *intending* it, as God.
A very few, as heroes, patriots, martyrs, reformers in the
great sense, and *men,* serve the State with their consciences
also, and so necessarily resist it for the most part; and they
are commonly treated by it as enemies. A wise man will
only be useful as a man, and will not submit to be "clay,"
and "stop a hole to keep the wind away," but leave that
office to his dust at least:—

> "I am too high-born to be propertied,
>   To be a secondary at control,
>   Or useful serving-man and instrument
>   To any sovereign state throughout the world."

He who gives himself entirely to his fellow-men appears
to them useless and selfish; but he who gives himself
partially to them is pronounced a benefactor and philanthropist.

How does it become a man to behave toward this
American government to-day? I answer that he cannot
without disgrace be associated with it. I cannot for an
instant recognize that political organization as *my* government which is the *slave's* government also.

All men recognize the right of revolution; that is, the
right to refuse allegiance to and to resist the government, when its tyranny or its inefficiency are great and
unendurable. But almost all say that such is not the case
now. But such was the case, they think, in the Revolution of '75. If one were to tell me that this was a bad
government because it taxed certain foreign commodities brought to its ports, it is most probable that I should
not make an ado about it, for I can do without them:
all machines have their friction; and possibly this does
enough good to counterbalance the evil. At any rate, it
is a great evil to make a stir about it. But when the
friction comes to have its machine, and oppression and
robbery are organized, I say, let us not have such a machine any longer. In other words, when a sixth of the
population of a nation which has undertaken to be the
refuge of liberty are slaves, and a whole country is unjustly overrun and conquered by a foreign army, and

subjected to military law, I think that it is not too soon for honest men to rebel and revolutionize. What makes this duty the more urgent is the fact, that the country so overrun is not our own, but ours is the invading army.

Paley, a common authority with many on moral questions, in his chapter on the "Duty of Submission to Civil Government," resolves all civil obligation into expediency; and he proceeds to say, "that so long as the interest of the whole society requires it, that is, so long as the established government cannot be resisted or changed without public inconveniency, it is the will of God, that the established government be obeyed, and no longer."—"This principle being admitted, the justice of every particular case of resistance is reduced to a computation of the quantity of the danger and grievance on the one side, and of the probability and expense of redressing it on the other." Of this, he says, every man shall judge for himself. But Paley appears never to have contemplated those cases to which the rule of expediency does not apply, in which a people, as well as an individual, must do justice, cost what it may. If I have unjustly wrested a plank from a drowning man, I must restore it to him though I drown myself. This, according to Paley, would be inconvenient. But he that would save his life, in such a case, shall lose it. This people must cease to hold slaves, and to make war on Mexico, though it cost them their existence as a people.

In their practice, nations agree with Paley; but does any one think that Massachusetts does exactly what is right at the present crisis?

"A drab of state, a cloth-o'-silver slut,
    To have her train borne up, and her soul trail in the dirt."

Practically speaking, the opponents to a reform in Massachusetts are not a hundred thousand politicians at the South, but a hundred thousand merchants and farmers here, who are more interested in commerce and agriculture than they are in humanity, and are not prepared to do justice to the slave and to Mexico, *cost what it may.* I quarrel not with far-off foes, but with those who, near at home, co-operate with, and do the bidding of those far away, and without whom the latter would be harmless. We are accustomed to say, that the mass of men are unprepared; but improvement is slow, because the few are not materially wiser or better than the many. It is not so important that many should be as good as you, as that there be some absolute goodness somewhere; for that will leaven the whole lump. There are thousands who are *in opinion* opposed to slavery and to the war, who yet in effect do nothing to put an end to them; who, esteeming themselves children of Washington and Franklin, sit down with their hands in their pockets, and say that they know not what to do, and do nothing; who even postpone the question of freedom to the question of free-trade, and quietly read the prices-current along with the latest advices from Mexico, after dinner, and, it may be, fall asleep over them both. What is the price-current of an honest man and patriot to-day? They hesitate, and they regret, and sometimes they petition; but they do nothing in earnest and with effect. They will wait, well disposed, for others to remedy the evil, that they may no longer have it to regret. At most, they give only a cheap vote, and a feeble countenance and God-speed, to the right, as it goes by them. There are nine hundred and ninety-nine patrons of virtue to one virtuous man; but it is easier to deal with the real possessor of a thing than with the temporary guardian of it.

All voting is a sort of gaming, like chequers or backgammon, with a slight moral tinge to it, a playing with right and wrong, with moral questions; and betting naturally accompanies it. The character of the voters is not staked. I cast my vote, perchance, as I think right; but I am not vitally concerned that the right should prevail. I am willing to leave it to the majority. Its obligation, therefore, never exceeds that of expediency. Even voting *for the right* is *doing* nothing for it. It is only expressing to men feebly your desire that it should prevail. A wise man will not leave the right to the mercy of chance, nor wish it to prevail through the power of the majority. There is but little virtue in the action of masses of men. When the majority shall at length vote for the abolition of slavery, it will be because they are indifferent to slavery, or because there is but little slavery left to be abolished by their vote. *They* will then be the only slaves. Only *his* vote can hasten the abolition of slavery who asserts his own freedom by his vote.

I hear of a convention to be held at Baltimore, or elsewhere, for the selection of a candidate for the Presidency, made up chiefly of editors, and men who are politicians by profession; but I think, what is it to any independent, intelligent, and respectable man what decision they may come to, shall we not have the advantage of his wisdom and honesty, nevertheless? Can we not count upon some independent votes? Are there not many individuals in the country who do not attend conventions? But no: I find that the respectable man, so called, has immediately drifted from his position, and despairs of his country, when his country has more reason to despair of him. He forthwith adopts one of the candidates thus selected as the only *available* one, thus proving that he is himself *available* for any purposes of the demagogue. His vote is of no more worth than that of any unprincipled foreigner or hireling native, who may have been bought. Oh for a man who is a *man,* and, as my neighbor says, has a bone in his back which you cannot pass your hand through! Our statistics are at fault: the population has been returned too large. How many *men* are there to a square thousand miles in this country? Hardly one. Does not America offer any inducement for men to settle here? The American has dwindled into an Odd Fellow,—one who may be known by the development of his organ of gregariousness, and a manifest lack of intellect and cheerful self-reliance; whose first and chief concern, on coming into the world, is to see that the alms-houses are in good repair; and, before yet he has lawfully donned the virile garb, to collect a fund for the support of the widows and orphans that may be; who, in short, ventures to live only by the aid of the mutual insurance company, which has promised to bury him decently.

It is not a man's duty, as a matter of course, to devote himself to the eradication of any, even the most enormous wrong; he may still properly have other concerns to engage him; but it is his duty, at least, to wash his hands of it, and, if he gives it no thought longer, not to give it practically his support. If I devote myself to other pursuits and contemplations, I must first see, at least, that I do not pursue them sitting upon another man's shoulders. I must get off him first, that he may pursue his contemplations too. See what gross inconsistency is tolerated. I have heard some of my townsmen say, "I should like to have them order me out to help put down an insurrection of the slaves, or to march to Mexico,— see if I would go;" and yet these very men have each, directly by their allegiance, and so indirectly, at least, by their money, furnished a substitute. The soldier is applauded who refuses to serve in an unjust war by those who do not refuse to sustain the unjust government which makes the war; is applauded by those whose own act and authority he disregards and sets at nought; as if the State were penitent to that degree that it hired one to scourge it while it sinned, but not to that degree that it left off sinning for a moment. Thus, under the name of order and civil government, we are all made at last to pay homage to and support our own meanness. After the first blush of sin, comes its indifference; and from immoral it becomes, as it were, *un*moral, and not quite unnecessary to that life which we have made.

The broadest and most prevalent error requires the most disinterested virtue to sustain it. The slight reproach to which the virtue of patriotism is commonly liable, the noble are most likely to incur. Those who, while they disapprove of the character and measures of a government, yield to it their allegiance and support, are undoubtedly its most conscientious supporters, and so frequently the most serious obstacles to reform. Some are petitioning the State to dissolve the Union, to disregard the requisitions of the President. Why do they not dissolve it themselves,—the union between themselves and the State,—and refuse to pay their quota into its treasury? Do not they stand in the same relation to the State, that the State does to the Union? And have not the same reasons prevented the State from resisting the Union, which have prevented them from resisting the State?

How can a man be satisfied to entertain an opinion merely, and enjoy *it?* Is there any enjoyment in it, if his opinion is that he is aggrieved? If you are cheated out of a single dollar by your neighbor, you do not rest satisfied with knowing that you are cheated, or with saying that you are cheated, or even with petitioning him to pay you your due; but you take effectual steps at once to obtain the full amount, and see that you are never cheated again. Action from principle,—the perception and the performance of right,—changes things and relations; it is essentially revolutionary, and does not consist wholly with any thing which was. It not only divides states and churches, it divides families, aye, it divides the *individual*, separating the diabolical in him from the divine.

Unjust laws exist; shall we be content to obey them, or shall we endeavor to amend them, and obey them until we have succeeded, or shall we transgress them at once? Men generally, under such a government as this, think that they ought to wait until they have persuaded the majority to alter them. They think that, if they should resist, the remedy would be worse than the evil. But it is the fault of the government itself that the remedy *is* worse than the evil. *It* makes it worse. Why is it not more apt to anticipate and provide for reform? Why does it not cherish its wise minority? Why does it cry and resist before it is hurt? Why does it not encourage its citizens to be on the alert to point out its faults, and *do* better than it would have them? Why does it always crucify Christ, and excommunicate Copernicus and Luther, and pronounce Washington and Franklin rebels?

One would think, that a deliberate and practical denial of its authority, was the only offense never contemplated by government; else, why has it not assigned its definite, its suitable and proportionate penalty? If a man who has no property refuses but once to earn nine shillings for the State, he is put in prison for a period unlimited by any law that I know, and determined only by the discretion of those who placed him there; but if he should steal ninety times nine shillings from the State, he is soon permitted to go at large again.

If the injustice is part of the necessary friction of the machine of government, let it go, let it go; perchance it will wear smooth,—certainly the machine will wear out. If the injustice has a spring, or a pulley, or a rope, or a crank, exclusively for itself, then perhaps you may consider whether the remedy will not be worse than the evil; but if it is of such a nature that it requires you to be the agent of injustice to another, then, I say, break the law. Let your life be a counter friction to stop the machine. What I have to do is to see, at any rate, that I do not lend myself to the wrong which I condemn.

As for adopting the ways which the State has provided for remedying the evil, I know not of such ways. They take too much time, and a man's life will be gone. I have other affairs to attend to. I came into this world, not chiefly to make this a good place to live in, but to live in it, be it good or bad. A man has not every thing to do, but something; and because he cannot do *every thing*, it is not necessary that he should do *something* wrong. It is not my business to be petitioning the governor or the legislature any more than it is theirs to petition me; and, if they should not hear my petition, what should I do then? But in this case the State has provided no way: its very Constitution is the evil. This may seem to be harsh and stubborn and unconciliatory; but it is to treat with the utmost kindness and consideration the only spirit that can appreciate or deserve it. So is all change for the better, like birth and death which convulse the body.

I do not hesitate to say, that those who call themselves abolitionists should at once effectually withdraw their support, both in person and property, from the government of Massachusetts, and not wait till they constitute a majority of one, before they suffer the right to prevail through them. I think that it is enough if they have God on their side, without waiting for that other one. Moreover, any man more right than his neighbors, constitutes a majority of one already.

I meet this American government, or its representative the State government, directly, and face to face, once a year, no more, in the person of its tax-gatherer; this is the only mode in which a man situated as I am necessarily meets it; and it then says distinctly, Recognize me; and the simplest, the most effectual, and, in the present pasture of affairs, the indispensablest mode of treating with it on this head, of expressing your little satisfaction with and love for it, is to deny it then. My civil neighbor, the tax-gatherer, is the very man I have to deal with,—for it is, after all, with men and not with parchment that I quarrel,—and he has voluntarily chosen to be an agent of the government. How shall he ever know well what he is and does as an officer of the government, or as a man, until he is obliged to consider whether he shall treat me, his neighbor, for whom he has respect, as a neighbor and well-disposed man, or as a maniac and disturber of the peace, and see if he can get over this obstruction to his neighborliness without a ruder and more impetuous thought or speech corresponding with his action? I know this well, that if one thousand, if one hundred, if ten men whom I could name,—if ten *honest* men only,—aye, if *one* HONEST man, in this State of Massachusetts, *ceasing to hold slaves,* were actually to withdraw from this copartnership, and be locked up in the county jail therefor, it would be the abolition of slavery in America. For it matters not how small the beginning may seem to be: what is once well done is done for ever. But we love better to talk about it: that we say is our mission. Reform keeps many scores of newspapers in its service, but not one man. If my esteemed neighbor, the State's ambassador, who will devote his days to the settlement of the question of human rights in the Council Chamber, instead of being threatened with the prisons of Carolina, were to sit down the prisoner of Massachusetts, that State which is so anxious to foist the sin of slavery upon her sister,— though at present she can discover only an act of inhospitality to be the ground of a quarrel with her,—the Legislature would not wholly waive the subject the following winter.

Under a government which imprisons any unjustly, the true place for a just man is also a prison. The proper place to-day, the only place which Massachusetts has provided for her freer and less desponding spirits, is in her prisons, to be put out and locked out of the State by her own act, as they have already put themselves out by their principles. It is there that the fugitive slave, and the Mexican prisoner on parole, and the Indian come to plead the wrongs of his race, should find them; on that separate, but more free and honorable ground, where the State places those who are not *with* her but *against* her,—the only house in a slave-state in which a free man can abide with honor. If any think that their influence would be lost there, and their voices no longer afflict the ear of the State, that they would not be as an enemy within its walls, they do not know by how much truth is stronger than error, nor how much more eloquently and effectively he can combat injustice who has experienced a little in his own person. Cast your whole vote, not a strip of paper merely, but your whole influence. A minority is powerless while it conforms to the majority; it is not even a minority then; but it is irresistible when it clogs by its whole weight. If the alternative is to keep all just men in prison, or give up war and slavery, the State will not hesitate which to choose. If a thousand men were not to pay their tax-bills this year, that would not be a violent and bloody measure, as it would be to pay them, and enable the State to commit violence and shed innocent blood. This is, in fact, the definition of a peaceable revolution, if any such is possible. If the tax-gatherer, or any other public officer, asks me, as one has done, "But what shall I do?" my answer is, "If you really wish to do any thing, resign your office." When the subject has refused allegiance, and the officer has resigned his office, then the revolution is accomplished. But even suppose blood should flow. Is there not a sort of blood shed when the conscience is wounded? Through this wound a man's real manhood and immortality flow out, and he bleeds to an everlasting death. I see this blood flowing now.

I have contemplated the imprisonment of the offender, rather than the seizure of his goods,—though both will serve the same purpose,—because they who assert the purest right, and consequently are most dangerous to a corrupt State, commonly have not spent much time in accumulating property. To such the State renders comparatively small service, and a slight tax is wont to appear exorbitant, particularly if they are obliged to earn it by special labor with their hands. If there were one who lived wholly without the use of money, the State itself would hesitate to demand it of him. But the rich man—not to make any invidious comparison—is always sold to the institution which makes him rich. Absolutely speaking, the more money, the less virtue; for money comes between a man and his objects, and obtains them for him; and it was certainly no great virtue to obtain it. It puts to rest many questions which he would otherwise be taxed to answer; while the only new question which it puts is the hard but superfluous one, how to spend it. Thus his moral ground is taken from under his feet. The opportunities of living are diminished in proportion as what are called the "means" are increased. The best thing a man can do for his culture when he is rich is to endeavor to carry out those schemes which he entertained when he was poor. Christ answered the Herodians according to their condition. "Show me the tribute-money," said he;—and one took a penny out of his pocket;—If you use money which has the image of Caesar on it, and which he has made current and valuable, that is, *if you are men of the State,* and gladly enjoy the advantages of Caesar's government, then pay him back some of his own when he demands it; "Render therefore to Caesar that which is Caesar's, and to God those things which are God's,"—leaving them no wiser than before as to which was which; for they did not wish to know.

When I converse with the freest of my neighbors, I perceive that, whatever they may say about the magnitude and seriousness of the question, and their regard for the public tranquillity, the long and the short of the matter is, that they cannot spare the protection of the existing government, and they dread the consequences of disobedience to it to their property and families. For my own part, I should not like to think that I ever rely on the protection of the State. But, if I deny the authority of the State when it presents its tax-bill, it will soon take and waste all my property, and so harass me and my children without end. This is hard. This makes it impossible for a man to live honestly and at the same time comfortably in outward respects. It will not be worth the while to accumulate property; that would be sure to go again. You must hire or squat somewhere, and raise but a small crop, and eat that soon. You must live within yourself, and depend upon yourself, always

tucked up and ready for a start, and not have many
affairs. A man may grow rich in Turkey even, if he will
be in all respects a good subject of the Turkish government. Confucius said,—"If a State is governed by the
principles of reason, poverty and misery are subjects of
shame; if a State is not governed by the principles of
reason, riches and honors are the subjects of shame."
No: until I want the protection of Massachusetts to be
extended to me in some distant southern port, where my
liberty is endangered, or until I am bent solely on building up an estate at home by peaceful enterprise, I can
afford to refuse allegiance to Massachusetts, and her
right to my property and life. It costs me less in every
sense to incur the penalty of disobedience to the State,
than it would to obey. I should feel as if I were worth
less in that case.

Some years ago, the State met me in behalf of the
church,and commanded me to pay a certain sum toward
the support of a clergyman whose preaching my father
attended, but never I myself. "Pay," it said, "or be
locked up in the jail." I declined to pay. But, unfortunately another man saw fit to pay it. I did not see why
the schoolmaster should be taxed to support the priest,
and not the priest the schoolmaster: for I was not the
State's schoolmaster, but I supported myself by voluntary subscription. I did not see why the lyceum should
not present its tax-bill, and have the State to back its
demand, as well as the church. However, at the request
of the selectmen, I condescended to make some such
statement as this in writing:—"Know all men by these
presents, that I, Henry Thoreau, do not wish to be regarded as a member of any incorporated society which
I have not joined." This I gave to the town-clerk; and
he has it. The State, having thus learned that I did not
wish to be regarded as a member of that church, has
never made a like demand on me since; though it said
that it must adhere to its original presumption that time.
If I had known how to name them, I should then have
signed off in detail from all the societies which I never
signed on to; but I did not know where to find a complete list.

I have paid no poll-tax for six years. I was put into a

jail once on this account, for one night; and, as I stood considering the walls of solid stone, two or three feet thick, the door of wood and iron, a foot thick, and the iron grating which strained the light, I could not help being struck with the foolishness of that institution which treated me as if I were mere flesh and blood and bones, to be locked up. I wondered that it should have concluded at length that this was the best use it could put me to, and had never thought to avail itself of my services in some way. I saw that, if there was a wall of stone between me and my townsmen, there was a still more difficult one to climb or break through, before they could get to be as free as I was. I did not for a moment feel confined, and the walls seemed a great waste of stone and mortar. I felt as if I alone of all my townsmen had paid my tax. They plainly did not know how to treat me, but behaved like persons who are underbred. In every threat and in every compliment there was a blunder; for they thought that my chief desire was to stand the other side of that stone wall. I could not but smile to see how industriously they locked the door on my meditations, which followed them out again without let or hindrance, and *they* were really all that was dangerous. As they could not reach me, they had resolved to punish my body; just as boys, if they cannot come at some person against whom they have a spite, will abuse his dog. I saw that the State was half-witted, that it was timid as a lone woman with her silver spoons, and that it did not know its friends from its foes, and I lost all my remaining respect for it, and pitied it.

Thus the State never intentionally confronts a man's sense, intellectual or moral, but only his body, his senses. It is not armed with superior wit or honesty, but with superior physical strength. I was not born to be forced. I will breathe after my own fashion. Let us see who is the strongest. What force has a multitude? They only can force me who obey a higher law than I. They force me to become like themselves. I do not hear of *men* being *forced* to live this way or that by masses of men. What sort of life were that to live? When I meet a government which says to me, "Your money or your life," why should I be in haste to give it my money? It may be in a great strait, and not know what to do: I cannot help that. It must help itself: do as I do. It is not worth the while to snivel about it. I am not responsible for the successful working of the machinery of society. I am not the son of the engineer. I perceive that, when an acorn and a chestnut fall side by side, the one does not remain inert to make way for the other, but both obey their own laws, and spring and grow and flourish as best they can, till one, perchance, overshadows and destroys the other. If a plant cannot live according to its nature, it dies; and so a man.

The night in prison was novel and interesting enough. The prisoners in their shirt-sleeves were enjoying a chat and the evening air in the doorway, when I entered. But the jailer said, "Come, boys, it is time to lock up," and so they dispersed, and I heard the sound of their steps returning into the hollow apartments. My roommate was introduced to me by the jailer, as "a first-rate fellow and a clever man." When the door was locked, he showed me where to hang my hat, and how he managed matters there. The rooms were whitewashed once a month; and this one, at least, was the whitest, most simply furnished, and probably the neatest apartment in the town. He naturally wanted to know where I came from, and what brought me there; and, when I had told him, I asked him in my turn how he came there, presuming him to be an honest man, of course; and, as the world goes, I believe he was. "Why," said he, "they accuse me of burning a barn; but I never did it." As near as I could discover, he had probably gone to bed in a barn when drunk, and smoked his pipe there; and so a barn was burnt. He had the reputation of being a clever man, had been there some three months waiting for his trial to come on, and would have to wait as much longer; but he was quite domesticated and contented, since he got his board for nothing, and thought that he was well treated.

He occupied one window, and I the other; and I saw, that, if one stayed there long, his principal business would be to look out the window. I had soon read all the tracts that were left there, and examined where former prisoners had broken out, and where a grate had been sawed off, and heard the history of the various occupants of that room; for I found that even here there was a history and a gossip which never circulated beyond the walls of the jail. Probably this is the only house in the town where verses are composed, which are afterward printed in circular form, but not published. I was shown quite a long list of verses which were composed by some young men who had been detected in an attempt to escape, who avenged themselves by singing them.

I pumped my fellow-prisoner as dry as I could, for fear I should never see him again; but at length he showed me which was my bed, and left me to blow out the lamp.

It was like travelling into a far country, such as I had never expected to behold, to lie there for one night. It seemed to me that I never had heard the town-clock strike before, nor the evening sounds of the village; for we slept with the windows open, which were inside the grating. It was to see my native village in the light of the middle ages, and our Concord was turned into a Rhine stream, and visions of knights and castles passed before me. They were the voices of old burghers that I heard in the streets. I was an involuntary spectator and auditor of whatever was done and said in the kitchen of the adjacent village-inn,—a wholly new and rare experience to me. It was a closer view of my native town. I was fairly inside of it. I never had seen its institutions before. This is one of its peculiar institutions; for it is a shire town. I began to comprehend what its inhabitants were about.

In the morning, our breakfasts were put through the hole in the door, in small oblong-square tin pans, made to fit, and holding a pint of chocolate, with brown bread, and an iron spoon. When they called for the vessels again, I was green enough to return what bread I had left, but my comrade seized it, and said that I should lay that up for lunch or dinner. Soon after, he was let out to work at haying in a neighboring field, whither he went every day, and would not be back till noon; so he bade me good-day, saying that he doubted if he should see me again.

When I came out of prison,—for some one interfered, and paid that tax,—I did not perceive that great changes had taken place on the common, such as he observed who went in a youth, and emerged a tottering and gray-headed man; and yet a change had to my eyes come over the scene,—the town, and State and country,—greater than any that mere time could effect. I saw yet more distinctly the State in which I lived. I saw to what extent the people among whom I lived could be trusted as good neighbors and friends; that their friendship was for summer weather only; that they did not greatly propose to do right; that they were a distinct race from me by their prejudices and superstitions, as the Chinamen and Malays are; that, in their sacrifices to humanity, they ran no risks, not even to their property; that, after all, they were not so noble but they treated the thief as he had treated them, and hoped, by a certain outward observance and a few prayers, and by walking in a particular straight though useless path from time to time, to save their souls. This may be to judge my neighbors harshly; for I believe that many of them are not aware that they have such an institution as the jail in their village.

It was formerly the custom in our village, when a poor debtor came out of jail, for his acquaintances to salute him, looking through their fingers, which were crossed to represent the grating of a jail window, "How do ye do?" My neighbors did not thus salute me, but first looked at me, and then at one another, as if I had returned from a long journey. I was put into jail as I was going to the shoemaker's to get a shoe which was mended. When I was let out the next morning, I proceeded to finish my errand, and, having put on my mended shoe, joined a huckleberry party, who were impatient to put themselves under my conduct; and in half an hour,—for the horse was soon tackled,—was in the midst of a huckleberry field, on one of our highest hills, two miles off, and then the State was nowhere to be seen.

This is the whole history of "My Prisons."

I have never declined paying the highway tax, because I am as desirous of being a good neighbor as I am of being a bad subject; and, as for supporting schools, I am doing my part to educate my fellow-countrymen now. It is for no particular item in the tax-bill that I refuse to pay it. I simply wish to refuse allegiance to the State, to withdraw and stand aloof from it effectually. I do not care to trace the course of my dollar, if I could, till it buys a man, or a musket to shoot one with,—the dollar is innocent,—but I am concerned to trace the effects of my allegiance. In fact, I quietly declare war with the State, after my fashion, though I will still make what use and get what advantage of her I can, as is usual in such cases.

If others pay the tax which is demanded of me, from a sympathy with the State, they do but what they have already done in their own case, or rather they abet injustice to a greater extent than the State requires. If they pay the tax from a mistaken interest in the individual taxed, to save his property, or prevent his going to jail, it is because they have not considered wisely how far they let their private feelings interfere with the public good.

This, then, is my position at present. But one cannot be too much on his guard in such a case, lest his action be biased by obstinacy, or an undue regard for the opinions of men. Let him see that he does only what belongs to himself and to the hour.

I think sometimes. Why, this people mean well; they are only ignorant; they would do better if they knew how; why give your neighbors this pain to treat you as they are not inclined to? But I think, again, This is no reason why I should do as they do, or permit others to suffer much greater pain of a different kind. Again, I sometimes say to myself, When many millions of men, without heat, without ill-will, without personal feeling of any kind, demand of you a few shillings only, without the possibility, such is their constitution, of retracting or altering their present demand, and without the possibility, on your side, of appeal to any other millions, why expose yourself to this overwhelming brute force? You do not resist cold and hunger, the winds and the waves, thus obstinately; you quietly submit to a thousand similar necessities. You do not put your head into the fire. But just in proportion as I regard this as not wholly a

brute force, but partly a human force, and consider that
I have relations to those millions as to so many millions
of men, and not of mere brute or inanimate things, I see
that appeal is possible, first and instantaneously, from
them to the Maker of them, and, secondly, from them
to themselves. But, if I put my head deliberately into
the fire, there is no appeal to fire or to the Maker of
fire, and I have only myself to blame. If I could convince
myself that I have any right to be satisfied with men as
they are, and to treat them accordingly, and not according, in some respects, to my requisitions and expec-
tations of what they and I ought to be, then, like a good
Mussulman and fatalist, I should endeavor to be satisfied
with things as they are, and say it is the will of God.
And, above all, there is this difference between resisting
this and a purely brute or natural force, that I can resist
this with some effect; but I cannot expect, like Orpheus,
to change the nature of the rocks and trees and beasts.

I do not wish to quarrel with any man or nation. I do
not wish to split hairs, to make fine distinctions, or set
myself up as better than my neighbors. I seek rather, I
may say, even an excuse for conforming to the laws of
the land. I am but too ready to conform to them. Indeed,
I have reason to suspect myself on this head; and each
year, as the tax-gatherer comes round, I find myself disposed to review the acts and position of the general and
State governments, and the spirit of the people, to discover a pretext for conformity.

> "We must affect our country as our parents,
>   And if at any time we alienate
>   Our love or industry from doing it honor,
>   We must respect effects and teach the soul
>   Matter of conscience and religion,
>   And not desire of rule or benefit."

I believe that the State will soon be able to take all
my work of this sort out of my hands, and then I shall
be no better a patriot than my fellow-country-men. Seen
from a lower point of view, the Constitution, with all
its faults, is very good; the law and the courts are very
respectable; even this State and this American govern-

ment are, in many respects, very admirable and rare things, to be thankful for, such as a great many have described them; but seen from a point of view a little higher, they are what I have described them; seen from a higher still, and the highest, who shall say what they are, or that they are worth looking at or thinking of at all?

However, the government does not concern me much, and I shall bestow the fewest possible thoughts on it. It is not many moments that I live under a government, even in this world. If a man is thought-free, fancy-free, imagination-free, that which is *not* never for a long time appearing *to be* to him, unwise rulers or reformers cannot fatally interrupt him.

I know that most men think differently from myself; but those whose lives are by profession devoted to the study of these or kindred subjects, content me as little as any. Statesmen and legislators, standing so completely within the institution, never distinctly and nakedly behold it. They speak of moving society, but have no resting-place without it. They may be men of a certain experience and discrimination, and have no doubt invented ingenious and even useful systems, for which we sincerely thank them; but all their wit and usefulness lie within certain not very wide limits. They are wont to forget that the world is not governed by policy and expediency. Webster never goes behind government, and so cannot speak with authority about it. His words are wisdom to those legislators who contemplate no essential reform in the existing government; but for thinkers, and those who legislate for all time, he never once glances at the subject. I know of those whose serene and wise speculations on this theme would soon reveal the limits of his mind's range and hospitality. Yet, compared with the cheap professions of most reformers, and the still cheaper wisdom and eloquence of politicians in general, his are almost the only sensible and valuable words, and we thank Heaven for him. Comparatively, he is always strong, original, and, above all, practical. Still his quality is not wisdom, but prudence. The lawyer's truth is not truth, but consistency, or a consistent expediency. Truth is always in harmony with herself, and is not concerned chiefly to reveal the justice that may consist with wrong-doing. He well deserves to be called, as he has been called, the Defender of the Constitution. There are really no blows to be given by him but defensive ones. He is not a leader, but a follower. His leaders are the men of '87. "I have never made an effort," he says, "and never propose to make an effort; I have never counte-nanced an effort, and never mean to countenance an effort, to disturb the arrangement as originally made, by which the various States came into the Union." Still thinking of the sanction which the Constitution gives to slavery, he says, "Because it was a part of the original compact,—let it stand." Notwithstanding his special acuteness and ability, he is unable to take a fact out of its merely political relations, and behold it as it lies absolutely to be disposed of by the intellect,—what, for instance, it behooves a man to do here in America to-day with regard to slavery, but ventures, or is driven, to make some such desperate answer as the following, while professing to speak absolutely, and as a private man,—from which what new and singular code of so-cial duties might be inferred?—"The manner," says he, "in which the governments of those States where slavery exists are to regulate it, is for their own consid-eration, under their responsibility to their constituents, to the general laws of propriety, humanity, and justice, and to God. Associations formed elsewhere springing from a feeling of humanity, or any other cause, have nothing whatever to do with it. They have never re-ceived any encouragement from me, and they never will."[1]

They who know of no purer sources of truth, who have traced up its stream no higher, stand, and wisely stand, by the Bible and the Constitution, and drink at it there with reverence and humility; but they who behold where it comes trickling into this lake or that pool, gird up their loins once more, and continue their pilgrimage toward its fountain-head.

No man with a genius for legislation has appeared in America. They are rare in the history of the world.

---

[1]These extracts have been inserted since the lecture was read.

There are orators, politicians, and eloquent men, by the thousand; but the speaker has not yet opened his mouth to speak, who is capable of settling the much-vexed questions of the day. We love eloquence for its own sake, and not for any truth which it may utter, or any heroism it may inspire. Our legislators have not yet learned the comparative value of free-trade and of freedom, of union, and of rectitude, to a nation. They have no genius or talent for comparatively humble questions of taxation and finance, commerce and manufacturers and agriculture. If we were left solely to the wordy wit of legislators in Congress for our guidance, uncorrected by the seasonable experience and the effectual complaints of the people, America would not long retain her rank among the nations. For eighteen hundred years, though perchance I have no right to say it, the New Testament has been written; yet where is the legislator who has wisdom and practical talent enough to avail himself of the light which it sheds on the science of legislation?

The authority of government, even such as I am willing to submit to,—for I will cheerfully obey those who know and can do better than I, and in many things even those who neither know nor can do so well,—is still an impure one: to be strictly just, it must have the sanction and consent of the governed. It can have no pure right over my person and property but what I concede to it. The progress from an absolute to a limited monarchy, from a limited monarchy to a democracy, is a progress toward a true respect for the individual. Even the Chinese philosopher was wise enough to regard the individual as the basis of the empire. Is a democracy, such as we know it, the last improvement possible in government? Is it not possible to take a step further towards recognizing and organizing the rights of man? There will never be a really free and enlightened State, until the State comes to recognize the individual as a higher and independent power, from which all its own power and authority are derived, and treats him accordingly. I please myself with imagining a State at last which can afford to be just to all men, and to treat the individual with respect as a neighbor; which even would not think it inconsistent with its own repose, if a few were to live aloof from it, not meddling with it, nor embraced by it, who fulfilled all the duties of neighbors and fellow-men. A State which bore this kind of fruit, and suffered it to drop off as fast as it ripened, would prepare the way for a still more perfect and glorious State, which also I have imagined, but not yet anywhere seen.

Sic Vita

I am a parcel of vain strivings tied
  By a chance bond together,
Dangling this way and that, their links
  Were made so loose and wide,
    Methinks,
  For milder weather.

A bunch of violets without their roots,
  And sorrel intermixed,
Encircled by a wisp of straw
  Once coiled about their shoots,
    The law
  By which I'm fixed.

A nosegay which Time clutched from out
  Those fair Elysian fields,
With weeds and broken stems, in haste,
  Doth make the rabble rout
    That waste
  The day he yields.

And here I bloom for a short hour unseen,
  Drinking my juices up,
With no root in the land
  To keep my branches green,
    But stand
  In a bare cup.

Some tender buds were left upon my stem
  In mimicry of life,
But ah! the children will not know,
  Till time has withered them,
    The woe
  With which they're rife.

But now I see I was not plucked for naught,
   And after in life's vase
Of glass set while I might survive,
   But by a kind hand brought
     Alive
   To a strange place.

That stock thus thinned will soon redeem its hours,
   And by another year,
Such as God knows, with freer air,
   More fruits and fairer flowers
     Will bear,
   While I droop here.

Winter Memories

Within the circuit of this plodding life
There enter moments of an azure hue,
Untarnished fair as is the violet
Or anemone, when the spring strews them
By some meandering rivulet, which make
The best philosophy untrue that aims
But to console man for his grievances.
I have remembered when the winter came,
High in my chamber in the frosty nights,
When in the still light of the cheerful moon,
On every twig and rail and jutting spout,
The icy spears were adding to their length
Against the arrows of the coming sun,
How in the shimmering noon of summer past
Some unrecorded beam slanted across
The upland pastures where the Johnswort grew;
Or heard, amid the verdure of my mind,
The bee's long smothered hum, on the blue flag
Loitering amidst the mead; or busy rill,
Which now through all its course stands still and dumb
Its own memorial,—purling at its play
Along the slopes, and through the meadows next,
Until its youthful sound was hushed at last.

In the staid current of the lowland stream;
Or seen the furrows shine but late upturned,
And where the fieldfare followed in the rear,
When all the fields around lay bound and hoar
Beneath a thick integument of snow.
So by God's cheap economy made rich
To go upon my winter's task again.

To the Maiden in the East

Low in the eastern sky
Is set thy glancing eye;
And though its gracious light
Ne'er riseth to my sight,
Yet every star that climbs
Above the gnarled limbs
  Of yonder hill,
Conveys thy gentle will.

Believe I knew they thought,
And that the zephyrs brought
Thy kindest wishes through,
As mine they bear to you,
That some attentive cloud
Did pause amid the crowd
  Over my head,
While gentle things were said.

Believe the thrushes sung,
And that the flower-bells rung,
That herbs exhaled their scent,
And beasts knew what was meant,
The trees a welcome waved,
And lakes their margins laved,
  When thy free mind
To my retreat did wind.

It was a summer eve,
The air did gently heave

While yet a low-hung cloud
Thy eastern skies did shroud;
The lightning's silent gleam,
Startling my drowsy dream,
　　Seemed like the flash
Under thy dark eyelash.

Still will I strive to be
As if thou wert with me;
Whatever path I take,
It shall be for thy sake,
Of gentle slope and wide,
As thou wert by my side,
　　Without a root
To trip thy gentle foot.

I'll walk with gentle pace,
And choose the smoothest place,
And careful dip the oar,
And shun the winding shore,
And gently steer my boat
Where water-lilies float,
　　And cardinal flowers
Stand in their sylvan bowers.

Smoke

Light-winged Smoke, Icarian bird,
Melting thy pinions in thy upward flight,
Lark without song, and messenger of dawn,
Circling above the hamlets as they nest;
Or else, departing dream, and shadowy form
Of midnight vision, gathering up thy skirts;
By night star-veiling, and by day
Darkening the light and blotting out the sun;
Go thou my incense upward from this hearth,
And ask the gods to pardon this clear flame.

Mist

Low-anchored cloud,
Newfoundland air,
Fountain-head and source of rivers,
Dew-cloth, dream drapery,
And napkin spread by fays;
Drifting meadow of the air,
Where bloom the daisied banks and violets,
And in whose fenny labyrinth
The bittern booms and heron wades;
Spirit of lakes and seas and rivers,
Bear only perfumes and the scent
Of healing herbs to just men's fields!

Inspiration

Whate'er we leave to God. God does,
    And blesses us;
The work we choose should be our own,
    God lets alone.

If with light head erect I sing,
    Though all the Muses lend their force,
From my poor love of anything,
    The verse is weak and shallow as its source.

But if with bended neck I grope,
    Listening behind me for my wit,
With faith superior to hope,
    More anxious to keep back than forward it,

Making my soul accomplice there
  Unto the flame my heart hath lit,
Then will the verse forever wear,—
  Time cannot bend the line which God hath writ.

Always the general show of things
  Floats in review before my mind,
And such true love and reverence brings,
  That sometimes I forget that I am blind.

But now there comes unsought, unseen,
  Some clear, divine electuary,
And I, who had but sensual been,
  Grow sensible, and as God is, am wary.

I hearing get, who had but ears,
  And sight, who had but eyes before,
I moments live, who lived but years,
  And truth discern, who knew but learning's lore.

I hear beyond the range of sound,
  I see beyond the range of sight
New earths and skies and seas around,
  And in my day the sun doth pale his light.

A clear and ancient harmony
  Pierces my soul through all its din,
As through its utmost melody,—
  Farther behind than they, farther within.

More swift its bolt than lightning is,
  Its voice than thunder is more loud,
It doth expand my privacies
  To all, and leave me single in the crowd.

It speaks with such authority,
  With so serene and lofty tone,
That idle Time runs gadding by,
  And leaves me with Eternity alone.

Then chiefly is my natal hour,
  And only then my prime of life,

Of manhood's strength it is the flower,
  'Tis peace's end and war's beginning strife.

'T hath come in summer's broadest noon,
  By a grey wall or some chance place,
Unseasoned time, insulted June,
  And vexed the day with its presuming face.

Such fragrance round my couch it makes,
  More rich than are Arabian drugs,
That my soul scents its life and wakes
  The body up beneath its perfumed rugs.

Such is the Muse—the heavenly maid,
  The star that guides our mortal course,
Which shows where life's true kernel's laid,
  Its wheat's fine flower, and its undying force.

She with one breath attunes the spheres,
  And also my poor human heart,
With one impulse propels the years
  Around, and gives my throbbing pulse its start.

I will not doubt forever more,
  Nor falter from a steadfast faith,
For though the system be turned o'er,
  God takes not back the word which once he saith.

I will then trust the love untold
  Which not my worth nor want has bought,
Which wooed me young and woos me old,
  And to this evening hath me brought.

My memory I'll educate
  To know the one historic truth,
Remembering to the latest date
  The only true and sole immortal youth.

Be but thy inspiration given,
  No matter through what danger sought,
I'll fathom hell or climb to heaven,
  And yet esteem that cheap which love has bought.

Fame cannot tempt the bard
   Who's famous with his God,
Nor laurel him reward
   Who hath his Maker's nod.

AFTERWORD

Walden—The Secret Center

In his own lifetime Henry Thoreau published only two volumes. From a commercial point of view both were abysmal failures. *A Week on the Concord and Merrimack Rivers* came out in 1849, Thoreau paying the cost of printing out of his meager earnings. He was then so confident of a literary career that he appended an announcement, "soon to be published: *Walden.*" By 1853, the printer had 706 copies of the *Week* unsold, out of a printing of 1,000, and wanted to get the dead weight out of his storehouse. They were shipped to Concord; Thoreau carried the mass up to the attic of his parents' house and then boasted in the privacy of his *Journal,* "I have now a library of nearly nine hundred volumes, over seven hundred of which I wrote myself." Not until the next August, in 1854, would Ticknor and Fields venture, without enthusiasm and with no expectation of profit, to produce 2,000 copies of *Walden.* It caused scarcely a ripple in literary circles and never yielded Thoreau financial recompense.

In addition he did manage to get into print several poems, though most of these were taken by *The Dial,* the organ of New England transcendentalism issued between 1840 and 1844. During its last two years *The Dial* was edited by Thoreau's patron and instructor, Ralph Waldo Emerson. Thoreau also produced about twelve essays, five of which were charitably received by *The Dial,* the others in a grudging and unremunerative market of struggling magazines. Shortly after his death in 1862, at the age of forty-four, his family and friends contrived to issue several other essays and to put together, out of his notes, travel books on Maine and Cape Cod. That seemed the end of Thoreau's story. Except that he also left thirty-nine notebooks of daily jottings (some of these he pillaged for the books), which we know as his magnificent *Journal* but which in 1862 were, of course, not in the public domain. They seemed destined to slumber forever within a pine-box coffin the dying compiler had himself constructed to contain them. To them he refers ironically, and with a characteristic pun, in the opening of *Walden* by telling how he was long a reporter for a journal of no very wide circulation whose "editor" seldom saw fit to print his contributions. He got, he says, only labor for his pains, and so insists that pains were adequate reward. In his declining months Thoreau had constantly to face the crushing reality of his failure, to reconcile himself to oblivion. As on the evening of the shattering day in which he had piled up unwanted copies of the *Week,* he fell back upon swagger: "Indeed, I believe that this result is more inspiring and better for me than if a thousand had bought my wares. It affects my privacy less and leaves me freer." We should be naïve indeed were we convinced by such bluff, though Thoreau may just possibly have persuaded himself.

The world decided—insofar as it bothered about him—that he would figure as a minor naturalist in a literature where the giants were Irving, Longfellow, Lowell, and Dr. Holmes. As for Thoreau's ideas, this same world assumed that the few he displayed were borrowed from Emerson and declared them reproduced in a clumsy awkwardness which, perhaps momentarily engaging, bespoke the bumpkin.

And this man has now become a god in modern literature. Wherever English is read, or can be translated, Thoreau is one of the major voices of the nineteenth century, who speaks to the twentieth in India, Japan, and West Africa as much as in the United States, with more and more resonance. The two books, plus four volumes of reverently collected pieces, constitute his writings, and to these are added fourteen thick volumes of the *Journal,* at last circulated widely. As though enacting a penance for the neglect which intellectuals of the time heaped upon *Walden,* the presses of scholarly and critical publications pour out essays, estimates, and footnotes until the literature concerning this single work, let alone the whole of Thoreau, has become too vast for one student to encompass. The disciple now shines a greater luminary than the master: Thoreau is more alive in popular estimation than Emerson, and Longfellow, Lowell, or Holmes have become hobbies for antiquarians. The history of the growth of Thoreau's reputation is documentation for an intellectual revolution throughout the last century which would be altogether staggering did we not also inherit from that confused era the equally amazing example of the rediscovery of Herman Melville.

We may imagine that Thoreau would have come somehow into his own had he never written *Walden,* had we had nothing but the *Journal* to go upon. Yet such a process of recognition would have been indeed slow. The *Journal* might never have come into print had not the increasing popularity of *Walden* engendered a passion for every available scrap of Thoreau's writing. It can no longer be denied that *Walden* is a masterpiece. The number of editions, including this one, are proof of a demand—or at least an awareness—so extensive as to suggest that could Thoreau's contemporaries, even such an infatuated disciple as H. G. O. Blake, be brought back to consciousness long enough to observe the scene, they would be utterly bewildered. This observation remains true, and even more bewildering, today, because with the intensification of our material order, the augmentation of machines, luxuries, devices, media, gadgets, *Walden* is infinitely more antagonistic to the dominant pattern of our civilization than it was to the relatively pastoral America of 1854. Maybe it now offends as many readers as it delights. The point, however, is that today both sorts of persons are obliged to listen. (Whosoever would be a man, Emerson had said, must be a nonconformist. Among us, those who would be Americans, though the most abject of conformists, must face the challenge that they cannot push away Thoreau's assertion of a supreme and uncompromising nonconformity.)

In this way *Walden*—leaving aside inquiries into Thoreau's perverse psychology or into the peculiar reasons why he particularly rejected the American dream of success—tells us of some Eden of the soul in which at least one American held off the pressures of materiality and mediocrity. The more harassing these confinements become—and the less it seems possible for the sentient spirit to escape them, short of some tawdry melodrama of the beatniks—the more Thoreau's report takes on qualities of a symbolic serenity. One can read *Walden* in the midst of the rush hour at Grand Central Station. Even there it communicates inward detachment, a genial solipsism.

Yet we must note that Thoreau is no pietistic exhorter. He does not preach imperviousness. He is aware of the world about him. He tells just how he fought for his emancipation. So nothing is to be gained by discounting him as an individualist born in a happier time which could tolerate his queerness. True, there was no Internal Revenue Bureau then, as there were no traffic jams, but Thoreau never earned enough cash to be worth the notice of the tax collector, nor did he travel on throughways. Amid the distractions of our industrial America, the image of the youth beside Walden Pond who cried only for simplification becomes for thousands the dream of a green isle in the sea, a surcease from distraction, imparting energy to those who admit to themselves, in sleepless nights, that they do after all lead lives of quiet desperation.

Those thus aware, however sporadically or faintly, are bound by the code of modern America to confess their grief only moderately. Since they are surrounded by colleagues who publicly deny the accusation, they are tempted to dismiss Henry Thoreau by calling him a village eccentric who, in a less regimented era, retreated from Main Street to a shack in the woods. He was still near enough to depend on the village and his friends. He was not a spectacular rebel, he was only a loafer and a parasite who ran no serious risks compared with those of a trapper or forest ranger.

Curiously, there always seems to be something hollow in this criticism of Thoreau. Why it proves ineffective may be variously explained, but the principal bulwark of Thoreau's irresistible appeal to the anxieties of our distracted age is not so much the content of his writing (substantial as that is) but the method of his presentation. He is as beguiling for the *how* of his utterance as for the *what*. *Walden* may well be, on an elementary level, a manifesto of Yankee cussedness, but it is a great

deal more. It is a poem about the bitter tension between
self and society, between the one and the many. Consequently, it becomes a hymn to the victory of life over
death. It has won attention not alone because it is propa-
ganda, though it does propagandize; it scores chiefly because in the face of powerful discouragements, of the
failure of public acclaim, before the footlights of nature,
Thoreau affirms and demonstrates the indestructibility
of the human consciousness. He permits no lapse in
awareness. He could therefore dispense with the emolu-
ments of material success in order to record the mightier
triumph that reduces those acquisitions to insignificance.
Walden accomplishes this end by a style in which substi-
tutions for the ephemeral goods accumulated through
life-killing routines of labor and business become the
only permanent values.

After several rereadings of *Walden*—generally one
needs several—the reader discovers a key to its riddle in
the form of Thoreau's address to him. While the account
purports to be the solitary meditations or reminiscences
of a hermit beside a pond of water, the prose is actually
written in the rhythms of public speech. Thoreau is not
musing, he is orating. When he addresses the reader as
"you," he is not speaking softly to one person, but ha-
ranguing multitudes. Look, for instance, at the summons
in Chapter 2 to "Simplify, simplify." One cannot read
that paragraph quietly any more than one can murmur
a speech of Daniel Webster's.

As we gradually penetrate the subtlety of this rhetori-
cal gambit, we realize that *Walden* is a highly contrived,
exquisitely organized creation. Perhaps we should be
grateful to the stupidity of the American public in 1849
for its neglect of the *Week*: their callousness caused Thoreau to wait until 1854 to find a publisher for his second
production. This gave him five years in which to work
over and over a text that otherwise he might have let
go prematurely. The *Journal* records how, up to the very
last moment, he was polishing nuggets of thought and
observation and ingeniously revising the book. The completed version of *Walden* is a mosaic incorporating bits
of the *Journal* written as far back as fifteen years previously. James Lyndon Shanley, in a fascinating study,

The Making of Walden (1957), has convincingly shown that there are at least seven distinct layers in the book, rising in sequence as discernible to the analytic eye as do geological strata in a ravine. Yet the topmost of these, the seventh recasting which we read, is the tightest of them all. We know, for instance, that Thoreau spent over two years at the Pond (1845 to 1847), and that within that period he left it for his first expedition to Maine. Yet *Walden* is placed within the frame of a single year, and progresses through summer and autumn to the corpse-cold pallor of winter, and at last to a climax in the renascence of spring. There obviously can be only one climax. "Walden was dead and is alive again" must be seen as the basic sentence in the chronicle, a summary and revelation of its concealed coherence.

Another way of expressing the point is to say that *Walden* is pre-eminently an ecstatic book. It is not perfunctorily optimistic, not "inspirational." It comes to a jubilation that had to be won by heroic exertion, for which a large price had to be paid. The "strong and beautiful bug" who in the next-to-last paragraph gnaws his way out of the dry wood of an old apple-tree table arouses in Thoreau an ultimate shout of joy: "Who does not feel his faith in a resurrection and immortality strengthened by hearing of this?" However, by this time Thoreau has so deeply involved us in the cycle of nature that the resurrection we proclaim, the immortality we assume, has nothing to do with mere personal survival. Somewhere along the way we have shuffled off individuality without a pang. Thoreau has steadily reached men and women in our noisy age not merely because he describes a haven of serenity in the midst of hubbub but because his artistry makes wholly plausible a declaration of life that truly does "transcend" the trivialities of daily existence.

Actually it is not paradoxical to contend that *Walden* is the most egotistical work of art ever constructed and yet that its movement from "Economy" to "Conclusion" is a surgical excising of selfhood. We look back from the final illumination to the opening pages and in that golden light perceive, to our amazement, that the dissonant emphasis upon "the *I*, or first person" with which the work commenced is something more than humorous arrogance. Now we understand that when he arrested our attention by declaring he would not talk so much about himself if he knew anybody else as well, that he was "unfortunately" limited by the narrowness of his experience, he was luring us into a course of discipline that would imperceptibly compel us to advance within ourselves from the particular to the universal, from the inert finite to the resurgent infinite. Day in and day out, if we look frankly at ourselves, we are sterile inhabitants of the "wasteland," and our identities are burdened with commonplace impressions and dull concerns. We doubt whether such creatures as we are worthy of redemption. In *Walden* our lumpish humanity becomes glorious even unto itself as it is suffused with the profound self-knowledge that Henry Thoreau discovered beside the pond.

This discovery, which he earnestly and skilfully reveals to us, reduces to nonsense the objection often uttered by those incapable of grasping his meaning, that Thoreau was selfish, indulgent, unsocial, unproductive, that he criminally evaded the duties and responsibilities of citizenship. What, cry the mob, would happen to the country if everybody ran away to a pond? Who then would raise the crops, tan the shoe leather, print the books, or produce the television shows? The answer, of course, is that only a unique Henry Thoreau has the courage to undertake the perilous quest. Here was the "private business" that summoned him from the town and the comforts of civilization into the woods. He did not need to go far. He was no scout exploring unmapped Rockies. It was enough that the pond lay only two miles south of Concord common. In *Walden* distance is not measured by spatial units. It has taken us a hundred years to apprehend a little of what Thoreau's dimension means; today we are still learning more and more about its implications.

The short piece now known as "Civil Disobedience" has through the years come to be thought of as an adjunct to *Walden*, so much so that a reprint of the book seems incomplete unless the essay accompanies it. To some extent this connection is entirely justified, because the episode which triggered the discourse, Thoreau's imprisonment in Concord jail for refusing to pay his tax, occurred in July, 1846, while he was living at the pond. Hence the anger against organized society which burns in these sentences must throw some light on the complex of motives and emotions which inspired his withdrawal. In the rewritings of *Walden* Thoreau muted his rage, so that many admirers still cherish it as a nature idyl rather than a social tract. We do well, therefore, to read "Civil Disobedience" as a reminder of how genuinely recalcitrant he was.

Thoreau delivered a first draft of the manifesto to the Concord Lyceum on January 26, 1848, and so it fundamentally is an oration and not at all an essay. It was published in the one and only issue of *Aesthetic Papers*, which in 1849 Elizabeth Peabody hoped would become a magazine to carry on the work of *The Dial.* It was entitled "Resistance to Civil Government," but has subsequently been called by the present title, given it by the editors of Thoreau's collected works.

In another sense, however, "Civil Disobedience" has been forcibly and wrongly united to *Walden,* because it has had a career of its own and acquired a distinct reputation. This has mainly come from Gandhi's use of it as the textbook for his campaign of passive resistance in India. The notoriety he gave the piece made it further used by the British Labour Party. Later, among resisters of the Nazi occupations in Europe, it became a rallying tract. It has been remarked that outside the United States Thoreau is generally more famous for "Civil Disobedience" than for *Walden.* The rest of the world immediately comprehends what seems a program for radical political action, but the flight from an advancing civilization to a communion with a patch of still unspoiled nature is something so peculiar to American experience that few Europeans or Asians quite understand it.

When we read "Civil Disobedience" immediately after living through *Walden,* we must, I believe, conclude that it really is not primarily a social protest any more than is the book. Thoreau resisted all temptations to become a reformer as energetically as did any businessman. He simply demanded of American democracy a right to go his own way at his own gait. He would not permit his conscience to be burdened with the responsibility of conducting himself according to standards that were not his. *Walden,* of course, proclaims this same intransigent individualism, though in the larger context of a spiritual research. So one does come deeper into Thoreau's thought by comparing the book and the essay.

—Perry Miller

SELECTED BIBLIOGRAPHY

Writings by Henry David Thoreau

A Week on the Concord and Merrimack Rivers, 1849 Travel book
"Civil Disobedience," 1849 Essay (Signet Classic 0451-523776)
Walden, 1854 Prose (Signet Classic 0451-523776)
"Slavery in Massachusetts," 1854 Essay
"A Plea for John Brown," 1859 Essay
Excursions, 1863 Posthumously collected essays
The Maine Woods, 1864 Posthumously edited travel book
Cape Cod, 1865 Posthumously edited travel book
The Writings of Henry David Thoreau, 1906 (Vols. VII–XX contain the Journals)
Collected Poems of Henry Thoreau, 1943; revised and enlarged, 1964
Consciousness in Concord, 1958 Early journal
Selected Journals of Henry David Thoreau, 1967 (Meridian Classic 0452-007496)

Biography and Criticism

Anderson, C. R. *The Magic Circle of Walden.* New York: Holt, Rinehart and Winston, 1968.

Buell, Lawrence. *Literary Transcendentalism.* Ithaca: Cornell University Press, 1973.

Cavell, Stanley. *The Senses of Walden.* New York: Viking, 1972.

Christie, J. A. *Thoreau as World Traveller.* New York: Columbia University Press with the cooperation of the American Geographical Society, 1965.

Harding, Walter. *The Days of Henry Thoreau: A Biography.* New York: Knopf, 1965. Reissued by Princeton University Press, 1982.

———. *A Thoreau Handbook.* New York: New York University Press, 1959.

Hicks, John H., ed. *Thoreau in Our Season.* Amherst: University of Massachusetts Press, 1966.

Lebeaux, Richard. *Young Man Thoreau.* Amherst: University of Massachusetts Press, 1977.

Matthiessen, F. G. *American Renaissance.* New York and London: Oxford University Press, 1941.

Meltzer, Milton, and Walter Harding. *A Thoreau Profile.* New York: Crowell, 1962.

Porte, Joel. *Emerson and Thoreau: Transcendentalists in Conflict.* Middletown, Conn.: Wesleyan University Press, 1966.

Richardson, Robert D. *Henry Thoreau: A Life of the Mind.* Berkeley: University of California Press, 1986.

Shanley, J. L. *The Making of Walden; With the Text of the First Version.* Chicago: University of Chicago Press, 1957.

Sherman, Paul, ed. *Thoreau: A Collection of Critical Essays.* Englewood Cliffs, N.J.: Prentice-Hall, 1962.

Taylor, Bob Pepperman. *America's Bachelor Uncle: Thoreau and the American Polity.* Topeka: University Press of Kansas, 1996.

Van Doren, Mark. *Henry David Thoreau: A Critical Study.* Boston and New York: Houghton Mifflin, 1916.